Cold Blooded Liar

By Karen Rose

The Raleigh Series
Have You Seen Her?

The Chicago Series
Don't Tell
I'm Watching You
Nothing to Fear
You Can't Hide
Count to Ten

The Philadelphia/Atlanta Series
Die For Me
Scream For Me
Kill For Me

The Minneapolis Series
I Can See You
Silent Scream

The Baltimore Series
You Belong to Me
No One Left to Tell
Did You Miss Me?
Watch Your Back
Monster in the Closet
Death is Not Enough

The Cincinnati Series
Closer Than You Think
Alone in the Dark
Every Dark Corner
Edge of Darkness
Into the Dark

The Sacramento Series
Say You're Sorry
Say No More
Say Goodbye

The New Orleans Series
Quarter to Midnight

The San Diego Case Files
Cold Blooded Liar

Novellas available in ebook only
Broken Silence
Dirty Secrets

KAREN

ROSE

Cold Blooded Liar

First published in the USA in 2023 by
BERKLEY
An imprint of Penguin Random House LLC

First published in Great Britain in 2023 by
HEADLINE PUBLISHING GROUP

1

Cataloguing in Publication Data is available from the British Library

Hardback ISBN 978 1 4722 9681 8
Trade paperback ISBN 978 1 4722 9682 5

Typeset in Palatino by Avon DataSet Ltd, Alcester, Warwickshire

Printed and bound in Great Britain by Clays Ltd, Elcograf S.p.A.

Headline's policy is to use papers that are natural, renewable and recyclable products and made from wood grown in well-managed forests and other controlled sources. The logging and manufacturing processes are expected to conform to the environmental regulations of the country of origin.

HEADLINE PUBLISHING GROUP
An Hachette UK Company
Carmelite House
50 Victoria Embankment
London EC4Y 0DZ

www.headline.co.uk
www.hachette.co.uk

To Margaret Taylor.
Thank you for your help on this book and
for your service to your community over the years.
But mostly I thank you for your friendship.

And, as always, to Martin. I love you.

Prologue

Carmel Valley, California
Wednesday, 2 April, 3.00 A.M.
Sixteen years ago . . .

She's gone.

Katherine's hand trembled as she gripped the barn door handle. Her whole body trembled. Her stomach churned so violently that she thought she'd be sick.

She's gone.

And it's all my fault.

So many things she could have done. Should have done.

Will do. But she didn't know where to start.

However, she did know where she needed to be.

Alone. In the barn. In the place where they'd first huddled together as frightened twelve-year-old runaways to get out of the cold night. In the place where – much later – they'd come to talk about . . . everything.

Well, Wren would talk. Katherine would listen.

Katherine was a good listener. She'd had to be. She'd learned to hear the nuances in a person's speech. To know if they'd help. Or hurt.

To know if they were lying or telling the truth.

She didn't want to listen now. She wanted to be alone where she could scream her fury, where she could unleash her rage. Where she couldn't hurt anyone else.

Because Wren was gone.

Her eyes burned and she swallowed the sob that rose in her

throat as she slid the barn door open just enough to slip inside. She was so skinny, she didn't need it to open much and she knew just how far she could slide the door before it creaked.

She didn't let it creak. It would be all right if she did, but she still found something satisfying about sneaking in where she wasn't supposed to be. At least not right now. She was allowed to be in the barn anytime she wished, but she was supposed to be sleeping right now.

Except she hadn't slept in nearly two weeks. Tonight would be no different, so she'd given up trying.

Someone had turned the night-light on, its soft glow spreading through the barn, leaving shadows lurking in the corners. She wasn't afraid of the shadows. She knew every one. This was her place. This was where she came to think.

Now it was where she came to grieve.

She breathed deeply, drawing in the scents of horses and fresh hay – and even fresher motor oil. The latter was unexpected. Usually the motor oil smelled old.

Tools were strewn on the floor around the old tractor that sat parked along the far wall. It had been broken for months. No one had had the time to fix it.

Looked like someone had been working on it tonight.

Someone who was still here.

She tensed, hearing the labored breathing coming from one of the empty stalls.

No, not breathing. Someone was crying.

She started to turn and run, but the cries became sobs. Deep, racking sobs that ripped at her heart.

At least someone else is missing Wren. Which wasn't fair, she knew. Everyone in the big house missed Wren. How could they not?

She crept farther into the barn, listening intently, ready to flee at a moment's notice, but now needing to know who'd come to her private place to grieve, even though she thought she knew.

The tuned-up tractor had been her first clue.

A big, burly man sat on the floor of an empty stall, back against the wall, shoulders heaving as he cried. In one of his massive hands was a piece of wood. In the other, his carving knife.

Harlan McKittrick. Her foster father.

She'd never seen him cry, not in the three years that she'd lived here, not even at the funeral today. He'd been stoic, his expression immovable, like a statue's. He'd held his arm around Mrs McK as she'd cried her eyes out. He'd spoken a few words over Wren's coffin in his deep, gravelly voice, about peace and eternity and God.

Katherine had wanted to scream then. She'd wanted to hit someone.

She'd wanted to hit Mr McK for being so . . . together. For being unfeeling.

But she could see now that she'd made a big mistake. The man was not unfeeling. He'd just saved his grief for when he was alone.

Just like I did.

She took a step back, intending to leave him in peace, to find somewhere else to scream her rage, but his head shot up and he met her eyes in the dim light.

For a long moment, neither of them moved. His tears continued to fall and she was poised to run. Finally, he wiped his face with his shirtsleeve.

'Kit,' he said gruffly.

'I'm sorry,' she whispered. 'I'll go.'

He shook his head. 'No, you don't have to. This was your place, hers too. I should have known you'd come here tonight.'

Her cheeks heated. She'd been caught out of bed at three a.m. There were rules, even here. 'I'll go.'

'No, honey. I'll go. Mrs McK is probably wondering where I've got myself off to. You can stay.' He rose, wincing as he stretched his back. 'I'm too damn old to be sitting on barn floors. I came out here to do some whittling, but . . .' He trailed off with a sigh. 'It kind of hit me. You know how it goes, huh, Kitty-Cat?'

He always called her Kit or Kitty-Cat. Not ever Katherine, and she'd often wondered why. But she didn't hate it. She might have even liked it. A little.

Talk to him. Say something to make him feel better. Because Mr McK was a nice guy. And McKittrick House was so much nicer than any other place she'd ever lived. And she'd lived in a lot of places.

Mr and Mrs McK were good people. They never yelled, never hit. Never . . . took advantage of the girls or the boys, like so many of the other fosters had.

They'd let her stay even though she was not . . . good. They'd let her stay and they'd told her to call them Mom and Pop McK if she wanted to, just like all the other kids did who'd come through their big, warm house that always smelled like apple pie and clean laundry and lemon furniture spray.

She never had, though. She'd stuck with 'Mr' and 'Mrs', anything to keep them at arm's length. They'd never made her feel bad for doing so.

Now she wanted to make him feel better, because he was crying and it shook her hard. He was big and rough and gruff, but he was crying.

For Wren.

She pointed to the carved wood in his hands. 'What are you making?'

He seemed surprised that she'd asked. Which was fair. Katherine didn't talk much. She never asked anyone anything remotely personal. Never answered any question with more than 'Fine' or 'Okay'. And when they'd offered to adopt her, to make her an official McKittrick, she'd said only 'No, thank you'.

Because nobody was that nice. Nobody really cared. It would end. They'd grow tired of her and make her leave, and then she'd be even worse off.

Mr McK stared down at the carving in his hands. 'A wren. You know, like the bird.'

A sob flew from Katherine's throat before she could shove it back in. 'A wren?' she asked, her voice breaking.

He nodded, his eyes on the little bird. 'I put one in her coffin, y'see. In her hands, so she'd have something to hold.' His smile was wobbly. 'To maybe remember us by. So she wouldn't be alone.'

Katherine pressed her hand to her mouth. *Keep it in. Keep it all in*. 'You did?' she asked, the words muffled.

'I did. And, um, this one is done.' He held it out to her. 'It's for you. To remember her.'

For a moment she didn't move. Couldn't move. Just stared at Mr McK's outstretched hand holding the small bird.

She could see it clearly now, delicate and beautiful. Like Wren had been.

Mr McK was still holding the carving on the flat of his palm, so that she could take it without touching him. They knew that she didn't like to touch anyone.

Wren had been the exception. Her sister, even though they'd shared no blood.

Katherine's hand crept forward, one finger extended. She stroked the little bird, expecting a rough surface but feeling only smooth wood. Mr McK simply stood there, the bird on his palm.

She gingerly picked it up and held it tightly against her chest. 'To remember her,' she whispered. Like she'd ever forget. Wren was all the good, sweet things.

Everything that Kit was not.

Mr McK smiled down at her, so sadly. 'We'll always remember her, Kit. She was so special and deserved to have the best life.'

'But now she's *dead*,' Kit choked out, clutching the little bird so tightly that even the smooth edges cut into her hand. 'Someone *killed* her and *no one cares*.'

'We care,' Mr McK whispered back fiercely.

'Nobody else does,' she snapped, her voice echoing off the barn walls. 'None of those cops who came and asked questions. None of them cared.'

'I don't know. I can't see their hearts. I only know my own and Mrs McK's.'

Now the rage was back. Now the rage was building. She wanted to throw something, but the only thing she could throw was the little bird and she clutched it even tighter. She'd never throw the bird away.

She'd never throw Wren away.

'They said she was a runaway. That she'd come back!' Katherine was shouting now and couldn't stop herself. The horses shifted in their stalls, one whinnying in dismay, but Katherine couldn't stop herself. 'They said she wanted to go. They said she was probably on the streets, taking drugs. They didn't care!'

Katherine took a step back, then another.

Mr McK continued to stand there, watching her with eyes so brokenhearted that she wanted to scream at that, too.

'Then they found her body in a dumpster and didn't even tell us for *five days*!' she screamed. 'Like she was *trash* and it was *okay* that she's dead!'

'They said,' he said calmly, 'that it took them five days to ID her.'

'That was five days too long! Five days that she lay there in the cold morgue *all alone*.' Her shouts became choked and finally, finally the tears came. Like a dam had burst and she couldn't stop the flow. 'They said they were *busy*. That they were *backed up*. That they were *sorry* for our goddamn loss.'

Mr McK wiped his eyes again. 'I know, Kit.'

'They're not even looking for who did this. No clues. Case has gone cold. It's been a week since they found her, and they're not even pretending to look.' She dropped her gaze to the little wooden bird in her hand. 'Well, *I'm* going to look. I'm going to find out who did this. Who took her from us.' *From me.*

Mr McK opened his mouth, then closed it, saying nothing.

She stared up at him defiantly. 'What? Not gonna tell me it's too dangerous? Not gonna tell me that I'm too young? That I'm only fifteen? Not gonna tell me it could be me next?'

He exhaled quietly. 'Why should I tell you any of those things? You already know them.'

She looked away, knowing that he was right and hating it. 'I should have watched her better. It should have been me.'

He sucked in a harsh breath. 'No, Kit. *No*. It shouldn't have been either of you. It should never be *anyone*'s child. Please. It should never have been you.'

She shook her head, all of her words gone now. All used up.

'You're ours,' he said, his voice ringing so true that she almost didn't doubt him. She didn't want to doubt him. 'You might not think so or you might not want it official on paper, but you are ours, Kit Matthews. You are ours to protect. Ours to love. Whether you want that love or not. That we didn't protect Wren will haunt me until the day I die. Please don't make me mourn you, too. I can't do this again.'

She looked up at him then, hating the tears that she couldn't stop. But he was crying, too, and that shook some more words loose. 'What are we gonna do, Mr McK?' she whispered. 'She's gone. And she's never coming back.'

He took a step forward, giving her a chance to step away.

But she didn't. She couldn't. Her feet were frozen.

Her heart was frozen.

Finally, he brushed his fingers over her hair. 'We go on, Kit. We'll remember her always, but we go on. It's what we have to do.' He hesitated for a long moment, then cupped her cheek in his big hand. 'We'll cry for her, but we'll also live for her. *You'll* live for her. You'll make yourself a good life, Kit Matthews. We'll make sure of it, me and Mrs McK. You will *live*.'

Katherine closed her eyes then and leaned into Mr McK's warm palm. *Just for a second*. He was . . . safety. Security. Strength. And affection she didn't need to repay. She'd take just a little. *Just for a second*. 'I want to make whoever hurt her pay. I want them to die.'

'Me too, Kit. Me too. But we'll do it right. We won't be stupid. We won't take any chances. We won't be reckless and get killed and leave Mrs McK all alone.'

She chanced a look up at him. He was serious. 'You'll help me?'

'I'll help you. I'd search for her killer even if you didn't want to.' One of his wide shoulders lifted in a half shrug. 'I'd already planned on it. But I'm a farmer, not a cop. It's not going to be easy.'

She met his eyes directly. 'And if I want to be a cop?'

'You'll be a damn good one. You'll never make any family feel like their loved one didn't matter.'

She scoffed. 'You sound pretty sure of yourself, Mr McK.'

He withdrew his hand, stooping down to pick up the carving knife that he'd dropped at some point. He slid it into its sheath and dropped it into his pocket. 'I'm pretty sure of you, Kit.'

She took a step back, her chest too full of feelings.

She hated feelings.

'Thank you, Mr McK. For the bird. I'll see you in the morning.'

She turned and ran for the house, tiptoeing up the stairs and slipping into her room. With the twin bed with messed-up sheets because she'd tossed and turned. And with the other twin bed, neatly made with the quilt with bright yellow sunbursts. The empty bed.

Because Wren was gone.

Carefully she put the little wooden bird on her nightstand where she'd see it at first light. Then she climbed into bed and lay there, staring at the ceiling.

I'm pretty sure of you, Kit.

She sighed.

Well, that makes one of us.

One

San Diego Police Department
San Diego, California
Monday, 4 April, 11.30 A.M.
Present day

'Hey, McKittrick.'

Kit swiveled in her desk chair, raising an eyebrow at Basil 'Baz' Constantine, her partner of four years. 'You rang?'

Baz pointed to the double doors leading into the San Diego Police Department's homicide division. 'You got company.'

Kit turned in time to see the doors close behind familiar wide shoulders. Harlan McKittrick ambled toward her, his gait as smooth and his smile as wide as it had been for the nineteen years that she'd been privileged to know him.

'Pop!' She pushed away from her desk, walking into his outstretched arms. She still didn't like to be touched, but she made exceptions for Mom and Pop McK. The contact seemed to make them happy.

Kit would do nearly anything to make those two happy.

'Kitty-Cat,' he said, tightening his arms until her ribs protested. He let her go when she grunted, his expression sheepish. 'Sorry. Haven't seen you in too long.'

'It's been two weeks,' she said dryly, but leaned up to peck his cheek, her heart warming at his pleased look. 'What brings you into the city?'

Because Harlan McKittrick hated the city. He was made for wide open spaces, not high-rises and traffic.

'We're getting a new kid. Mom is meeting with the social worker and I thought I'd stop in and say hi.'

'Well, hi. Come and sit with me. I can take a short break.'

He looked around as he followed her back to her desk, curious as always. He was no stranger to the homicide division, having haunted its halls for years after they'd lost Wren. He'd kept the promise he'd made after Wren's funeral, helping her search for the man who'd killed her sister. They'd been unsuccessful in finding the monster, but even after sixteen years they still searched.

She wondered if he'd come with a new lead. If so, it would be the first one in five years.

'Nope,' he said as he eased his six-foot-two frame into the chair next to her desk. 'Nothing new.'

He'd always been able to read her mind. It had been maddening in her teenage years. He'd always known when she was ready to bolt or if she was telling anything less than the total truth. Now it was a comfort that someone knew her so well.

'Me either. So tell me about the new kid.'

'Thirteen-year-old girl.' His shoulders drooped. 'She was scared of me.'

She squeezed his hand. 'She'll see that you're different. They always do.'

One side of his mouth lifted. 'You did.'

'I did, indeed.'

He sat quietly for a moment, then dug something from his pants pocket. Kit tensed, knowing what it would be even before the little carving appeared.

It was that time of year. Again.

Sixteen anniversaries of Wren's murder and still no closure. But true to his word, Pop McK had never forgotten the little girl who'd been such a bright light.

He held out his offering on his flat palm, just as he always did, year after year. It was always a little bird. Kit had a special shelf in her bedroom for the birds, placed where she could see them when she opened her eyes each morning.

They were the only things in her home that she routinely dusted.

Except today it wasn't a bird – or not just a bird. It was a cat with a bird perched on its head. The bird looked quizzical. The cat looked . . . content. Three inches long and an inch wide, it was intricate and detailed and beautiful.

'Pop,' she breathed. Gingerly, she took it from his hand. At one time, it had been because she was touch averse. Now it was because it looked like the little figurine would snap if she gripped it too firmly. 'Thank you.'

'It won't break,' he told her. 'You can carry it in your pocket if you want to. For luck.'

'I will.' But she didn't, not yet. She held the small carving up to the light, marveling at his skill as she always did. 'It's amazing.'

His smile was shy, an adorable look on a man as big as he was. He dug in his pocket once again, bringing out another carving. This one was just a bird. It was still beautifully done, but the bird sat alone on a twig.

'For your shelf.'

She took it from his palm. 'Thank you, Pop.'

'You're welcome, Kitty-Cat,' he murmured, running a hand over her hair. 'I have something for you, Baz.'

Baz got up from his desk to sit on the corner of Kit's. He hadn't even been pretending not to listen. 'Yes, please.'

Harlan produced a small carved horse, making both Kit and Baz frown. It wasn't a bird. They both always got birds.

'It's for Luna,' Harlan explained. 'She saw me carving the last time you brought her out to the farm and asked if I'd make her one for her birthday.'

Baz's face softened at the mention of his five-year-old granddaughter. 'She's going to love it, Harlan. Thank you.'

'Well.' Harlan cleared his throat gruffly. 'You've been there for us more times than I can count. So thank you.' He held out a fourth carving. A bird. 'For you.'

Harlan had started giving Baz and Kit carvings at the same time. Kit, so that she could remember Wren. Baz, so that he wouldn't forget about the victim whose murder he'd never solved.

Baz didn't try to aw-shucks his way out of the gratitude. He'd been the detective who'd worked Wren's case and was not as callous as fifteen-year-old Kit had assumed.

Wren's murder had been Baz's very first homicide case. It had shaken him, and his attempts to distance himself from their grief so that he could do his job had come off as cold and unfeeling. He'd been anything but, having helped them track down every lead ever since.

That they hadn't found Wren's killer was not from lack of trying.

Baz slipped the carvings into his own pocket. 'I'll make a video when we give Luna's to her. Be prepared for squeals that could break glass.'

A door opened behind them and their lieutenant's voice cut through the bullpen noise. 'Constantine, McKittrick. With me. Now.'

A chorus of *ooooh* came from their fellow detectives, like they were all in middle school. Which wasn't far off for many of them – behaviorally speaking – despite being mostly middle-aged men. It was how they coped.

'Gotta go,' Kit said. 'Sorry, Pop.'

'I need to pick up your mom and our new kid. Wish me luck.'

'You won't need it,' she said. 'I give the kid a week before she's calling you Pop.'

'Unless she's like you,' he teased. 'Then it'll be four years.'

'I was a little stubborn,' she admitted.

Baz snorted. 'A little?'

'Shut up,' she told him without heat. 'Pop, I'll be there on Sunday for dinner.'

Harlan gave her another rib-crushing hug. 'See that you are. Your mother worries.'

Betsy McKittrick did worry about her. She and Harlan had been the only ones who ever had.

'I'll be there.' She started walking backward toward her lieutenant's office, not turning until Harlan had passed through the double doors.

Straightening her spine, she slid both carvings into her pocket before opening the lieutenant's door. 'What's up, boss?'

Reynaldo Navarro gestured to the chairs across from his desk, handing them each a sheet of paper. 'Transcript of an incoming call. Audio's been sent to your email for your listening pleasure.'

Kit scanned the transcript before looking up with a frown. 'He mentioned me?'

'In particular,' Navarro said. 'Listen.' He hit a button on his computer and the voice of a very nervous-sounding man filled the air.

'Hi. This message is for homicide detective Kit McKittrick. I have reason to believe you'll find the victim of a murder in Longview Park at the following coordinates.' He rattled off a string of numbers and the call ended.

Kit tried to place the voice but came up empty. 'I don't think I've ever met him before.'

Navarro shrugged. 'Well, if he hasn't met you, he at least knows of you. I want you two to check it out. Report back. Baz, you can go. Kit, stay.'

Damn. Kit had a feeling she knew what was coming.

When Baz was gone, Navarro sighed. 'You skipped your appointment. Again.'

Yep, this was what she'd expected. 'I thought it was optional.'

Navarro gave her his I'm-disappointed-in-you look. She was almost immune to it. 'You promised,' he said. 'That's why I made it optional.'

She had promised. 'I'm sorry. I just hate going.'

'None of us likes going to the department shrink, Kit, but we've talked about this every year for the past four. Every one of your bosses before me has talked to you about it, too. This time of year, you work yourself into near exhaustion and we all know why.'

Well, yeah. That she'd lost Wren this time of year wasn't a secret. Especially in the homicide department.

'Working helps. And I can handle it.'

'Maybe this year you can. Maybe next year, too. But sooner or later, it will become too much. Your performance will drop. You'll lose your edge.'

She ground her teeth. He knew her too well, because losing her edge was one of the things she feared most.

'Go to your appointments, Kit. You might be surprised. Dr Scott may actually be able to help you.'

'And if he doesn't?'

'You mean if you don't want to tell him anything personal?'

'Yes.' Because she didn't. She didn't dislike Dr Scott. She just didn't want to bare her soul. Like any normal person wouldn't.

'Then you can sit and talk about your cases for an hour. It's one hour a week, Kit. It's not going to kill you.' He dropped his gaze to the paperwork in front of him, effectively dismissing her.

She wasted no time leaving his office.

'This anonymous guy sounds like a kook,' she grumbled to Baz when she was back at their desks. 'We've got better things to do than chase after anonymous tips all day.'

'No, we've got a mountain of reports to write. It's a beautiful day. Let's go check it out and then we can grab some lunch.'

'It's always a beautiful day. It's freaking San Diego.'

'Stop whining, McKittrick. I've got a craving for Vietnamese.'

Rolling her eyes, Kit followed him out. 'Waste of time.'

Luckily, she liked Vietnamese food.

Longview Park, San Diego, California
Monday, 4 April, 5.30 P.M.

Kit pulled the handkerchief across her nose and mouth as she watched the two CSU techs meticulously uncovering what was, indeed, a grave. Based on the odor, the body had been there a while.

They'd arrived at the mystery caller's coordinates to find that the ground had settled somewhat, creating a slight depression that measured five and a half by two and a half feet.

Ground-penetrating radar had shown a body.

The victim had been small.

Kit slipped her hand into her pocket, finding the little cat-bird figurine. Stroking it with her thumb. *Please don't be a child.*

'I hope it's not a kid,' Baz murmured, echoing her thoughts.

All homicides were difficult. Even drug dealers murdered on the street had been loved by someone. Were missed by someone.

But the child homicides were a completely different level of hell.

She looked away from the grave to where Sergeant Ryland, the CSU leader, was making a plaster cast of the only footprint they'd found in the area. It was a man's shoe, size eleven.

'You got anything for us, Ryland?' she called.

'I just might.'

She and Baz walked from the grave site to where someone had stepped off the asphalt path, leaving the single footprint in the strip of ground between the path and the field of grass.

Ryland finished pouring the plaster over the footprint, smoothed it out, then set the timer on his phone. 'Thirty minutes for the plaster to set. Come see the photos I took of the print while I wait.' He retrieved his camera and beckoned them closer. 'There was lettering on the sole of the shoe – likely a brand name. I can't quite make it out in the photo, but I'm hoping to get detail from the plaster cast.'

'So it'll be seventy-two hours or so,' Baz said and Ryland nodded.

Kit leaned closer to the screen. 'Can you zoom in on it?'

Ryland did, handing the camera to Kit. 'I can make out what looks like a Y at the end of the brand name, but—'

'Sperry,' Kit said. 'Sorry to interrupt, Sergeant. I recognize the logo. They're Sperry Top-Siders.' She gave him back his camera. 'My sister runs a charter fishing business and sometimes I first mate for her on my days off. A lot of her customers wear them.'

Ryland studied the photo. 'You could be right.'

She was, Kit was certain. 'Trouble is, that's a popular shoe. I've even got a pair.'

'So do I,' Baz said. 'Tracking those will be nearly impossible.'

Kit shrugged. 'But when we find the guy who owns these shoes, we can put him at the scene. Any way to get a weight estimate on the wearer?'

Ryland shook his head. 'Ground's too hard. Barely enough sinkage to get the plaster cast. I'll let you know when I have something definite.'

'Detectives?' one of the techs at the grave called, his tone urgent. 'Something over here you need to see.'

'Thank you, Sergeant,' Kit said, then approached the grave alongside Baz, schooling her expression. If it was a child's grave, she would maintain her professionalism. She'd let herself react later, when she was alone.

'Victim's a postpubescent female,' the tech said when they were graveside. 'The ME will be able to give you a better age than I can, but I'm guessing somewhere between fourteen and eighteen.'

Feeling Baz's eyes on her, Kit reassured him with a quick glance. She was fine.

He always worried about her reaction when the victim was the same age that Wren had been when she'd been murdered, but after four years as a homicide detective, Kit had seen far too many victims who'd been Wren's age. It never got easier.

She hoped that it never would.

But at least she no longer wondered if it was the same guy who'd done it. That had been her first thought earlier in her career. She'd never stop looking for Wren's killer, but she'd made her peace with the fact that she might never find him.

The CSU techs had uncovered the victim's head and torso. The remains were badly decomposed, but some of the girl's basic features were identifiable. She'd been Caucasian with shoulder-length blond hair.

She was clothed in a pink T-shirt and jeans, the waistband of which was just visible with her lower body still covered by dirt.

Big gold hoop earrings shone against the dirt, her earlobes having decomposed long before. There was a necklace around her neck, a thick ring hanging from the chain. A class ring of some kind.

High school or college? she wondered.

A second later Baz gasped. He was staring at the remains, his eyes wide behind his bifocals, so she looked back.

And abruptly understood her partner's shock.

'Fucking hell,' she whispered.

The victim's wrists were restrained with a pair of pink handcuffs that still managed to sparkle despite the coating of dirt.

'Pink,' Baz said hoarsely.

Kit swallowed hard. 'Sparkly pink.'

The tech was masked and goggled, but his eyes still showed grim recognition.

His much younger assistant did not understand, however. She looked up from where she was removing the lower-body dirt with a small brush. 'What am I missing?' she asked hesitantly.

'Old serial killer case,' her supervisor said quietly. 'Always left the bodies cuffed with pink handcuffs. The last body found was five years ago. The first was found fifteen years ago, and two were found in between. This could be the fifth victim.'

Her eyes widened. 'Oh. Shit.'

Indeed. 'The pink handcuffs detail was not released to the press.' Kit met the young tech's eyes, silently warning her to keep her mouth shut.

'I won't say a word,' the younger woman promised. 'Holy cow. So it's not likely to be a copycat.'

Baz exhaled, a frustrated sound. 'That's what we have to find out.'

Kit tilted her head toward their vehicle. 'We need to call the boss.'

Baz grimaced. 'Rock, paper, scissors. Loser makes the call.'

Kit rolled her eyes. 'You're ridiculous. I'll make the call.' She waited until they were both in the car with the doors closed before dialing Navarro and putting him on speaker.

'It's Kit and Baz,' she said when he answered. 'Is anyone with you?'

'No,' Navarro replied slowly. 'Why?'

'Because the victim was buried with pink handcuffs.'

There was a beat of silence. 'Motherfucker,' Navarro growled. 'Not again.'

'Yeah,' Baz agreed. 'That was our reaction, too. She fits the profile – young, blond, and petite. She's been in the ground a year or two based on decomp. ME'll give us a range for time of death, but she's wearing a class ring on a chain. Hopefully that'll help narrow things down and maybe even ID her.'

'Any evidence of the doer?'

'A footprint,' Baz said. 'Either the doer or the caller or both, if he called it in himself for the attention. But it's probably a Top-Sider. Kit recognized the logo.'

'Hell, even I have a pair of those,' Navarro muttered. 'That's no help.'

'Not to trace him, no,' Kit agreed. 'We're going to pull missing-person reports for teenage blondes over the last few years and get IT to trace the anonymous call. What we wanted from you is direction on the pink handcuffs. Keep it confidential?'

'Absolutely. Last thing we need is for the press to get their hands on this. It'll go viral and we'll have copycats and fake sightings and . . . hell. ID the victim and trace the caller. Then we'll go from there.'

'Yes, sir,' Kit said. 'We're heading back now.' She ended the call and looked at Baz, who was driving this week. 'I don't feel much like eating.' They'd missed lunch and it was now dinnertime, but she still wasn't hungry.

Baz started the car. 'Now that I'm not downwind from a body, my stomach is growling. We can order something back at the office.' He shot her an arch look. 'You will eat.'

She didn't argue because Baz was right. Plus he'd tell on her to Mom McK. 'Fine.'

Accepting his victory with a smirk, he handed Kit his phone. 'Text Marian, please. Tell her I'll be late tonight.'

Kit did so, grateful that she didn't have a spouse to disappoint with her late nights. 'She says you owe her "stuff". She used quotes. Do I want to know?'

He chuckled, a rich sound that normally made Kit happy, but at this moment, it was TMI. 'No, Kit. You do not want to know.'

'Old-people sex,' she teased with an exaggerated shudder. 'Let me get Snickerdoodle settled for the night.'

She texted her sister Akiko: ***Caught a case. Can u keep Snick*** *tonite?* Her standard poodle Snickerdoodle would need to be walked long before she got home.

Akiko responded immediately. ***Will do. You okay?***

Just fine. It's going to be a busy night, that's all.

We on for Saturday? Saturdays were Akiko's busiest day, with fishing charters scheduled for morning and afternoon. This time of year, her guest roster was always packed. Kit gave her a hand whenever she could. It was a win-win. Akiko got the help and Kit got a day on the water to unwind, catching fish instead of murderers.

And Snickerdoodle got head scritches from the guests. Everyone was happy.

Yes for now. May change. Will let you know.

A thumbs-up emoji was Akiko's answer.

Baz headed out of the park, nodding to the officers who'd cordoned off the crime scene. 'Snickerdoodle taken care of?'

'Yep. Akiko's got her. Snick gets spoiled at her place, so she'll be happy.'

Baz snorted. 'She gets spoiled at your place, too. Don't front.'

'I spoil her with attention. Akiko spoils her with cheese.'

Baz frowned. 'I thought Akiko was vegan. Is she giving her vegan cheese?'

Kit chuckled. 'Akiko is not vegan, just a pescatarian who's lactose intolerant. She buys cheese especially for Snickerdoodle.' She looked into her side mirror, watching the crime scene disappear from view. 'She was young.'

Baz nodded, rolling with the subject change. 'I hope someone reported her missing.'

Kit hoped so. While it would have been hell on the girl's family to lose her, Kit hoped someone had genuinely loved the girl before she'd been killed. 'Her T-shirt was from an Ariana Grande concert, three or four years ago. If we can't ID her from either her fingerprints or from the ring around her neck, we can search missing-person reports for what she was last wearing.'

'He didn't take her jewelry.'

'No.' Which was kind of unusual. 'Were the other victims found with jewelry?'

'At least two of them were,' Baz said. 'One of them – the third one – was even ID'd through a necklace with her name on it. That was Ricki Emerson. The first victim was wearing a cross on a chain.'

'She was never identified.'

Baz sighed. 'No. We canvassed the area where she was found for miles, but no one remembered seeing her.'

'She'd also been dead a good while longer.'

'True. At least two years, the ME said. Maybe as many as five. The neighborhood where she was found had a number of Coronado families.'

'High turnover,' Kit murmured. The naval base on Coronado Island housed more than thirty thousand personnel and their families. Transient by definition.

'Yep. Most of the residents we talked to hadn't lived there two years before.'

'Maybe we'll be lucky with this girl and somebody will remember seeing her and who she was with before she disappeared. And if we are *supremely* lucky, we can trace that call and work the case from both ends.'

Baz held up crossed fingers. 'Which ID do you want? The vic or the caller?'

'Since he specifically asked for me, I'll take the caller.'

And when she found him, he'd better have some very good answers to a lot of very hard questions.

Shelter Island Marina, San Diego, California
Monday, 4 April, 11.45 P.M.

Kit pulled into her parking place, exhausted. It had been a very long day and all she wanted was to curl up with a cup of tea and snuggle her dog. Unfortunately, Snickerdoodle was with her sister on the other side of town. Akiko would be asleep by now, and Kit wouldn't wake her. Her sister had a full fishing charter tomorrow and needed her rest.

The IT guys had given Kit bad news. The call had come in on

a burner phone and there was no way to trace it. So that was a dead end.

Frustrated, Kit had joined Baz's search for the victim. They'd hoped that the high school class ring the girl had worn on the chain around her neck would allow for a quick ID, but that hadn't panned out. No young women had disappeared from that high school, and they'd have to wait until morning to trace the ring itself, so they'd printed up the missing-person reports for young women – blond, petite – who'd gone missing between one and two years ago.

It had been a tragically big stack. Most had been labeled as runaways. Which, of course, brought back memories of Wren. The cops had initially said she'd run away, too, because she'd had a 'history' of it.

A history of one fucking time. Wren and Kit had run from their foster home when they'd been twelve years old. Before Kit had arrived in the home, Wren had been too scared to run alone. Then they'd landed in McKittrick House, and there had been no reason for either of them to run ever again.

After reviewing the missing-person reports, she and Baz had ID'd the victim in the grave in the park by the Ariana Grande T-shirt she'd been wearing when last seen. Jaelyn Watts, age sixteen. Her family had been frantic when she'd disappeared. But she'd recently snuck off to Los Angeles with her friends to try out for a sitcom in an open casting call and had, therefore, been labeled a runaway, the investigation going cold. Kit would make sure to call the officer who'd taken the report to tell him that she'd been found in an unmarked grave. She hoped it would make him think twice in the future about dismissing a missing child as a runaway.

Sighing, she gathered her things and locked her Subaru. Parking wasn't cheap in the marina, but it was one of the few expenses she had, so she'd paid extra for a spot close to her boat. It helped when she got called to a crime scene in the middle of the night.

She frowned as she approached her boat. There was a light burning in the portlight window. Akiko must have left it on when she picked up Snickerdoodle that afternoon.

Kit couldn't complain about the wasted electricity, though. Not when Akiko was nice enough to take care of her dog.

She did a visual check of the deck as she boarded, making sure everything was where it was supposed to be. The marina had excellent security, but this was her older brother Arthur's sailboat and she would be a good tenant.

She heard the music as soon as she opened the cabin door. Faint at first, the sound of twanging guitars grew louder as she descended. Country music.

Akiko was here. Which meant Snickerdoodle was, too.

Kit felt instantly calmer.

One thing about living on a thirty-eight-foot boat was that everything was within sight. Akiko was sitting on the bed, reading a book. She gave Kit a wave as Snickerdoodle bounded off the bed, coming to meet her with tail-wagging joy, just as she did every day.

Kit knelt on one knee to hug her, absorbing the welcome. 'What are you guys doing here?' she asked, giving Snick a scratch behind the ears where she liked it best.

Akiko followed Snickerdoodle into the main cabin. 'I had a cancellation tomorrow, so I figured I'd bring Snick back and wait for you.'

Kit rose, frowning. Tomorrow's trip was an all-day charter. 'How rude to cancel on you last minute like that. I hope they don't get their money back.' Because Akiko had too many expenses to lose so much cash.

'They won't, and they didn't fight me over it. It was a bachelor party, but the groom caught the bride in bed with her ex and . . .' She shrugged. 'The best man is taking care of canceling everything because the groom is in shock. I told the best man that when the groom feels better, they can rebook at a discount.'

Her sister had a soft heart. 'It's a wonder you make a profit at all,' Kit grumbled.

'Being kind gets me return customers. The best man's already booked a spot on one of my regular fishing cruises.'

'Okay.' Kit inhaled and her stomach growled loudly. Something smelled good. 'Did you cook?'

'I did. I grilled up some of yesterday's catch at my place and brought it over. You want me to zap it for you?'

'Do you mind?'

'Of course not. Sit down, Kit. You look tired.'

'I am.' She sank onto the sofa, patting her lap. Snickerdoodle jumped up and cuddled, instantly making her feel a little better.

Within minutes, she had a plate filled with bluefin tuna, buttery potatoes, and fresh snap peas. The potatoes and peas had come from Harlan and Betsy's farm, so they'd be delicious.

Akiko curled up on the sofa beside her, cradling a cup of tea. She waited silently as Kit ate, knowing it wasn't worth asking questions until the plate was clean.

Kit swallowed the last bite and sighed. 'Thank you. I was so hungry and dreading a microwave meal.' The microwave oven had been one of the few appliances she'd added since moving onto the boat two years before. It worked well here in the marina with the electrical hookup. It was harder to power when she took the boat out on the open water, so those days she ate sandwiches.

Arthur had taken most of his meals at the naval base when he'd lived here, as had Kit when she'd been with the Coast Guard. Unfortunately, her schedule as a detective didn't always mesh with take-out places, so she depended on that microwave at the end of a long day.

'I told you that I'd cook for you,' Akiko said mildly. 'I'm cooking for myself anyway, and I don't mind doubling up for you.'

Kit got up to wash her dishes. It was an old argument. Akiko always offered, but Kit never wanted to put her out. 'I hate to put you to the trouble.'

Akiko shook her head. 'I like to cook, unlike you. I don't mind, Kitty-Cat. I really don't. In fact, I think I'm going to take the decision out of your hands. From here on out, I will double whatever dinners I make and just bring them out to you. I'll send you a bill for your share of the groceries at the end of the month.'

Kit smiled over at her. 'You're too good to me.'

Akiko smirked. 'I know.'

Kit finished the cleanup – there was no room in the galley for dirty dishes to pile up – and made herself a cup of tea. 'Today sucked. And I can't tell you much about it.'

'Well, I figured there was a murder,' Akiko said dryly as Kit reclaimed her place on the sofa. 'Considering you're Homicide and all.'

'Yeah,' Kit murmured, thinking of the body in Longview Park, buried in an unmarked grave, her hands restrained in sparkly pink handcuffs. Jaelyn Watts, on the cusp of starting her life. 'We ID'd the vic. I hate it when they're young.'

'How young?' Akiko asked, sympathy in her dark eyes.

Kit hesitated. The girl's age wasn't going to be a secret when the details were released. She could share that much. 'Sixteen.'

'Oh.' There was a wealth of understanding in that single syllable.

Akiko had never known Wren, having come to live with the McKittricks shortly after the murder, but she knew all about it. She knew how much it had ripped Kit apart. She, along with Harlan and Betsy, had been responsible for stitching Kit back together.

In the years that followed, Akiko had become Kit's very best friend.

'Yeah, oh.'

'You'll find who did it,' Akiko said with unshakable confidence. 'And if you don't, no one else could've, either.'

Akiko always knew the right thing to say. 'Thank you.'

'You're welcome. I just walked Snick before you got home, so she's good for the night. Get to bed. If I know you, you'll be back at the station first thing in the morning.'

That was the truth. 'Stay tonight. I don't like you driving home alone so late.'

Akiko laughed. 'It's only midnight, Kit, and I don't turn into a pumpkin. I can take care of myself, you know. But I'll stay, if for no other reason than to make you a decent breakfast before you head back.' She pointed an accusing finger. 'I saw those Pop-Tarts in your cupboard.'

'Hey. They're fortified with vitamins and minerals.'

Akiko snorted. 'Right.'

'You don't have to get up and make me breakfast. Sleep in on your day off.'

'I'll go back to bed after you have some nutrition, then I'll take Snick and go to Mom and Pop's. I don't get a day off very often, and I think I'll spend it weeding.'

While the McKittricks never asked for help, the majority of their former fosters regularly returned to the farm to assist with the never-ending chores.

Kit hadn't been out to the farm in too long, though. Not for a whole day. She'd been working, investigating cold cases when she'd closed the current ones.

Navarro was right. She did work nonstop this time of year. She figured that Harlan, Betsy, and the rest of the family understood, but maybe she shouldn't expect them to.

She showered and changed into her pj's, taking a moment to retrieve the carved figurines from her pocket before shoving the day's clothes into a laundry bag. She held the little wooden cat-and-bird, studying the bird perched on the cat's head.

Akiko, already on her side of the bed, took off her headphones. 'Pop gave it to you.'

'Yeah. He came by today. He and Mom were picking up a new kid downtown. He said I could keep it in my pocket. For luck.'

'I saw it last Sunday at dinner. It's different from your usual Wren carving.'

'He gave me one of those, too. And one to Baz.' She placed the other carving, the lone bird, on the shelf with the others. 'I'm going to need a bigger shelf.'

Akiko didn't say anything because there really wasn't anything to say. Kit loved that about her. Her sister didn't fill silences when she didn't need to.

Kit locked up her gun and put the cat-and-bird on the table with her keys and wallet. It would go into her pocket tomorrow and every day thereafter. 'Come on, Snick. Time for bed.'

The dog jumped up onto the bed, snuggling between her and Akiko. Kit set an alarm on her phone, then stared at the audio app she still had open. She'd been listening to the anonymous call off and on all day. She still didn't recognize the voice. Slipping in her earbuds, she got under the covers and started the recording again, putting it on repeat.

Hi. This message is for homicide detective Kit McKittrick. I have reason to believe you'll find the victim of a murder in Longview Park at the following coordinates.

He sounded nervous. And maybe scared, as well.

Who was he? *Why did he pick me? Do I know him?*

How did he know about the grave?

Could he be the killer?

Kit found herself not wanting him to be. He sounded . . . sincere.

Rookie mistake, assuming a person's sincerity.

She petted Snick, long strokes over her curly cream-colored coat. And listened to the caller's voice over and over until she finally fell asleep.

Two

SDPD, San Diego, California
Tuesday, 5 April, 8.05 A.M.

'Well?' Navarro asked when Baz and Kit were sitting in his office the next morning.

'We're ninety-nine percent certain that the vic's name is Jaelyn Watts,' Baz said. 'She was sixteen years old when she disappeared last February, fourteen months ago. We're going out later this morning to see the family. Hopefully their dentist will have dental records or the parents will have saved her toothbrush or hairbrush for DNA confirmation.'

'Her parents filed a missing-person report the same day she disappeared,' Kit said, placing a copy of it on Navarro's desk. 'But she'd recently played hooky to go to LA to try out for a part in a sitcom, so she was treated as a runaway. Parents contacted LAPD, who checked with the production company that had held the audition. They had no record of seeing her after she'd disappeared.'

'She obviously never made it to LA.' Baz sighed. 'She never made it out of San Diego.'

Navarro's jaw tightened. 'Sixteen. That was the average age of the other victims.'

Baz nodded. 'Yes. Ricki Emerson was sixteen and the ME estimated the others around the same. And now Jaelyn.'

'Cause of death?' Navarro asked.

'ME suspects strangulation,' Baz said, 'but she needs time for the autopsy.'

'Strangled like all the others,' Navarro muttered. 'Did the ME find evidence of sexual assault?'

Both Kit and Baz nodded silently, and Navarro's shoulders sagged. 'Dammit.' He looked at Kit. 'The caller?'

Kit scowled. 'So far, nothing. IT can't trace the burner. They say they'll do an analysis of the audio to see if there are any identifying factors, but they didn't have a lot of hope. We didn't put a high priority on the analysis yet and there's a long queue. We wanted to give you time to update the brass before we tagged the investigation as a serial killer.'

'You're sure you don't recognize the man's voice?' Navarro pressed.

Kit shook her head. 'I listened to that tape at least fifty times last night.' She'd even dreamed the guy's voice when she'd finally gone to sleep. 'If I've met him, I can't remember it.'

Navarro shrugged. 'It's just as likely that he read about you online. If he's a serious witness, it would make sense to choose you for first contact. If he's the killer and just playing us, same holds true.'

Because Kit had a reputation for caring about the cold cases involving teenagers, closing nearly a dozen in the four years she'd been a homicide detective. One of the city's online papers had done a profile on her two years before, resulting in a lot of unwanted attention.

Kit hated attention at the best of times, but the interviewer had been intrusive and far too personal. Tamsin Kavanaugh had made it her personal mission to follow Kit around ever since, reporting on her homicide cases.

'Maybe,' she said. 'We pulled case files on the previous four victims and made a comparison chart for your meetings upstairs.' She gave him the chart. 'I know that you know the details, but it might help the brass.'

Navarro had been involved in the first four investigations, first as a detective, then as their boss. 'Thank you. I've been getting calls since yesterday afternoon. Walk me through this.'

'All five victims were found with the pink handcuffs,' Baz began. 'The first four had been painted with Krylon glitter spray paint, available in any craft store. We're waiting on lab results for the fifth pair of cuffs. The first two, found fifteen and thirteen years ago, were painted with paint from the same lot, probably the same can. The second two, found eight and then five years ago, were painted with the same lot, but different than the first two. The paint itself is pretty much untraceable.'

'I remember,' Navarro murmured, looking over their analysis.

'All were buried in parks,' Kit continued, 'all around San Diego County. The first was found in a downtown park by a man whose dog found the victim's tibia bone. The rest were found in different parks by random people with metal detectors. Fortunately, two of those three people hadn't actually uncovered the handcuffs. They backed away after exposing one of the victims' bony fingers and the other victim's decomposed face.'

Kit often wondered about the subsequent mental health of those random people who discovered bodies. They were a catalyst for the murder investigation, but most had never seen an actual body outside of a funeral before discovering the grisly remains.

The few she'd interviewed while working cold cases still had nightmares, years later. Just another ripple effect of a killer's cruelty.

'One of the guys with a metal detector did find the pink handcuffs,' Navarro recalled.

'Yes,' Baz agreed, because he'd worked that case, too. 'But he seemed to be a stand-up guy. Promised he wouldn't divulge the detail.'

Navarro looked up, his eyes sharp. 'Find out if he continues to be a stand-up guy. We'll address this differently if it's a copycat killer.'

'On our list, boss,' Baz said. 'We'll seek him out today.'

'So this victim is the first one called in by a potential witness,' Navarro said thoughtfully. 'Killer or caller?'

'We don't know yet,' Kit confessed. 'His nervousness could be an act. This doer has been killing for between seventeen and twenty years – that first victim found fifteen years ago had been in the ground for a while. Maybe he's bored of anonymity and wants some media exposure. Or the caller could be a legit witness.'

Navarro grunted his acknowledgment as he returned his attention to the analysis. 'All the victims had jewelry, none of it expensive. So he's not taking jewelry as souvenirs.'

'It's kind of weird that he doesn't dispose of the jewelry,' Kit said. 'One of the first four victims – Ricki Emerson – was ID'd through her jewelry.' She was the only other victim they'd ID'd before Jaelyn. 'You'd think he'd have learned his lesson, assuming he knows that Ricki was found.'

'Unless he's not worried about that,' Navarro said. 'Levinson seems to think that he wants it known.'

Dr Alvin Levinson was their criminal psychologist. He'd consulted on establishing the killer's profile – middle-aged white guy with a flair for the dramatic – but it was too vague to be of any real use. Not anyone's fault. They just didn't have the evidence for anything more.

'Part of his thrill,' Baz said. 'Will they be found or won't they? If they are, can the cops figure out who she is? If they get an ID, will they trace her to me?'

'Something like that.' Navarro shrugged. 'It's a theory.'

'It's what I'd do if I were a killer,' Kit agreed. 'Especially a cocky killer. I'd want to play with the police. It'd be part of the game.'

'You *would* be a cocky killer,' Baz said with a fond nod. 'No question.'

Kit rolled her eyes. 'The victims were all between five feet tall and five-three,' she said, getting them back on track. 'Weighed between a hundred and a hundred twenty pounds. Jaelyn is five-one and weighed one fifteen, so she's right in his range. She and Ricki Emerson went to different high schools, so there's no overlap there.'

'Dammit,' Navarro muttered.

'But,' Kit said, raising a finger, 'both Ricki Emerson and Jaelyn Watts were in their schools' drama clubs. We're going to talk to Ricki's family and friends again to hopefully find more commonalities with Jaelyn. Of course, it's been ten years since she disappeared – eight since her body was discovered – so getting good recollections isn't guaranteed.'

'If anyone can do it, you two can,' Navarro said. 'I remember that Ricki disappeared in September, so there's no pattern to his abductions, either.' He tapped the page in front of him. 'I like this format. It'll make my conversation with the captain much more straightforward.'

'All Kit,' Baz said with a hint of pride.

Kit's cheeks heated, but she wasn't going to deny it. One of her strengths was communicating ideas in a clear manner. No one ever left any of her briefings confused.

One side of Navarro's mouth lifted. 'Thank you, Mr Miyagi. Are you going to make her wax on and wax off during her lunch break?'

Baz laughed at the gentle *Karate Kid* ribbing. That he was Kit's mentor had always made him proud, and she treasured their relationship.

'If I thought I could get away with it, I would,' Baz said. 'My car needs a good waxing. Marian's been nagging me about it for weeks now.'

'Don't even think about it,' Kit said. 'Our first priority is a positive ID on the victim. Then checking with the only witness to see the pink handcuffs to make sure he hasn't told anyone. He found the second victim thirteen years ago, so again, we're talking a lot of years in between.'

'A lot of years that this killer could have been killing other victims we've never found,' Baz said soberly. 'We're requesting any missing-person reports that fit the profile from all the neighboring precincts going back twenty years. We might need help running down leads, depending on what we find. I've been through a lot of those reports already over the years, trying to ID our three Jane Does, but Kit and I are going to take a fresh look together.'

'I can get you help. Just keep me updated. Call me with anything you find.'

Their plans approved, Kit and Baz went back to their desks, where Kit checked her phone for the directions to Jaelyn Watts's house. 'I'm ready to go whenever you are.'

Baz closed his eyes, looking abruptly old. 'I hate meeting with the families.' He'd gotten much better at it since delivering the news of Wren's death sixteen years before. He'd probably swung too far in the other direction, growing more emotional about each victim than was probably wise.

Kit sighed. 'Me too.'

San Diego, California
Friday, 8 April, 1.45 P.M.

Dr Sam Reeves paced back and forth across his boss's office, glancing at his phone.

'Has it changed?' Vivian asked.

Sam stopped pacing, turning to glare at the stylish woman behind the desk. He'd done the math to estimate her age when he'd first met her. Dr Vivian Carlisle looked to be in her midfifties, but if she'd earned her bachelor's degree at twenty-one, she was now sixty-five. Or at least he thought so.

Sam had never asked her age. His mother had raised him right. And he was not stupid.

Normally.

Today, he felt stupid. Today, he felt powerless.

'No. Still no news.'

'Sam,' she said warmly, 'sit down. Talk to me.'

It was her therapist voice. Sam was quite familiar with the therapist voice since he was a goddamn therapist, too.

A goddamn therapist stuck between his personal and professional ethics. Classic rock and a hard place.

'I haven't slept in days,' he confessed, scrubbing his palms over his face. 'I keep wondering if I've done the right thing.'

'We agreed together that what you did was the right thing. That it was the only thing you really could do.'

Sam nodded, then slid down in his chair, letting his head fall back to rest against the cushion. Vivian's chairs were more comfortable than his were. He needed to request an upgrade.

If he still had a job after this was over.

The alternative turned his stomach. He'd dedicated the past seventeen years of his life to becoming a respected clinical psychologist. He'd wanted to help people, help his clients.

He still did. He just wasn't sure who to help in this case.

'Did you go back to the park to see if the police had done any digging?' she asked.

'No. I haven't been back since I checked the place out four days ago.' It had been four agonizingly long days since he'd made his anonymous call to SDPD. 'If they're digging, I certainly don't want them to ask me what I'm doing there. I don't want to lie.'

Ironic, of course, since it was a compulsive liar who'd gotten him into this mess.

'Understandable. So, what did you say when you made the call?'

Sam tapped his phone screen, opening the Notes app. '"Hi. This message is for homicide detective Kit McKittrick",' he read. '"I have reason to believe you'll find the victim of a murder in Longview Park at the following coordinates". I gave the coordinates, then I hung up.'

Her dark brows lifted. 'You prepared a script?'

'I did. I get flustered sometimes and I didn't want to ramble or say too much.'

'Like "Hi, I'm Dr Sam Reeves and one of my clients – who is a pathological liar, by the way – may have killed a young woman and buried her in Longview Park. Please dig her up and let me know if he's telling the truth".'

Sam found himself chuckling, because those were the exact words that would have come out of his mouth. 'Yeah. Like that.' He sighed. 'When I was in grad school, I wondered what I'd do in this situation. I mean, I get the rules. I do. If our clients believed that we might spill their secrets to the police, we wouldn't achieve any kind of trust. But this is murder, Vivian.'

And past murders were covered under therapist-client confidentiality. Sam was not only not required to report a murder, he was not allowed to do so, except under very specific circumstances. Failure to comply risked his license and even opened him up to civil litigation.

'*If* Colton Driscoll is telling the truth,' she commented.

'*If*,' Sam agreed. 'I mean he goes from talking about having dinner last night with Katy Perry to saving a busload of nuns to putting flowers on the grave of the "pretty young thing" who loved him so. I tried to get him to focus on that – on the grief of whoever he'd lost, thinking that might be a key to his anger issues – but he kept bouncing along. Tea with William and Kate to winning the lotto to playing a round of golf with Tiger Woods and Tiger asking him for pointers. He's exhausting.'

'Pathological liars usually are. You were smart not to confront his lies.'

Sam shrugged. 'He won't admit to them. But I did talk about how he'd felt when his neighbor confronted his lie, trying to direct him toward his anger triggers so that we could explore them. I mean, he's here because he's been court ordered for anger management.' Colton had beaten his neighbor to a bloody pulp after the man exposed one of his lies to their neighborhood. Colton had broken the man's jaw and bruised several of his ribs. The victim had been lucky not to lose his eye. 'He did get angry with me about that. Doubled down on the lie, which was so easily disprovable. But every time I get him focused on the anger, he pops back with more fabrications. He's doing this to confuse me and sidetrack me from the anger problem, I get that. When it was just Katy Perry and British royalty, I could shrug it off, but now . . .'

Colton had started talking about terrible things that could be true.

'We've talked about this,' Vivian said. 'You're doing the right things, Sam. Colton is a difficult case. That he's talked about this "pretty young thing" at all is probably significant. That he's referred to multiple girls this way is even more concerning.'

Colton had returned to the pretty young thing – the one whose grave he visited – in all their sessions thus far, usually only once or twice. But last week he'd talked about the dead pretty young thing several times, adding details that had caused the hairs on Sam's neck to rise. Things like how the grave looked in the springtime and the tree he'd sat under that was near a pond and the scent of strawberries in the air when the wind blew from the artificial flavor factory.

Sam had smelled that strawberry in the air on the days the factory made that flavor. He'd walked his dog on the path around that pond.

It was the first time that Colton had referenced anything remotely real.

And then he'd talked about his new pretty young thing. How she was blond and petite. How cute she was when she was studying her geometry. How she defied curfew to be with him. How she 'loved him so' but that 'sometimes she was bad and needed to be punished.' His words had been alarming enough, but Colton's hands had been clenched around a water bottle, twisting violently as his eyes had grown hard and angry.

Sam had seen that expression before, many years ago. He'd seen hands around a young woman's throat, twisting just like Colton's had. That young woman had died. Sam's old nightmares had been renewed since that session with Colton.

Instinct had told him to be very careful after seeing Colton strangle a bottle. He'd quietly asked Colton to tell him more about his new pretty young thing, because she did indeed sound young. Like, minor young.

Young enough that Sam might have a duty to report child abuse.

Colton had frozen for a brief moment, fear and realization flitting through his eyes. Like he'd realized what he'd revealed.

Like it was true.

But as quickly as it had come, the fear was gone, replaced with cocky laughter as Colton launched into how he'd taught a famous actor how to ride a horse.

Sam blew out a breath. 'His pretty young things are his only topics that don't involve celebrities. She sounds like a teenager, Vivian. She sounds *real*.'

Vivian nodded. 'You were right to pick up on that. If she is real, we have a duty to warn.'

She was soothing him. Building up his confidence. Things that after four years of private practice, he should not need.

Sam's cheeks heated. 'I'm sorry. You have better things to do than hold my hand and tell me I did the right thing.'

One side of her mouth lifted. 'That's kind of my job, Sam. I'm your supervisor. You have done all the right things. I've confirmed it with *my* supervisor.'

Vivian owned and ran the therapy agency, but like other senior practitioners, she had her own therapist to confide in and to check her process. That person had approved Sam's conclusions and his need to know if the grave was real or not.

Sam had dotted his *i*'s and crossed his *t*'s.

He straightened in the chair so that he felt like the professional he was. 'I have two more sessions with Colton. My goal is to focus on his anger so we can work on his triggers. That is the reason for his court-ordered therapy. But if he gives me more about the young women, I'll listen. And if the cops find a body where he described, I'll know he's telling the truth about this and that there is clear and present danger to his newest victim.'

'That sounds like the right way to go.' Vivian folded her hands on her desk. 'I am curious about one thing, though. Why Detective McKittrick? Why did you choose her for your anonymous message? You didn't have to ask for any particular detective.'

'Two reasons, actually. I heard about her initially from my friend, Joel Haley.'

She looked surprised. 'The prosecutor?'

'One and the same. He'd talked about this homicide detective he wanted to date. But she said no. Firmly. Said that they could be friends, but no more. And now they're friends. I've never met her, but he respects her and I respect Joel, so . . .'

She smiled at him fondly. 'That's nice. What's the second reason?'

'I got curious about her after Joel sang her praises, so I looked her up. She's got a stellar record. Served in the Coast Guard, then joined SDPD. She's been a homicide detective for four years now and has closed some cold cases from ten, fifteen years ago. All of them were murders of young women. Teenagers.' There had been a video of her being interviewed, and there'd been a passion in her voice, a determination to stand up for the dead that had spoken to him. 'So when Colton started talking about the grave of his pretty young thing, I wanted her to be the one to look.'

'Good choice. Do you want me to drive by the coordinates to see if anyone's been digging?'

'Would you?'

'I would. Richard and I have a commitment tonight, but we'll go first thing in the morning, and I'll let you know. Call me if you hear anything.'

'I will.' Sam stood, smoothing his tie. 'Thanks, Vivian.'

'You're welcome. Try to get some rest.'

He'd try, but every time he closed his eyes, he could see that slight depression in that grassy field. Not enough to be noticeable unless one was looking for it.

It was a small grave, because – if Colton was telling the truth – he liked his victims small.

'I can't rest yet. I'm meeting my folks for dinner.'

'How's that going, having them living so close by?'

His parents, much to Sam's chagrin, had recently rented an apartment in his building. *For weekend getaways*, they'd claimed, but they spent more time in California than they spent back home in Arizona. On one hand, it was stifling, having his parents hovering so close. On the other, though . . .

He loved them. Plus, his dad had had a mild stroke recently and seemed to need to be near his only son. Sam could oblige them a little hovering.

'Not too bad. I get home-cooked meals once a week, and Dad's an amazing cook.' Tonight was going to be lasagna, which was Sam's favorite.

'They're happy with seeing you only once a week?'

'I didn't say we saw each other once a week, only that Dad cooks for me that often. I see them nearly every day, but they'll be going back to Scottsdale soon. Dad has some big golf tournament, so I'll get some peace.'

'Offer stands.'

Sam chuckled. Vivian had set up a code word. When Sam texted it to her, she'd promised to call and say he had to come into the office ASAP. They hadn't used it yet, but Sam had been tempted a time or two or six.

'Thank you. Call me when you've checked out the park?'

'Of course I will. Try not to worry.'

Sam headed for his own office, checking his phone for news of a body.

Still nothing.

Dammit.

San Diego, California
Friday, 8 April, 3.00 P.M.

'Good afternoon, Mr Driscoll.' Sam gestured to the sofa. 'Please have a seat.'

Colton Driscoll made a show of sitting in the middle of Sam's sofa, resting one ankle on the other knee as he spread his arms wide, resting them on the cushion, palms out. It was classic manspreading and Sam pitied any poor soul who sat next to this man on the city trolley.

Which Colton had to take to get here since his license had been suspended as punishment for nearly running his neighbor over after breaking the man's jaw.

Sam had never felt personally afraid of Colton Driscoll. Colton didn't see him as a real threat but merely an impediment, a court-ordered boulder thrown in his road. Not worth expending the energy over. And even when Sam succeeded in getting a rise out of him, Colton squashed the reaction quickly.

Some pathological liars were unaware of their lies, but Colton was very aware of his. He used them as both sword and shield, deflecting any serious attention from himself.

Unless he was talking about his pretty young things. Then he was almost . . . dreamy.

That scared Sam a lot.

Sam hoped that these young women – whatever their age – were merely figments of Colton's imagination. Images he'd perhaps seen in a movie, weaving them into the stories he told his court-ordered therapist because he had a compulsion to do so.

But Sam didn't think that was the case.

He sat in his own chair in the treatment area, always avoiding sitting behind his desk during sessions. 'So, Mr Driscoll, tell me about your week.'

About six feet tall with a lean, wiry build, Colton was forty-five years old, had been married four times, and had no children. He wasn't model-handsome, but when he smiled, he was oddly compelling.

Sam suspected that was how he'd been married four times, his brides always eighteen years old. Another red flag. Colton liked them young. He'd charmed his wives, but they'd all left after learning that nearly every word out of his mouth was a self-serving lie.

Colton shrugged stiffly. 'Same old, same old.'

That was new. Usually he'd have claimed that he'd had dinner with royalty by now.

'Nothing new or interesting?'

'Nope.'

Ah. Colton was stonewalling. Maybe because he'd scared himself last session by talking too freely.

A tiny part of Sam was relieved. He didn't want to know about Colton's pretty young things. But a bigger part of him needed to know. If Colton had his sights set on a new victim, he needed to know who that victim would be. He had a duty to warn.

'Any major blowups this week? Losing your temper?'

'Nope.'

'I see. Okay. Well, you have to engage with me during the session or I can't check it off your list. If you don't complete the therapy, you'll—'

'I know,' Colton snarled quietly. 'I'll violate my probation and I'll go to fucking jail.'

'That's right,' Sam said cheerfully. 'So . . . talk to me.'

Colton seethed quietly. 'I have nothing to say.'

'No dinners with the Hollywood A-list? B-list?' he added when Colton remained stubbornly silent. 'Z-list?'

Colton looked dead ahead. 'This sucks.'

'I suppose it does. What about your work? How are you getting along with your coworkers?'

'Fucking morons,' Colton muttered. 'I do all the work there. All those damn millennials sit around on their asses and watch me.'

Colton worked in the mail room at one of the high-rise office complexes downtown. Sam had no idea if him doing all the work was the truth, but it was the first time Colton had complained about his coworkers.

'I think that would make me angry.'

'Damn straight.'

'What do you do when they make you angry?'

Colton's expression shut down. 'I don't hit them.'

'That's good to hear. So . . . do you talk to them? Glare at them? Shake their canned sodas?'

Colton chuckled. 'I like the idea of the canned sodas.'

'That would get you into trouble, I suspect.'

'Not if they don't catch me. I'd wear gloves. Go in after hours.' He mimed shaking a can. 'Watch them be angry the next day.'

'The carbonation will have calmed down by the next day.'

Colton slumped. 'Well, damn.'

'Does your supervisor see that the others are lying down on the job?'

'Nah. He's busy spying on all those rich people who pay through the nose to rent office space in the building.'

'I see. Maybe make him aware. Ask him for ideas on how to get the others to do their fair share. Even if he says no, you've put the seed into his mind.'

A lackluster shrug. 'Maybe.'

This was going nowhere. 'What's going on at home? You mentioned a new relationship last week. How's that going?'

Colton seemed to relax. 'Really well. She loves me.'

'That's good. Having someone who loves you might not make

all the frustrating things go away, but that person can share your burden. Does she do that for you?'

'I don't have any burdens for her to share,' he said defiantly. 'I leave those at the front door. When I'm with her, I'm one hundred percent focused on her.'

A shiver of distaste rippled across Sam's skin. Colton's words themselves were a lie, of course, but the tone with which he'd said them was downright creepy.

'What kind of things do you do?'

'We watch TV. Have supper at my place.' He lifted a brow. 'Then other things.'

Sam managed to keep his expression neutral. He didn't want to think about what *other things* Colton could mean. 'What kind of TV?'

Colton thought for a moment. 'She likes *Avondale*.'

Sam's heart sank. Teenagers had been *Avondale*'s target audience.

Although maybe Colton's pretty young thing was legal now and just enjoyed watching shows from her past. 'That show's been off the air for a few years now. You must have found reruns.'

'I did.' He crossed his arms over his chest, tucking his hands into his armpits and staring straight ahead.

Oh good. I yanked him back under the cone of silence. 'Does she know about this? About your therapy?'

Colton was shocked out of his silence. 'God, no. I would never tell her about this. She wouldn't understand.' He shrugged. 'Besides, I'm okay now. It's not like I'll have another incident. She won't need to worry about me getting mad.'

Yeah, right. 'She never makes you angry?'

'Nope.' Colton cast him a smug look, like he knew that Sam was becoming desperate for his answers.

Back away. In previous sessions, Sam would sit quietly until Colton could be silent no longer. The man hated silences.

Sam was off his game today, too worried about a potential victim to do his job properly. So he arranged his lips into a slight smile, exuding calm and patience.

I've got all the time in the world.

Even though he didn't if a minor child was in jeopardy.

They sat that way for about five minutes and Sam was both impressed and frustrated. Colton's previous record was two minutes and forty seconds. But maintaining silence wasn't easy for him. He was biting at his lips and crossing, uncrossing, and recrossing his legs.

'I might miss next week's session,' he blurted out. 'I'm going to England.'

This, unfortunately, was more normal. 'Why?' Sam asked congenially.

'A movie premiere,' he said. 'I'm invited to an after-party.'

Sam nodded. 'Well, we'll need to get permission from your probation officer for the absence, but if he's okay with it, bon voyage.'

'Everyone who's anyone will be there,' Colton went on, completely ignoring the statement about his probation officer. 'It's black tie.'

'Do you have a tuxedo?'

'I do. It's Tom Ford.'

'And will you bring a plus-one?'

Colton blinked. 'A plus-one?'

'A guest. Will you be bringing your girlfriend with you?'

A wistful smile bent Colton's lips. 'I wish I could, but Lilac has a game.'

'What kind of game?' Sam asked mildly, but his heart had started to beat harder. *Lilac.*

'She plays lacrosse. She's the prettiest one on the team, even though I like her better with her hair down. She wears it in a ponytail when she plays. But purple is her color.'

'Her hair is purple?' Sam asked in surprise.

Colton laughed. 'No, her uniform is purple. Her hair is blond.' His eyes widened and flickered with something that looked like panic. Again, he'd become aware that he'd said too much. 'I'm not feeling well. Can we reschedule this session?'

'If we must. I'll have to report your partial absence to your probation officer.'

Colton's eyes narrowed. 'I've been here for more than half an hour.'

'You're court ordered to be here for a full hour,' Sam said, keeping his voice level. Colton hated that.

Colton sprang from his chair, fists clenching, eyes abruptly wild with fury. 'You sanctimonious little—' He cut himself off, shaking his head. Drawing a deep breath, he relaxed his fists and sank back into his seat, flattening his hands on his thighs. 'I apologize,' he said stiffly.

Sam exhaled quietly. That had been unnerving – and the first time Colton had acted violently toward him.

Steadying himself, he focused his attention on Colton's hands. *Well, shit*. The knuckles on his right hand were raw with open abrasions. He'd hit something – or someone – hard.

'This is what we need to discuss,' Sam said seriously. Because he'd let Colton ramble longer than he usually did. He'd check out local girls' lacrosse teams later. 'You losing your temper just now.'

'I didn't lose control,' Colton said from behind clenched teeth.

'No, you didn't.' Although it appeared he had at some time in the recent past. 'What stopped you?'

'You did.'

'How did I do that?'

A sneer twisted Colton's features. 'Because as soon as I step out of line, you'll rat me out. I can't trust you.'

'What stops you when you're at work?'

'Don't wanna lose my job,' Colton said with a small snarl.

'Who did you hit?' Sam asked quietly, pointing to Colton's hand.

Colton's nostrils flared. 'A wall.'

That was plausible. 'Not a person?'

'No,' Colton spat. 'I wanted to, trust me. But I didn't.'

'Who did you want to hit?'

'Guy at work. Just an asshole. Tried to get me riled up so I'd hit him. He wants my job.'

Sam didn't know if that was true or not, but if Colton *had* hit a wall, he was at least trying to manage his anger in his own way. An unsuccessful way, to be sure, but he had redirected his rage.

'That had to have hurt,' Sam said gently. 'I'd like to help you find other ways to deal with your anger that don't hurt you.'

Colton looked down at his damaged hand and sighed. 'Maybe.'

That was the most positive response Sam had gotten in the four weeks he'd been seeing Colton Driscoll. 'Then let's talk about that.'

The rest of the session passed with no other issues.

'I'll see you next week,' Sam said as he walked Colton to the door.

'Yeah, yeah,' Colton muttered.

When he was gone, Sam closed his office door and went to his computer. Normally, he'd type up his personal notes from the session, but not now.

Pulling up a browser window, he typed 'women lacrosse San Diego purple uniforms.'

He crossed his fingers, hoping for a purple-uniform-wearing adult intramural league or a college league. *Don't let her be a teenager. Please.* He'd have a duty to warn regardless of the victim's age, but if she was a minor, it made his involvement even more urgent.

He exhaled heavily at the search results. There were only two teams with purple uniforms, both at the high school level.

Sam clicked on both links and studied the photos of the girls' teams. One team's uniforms were dark purple, the other a lighter shade. *Lilac.*

The Tomlinson Wolverines lacrosse team lined up in the photo arm in arm, smiles on their faces. Several of the girls wore their long hair up in ponytails. About half of them were blond, but only two of them were petite – Destiny Rogers and Alyssa Newman.

If the depression in the ground at Longview Park that Sam had seen truly had been a grave, Colton liked his pretty young things small.

Sam stared at their faces, hoping that he wasn't too late, hoping that Colton hadn't hurt his most recent conquest. *I have to report this.*

But he'd thrown the burner phone away. Which seemed silly now but had seemed like the right thing to do four days ago. He could buy another, but that would take time and he was feeling each tick of the clock.

Tearing his gaze away from the Tomlinson High School team photo, he brought up another browser screen and typed 'pay phones near me'. They had to still exist somewhere, didn't they? Luckily they did, and there was one only five miles away. He had time to make the call before meeting his parents for dinner.

Three

SDPD, San Diego, California
Friday, 8 April, 4.30 P.M.

Kit went straight to her desk and opened the drawer, cursing quietly when she found it empty. She'd forgotten to refill her stash.

Bracing her hands on the desk, she hung her head and closed her eyes. Then flinched when something landed in front of her.

Opening her eyes, she found a king-sized Snickers bar. Raising her gaze, she saw her boss leaning against the corner of her desk, his expression sympathetic.

'Rough one?' Navarro asked.

She nodded, ripping the wrapper from the candy bar and taking a generous bite. Lowering herself into her chair, she let the chocolate, caramel, and peanuts work their magic on her frazzled nerves.

'Jaelyn Watts's parents got home from their vacation this afternoon,' she finally said after chewing and swallowing.

'They were in Africa, yes?'

'Yes, on a photo safari in Tanzania. It was a gift from the rest of their children, for their anniversary. It was also the first time they'd left town since Jaelyn was taken – which took a lot of convincing by their surviving kids. They just knew that as soon as they left the area, there'd be news.'

'Parental intuition?' Navarro murmured. 'Or just wishful thinking?'

She shrugged. 'Either way, they were right.' Eyeing the rest of the candy bar wistfully, she set it aside and met her boss's eyes. 'Mrs Watts was certain we were wrong, that it couldn't be Jaelyn.

She and her husband rushed back, but it was still a long trip after they made it back to the nearest airport.'

'But you had the dental comparison.'

The surviving siblings had cooperated fully, desperate for closure of some kind. 'It's Jaelyn, no doubt. But Mrs Watts wouldn't believe us, not until she saw the body.'

Navarro sighed. 'Unfortunately, I get it.'

'So do I.' Kit had insisted on identifying Wren's body, after all. 'The ME didn't do a full reveal, of course. Jaelyn had a birthmark on her leg and a scar on her elbow. There was enough left for the parents to ID her based on those. Mrs Watts . . . well, she was as you'd expect. Devastated. Weeping. Her husband was stoic until we'd left the morgue, then he collapsed, too.'

It always brought back the memories of Harlan McKittrick's sobs in the barn that night, whenever she saw a big man cry like his heart was breaking.

Because Harlan's had been. So had Jaelyn's father's.

She took another bite of chocolatey goodness, trying to rid herself of the acrid taste of fury at what had come next. 'And then we were ambushed by Tamsin Kavanaugh outside the morgue.'

Kit had good relationships with several of San Diego's reporters, but not Tamsin Kavanaugh. The woman was a thorn in her side, going out of her way to get Kit's statement on every case. Kit said 'no comment' ninety-nine percent of the time, but Kavanaugh was undeterred.

'Oh, for God's sake,' Navarro muttered. 'How did she know you were there?'

'She followed me. She does that sometimes, when she's hard up for a story. Usually I can lose her, but I was distracted today.'

'Parents' grief will do that,' he said gently.

'Yeah, but my distraction meant she put her microphone in their faces. I wanted to hit her.'

'Please tell me you didn't.'

'I didn't, but it was close. "Why are you here? What did you see? Who did you lose? How do you feel?"' she said, her tone mocking. 'How the hell did she think they felt? They were coming out of the *morgue*, for fuck's sake. They were crying and she badgered them and it was so cruel. Luckily Baz kept his head and distracted her while I got the Wattses into our car.'

'Where's Baz now?' Navarro asked.

'He went home. I told him to go,' she added when Navarro frowned. 'They're having his granddaughter's birthday party tonight. I escorted the Wattses home and made sure they weren't alone. Their other children were there, waiting for them. They'd already accepted Jaelyn's death.'

'So what's next?'

'This morning, we finally tracked down the Good Samaritan who found the second victim thirteen years ago. The only one who saw the pink handcuffs. He's dead. Has been for ten years. His wife said that she knew something was wrong, but he never told her specifically.'

Navarro's brows shot up. 'Define "specifically".'

'She thought he was having an affair because his behavior had changed so radically. He told her that he'd found a body and couldn't get it out of his head. He gave her the name of Detective Hammond so that she could verify.'

'Hammond retired, what, eleven years ago?'

'Twelve, sir. She called him and he verified that her husband was telling the truth. That's all she needed to know. She said she never bugged her husband about it again. I called Hammond and he confirmed that she'd called him.'

'So the only civilian who knew about the pink handcuffs didn't spill the beans.'

'And he was dead by the time the last three of five victims were found.' She nibbled the corner of the candy bar. Not enough to fill her mouth, but enough to let the chocolate coat her tongue. 'He wasn't able to sleep after finding that body. His wife said that his doctor cautioned him about his stress levels. She thought it accelerated his heart attack – which was what killed him.'

'Ripples,' Navarro said quietly.

'Exactly.' The depraved actions of one killer affected so many other lives. 'We may have ID'd one of the three remaining Jane

Does, the one between Ricki Emerson and Jaelyn Watts.'

Navarro pulled a folded piece of paper from his pocket. Smoothing it flat on her desk, Kit saw that it was the grid she'd prepared. It was already worn at the folds. Navarro had been consulting it often, it appeared. There were notes along the margins in his chicken-scratch handwriting.

He poised his pen next to the line for the fourth victim. Fourth known victim, anyway. 'She was found five years ago and the ME estimated her age at fifteen,' he read from the grid. 'Who do you think she was?'

'Miranda Crisp.' Kit handed him the missing-person report. 'She matches the victim profile, and the date she went missing was consistent with the ME's estimated time of death.'

'Seven years ago.'

'Yes, sir. She was blond, petite, and a cheerleader at a high school in Chula Vista. Also considered a runaway. She was a foster kid. Had run before.'

Navarro exhaled wearily. 'We've done a shitty job with these so-called runaways. Laziness.'

Kit could only agree. The cops who'd taken Wren's missing-person report had been equally dismissive. *Just a runaway. She'll come back.*

Wren hadn't and neither had Miranda. Or Ricki. Or Jaelyn.

'Her foster parents did all the right things,' Kit said. 'They reported her missing the very night she didn't come home from school and cooperated with the police. They were never suspects.'

Navarro scanned the report. 'She wanted to go to LA, to be in movies.'

'Yep, just like Ricki and Jaelyn.'

He looked up, a gleam in his eye. 'So a legit pattern.'

'Yes. We still don't know how it connects to their killer, but it's more than we knew yesterday.'

'Good work, Kit.'

'Thank you, sir, but Baz found this one. I'm going to visit the family who reported her missing when I'm done here, to ask for anything they might have kept. It was a foster placement, so the chances that they kept anything of Miranda's is low. She went missing nearly seven years ago. I'm sure they've had a lot of kids pass through in the meantime.'

'It's worth a try.' He handed the report back to her and started for his office. 'Call me if you learn anything new.'

'Will do. Thanks, boss,' she called.

He turned, a small smile on his face. 'For what?'

'The candy bar. I needed it.'

'I know.'

'Is it from your personal stash? I'll replace it.'

He chuckled. 'No, it's from my person*nel* stash. I keep something in there for every detective in the division. You're not the only one who embraces chocolate when they're having a rough day. If you want to replace it, fine, but it'll sit there until you or someone else needs it. Maybe even me.'

'Well, thanks anyway. I—' She stopped when the landline on her desk rang. 'This is Detective McKittrick,' she answered.

'Detective, this is the downstairs desk. A call came in for you. Caller wouldn't give his name. You asked to be warned if it happened. Should I put him through?'

A shiver of anticipation raced down her spine.

'Boss,' she called. 'This may be my caller.'

He was at her desk in two strides. 'Put it on speaker.'

'Yes, please,' she told the clerk. 'But first, what number is he calling from?' The clerk told her and she noted it. 'Thank you. Please, put him through.' She activated the recorder, then exhaled quietly before answering. 'This is Detective McKittrick. How can I help you?'

'Detective.' It was him. The voice she'd listened to dozens of times. 'I have a tip for you.'

'Another one?'

'You got my previous message?'

'I did.'

'Did you find anything?'

Navarro shook his head, confirming the response she'd planned. 'How can I help you, sir?'

The man huffed. 'You can tell me if you found anything.'

She waited a beat, then repeated, 'How can I help you, sir?'

He muttered something under his breath that sounded like a curse. 'I want to report a possible threat to a student at Tomlinson High School. She'll be blond and small. Plays lacrosse.'

Kit barely managed not to gasp. Quickly she pulled up the list of missing-person reports on her computer and motioned for Navarro to look.

Cecilia Sheppard had gone missing eight months ago. She was sixteen years old, blond, petite, and had played lacrosse at Tomlinson High.

'How do you know this young woman?' she asked calmly.

'Just . . . take care of her, okay?'

And then he ended the call.

'Dammit,' Kit hissed. 'I wanted to keep him talking.'

'Doesn't matter,' Navarro said, satisfaction in his tone. He'd been typing into his phone while she'd been talking. 'The number he called from is a pay phone at the trolley station at the junction of I-8 and I-15.'

'I'll get surveillance tapes of the area,' Kit said, excited once more. 'What is this guy's game? Cecilia Sheppard went missing eight months ago. Why would he be worried about her now? Is he taunting us?'

'Didn't sound like it, but if he's been killing for twenty years – at least – he's got to be good,' Navarro said grimly. 'Let's go check for security footage.'

She looked up at him with surprise. 'You're coming with me?'

'Yeah. I want to know who this bastard is. Was Cecilia into drama?'

'Yep. Wanted to be in movies. Had taken a few trips to LA with friends for tryouts in the past. Her parents had grounded her, but she'd left the house anyway. Goddammit. We're going to be too late for her.'

'Probably. Let's find out what this caller of yours knows.'

San Diego, California
Friday, 8 April, 9.10 P.M.

'Well?' Baz asked as he jogged into the bullpen. 'What did you find?'

Kit looked up at him sharply. 'You were supposed to stay at Luna's birthday party.'

Baz pulled his desk chair next to hers. 'I did. She's five, Kit. The party lasted two hours. After the cake, the parents took the other kids home and my daughter took Luna home, too. She's probably tucked into bed, getting her daddy to read her favorite book three times as we speak.'

Kit's lips curved. 'She got me to read it four times the last time I was there.'

Baz grinned, unrepentant. 'Five is my record. She loved Harlan's horse carving, by the way. I got video of her opening the box. Which I will show you after you share all.' He pointed to her computer screen. 'So, the mystery man called back? Have you ID'd him yet?'

'Not yet. He's wearing a funky hat that hides his face.' She toggled to the security footage that offered the clearest view of the man's face. 'He looks like he's acting in some kind of desert flick.' The hat's brim hid the top half of his face, the flap hanging at the back hid his cheeks and neck.

'Did you pull the coins from the phone?'

'I did. Navarro got Latent to do a rush analysis. None of the prints popped in AFIS. Well, that's not true. Three of the prints popped, but they were for people who didn't match this guy's description. Our guy either isn't in AFIS or he wiped the coins.'

'Not a huge surprise. If he's been killing for twenty years, he's smart enough not to leave prints. What are you doing now?'

'Trying to get a license plate. After making the call, he got into a gray Toyota RAV4 parked about a block away, but none of the security cameras were angled to get his plates. I've been looking at footage from cameras up and down the nearby streets to see if I can find him.'

'Good thinking. Send me some of the footage and I'll do the same.'

For the next hour, they worked steadily, reviewing the footage from traffic cams along the most-used routes away from the trolley station. Finally, Kit spied the man's SUV.

'Got him,' she crowed. 'Tinted windows, so I can't see his face, but I got his license plates.' Baz came around their desks to perch on the corner of hers, waiting as she typed the license plate number into the DMV database.

Then she sat back and stared at the man's photo.

'Samuel C. Reeves,' Baz said quietly. 'They always look so normal.'

Yes, they did. But Samuel Reeves didn't look normal. He looked . . .

She wasn't sure. Extra, somehow.

His eyes were green, his hair a dark brown that was almost black. His mouth had a serious set, but there was a sparkle in his eyes. If she saw him on the street, she just might pause and take a second look. He had a nerdy Clark Kent vibe that was earnestly appealing.

'He wears glasses, according to his license,' she said, even though he had none in the photo. There were, however, little indentations on the sides of his nose. 'Heavy ones from the look of it. He's also an organ donor.'

'No traffic citations, either. Not even a parking ticket. Guy's as clean as a whistle.'

'He's probably too young,' Kit observed, pointing to his birth date. 'He's thirty-five. He'd have been between fifteen and seventeen at the time of the first murder.'

'Old enough to kill,' Baz said. He tilted his head, studying her. 'What's wrong? You sound like you don't want it to be him.'

Kit blinked. 'I . . . I don't *not* want it to be him. He just doesn't look the part. Although I guess that's how serial killers stay under the radar.'

'This is your first serial,' Baz said knowingly. 'I thought the same thing the first time I ran across one. He looked like he could have been my next-door neighbor, but he'd brutally murdered nearly a dozen children. That we knew of.'

Kit shuddered at the thought. 'You've mentioned him before.'

'It changed me, seeing those dead kids. Made me not trust anyone that looked normal.'

That she shouldn't either was unspoken in his gentle rebuke.

Kit opened a new browser window and typed in *Samuel Reeves*. 'He has a Facebook account.'

'Whoa,' Baz said, pointing at the third search result. 'Hold on before you click on his Facebook. Look at that article. He's a shrink.'

He was indeed. Dr Sam Reeves, Kit read after clicking on the article, had delivered a keynote speech to a gathering of psychologists on serving homeless populations. 'He also works pro bono at a teen shelter according to the bio on this site.'

'And volunteers at a retirement home,' Baz added, his voice heavy with derision. 'He's a regular humanitarian.'

Kit frowned at her screen, thinking about the short conversation she'd had with Dr Sam Reeves. He'd sounded uncertain and almost panicked. She replayed the recording, listening to his words once again. When she finished, she shook her head. 'I don't think he was fucking with us.'

That wasn't exactly true.

I don't want to believe that he was fucking with us.

And that was disturbing. She never, ever allowed herself to be swayed by a suspect, but this man . . . *I don't want to believe he's a killer.*

Baz grabbed a chair and sank into it. 'Talk to me, Kit. What's on your mind?'

Staring at Sam Reeves's photograph, she shook her head again. 'I don't know.'

Yes, you do. You like his face and you don't want to believe he's bad.

Which . . . was bad.

'You don't think he's guilty,' Baz stated.

'I don't know,' she said again. 'He sounds sincere.' She held up a hand to silence her partner. 'I know that's foolish. The best killers sound sincere. They sound innocent. Otherwise we'd catch them faster. But this guy . . .' She glanced over at Baz. 'It's possible this was a simple anonymous tip. Maybe one of his clients confessed something that he couldn't allow to go unreported.'

Baz made a disgruntled noise. 'Maybe. How long has he been in the city?'

Kit ran a standard background check, drumming her fingers on her desk as she waited for the results. 'Four years,' she said when the report filled her screen. 'Not long enough to be our killer.'

'He could always be an accomplice who felt so guilty that he had to call,' Baz said reluctantly.

Kit almost chuckled. Baz sounded so disappointed.

He did have a decided bias against psychologists and psychiatrists. He felt that they chose their occupations at best to fix themselves or because they were arrogant. At worst to hide a more perverse nature under the guise of helpfulness. He didn't trust any of them.

Thinking of her 'optional' appointment with Dr Scott, Kit was inclined to agree. The man was somehow able to burrow under her defenses, getting her to share feelings she'd rather have kept hidden. Feelings about Wren.

Suspiciousness of shrinks was normal among cops. Her *lack* of suspiciousness concerning this one shrink was not.

Baz pointed to Dr Reeves's current address. 'Look at this.'

Samuel Reeves lived in one of the high-rises downtown. She sighed, immediately seeing the connection. 'That's only a few blocks from where the first body was found.' The woman had been buried in a downtown park, which brought to mind a question she'd been meaning to ask. 'How could her killer have buried her in a park in the middle of downtown? Surely someone must have seen him.'

Baz shrugged. 'We asked that question when we found her, but not knowing exactly when she was killed made it hard to even speculate.'

Kit noted the question and returned her attention to the photo of Sam Reeves. 'He was twenty when the first body was found, between fifteen and seventeen when she was killed.' She clicked on the link for his Facebook account. People put a lot of personal information in their social media profiles. Sam Reeves was no exception. 'He grew up in Scottsdale, Arizona, went to high school there.' He'd attended Stanford University for his undergrad and UCLA for his doctorate. 'He's not from San Diego.'

'He has a car.'

She sighed again, because she wasn't going to convince him and she didn't think she should even be trying. Baz could be right, after all. 'Okay. Let's dig into him a little more. Then pay him a visit.'

'Fine.' He pointed at her screen. 'There's the hat he was wearing today.'

Kit nodded. She'd seen it the moment she'd opened his Facebook page. His profile photo was him wearing the hat. He appeared to be somewhere dry and hot with scrubby plants. There was a tent behind him and the sun was setting in the background.

A cute brown-and-white dog sat at his side, some kind of Lab mix. The dog held a stick in his mouth, looking for all the world like a cigar.

She clicked on the photo. 'He uploaded this as his profile pic two weeks ago.' Scrolling down, she found the photo again, this time as a post. '"Camping at Joshua Tree with Siggy",' she read. 'Lots of photos of him with the dog.'

'Lots of photos of him camping,' Baz noted. 'Lots of places to hide other bodies.'

Which Kit hadn't thought about. Usually she was the first to think something like that. *Get your head back in the game.*

'Oh.' She swallowed hard as a familiar scene hit her screen. It was a selfie taken at Longview Park, where they'd found Jaelyn Watts. Dr Reeves was crouched at the edge of a pond, his dog at his side once again. 'He was there just a few weeks ago.'

'Hmmm,' Baz hummed noncommittally. 'Lots of folks use that park, though.'

'I know,' she said, troubled. A thought struck her and she made another note. 'I'm going to call the parks department first thing tomorrow. We know when Jaelyn went missing. I'm going to ask for maintenance records for the weeks immediately after her disappearance. It's been less than two years, so they might have the records handy.'

Baz nodded. 'Makes sense. If they'd closed off part of the park for some reason, that would give Dr Reeves opportunity to bury the body.'

'Or someone else,' Kit countered, wincing even as she did so.

Baz tilted his head. 'You really don't want it to be him, do you?'

'No,' she confessed. 'And I don't know why. Just a gut feeling based on no data whatsoever.'

Baz studied the photo, his expression as troubled as she felt. 'You've got a good gut. Go back to the background check.'

Kit toggled to the correct tab. 'What are you looking for?'

'Weapons. None registered to him.'

She frowned. 'The victims were strangled. No bullet wounds.'

'I know. But I don't want to be surprised when we knock on this guy's door. Let's go pick him up.'

'Fine, but for now we look at him as a witness versus a suspect.'

Baz shrugged. 'I hope you're right.'

San Diego, California
Friday, 8 April, 11.45 P.M.

Sam turned from his 'crime board' to look down at Siggy with a tired sigh. 'It's not going to make any more sense no matter how long I stare at it, is it?'

Siggy just stared up at him adoringly, his tongue lolling.

'You're no help at all,' Sam grumbled. 'But you're a good boy.'

It had been a ridiculous thought, that maybe he could create a crime board with maps and pictures like the cops used. But he couldn't get those two young women out of his head. They were in danger. Or one of them was, at least.

As much as he'd hoped Detective McKittrick would have leapt on his second tip this afternoon, she hadn't. He'd heard suspicion and distrust in her voice.

His disappointment was . . . huge. He'd had such high hopes that she'd be eager for information. She was dedicated to finding justice for the dead and he'd admired her for that. He'd even liked her – or what he knew about her, anyway.

But even bigger than his disappointment in Detective McKittrick was his fear for whichever young woman Colton Driscoll had chosen as his newest pretty young thing.

I have to do *something*. The phrase had been thrumming in his head for hours on an infinite loop. Even his mother noticed he'd become lost in thought at dinner, tuning his parents out, which was something he never did. It wasn't like he could tell his parents what was going on, after all.

His mom had sent him home with chicken soup when he'd claimed a headache.

He glanced wryly at the can of Campbell's chicken noodle soup on his dining room table. His mother meant well, but she wasn't the best cook. Luckily his father was, but as delicious as Sam was sure the lasagna had been, he'd picked at his portion, not tasting any of it.

I have to do *something*.

So he'd taken the elevator three stories up from his parents' apartment to his own, planning the crime board. He'd propped a piece of poster board on the dining room sideboard and fired up his laptop, searching for information on Colton's potential victim.

So far, he'd taped up a photo of the lacrosse team that he'd printed from the school's website. He'd zoomed in on the two petite blondes, printing their faces as well. They went up on the board, along with their addresses. He'd printed a map of the city, marking their homes and Longview Park, where Colton had claimed to visit his last pretty young thing's grave. He'd even added Colton's home address, hoping to see a pattern, but there was nothing.

He'd checked the social media accounts of the two young women, hoping for something that would connect with Colton's ramblings during their session. He'd pulled up his personal notes from the man's sessions, poring over every detail, willing something to jump out and say *It's me. I'm in danger*.

He'd checked the young women's social media for any mention of *Avondale*, the show that Colton claimed to watch with his newest 'love', but he hadn't found anything. Both teenagers had boyfriends at school – within their grade level. No older men. No mention of older men. Not even any posts about any famous actors that were older.

There was nothing whatsoever to indicate that either young woman was being pursued by a mysterious man of Colton Driscoll's age. Of course, they might be hiding the relationship from their family and friends. That was probable, even.

Sam wished that his boss had been able to drive to the park tonight, but she would tomorrow and they'd find out if there was any sign that the cops had listened to his first tip. If they hadn't, they weren't likely to have acted on his tip this afternoon.

If the cops didn't move to protect those young women, Sam would have to find a way to warn them himself. If he couldn't figure out which teenager was Driscoll's likely target, he'd warn them both. He wasn't sure how he'd manage it within the confines of ethics and the law, but he was certain that he couldn't live with himself if either young woman was hurt – or worse – because he'd done nothing.

Sam sighed again. 'I think it's time for bed, boy.' He'd already walked Siggy for the night, so he could just go to sleep. If he was able to sleep.

He turned from his attempt at investigating, then paused, eyeing his gun safe. He remembered that brief moment during Colton's session when the man had been poised to strike him. Colton had recovered quickly, controlling himself, but it had left Sam more shaken than he'd wanted to admit.

What if the cops had acted on his tip this afternoon? What if they'd already warned the teenagers on the lacrosse team? That would be good for the young women, but if Colton figured out that Sam had been the tipster . . .

The man had beaten his neighbor for confronting one of his many lies. If he discovered that Sam had been the one to turn him in, he might strike out. Sam didn't intend to be Colton's next assault victim. He drew the gun from the safe. It was loaded, with a bullet in the chamber.

He'd had the gun for years, normally only carrying it with him when he went camping, just in case he met with trouble. He'd never fired it outside a target range and hoped he'd never have to.

He'd had alarming clients in the past, of course. He'd even been worried that clients would come after him before. But this was different. If Colton wasn't lying, if he was guilty of sexual assault or even murder, Sam would be the one responsible for turning him in to the police.

Sam couldn't carry a weapon into the office, but he could put it on his nightstand for his own peace of mind. If the police had taken his tips seriously, they'd hopefully take Colton into custody and Sam wouldn't have to worry about him.

It wouldn't be as simple as that, Sam knew. Colton might not be arrested, and if he was, he might be released on bail within a day.

I'll cross that bridge when I get there.

A sharp rap on his door had him freezing, then glancing at his phone for the time. It was almost midnight. Neither of his parents would be knocking this late, and they did a little shave-and-a-haircut knock anyway, so it couldn't be them.

A shiver of trepidation slithered down his spine. It couldn't be Colton. *I'm being ridiculous. I've got myself worked up over nothing.*

But just in case . . . Sam pointed the gun toward the floor, crept to the door, and put his eye to the peephole.

Then exhaled in a swift rush of relief. Two people stood on his doorstep – a tall man with graying hair and a thirtyish woman of medium height with a sweet face devoid of makeup, her strawberry blond hair pulled back in a no-nonsense ponytail.

Detective McKittrick. The man was her partner, Basil Constantine. Sam recognized him from the articles he read.

They'd followed up on his tips. *Thank you, God.*

Sam opened the door. 'Detectives. I—'

He froze once again when both detectives abruptly drew their weapons and pointed them. *At me.*

'Drop the weapon,' Constantine barked.

McKittrick appeared grim. And maybe disappointed?

Sam didn't have time to analyze her expression, remembering too late the gun he'd brought to the door. *Shit, that was stupid*. But he could explain. They'd understand.

Slowly he lowered the gun to the floor and took a step back, his hands held in front of him, palms out. 'I can expl—'

McKittrick's soft gasp cut him off. 'What the hell?' she murmured, her eyes wide and focused behind him.

Sam looked over his shoulder. His crime board. *Shit*. 'I can explain.'

'I'll just bet you can,' Constantine snarled quietly. 'Trolling for your next victim, you sick sonofabitch. Hands out at your sides, *Dr Reeves*.' He spat Sam's name with contempt.

What? Oh. Oh no. Realization dawned and Sam took another step back. They thought he was involved. *They're here for me*. 'This is a misunderstanding.'

'It always is,' Constantine mocked.

McKittrick's jaw was squared, her eyes cold as she pulled handcuffs from her belt. 'You're coming with us.'

In shock, Sam opened his mouth. 'This is wrong. You're wrong.'

Ignoring him, she snapped a cuff on his right wrist, stepping behind him to cuff his left. Panic rose, clawing his throat.

No, no, no. Not his arms. They couldn't grab his arms. He couldn't let them.

'No!' He yanked free, taking a large step backward. 'This is a mistake. Let me explain.'

Then everything seemed to happen at once. McKittrick swept his legs out from under him and had him facedown on the floor of his own apartment. His glasses went skittering across the floor as she jerked his arms behind his back, slapping the other cuff on him.

'Your mistake was resisting, Dr Reeves,' she said coldly. 'Now you're under arrest.'

Arrest? I'm under arrest? Me? No. No. No. This is wrong. This can't be happening. But it was.

Siggy was growling, his teeth bared.

'Call off your dog,' Constantine demanded. 'If he attacks, I'll shoot him.'

'No!' Sam thrashed, trying to knock McKittrick off him, but she shoved her knee into his kidney. Pain flared but fear for Siggy kept him struggling. 'Don't hurt my dog! Please don't hurt him!'

Siggy was approaching, lowered in a crouch, snarling at McKittrick in a way that Sam had never heard before.

'I hate it when they have dogs,' Constantine muttered.

'Tell him "down," Dr Reeves,' McKittrick said calmly. 'You can call someone to come and get him.'

Mom and Dad. They'd come for Siggy. They could be here in two minutes.

And see me cuffed and arrested.

No. That wouldn't do. His father would have another stroke.

I'll sort this out. I'll explain and they'll let me go. Mom and Dad will never be the wiser.

He got control of his breathing and, as calmly as he could muster, told Siggy, 'Down, boy. It's all right. Down.'

Siggy dropped to his belly but continued to growl menacingly.

'Do you want to call someone to get him?' McKittrick asked, her knee still in his kidney.

Sam didn't like her so much anymore.

'Yeah,' he grunted out. 'I have a dog walker.' A college student who lived on his floor. But he'd never called her this late before.

McKittrick patted him down and pulled his phone from his pocket. 'Tell me your code and I'll call her for you.'

No. Clarity was returning with a rush of anger. *This is wrong. I was trying to help you and* this *is the thanks I get?*

Although he could see their point of view. It looked bad. *But I'm not bad*. He'd make them see that.

Still, he wasn't going to give the cops any more ammunition to use against him. Once he gave them his phone code, they'd have access to his personal life.

His personal session notes.

'No,' he said, trying for calm. He needed to see to Siggy's safety first. He didn't think Constantine would shoot his dog, but he couldn't be sure. 'If you'll let me put him in his crate, I'll call the dog walker when my hands are freed.'

'Suit yourself.' Her weight disappeared from his back and he drew a deep breath, fighting nausea. 'Up.' She grabbed his arm and hauled him to his feet.

If he weren't so furious and about to throw up, he'd be impressed. Sam was six feet tall and weighed one-eighty. McKittrick didn't look like she was big enough to manage him like that.

'If you'd let me explain, none of this will be necessary,' he said, using his therapist's voice.

She huffed a mirthless chuckle. 'Go ahead. I'm listening. You've called me twice, Dr Reeves, and neither time did you give me a valid explanation, but by all means, explain.'

'First, I need to know if you found anything in the park.'

'I'm not telling you anything. You wanted to explain. So explain.'

He closed his eyes for a moment, considering his options. He couldn't tell her anything until she confirmed that there was indeed a body. That was the point of this entire exercise. If he spilled everything now, he could lose his license, especially if Colton was lying.

'I can't. Not until I know what you found in the park.'

'Then we're at an impasse,' she said, still cold. 'Where is your dog's crate?'

Sam gritted his teeth. He'd be getting the biggest apology from SDPD when this was over. 'In my bedroom.'

'Will he go with me?'

'No. I'll have to walk him there.'

She looked at her partner. 'If you'll get the warrant started, I'll take care of the dog and then get CSU to process the creepy photos.' She drew her weapon once again and pointed it at Sam. 'Walk slowly, Dr Reeves. Do not incite your dog to violence and do not try to resist.'

Motherfuckers. His blood boiling, Sam obeyed. 'This is a mistake,' he hissed once again.

She sighed wearily. 'You have the right to remain silent, Dr Reeves. I'd exercise that right if I were you.'

He flashed her a look filled with all the venom burning inside his chest. 'Do I get my one phone call?' he asked, his teeth clenched. Vivian would clear this up.

'Depends on your behavior. Let's go. Call your dog.'

'Siggy,' he said, managing to keep his voice calm. 'Come on, boy. Time for night-night.' Siggy warily followed them to his bedroom where the crate door was open, his water bowl already filled. 'In, boy.'

Still wary, Siggy slunk into his crate and McKittrick fastened the closures with a practiced hand, making him wonder if she had a dog of her own.

'Do you put food in his crate with him?'

'No. He's eaten already.'

'Then let's go.' She hesitated, then gave the crate a pat. 'It'll be okay, Siggy,' she soothed, then turned to Sam. 'After you.'

Four

SDPD, San Diego, California
Saturday, 9 April, 5.45 A.M.

Sam's glasses were broken and his face hurt. Staring into the interrogation room mirror, he saw a bruise forming on his cheekbone where his face had hit his living room floor.

At least they'd taken off the handcuffs. He could breathe normally again.

They'd started to question him, but he'd immediately asked for a lawyer. He might have been stupid enough to think he could make a damn crime board, but he knew enough not to say another word without his lawyer present. Especially since they wouldn't address the one question he needed an answer to.

Except he didn't have a lawyer. He'd never needed one. He'd never even had a parking ticket, for fuck's sake. The only defense attorney he knew personally might not even take his calls anymore because their relationship had ended rather poorly, but he'd tried calling anyway.

Laura Letterman hadn't shown up yet, but the detectives weren't hurrying him into a holding cell. So there was that. He had a little time to figure out what to do.

It had to be close to dawn, but he didn't know the time because they'd taken his phone. He glared at the mirror, knowing they were there, watching him.

Damn detectives. He closed his eyes, trying for the umpteenth time not to let the panic overtake him. Vivian hadn't picked up the phone and the answering service said that she'd had a family emergency and was off call for the night.

They were supposed to forward her calls to him.

Ha! That had actually made him laugh.

He'd had to tell the answering service that he would also be unable to cover any after-hours calls. They had other therapists who could handle an emergency, so at least their clients wouldn't be negatively impacted.

He wanted to be worried about Vivian – and he was – but worry over his own situation eclipsed everything. He was on his own for now.

Opening his eyes, he fixed his gaze on the mirror. 'I can clear this up if you'd only answer my question. I can't divulge information until I know what you found – if anything – in the park. I figure you found something because I'm here, but I can't talk to you until I know for sure.'

No answer. He waited for what felt like an hour but must have been only a minute or two.

He sighed, exhausted. He had one more card to play before he let the panic have him. 'Fine. I assume you haven't heard from my attorney yet. Can I call another? His name is Joel Haley.'

The door opened and McKittrick strolled in like she had all the time in the world.

He *really* didn't like her anymore.

'Joel Haley?' she asked, looking mildly interested – on the surface. But her eyes were more expressive than she probably realized. She was very interested. 'The only Joel Haley I know is a prosecutor.'

'He's the one.'

She regarded him levelly for a long moment. 'Why Joel Haley?'

'Because he's my best friend.'

Her eyes widened at that. 'Really? Huh. Okay, then, I'll get your phone. You should have mentioned him earlier.'

He rolled his eyes. 'I was hoping I wouldn't have to. I was *hoping* you'd be *reasonable* and answer the one damn question I need you to answer.'

Her expression went cold once again. 'And until I know your game, Dr Reeves, I'm not telling you anything.'

He leaned back into the very uncomfortable chair, wishing he hadn't called from that damn pay phone. That had been a rookie move. 'Just let me call Joel.'

She left the room and he yawned, cracking his jaw and making his face hurt all over again. Dammit.

She returned a few minutes later with his phone in an evidence bag. After giving it to him, she watched him intensely as he tapped his security code onto his screen. He hunched over his phone as he typed in the numbers so no one could see the code – not Detective McKittrick, not anyone on the other side of the mirror, and not the damn camera on the wall with its blinking red light.

He dialed Joel, holding his breath that the man would answer. It was hit or miss with Joel, especially on the weekend. He worked his ass off during the week and played hard starting Friday night. Which meant hooking up with someone from his little black phone app.

'Yeah?' Joel answered groggily. 'What's wrong?'

Sam exhaled in relief. 'Joel, I need your help. I'm in some trouble.'

Taking a chair across the table, McKittrick snorted inelegantly. Sam ignored her.

'What kind of trouble?' Joel asked with a yawn. 'Can't it wait until later?'

'No, it can't. If it could, I would have waited until later. I'm at the police station downtown.'

'What?' Joel demanded, sounding more awake now. 'Sorry,' he murmured, presumably to his bedmate. 'Go back to sleep.'

There was the sound of rustling sheets and then that of a door closing. 'Okay,' Joel said. 'Talk to me, Sammy.'

'It's a long story and I can't tell anyone anything until the police answer a question for me.'

'Did you call an attorney?'

Sam winced. 'I called Laura. She's the only one I know.'

Joel barked out a harsh laugh. 'You *must* be desperate. Don't worry. I've got other contacts you can call. What do they think you did?'

That his best friend didn't automatically assume he was guilty made Sam feel a little better.

Sam focused on McKittrick's face when he answered Joel's question. 'I think they think that I murdered someone.'

McKittrick's mouth firmed. Yeah, that was it. *They think I killed someone.*

Maybe I was too late. Maybe Colton already killed the lacrosse player.

'What the actual fuck?' Joel exploded. 'Wait, what do you mean you can't tell them until they answer a question? Can't tell them what? What the hell's going on, Sam?'

'I can't tell you, either. I could lose my license.'

Joel huffed out a breath. 'So this is a client thing? Something one of your clients did?'

Sam sighed in relief once again. 'Yes.'

'I'll be there in half an hour. Are they treating you okay?'

'My face hurts because one of the detectives took me down in my own living room, but I'm otherwise unharmed.'

'Which detectives?'

'McKittrick and Constantine.'

'Fucking hell. They should know better. Is McKittrick there?'

Sam eyed the detective, who was studying him with what he hoped was a tad less animosity. 'She is.'

'Let me talk to her.'

Sam handed the detective his phone. 'Joel wants to talk to you.'

Warily she took it, lifting it to her ear. 'Hey, Joel.' She listened for about a minute, then rolled her eyes. 'Come on in, then. Hopefully your *friend* will tell us something useful.' She listened some more, rolled her eyes again, then handed the phone back to Sam. 'He wants to talk to you.'

'Don't talk to anyone until I get there,' Joel instructed. 'I'm calling a defense attorney as soon as I hang up. Do you need medical attention for your face?'

'Ice would be nice.'

'They'll get it for you. We'll get this cleared up, Sam. Don't worry.'

'Thanks, Joel. Sorry I ruined your night.'

'You can make it up to me with some of your dad's lasagna.'

Sam laughed softly. 'Deal.' He ended the call, locked his phone, then handed it back to the detective. 'Thank you.'

Rising, she shook her head. 'Don't thank me yet. Just because a prosecutor says you're a good guy doesn't let you off any hooks. I'll get you some ice for your face.'

He didn't say another word as she left the room. She was back quickly, some ice in a plastic baggie.

He took it with a nod of thanks. Pressing it to his face, he waited with her in tense silence. She looked as tired as he felt.

After a few minutes, she covered another yawn. 'Did you need to take care of your dog?' she asked.

'Depends on how long I'm here. What time is it?'

'Nearly six.'

'My dog walker waits tables in a bar. Puts herself through college that way. Saturday is her day to sleep in, so I won't bother her yet. If I'm still here by eight, I'll call her. She won't be happy that I woke her up, but she loves Siggy, so she'll do it.'

'She'll have to be escorted by an officer. She can't just let herself into your apartment. I stationed a uniform outside your door to guard the place after CSU was finished processing the scene.'

He stared at her, stunned once more.

A uniform was stationed outside his front door. The neighbors would be waking up soon. They'd see. They'd talk. They'd wonder if he was all right and once they saw that he was, they'd wonder what he'd done. They'd speculate, and word would spread, likely to his clients. It was going to be awful.

It had been one thing to be dragged out in handcuffs when everyone was asleep or out partying. No one had seen them coming down the elevator. But now . . .

'I was trying to do the right thing and still protect my career,' he said quietly. 'Now I'll be the subject of gossip and my career will be tarnished.'

Something changed in her expression, a flicker of emotion in her eyes. 'What was the right thing that you were trying to do?'

He pulled the ice pack from his face and set it on the table with a sigh. 'I told you that I could explain if you only told me what you found at the park. I didn't hurt anyone. I risked my career so that someone wouldn't get hurt.'

She held his gaze for a long moment, and he could practically see the wheels turning in her mind. 'A body,' she finally said very quietly.

He sucked in a breath, remembering the tiny sunken plot of earth. 'Dammit,' he breathed. He hadn't wanted to be right. He hadn't wanted Colton to have been telling the only truth of his miserable life.

'Is that enough information?' she asked.

The door opened, startling them both. 'Don't answer that question,' said a very familiar female voice.

Laura's here. And was she ever. She blew into the room, four-inch heels clacking on the cheap tile, and took the seat next to Sam. She looked as put together as always, her power suit intimidating, her makeup flawless, and her eyes bright, as if she'd had a full night's sleep. She probably hadn't. She'd been an incurable insomniac in the four years they'd been together.

'I didn't think you'd come,' Sam murmured, his feelings conflicted. On one hand, he was grateful she'd come. On the other, he'd honestly hoped he'd never have to see her again.

She shot him her don't-be-an-idiot look. He'd been on the receiving end of that look more times than he could count. 'I'm not going to let the cops railroad you.'

The detective cleared her throat. 'I'm Detective McKittrick.'

Laura gave the detective a brusque nod. 'I know. I'm Laura Letterman, Dr Reeves's attorney. This interview is over.'

'Laura, stop.' Joel strolled in and closed the door behind him. He met Sam's gaze, brows lifted. 'We met up in the lobby, but she walks too fast for me.'

It was a lie. Joel didn't like Laura any more than Sam did and had probably let her charge ahead so that he could put off having to interact with her for a few minutes longer.

Laura skewered Joel with a cutting glare. 'Sam doesn't say anything to the cops until I know what's going on.'

'That's fair,' Joel said mildly. 'But I think he wants to cooperate. Detective, can you give us a few minutes alone with Ms Letterman's client?'

Eyes narrowed, McKittrick looked from Joel to Laura to Sam, lingering on Sam's face. 'Of course. I'll be on the other side of the glass and I'll turn down the volume. Wave when you're ready to talk.'

When she was gone, Laura turned to Joel with a slight snarl. 'Why are you here?'

Joel smoothed a hand down his tie. He was also dressed in a snazzy suit, making Sam feel like a schlub in his sweatpants and T-shirt. 'Sam asked me to come.'

'Well, I'm here now,' she said coolly. 'You may go.'

'No,' Sam interjected, before their argument could gain steam. Sam's breakup with Laura had been cold and final, with no conversation. Joel's, on the other hand, had been explosive, with much shouting and gnashing of teeth. Which had always made Sam curious since he'd been with Laura for four years. Joel had only dated her casually for two months, but he'd been much more emotional about Laura's infidelity, which Sam now knew wasn't like him at all.

Laura bit back whatever she was about to say to Joel and turned to Sam. 'Explain, please.'

So he did. He didn't give specifics about Colton or what he'd suspected, but he did tell them that he'd had an ethical conflict and how he'd resolved it.

'So let me get this straight,' Laura said when he was finished. 'You suspect a client did something, you made two anonymous calls to McKittrick, and you only need her to tell you what she found in the park before you can tell all?'

'Basically, yes. If I'd just told her what I knew, I could lose my license. And the client could sue me in civil court on top of that. I didn't know if he was telling the truth or making up some grand story, so I couldn't spill until I knew.'

'Do you know now?' Joel asked.

'McKittrick said it was a body,' Sam said. 'Right before you came in, she finally told me.'

Laura tilted her head. 'Would you have spilled all without a lawyer?'

Sam shook his head. 'Not at this point. I was going to at least wait for Joel.' He stroked his thumb over his bruised cheekbone, some of the anger he'd suppressed roiling back to the surface. 'They were far more aggressive than they needed to be. Scared my dog.' He grimaced. 'Scared me, too.'

'I'd guess so,' she said sympathetically. 'You're like the quintessential Dudley Do-Right, and I'm not being mean. You've always done the right thing, Sam. Getting arrested has to have shaken you up.'

He nodded wearily. 'You have no idea.'

'So you think you know who this guy's next victim is?' Joel asked.

'I've narrowed it down to two teenagers. I couldn't wait any longer to find out what they found in the park. I couldn't have lived with myself if either girl was hurt.'

Laura's gaze softened. 'So what do you want me to do?' She glanced at Joel, a flash of regret in her eyes that she'd never aimed toward Sam. 'Or *us* to do, I guess.'

'I want you to get them to drop any charges once I tell them what I know,' Sam said to Laura, then turned to Joel. 'I'd like you to be a character witness. And if they don't let me go, I need you to take Siggy until I'm out of here. They can't keep me forever. I didn't do anything.'

'Oh, you sweet summer child,' Laura murmured. 'They can do whatever they want.' She glared at Joel again. 'Prosecutors and cops.'

'Not fair,' Joel said quietly.

She sighed. 'No, it wasn't. I'm sorry.'

Joel nodded tightly, then waved at the mirror to motion McKittrick back into the room. 'Why'd you pick Kit, Sam?'

'Because you respect her. You said that she was a good cop and a decent person. She's your friend. I hoped she'd take me seriously.' And it seemed that she'd done exactly that.

She'd found a body in Longview Park.

Colton Driscoll was a murderer.

At least now Sam knew for sure. He could turn Colton in with no guilt or career repercussions.

He only hoped he wasn't too late.

SDPD, San Diego, California
Saturday, 9 April, 6.30 A.M.

'What do you think?' Baz asked, standing next to Kit on the other side of the mirror.

'I don't know,' she admitted, studying the faces of the three people sitting around the interview room table. 'I know Joel, of course, as do you.'

'He's a good guy.'

And he was. Joel Haley was a hard-nosed prosecutor with a winning record. Kit both liked and respected him. She didn't think he'd lie. But he could be mistaken about his friend's character. If Samuel Reeves had committed a murder, Joel would have to recuse himself.

But Kit didn't think that Reeves had done it. She hadn't thought so when she'd first seen his photo.

And, because of that, Kit didn't trust herself. But she'd taken the chance. She'd answered his question.

When she'd told him that they'd found a body, his reaction had been one of pain. And resignation. Like he'd expected it but hadn't wanted it to be so.

'Reeves still has a lot to explain,' she murmured. 'Mainly the two photos he had taped up in his apartment.'

'Neither of the two girls had ever seen him before, nor had their parents.'

Baz had personally checked on the two teenagers after they'd deposited Reeves in the interview room. The two girls had been in their respective homes, one already in bed and the other watching TV with her boyfriend on the family's living room sofa.

They'd both known Cecilia Sheppard, the teen who'd gone missing eight months before. She'd played on their lacrosse team. They'd been friends.

'I want to hear his explanation,' Kit murmured.

Baz made a face. 'I know his attorney. Letterman's a real shark. She defended a guy I booked on aggravated arson five years ago and questioned me on the stand. She is very, very good. She tied me into so many knots that she almost had me second-guessing myself. We got a conviction, but it was close. Do not underestimate her.'

Kit would not. She'd never met a defense attorney whom she'd trusted. 'They have history,' she said, nodding at the three talking animatedly around the interview room table. 'All of them.'

'I figured the same. Letterman has feelings for both Reeves and Haley. Not necessarily good feelings, but feelings nonetheless.'

Kit had thought the same. It was in the way they'd greeted one another. It was as if Reeves hadn't wanted her to come, even though he'd also been grateful that she had. And Kit bet that Joel's casualness was a facade.

There was a story there, but for now she only wanted to get to the truth of *this* story. Jaelyn Watts and Cecilia Sheppard and four other young women had lost their lives.

The three ceased their conversation and Joel waved at the mirror.

'That's my cue.' Kit grabbed the case folder and went into the interrogation room, taking her seat across the table from Reeves, Joel Haley, and the shark attorney. Laura Letterman. *Don't underestimate her*.

Kit hit the record button on the room's video camera remote. 'I'm listening.'

'I'm a psychologist,' Reeves began. 'I have a court-ordered client who is a pathological liar. Talks about having tea with royalty, dinner with various Hollywood celebrities. But then he started talking about a grave he visited and how much he missed his "pretty young thing".' He used air quotes. 'This came up during more than one session, and I began to wonder if this was the one truth he was telling me.'

'The grave in the park?' Kit asked, and he nodded.

'I'm not allowed to report a client for a past murder, only one that's about to happen. In that case, I have a duty to warn, and I take that very seriously. But I didn't know if this was fabrication or truth. Even if it was true, I *still* couldn't divulge the past murder. Unless a minor was involved.' He tilted his head. 'Was the victim a minor?'

Kit nodded, relieved. He'd been telling the truth. He hadn't killed anyone. She hoped, at least. She wasn't going to let her gut lead her, though. She'd play this like he was still guilty until she was positive. 'Yes, she was.'

Reeves closed his eyes, his expression tight and pained. 'Was she a child? The grave looked small.'

'She was petite,' Kit agreed. Jaelyn had been barely five-one. 'A minor, but not a young child. What made you risk your career and make that first call?'

Reeves opened his eyes and they were filled with worry. 'He recently started talking about a new "pretty young thing". I shared my concerns with my boss and we decided the best way to proceed was to determine if he was lying or telling the truth.'

'So you told me to check for the grave.'

'Yes. I watched the news, but I saw nothing on any bodies being found in Longview Park. I'd planned to wait until I did before I did anything more, but then my client and I had a session today. I was able to glean enough information from his ramblings to know that the new young woman was a lacrosse player. He called her "Lilac". He said she had blond hair.' His shoulders sagged. 'I googled girls' lacrosse teams in the area and only one school has lilac uniforms.'

'Tomlinson High.'

He nodded. 'I assumed that because the last victim was petite, this was his type. Two girls on the Tomlinson team fit the profile. I couldn't live with myself if another girl got hurt because I was protecting my career. So I called you again.' He met her gaze, his own anguished and anxious. 'Are they all right? The two girls?'

'They're fine,' Kit said.

He slumped where he sat. 'Thank goodness.'

'Your boss can corroborate all of this?'

He nodded. 'She's not available right now, though. She was the first person I called, but the answering service says she's not taking calls. I'm not sure why.'

Suspicion pinged Kit's mind. That the one person who could corroborate his testimony wasn't available was too convenient. Apparently both Joel Haley and the defense attorney thought the same thing because they both winced.

'Is she the only one?' Kit asked.

Sam looked around the table, his brows furrowing at the expressions on their faces. 'No,' he said, his voice slightly strained. 'She told her therapist as well.'

'I'll need his name.'

Reeves hesitated. 'I don't know it. Her assistant probably would, or maybe even her husband, but I never asked and she never offered.'

Too fucking convenient. Kit sighed, disappointed in her gut once more. She'd really wanted to believe this man, which wasn't like her at all. 'What was with the photos you had taped to that board?'

'Stop, Sam,' his lawyer advised. 'I don't like the way this is going.'

Reeves looked at Joel. 'Do you agree with her?'

Joel waffled his hand in a so-so motion. 'I believe you, but that your boss is suddenly unavailable to corroborate doesn't look good.'

'She will, once she's back,' Reeves insisted. He turned to Kit, looking her in the eye. 'I didn't think you believed me. Four days passed from my first call and I'd neither seen nor heard anything about any bodies found in the park. I figured there'd be something about police digging a hole, at least, but there wasn't.'

This was true. They'd barricaded off the area when they'd started digging so that no one would witness the activity and had asked the park's management to say it was a broken pipe if anyone asked why the ground had been disrupted. Kit hadn't thought it would work, but there had been no media coverage, much to SDPD's relief.

'When I called a second time, you were suspicious,' Sam went on. 'I figured you hadn't taken me seriously, so I decided to figure out who the next victim was and warn her myself if I had to.'

He sounded so goddamn sincere. *Why does he have to be so goddamn sincere?*

'So you did what?' She smiled condescendingly, just to see his reaction. 'Thought you'd make a murder board like we use in Homicide?'

His cheeks flushed with color and he clenched his jaw for a second before answering. 'Yes. I told you that I take my duty to warn seriously. I'm glad you find this so amusing, Detective,' he said bitterly. 'At least "Lilac" is safe.'

Kit kept her gaze fixed on his face, watching for his reaction to her next disclosure. 'No, she isn't. The two teenagers you pointed us to are all right. But one of their teammates went missing eight months ago. She was blond and petite and played lacrosse wearing a lilac uniform.'

The color drained from Reeves's face. 'Oh my God,' he whispered. 'Did she like the TV show *Avondale*?'

Kit blinked at the question. 'I don't know. Why?'

'Because my client said they watched that show together. Did he kill her? Could she still be alive?'

'What is your client's name?' Kit asked, fully expecting him not to answer.

'Colton Driscoll,' he said, still appearing horrified. 'He was referred to me for anger management as a requirement of his probation after he beat his neighbor and tried to hit him with his car.'

Colton Driscoll. Excitement prickled over her skin. Now they had a name.

'And he got probation?' Joel demanded. 'What the hell? I hate the system sometimes.'

'Me too,' Kit said coolly. 'How old is Mr Driscoll?'

Reeves frowned at her, confused. 'Forty-five. Why?'

Old enough to have done all the murders. He'd have started when he was twenty-five. Maybe even earlier if there were victims they hadn't yet found.

'Is he from the area?' she asked, ignoring his question. 'Or did he move here from somewhere else?'

Reeves's confusion intensified. 'I don't know. According to him, he's from up north, the Midwest, out east, or from England, depending on which day it is. It changes from session to session. He's a pathological liar.'

'I got that part,' Kit said. 'Was there anything else that you remember about Mr Driscoll? Anything that you yourself observed?'

Reeves swallowed. 'When he talked about his "pretty young thing," he'd do this around the water bottle he was holding.' He squeezed his hands together, twisting them.

As if strangling someone. All the known victims had been strangled to death.

'It was . . . disturbing,' he added quietly. 'That was what initially caught my notice. He didn't make the hand motions when he was talking about his fabricated life. You know, the actors and the royalty.'

'I imagine that would be disturbing,' Kit murmured. 'Do you have his address in your client files?'

'I have the address he provided on his intake paperwork, but it wasn't the right one. When I started to become uncomfortable with his disclosures, I checked his address against his arrest report. I figured that was the correct one. The one he provided to us was a mansion in Del Mar, but he really lives in a two-bedroom in Mira Mesa.'

Kit drew in a slow breath as she understood. 'Mira Mesa was the fourth dot on the map.' He'd marked on his murder board the addresses of both young women and the park where Jaelyn Watts had been buried. The fourth dot had been unlabeled. It made sense now.

'Yes.'

She leaned back in her chair, studying him. 'Why did you mark his address on the map?'

He held her gaze. 'I thought it might show a pattern.'

No, she thought. That was a lie. His voice had gone slightly flat. Barely noticeable, if she hadn't been listening for it.

'Were you planning on following him?' she asked.

'Sam,' his lawyer broke in. 'I don't think you should say anything else.'

He flicked the woman a sharp look before locking Kit's gaze with his. 'I hadn't decided.'

Laura Letterman's head dropped back, and she stared at the ceiling. 'I'm clearly not needed here. I'm going home and back to bed.'

'I see,' Kit told Reeves levelly, ignoring the dramatic attorney, who made no move to leave. 'You were going to see if he went to either of the girls' homes?'

The attorney abruptly straightened in her chair. 'Do *not* answer that, Sam,' she hissed. 'I swear to God, you need to keep your mouth *shut*.'

He glanced at his attorney again before meeting Kit's eyes. 'Will you arrest Colton Driscoll?'

She wanted to say yes. His green eyes were so vivid. So goddamn sincere. *This is a genuinely good man.*

Who might be manipulating me right now. He was a shrink, after all. Baz was right not to trust them. They knew the human mind. They knew how to use their words, their voice, their body language to get people to say things they never would have otherwise said.

This Kit knew from experience. This was why she'd been avoiding Dr Scott.

'We'll check him out.' That was all she would commit to at this point.

Logically, Driscoll made a better suspect than Reeves. Driscoll was the right age and – if Reeves could be believed – had a history of violence. Both things were easily checked out.

'You'll have to remain here until we've investigated this lead,' Kit said, rising.

Reeves's jaw tightened and his eyes flashed with anger, but he said nothing.

'Arrest him or let him go,' Laura Letterman demanded.

'Oh, we already arrested him for resisting arrest,' Kit said dryly. 'That one doesn't go away.'

Letterman turned raised eyebrows to Sam.

He shrugged. 'I panicked. She . . .' He closed his eyes. 'She grabbed my arms.'

'Oh.' Letterman nodded, understanding softening her harsh expression. 'We can make that go away,' she said softly, then glared up at Kit. 'He was *trying* to *help* you.'

Kit felt a momentary pang of guilt, then shoved it away. Not yet. Not until she was certain that he wasn't involved. 'He was also in possession of an unregistered gun, which he was holding when he answered the door.'

Reeves frowned. 'It is registered.'

'In California?'

He winced. 'No. In Arizona. I inherited it from my grandfather. I only take it with me when I go camping.'

'Stop, Sam,' Letterman repeated with growing frustration. 'We will discuss your weapon once we are alone.'

Reeves sighed, his shoulders sagging. 'Fine.'

Kit looked down at Reeves, willing him to say something – anything – to make her believe him. But he looked away, his mouth tight.

'I'll need your boss's contact information.' She slid her notebook across the table. 'Name and number.'

'I'll need my phone.'

She returned it to him, noticing that both Joel Haley and Laura Letterman shifted to hide his hand while he tapped in his password.

Reeves engendered loyalty, even in someone with whom it appeared he had bad history. He wrote *Vivian Carlisle* in a neat, compact script, then paged through his contacts before adding a phone number and an address in La Jolla. Looked like Dr Carlisle did all right for herself. That was a nice part of town.

Wordlessly he pushed her notebook back to her. His expression, which had been so open, was now shuttered and cold.

It seemed he was finally taking his attorney's advice.

That left her feeling . . . sad.

Stop. Stop liking him. Stop wanting him to be innocent.

She slid her notebook into her pocket. 'Sit tight, Dr Reeves. I'll be back.'

San Diego, California
Saturday, 9 April, 7.20 A.M.

'What's wrong with you?' Baz asked as he pulled away from the department lot. Their boss had sent a small army of officers to back them up. They'd surround Colton Driscoll's house before knocking on his door.

This was the closest they'd come to solving a decades-old string of serial murders, and Lieutenant Navarro was unwilling to allow Driscoll to get away.

'I don't know what you mean.'

Baz snorted. 'Don't try that with me. I've known you too long. We're about to take down a notorious killer and you're all mopey. What's wrong?'

Kit should feel elated. They were about to take a monster off the streets.

But she just felt . . . off. 'I want Colton Driscoll to be the killer.'

'Because you want the doctor to be telling the truth,' Baz observed, not unkindly.

She didn't answer because she didn't want to admit it out loud, because it was true. But she also refused to be a victim of a shrink's manipulation, no matter how goddamn sincere Reeves appeared to be.

'Driscoll is a more logical choice than Reeves,' she said quietly. 'He's the right age and he has a history of violence.' She thumbed through the man's rap sheet displayed on her phone. 'His neighbor wasn't the first person he assaulted. He's been convicted of four additional misdemeanors – two bar fights and two counts of domestic violence with his first two wives. But he's never done a day of time. He's lived in San Diego since high school, at least, and he's worked in the mail room in the Ruby Building for five years. He was an IT professional before that.'

'So what feels wrong? About Driscoll, I mean.'

He'd left her reaction to Reeves unacknowledged, allowing her to focus on the man they were on their way to see. 'That a man with that history of violence – impulsive violence – has managed to stay under our radar for twenty years.'

'He's not stupid,' Baz said. 'He worked in IT.'

'For a lot of different companies. Never held a job for more than a few years. His temper kept getting him fired. He's supposed to be charming, though. Makes women fall for him. He's been married four times.'

'Where did you read that?'

'In his probation file.'

'Maybe you should be the one to question him, then. Pretend to fall under his charms when we get him into interview.'

'We'll see,' she said doubtfully.

Baz blew out an exasperated breath. 'Look a little more alive, will you? We're about to bag a serial killer. This will be a feather in both our caps.'

Kit straightened her spine. Baz was right. She needed her head in the game. 'More alive, coming up.'

They spent the rest of the drive going over Driscoll's file.

Kit frowned, her mind sorting through the data. 'He lured four barely legal wives into marriage. He'd certainly be able to charm a teenage girl with stars in her eyes. But how is he finding them? Did he lie and tell them that he was a talent scout or a producer?'

'That'd be my guess. We'll search him and his house and see what we find.'

Baz stopped the car in front of a dilapidated two-story house matching the address on Driscoll's police report. The house looked like it hadn't been touched in a decade, with peeling paint and sagging doorframes. The lawn was patchy and taken over by weeds.

The other houses nearby, in contrast, were well kept. Not new, but maintained with pride by their owners. It was still early enough that only one person was out on the street – a jogger who eyed them curiously as he passed.

'The probation file says that none of his neighbors like him,' Kit said. 'I mean, beating someone up aside, I can see why.'

'Wonder why he didn't try to charm his neighbors.'

Kit tugged on the straps of her tactical vest. All of them wore full tactical gear because they weren't sure what they'd find. 'Good question.'

Putting her reservations – and concerns about Dr Reeves – aside, she got out of the car, quieting her mind and readying herself to break into the house if need be.

Two uniforms headed out to the back of the house, guarding all the possible exits. Two more followed Baz and Kit up the front sidewalk.

The others stayed back, awaiting orders to move in if necessary.

'You good?' Baz asked.

She nodded resolutely, her head finally on straight again. 'Yes. Let's go.'

They approached the house carefully, watching the windows for any sign of Colton Driscoll. They'd been shot at from windows before and Kit wasn't keen on making that a regular thing.

They made it to the front door with no altercations and Kit rapped briskly. 'Mr Driscoll? It's San Diego PD. We want to talk to you.'

Nothing. Not a sound. No scurrying, no rustling. Nothing.

Kit and Baz frowned at each other.

'I don't hear anything,' Baz whispered.

A feeling of foreboding shivered down her spine. 'Me either.'

Baz motioned to the two officers standing behind them. 'If you would.'

The two men swung a battering ram at the door, breaking it open. Kit and Baz entered, guns drawn.

'Mr Driscoll,' Baz boomed loudly, 'San Diego PD.'

But then they froze, three feet into Driscoll's living room. Kit stared up into the cold eyes of Colton Driscoll.

Into his cold, dead eyes.

He swung from the rope tight around his neck, his face a purplish color, his tongue slightly extended, his head bent at an unnatural angle.

'Well, shit,' Kit muttered. She pressed gloved fingers to his wrist, just in case, then frowned. 'He's still a little warm. He hasn't been dead that long.'

'We must have been just too late.'

And Baz didn't sound too torn up about that. Kit understood, although the identities of the remaining victims would remain a mystery unless Driscoll had left records of some kind.

'We need to tell Navarro,' she said.

Their boss was anxiously awaiting news, hoping to tell the brass that they'd solved a cold serial murder case.

'He's going to be unhappy,' Baz murmured, still staring at Driscoll's face.

Kit dialed Navarro, who answered on the first ring. 'Did you get him?' he demanded.

'He's dead,' Kit said flatly. 'Hanged himself.'

'Motherfucker,' Navarro hissed. 'Is there a note? Anything?'

'We haven't looked around yet,' Kit told him. 'We'll search and call you back, but I thought you needed to know. More later.' She ended the call and turned to Baz. 'I'll call the ME, you call CSU.'

She and Baz made their calls, then began searching the house.

'There's a note on the printer,' Baz called and Kit hurried over to see.

'"To whom it may concern",' she read, '"I'm so sorry. I've done terrible things. I've killed five young women. Five innocents. I could no longer live with myself and knew I'd do it again and again, so I'm taking myself out of the equation. Please tell their parents that I'm sorry".'

'A confession,' Baz said, sounding stunned.

But Kit wasn't convinced. 'Five? What about Cecilia Sheppard? She should have been number six.'

Baz slid the note into an evidence bag. 'Maybe he didn't want to admit to all of his victims. We've always thought there were likely more than the bodies we found by accident. Or maybe Cecilia Sheppard was killed by someone else. She was only reported missing. We don't even know for sure that she's dead.'

That was technically true, but Kit didn't think Cecilia was still alive, or that she'd been killed by someone else. The lacrosse and lilac references had been too spot-on. 'Why admit to five, then? Why five? Could he know we'd found five victims? Did he know we'd just found Jaelyn's body in Longview Park? We've kept a tight lid on this information. Need-to-know only. Do we have a leak?'

'All good questions,' Baz acknowledged. 'Let's keep looking. We might find answers.'

Frowning, Kit went back to Driscoll's body, studying it as it lightly swung. 'He hit something recently.' His knuckles had abrasions, but they'd started to scab over. 'And he dressed up.' He wore a nice shirt, unbuttoned at the collar, along with trousers and a sport jacket. A folded tie peeked out of the jacket pocket, like he'd taken his tie off at some point. 'Did he dress up to kill himself or did he go somewhere last night and come home to kill himself?'

Her gaze stopped at his feet. He still wore his shoes.

'Baz, look at his shoes. Sperry Top-Siders.'

'Same as the prints we found at the Longview Park scene.' Baz lifted his eyebrows. 'Same as the shoes we found in Dr Reeves's closet. Looks to be about the same size, too, but Reeves's were more worn.'

Kit hunkered down until the shoes were at her eye level. 'These are new. Not even broken in. Forensics can tell us which shoe made the print.'

But she knew in her gut that these shoes wouldn't be a match. Besides, Dr Reeves had already admitted going to the park to see if there was a grave. He'd left the print.

She rose and began searching the kitchen. 'Wallet and keys are here on the counter. If he cooked anything last night, he tidied up afterward.'

'Everything's tidy,' Baz observed. 'Not even a speck of dust on the bookshelves.'

'He doesn't even have a junk drawer,' she said after opening all the kitchen drawers. She moved on to the cabinets but found nothing of immediate interest, so she went to the bedroom.

And froze at the first dresser drawer she opened.

'Holy fucking shit,' she muttered.

'What?' Baz asked, coming up behind her. Then he whistled softly. 'Bingo.'

Six pairs of brand-new handcuffs were piled in the drawer and, beside them, lying on its side, was a can of sparkly pink spray paint.

Five

La Jolla, California
Saturday, 9 April, 9.45 A.M.

'Just a minute,' Kit said as Baz stopped their car at the curb of Dr Reeves's boss's very posh street. They'd left the crime scene to CSU and the ME techs and headed to Dr Vivian Carlisle's home to check out the rest of Reeves's story. 'Incoming call from the ME.'

Baz turned to watch her, a frown on his face. 'Why?'

She held up a finger and answered, putting it on speaker. 'Alicia? I've got you on speaker. Baz Constantine is here, too.'

'Good morning.' Alicia Batra was not only one of Kit's favorite MEs, the woman had become a good friend. 'I'm at the scene. My assistant said that you needed to speak to me.'

'Yes. Can you run a tox screen on the victim? I'm specifically interested in any sedatives that would have a short half-life.'

Baz's brows shot up. 'What?'

'Why?' Alicia asked.

'Because I want to make sure someone didn't help him hang himself.'

Alicia was quiet for a moment. 'You don't believe this was suicide?'

'I don't know. I'm worried about the confession he left. There's a detail that doesn't fit.' Five young women. Not six. 'Having the tox screen will ease my concerns and I wanted to make my request while the body was still fresh.'

Baz shook his head, looking weary and impatient.

He didn't look like that often and it stung a little, but Kit's gut was not on board with Driscoll's confession. It was too neat – and missing a body.

'I can do that,' Alicia said. 'Anything else?'

'Yeah. Make sure that he died by the hanging and wasn't already dead.'

'I'd do that anyway. Did you find a specific sedative in the house?'

'No,' Baz inserted. 'There were *no* prescription drugs in the medicine cabinets or drawers.'

'I know that,' Kit snapped. 'Look, he's too big a man to have submitted to a hanging without some kind of a fight, and we didn't see any sign of defensive wounds, other than the skinned knuckles, and those looked older. I just want to make sure he wasn't chemically coerced. I'm dotting my *i*'s.'

'Got it,' Alicia said. 'I'll run the test and look for the shorter-lived drugs. It'll take about forty-eight hours.'

'Thanks, Alicia.' Kit ended the call and frowned at her partner. 'I'm not an idiot, Baz. I know the man is guilty of something, but I can't get past *five* young women.'

'We don't know that Cecilia Sheppard was number six.'

'I know. But do you honestly believe there were only five over fifteen years? Four of which just happened to be found by chance?' Three by metal detectors, the fourth by a dog digging for bones.

Baz's mouth firmed to a straight line. 'No. I think there were others. But he wouldn't admit to any more if he thought we only knew about five. We just found out about Cecilia last night. If he didn't know we knew about her, he wouldn't have admitted to it.'

'You could be right. But how did he know about Jaelyn?'

Baz shrugged. 'Maybe he went back to the scene of the crime and saw we'd been digging. Or maybe we have a leak. Enough people in the department know. It was going to get out.'

'Maybe.' The first answer was plausible, but she didn't like the second. If the discovery of Jaelyn's body had leaked, the use of the pink handcuffs might have as well. 'But it can't hurt to check for drugs in his system, can it?'

'No,' he admitted. 'What about Reeves? Do you believe him?'

'I still don't know. I want to believe him. He was right about Driscoll – if that confession note is genuine. But Reeves could be lying. We can verify his story with a few questions to Dr Carlisle.'

Which was why they were parked in front of her house.

'Let's get this over with.' Baz shoved his door open and got out of the car with a groan. 'I need to sleep.'

Kit studied him as they walked to the Carlisles' front door, worried. Partly because he seemed a lot more tired recently. Partly because she wondered if she was overthinking this case. And partly because Baz *wasn't* overthinking it.

She might have wanted Reeves to be innocent, but Baz really wanted Driscoll to be guilty. Which wasn't wrong in and of itself. Baz had been in homicide for sixteen years. He'd been around for the discovery of all five of the killer's victims. That he'd desperately want to have caught the perpetrator was natural.

That he wasn't concerned about the discrepancies in the letter bothered her.

She put that out of her head when they reached the front door. It was painted a cheerful red, contrasting with the beige stucco exterior. Kit knocked briskly and waited, breathing in the sea air. The house was a block away from the beach and this close she could hear the waves breaking. It would be peaceful if she weren't so keyed up.

The door opened, a woman about Kit's age eyeing them distrustfully. 'If you're selling something, we're not interested.'

The woman was too young to be Vivian Carlisle. The psychologist appeared to be at least sixty from her online bio. But the woman at the door had Vivian's eyes, so maybe she was the daughter.

Kit showed her badge. 'SDPD. We'd like to speak to Dr Vivian Carlisle.'

The woman blinked, then quickly regained her composure. 'She's not taking visitors right now. Can I help you?'

'No,' Kit said, kindly but firmly. 'It's imperative that we speak with her.'

'Who's at the door?' a man called, appearing behind the woman a few seconds later. He was older, his face bruised, his head bandaged, and his arm was in a sling. He gave Kit's badge a wary look. 'We gave a statement to the officer at the scene of the accident last night.'

An accident would explain why they weren't accepting calls all night. Another mark in Reeves's favor.

'I'm sorry, sir,' Kit said, assuming this was Vivian's husband. 'I hate to intrude, but I need to speak to your wife urgently. It's related to one of her employees.'

The man's eyes widened. 'Which one?'

'Sam Reeves,' Baz said. 'May we come in?'

'Is he all right?' the man asked, opening the door a little wider.

Kit gave him a neutral smile. 'He's unhurt. We really need to speak to Dr Carlisle.'

'For a moment only,' the younger woman said firmly. 'My mother needs her rest.' She aimed an arch look at the man. 'So does my father.'

He rolled his eyes and opened the door completely. 'Please come in. I didn't get your names.'

'I'm Detective McKittrick and this is my partner, Detective Constantine.'

'McKittrick?' another woman asked from inside the house. 'Richard, did she say her name was McKittrick?'

'Yes, dear. She says she needs to talk to you about Sam.'

Sam. Not Dr Reeves.

'Tell them to come in and hurry.'

Kit and Baz complied, following the husband into a comfortably furnished living room where Dr Vivian Carlisle sat on the sofa, elevating her leg that was encased in a plaster cast.

A serious accident, then.

Kit and Baz took the seats indicated, and Baz let out a quiet sound as he rested on a cushion that was much softer than it had looked.

He smiled ruefully at the older woman. 'Long night. Looks like you had one, too.'

'I did. I'm Vivian Carlisle. What happened to Sam?'

'We need to confirm his account of his dealings with one of his clients,' Kit said.

Vivian frowned. 'Where is Sam right now?'

'In an interview room at the precinct.' Kit watched the woman closely for a reaction. She didn't have to wait long.

'What the hell?' Vivian demanded. 'Why is he in an interview room?'

'Because he made an anonymous call to my direct line,' Kit said. 'He referenced an ongoing investigation and we wanted to question him.'

'Took you long enough. He called you on Monday.'

So Carlisle had known. The marks in Reeves's favor were piling up. 'Can you tell me what you know about Colton Driscoll?'

Vivian glanced at her daughter and husband. 'Can you two go in the study and close the door? I'd take them in there myself, but . . .' She gestured to her leg, waiting as they disappeared down a hall, their voices going silent after a door was closed. 'Dr Reeves has been concerned about Colton Driscoll for several weeks. He was worried when the man started talking about his "pretty young thing" and her grave. He became more worried when Driscoll mentioned a new young woman. Driscoll is a compulsive liar. We decided that an anonymous phone call to SDPD would be in order, to make sure that Driscoll was telling the truth. We've been waiting since Monday for some announcement of the discovery of a body in the park, but none came. Sam's become more and more concerned.' She tilted her head. 'Did you find a grave?'

Kit nodded once. 'We did. We brought Dr Reeves in because he refused to tell us how he knew about the grave until we confirmed we'd found a body. He finally told us this story and that you could verify it.'

'He's telling the truth. Sam Reeves is a good man. Too good, sometimes.'

'What does that mean?' Baz asked suspiciously.

Vivian's glare was frosty. 'It means that he has a huge heart and that he tends to invest too much personally in his clients. One has to maintain a professional distance to maintain good mental health in this field. Caring too much will eat you from the inside out.'

Something we have in common, Kit thought. 'Did Dr Reeves mention anything about lilac or lacrosse?'

'No, but he did have a session with Mr Driscoll yesterday after our meeting. He was planning to dig deeper and hopefully find out more. I guess he did. I was supposed to check on the potential grave site myself today, but my husband and I were struck by a car full of teenagers last night and . . . Well, I'm not going to be walking through any parks anytime soon. I suppose Dr Reeves found more information that was pertinent.'

'He did.' That was all Kit would say. 'Is there anything else you'd like to add?'

'Only that he picked you especially, Detective. I asked him why he called you, in particular. He said he'd heard about you from a friend and that you seemed to care about victims who'd been forgotten. He admired that about you.'

Kit wasn't sure what to say to that. She'd wondered why Reeves had chosen to call her. 'I appreciate your candor.'

'I'll also add that if he needs an attorney, I will provide one. Tell him to call the house phone. My cell was destroyed in the accident and I haven't gotten a replacement yet.'

'He has an attorney,' Kit said, 'but I'll let him know. He was worried about you.'

'Tell him I'm okay. Can you see yourselves out?'

Kit and Baz walked in silence to their car. 'Well?' she asked when they were both buckled in.

'Reeves was telling the truth,' Baz said and sounded so disappointed that Kit had to laugh.

'I'm so sorry.'

He tried to glare, but it ended up a sigh. 'At least we have our killer.'

Five young women, not six. 'Yeah.'

SDPD, San Diego, California
Saturday, 9 April, 11.05 A.M.

Sam paused his pacing, staring at the interview room mirror. If there was anyone still back there, he couldn't see them. 'What is taking them so long?' He turned to Laura. 'Is this good or bad?'

She lifted a shoulder in a very familiar shrug. He really hated that shrug, but he couldn't say anything because she was here, representing him. She could have chosen not to come, but she had, and he could be grateful for that and still wish she weren't here, in his space.

The scent of her perfume made his nose itch.

The sound of her voice made his ears want to bleed.

At one time, just the sight of her smile had been enough to make his heart pound with happiness. Now, he saw her smile for the cold, calculating thing that it was.

It had messed with his head for a long time, having been so wrong about her. Having trusted her.

It had been Joel who'd helped him see the truth – that people like Laura Letterman were experts at making you see what they wanted you to see.

He'd taken that experience and learned from it. It had made it easier for him to see similar characteristics in his clients.

So he guessed he could be grateful to her for that, too.

'It could be either, neither, or both good and bad,' she said. 'If they brought Driscoll in and are questioning him, it might just be that they're holding you here in case his interrogation raises questions you might be able to answer.'

He'd thought of that. He hoped that was all this delay was about.

'Has Joel texted you about Siggy?' he asked.

She tapped at her phone's screen, then nodded. 'About five minutes ago. He says Siggy is comfortable at his place. He's on his way back here.'

'He doesn't have to come back.'

Laura shot him that don't-be-an-idiot look again. 'He's your friend, Sam. He's worried about you. Let him fuss. He sent a pic of the dog.' She huffed a soft laugh. 'He's cute.'

She tilted her phone so that Sam could see the photo. Siggy was in his crate, his tongue lolling happily. At least he wasn't scared.

Sam hated the thought of his dog being scared.

'When did you get him?' Laura asked.

Sam leaned against the mirror, trying to put anyone watching him out of his mind. 'The day after I broke up with you.'

Her eyes widened, and then she smiled ruefully. 'He's probably better for you than I was.'

'No doubt,' Sam said, needing to change the subject. He wasn't comfortable with anyone behind the mirror knowing his personal business. Any more than they already did – and he was certain that they'd been digging deep. 'Have you worked with McKittrick and Constantine before?'

'Constantine, yes.' She made a face of distaste. 'He's a good cop. Very procedurally thorough. He was unshakable on the stand and my client is now serving life in San Quentin.' She tilted her head. 'He doesn't like shrinks. I remember that from the case because a shrink testified on my client's behalf.' Another shrug. 'We tried to go for a diminished capacity defense, but the prosecutor's shrink blew mine out of the water.'

'Unfortunate,' Sam said sarcastically.

'He was guilty as fuck, so I threw a Hail Mary. Sometimes they work and sometimes they don't. Just . . . be careful of Constantine and his partner. They're predisposed to suspect you, or at least Constantine is.'

Sam remembered the disappointment on McKittrick's face when she'd arrived at his apartment. She'd hoped he was on the level then, but his stupid crime board had sunk that ship. Not to mention the damn gun. He wished he'd never taken it out of the safe.

He could only hope that she'd be fair. He realized that he hated that she thought he could kill someone. He didn't so much care about Constantine's opinion of him, as long as the man believed he wasn't a murderer. But he wanted McKittrick to . . . what? Like him?

Well, yeah. He did. It was juvenile, but accurate.

'Thanks. I'll be careful. Have you been able to reach Vivian?'

'I would have told you if I did,' she said, not unkindly.

He knew that. 'Sorry.' Pulling out a chair, he sat and dropped his head into his hands. 'This is pretty awful.'

'You didn't do anything wrong,' she said in a practical voice that actually soothed him. 'Except for the resisting and the gun.'

He groaned. 'I'm an idiot.'

'Did you point it at them?'

'No. I had it pointed down when I answered the door.' He sighed. 'I thought, *What if it's Driscoll?*'

'I can't say that I blame you, especially knowing what he'd done to land in your office. Don't worry. We can fix that. The resisting arrest charge might depend on their generosity, though. They haven't booked you yet, so there's still time to work it out.'

'I can't have a record,' he mumbled. 'I just can't.'

'Look at it this way,' she said, sounding almost amused. 'You've led such a boring Boy Scout life up until now, this can be a story you tell at parties someday. You can make yourself out to be a real badass.'

He scowled. 'Boring isn't a bad thing.' It had been the reason she'd given for cheating on him, though, and that still rankled. 'I'm so *sorry* that I'm not *interesting* enough for you.'

She winced. 'Sorry, sorry. I'll just sit over here quietly and wait for the detectives to come back.'

'Fine.'

But he couldn't sit. He began to pace again, tempted to flip the bird to the mirror on principle alone. But he didn't. He couldn't make this worse.

He was pushing a hundred laps around the room when the door opened and McKittrick and Constantine filed back in.

For a moment McKittrick held his gaze, but he wasn't sure what she was thinking. She motioned to the chairs.

'Please have a seat, Dr Reeves. We have much to discuss.'

Heart pounding, he obeyed. 'Did you find Colton Driscoll?'

'You could say that,' Constantine said.

McKittrick sighed. 'He's dead.'

Shocked, Sam's mouth fell open. 'What? How? When?'

Oh shit. Do they think I did it?

'We found him in his house,' Constantine drawled, 'hanging from a rope.'

Sam felt like he'd been sucker-punched. 'Oh my God. Why?'

'He left a confession note saying he'd done the murders,' McKittrick said. 'ME places time of death sometime between three and seven a.m. What was he wearing when he came for his session yesterday afternoon?'

Sam's mind was reeling. 'His mail room uniform. Khakis and a polo shirt. It was blue.'

'Thank you,' McKittrick said. 'We stopped by your boss's house after we finished at Mr Driscoll's place. Dr Carlisle confirmed your story.'

Sam sagged in relief. 'Thank you. Is she all right?'

'She's fine,' McKittrick assured. 'She was in a car accident with her husband last night. Both were treated for minor injuries at the hospital, then released, but her phone was smashed up. She said to tell you that she is okay.'

Sam closed his eyes, feeling a little dizzy. Vivian was all right and the detectives believed him now. Everything might be okay.

Except for Colton. That bothered him more than he'd expected it would.

Sam opened his eyes and found McKittrick watching him, her gaze still unreadable. 'I'm surprised that Mr Driscoll killed himself,' he said. 'I wouldn't have taken him as the type to do so.'

'Does this mean that my client is free to go?' Laura inserted, giving him a shut-up-now look.

McKittrick nodded. 'We'll be dropping the charges on resisting arrest. You did us a favor by bringing Colton Driscoll to our attention, Dr Reeves, and we thank you. Please register your gun in California at the first possible opportunity.'

Sam shuddered out a breath. 'Yes, of course. I'll do that.'

'Then you're free to go,' she said. 'Baz, do you have his phone?'

'Yeah,' Constantine grunted. He handed Sam his phone. 'Here.'

'Thank you,' Sam said politely.

She produced a small Milk-Bone-style dog treat from her pocket, then stunned him by smiling. Sam couldn't rip his eyes away from her face. She was pretty in a cute-girl-next-door kind of way, but when she smiled, her whole face lit up.

'For Siggy,' she said. 'We didn't mean to frighten him.'

Sam's mouth curved as he took the treat. 'I'm sure he's forgotten all about it by now, but he'll enjoy the treat.'

Laura stood. 'I'll be taking my client home now. Sam?'

He gave a last nod to McKittrick, then followed Laura out into the hallway.

'Thank you,' he said to Laura. 'For coming. I appreciate it. How much do I owe you?'

'Nothing. I figure I owe you that much. You ready to go?'

He regarded her for a moment, this woman whom he'd once loved. There was good in her heart, but there was a lot of awful in there, too.

'Did you say Joel was on his way?'

Her expression faltered. 'Yes. You're going to wait for him?'

Sam almost said, *No, I'll go with you*, but then remembered how it had felt when he'd found her in bed with another man. How much it had hurt. He wouldn't beat himself up for loving her or leaving her. But he wasn't going to go down that road again.

'It's for the best. He's got Siggy at his place. We can get my dog, then he can take me home. Seriously, though, Laura, I do appreciate what you did today.'

'It wasn't really anything. It would have been okay without me. But better to have representation, just in case.' She took a step back, her gaze a little regretful. 'Take care of yourself, okay?'

'I will. You too.'

He watched her go, then realized a uniformed officer stood about a foot behind him.

'I'll escort you to the lobby,' the cop said.

'Oh, of course. What about my belongings? My laptop and my wallet?'

'They'll have those up at the front desk. You'll get them all back. This way, please,' the cop said and Sam followed.

But he felt eyes on him. A look over his shoulder revealed McKittrick standing in the doorway to the interview room, silently watching.

He raised the hand that held the dog treat, then didn't look back again.

SDPD, San Diego, California
Saturday, 9 April, 11.25 A.M.

Baz lifted a brow when Kit came back into the interview room. 'What was that?'

She didn't blink. 'What?'

'That smile. And a dog treat?' He made a face. 'You carry dog treats in your pockets?'

'Of course I do. Snickerdoodle loves them. And we did scare his dog.'

Baz had the good grace to look a little shamefaced. 'I'm sorry about that part. But not the rest.'

'He gave us a killer.'

Baz leaned back in his chair, studying her. 'A killer you still seem to doubt. Why?'

She sat on the corner of the table. 'Five murders. Why five? Why not six, including Cecilia Sheppard? Why not ten? Do we think we really found all his victims over the years? That's taking coincidence to ridiculous levels.'

'Like I said, maybe he didn't want to admit to all the people he killed.'

'He's a pathological liar who claims to party with Hollywood stars. I can't believe he didn't claim to have killed a hundred people. Or that he showed enough remorse to kill himself.'

Baz grimaced. 'Point. But is that your only concern?'

She shrugged fitfully. 'I don't know. It feels . . . off.'

'He knew about Cecilia,' Baz said, counting on his fingers. 'He knew she wore a lilac uniform. He knew about Jaelyn's grave.

He confessed. And for fuck's sake, he had handcuffs *and* pink spray paint when we've kept that detail from the press. What more do you want to see?'

'I don't know,' she said and meant it. She *didn't* know. That bothered her a whole hell of a lot.

'I'd say we've closed this case. And we'll get credit for catching a serial murderer, Kit. This is a huge feather in your cap this early in your career.' He frowned. 'Is this a fear of success?'

She scoffed at the notion. 'No. It feels too convenient. Too easy.'

His smile was kind. 'Sometimes it is easy. Not every case is like Wren's. Sometimes we get the bad guy. You know this. You've closed more than your share of cases since you joined Homicide.'

She sighed. 'You're right. I'm making this too hard. Let's call Navarro.'

'We will. But first . . . what was with the smile at Reeves, Kit? I'm serious.'

'I don't know,' she murmured once again. 'I was . . . glad. Glad he was telling the truth. Glad he wasn't a fraud, doing charity work to make himself look less guilty. Glad he was truly sincere and not some fake.'

'You like him,' Baz said quietly.

Her mouth tightened. 'I don't know him.'

'You like the idea of him, then.'

That wasn't untrue. 'I like the idea that someone is good and kind – and who they claim to be. I respect that he risked his career for young women he'd never met.'

The man also engendered loyalty from so many people – from his boss and her husband, from Joel Haley, and even from the shark attorney who'd looked so sad when he'd declined her offer of a ride home.

That piqued Kit's curiosity. There was a story there, she was certain.

Too bad she'd never know what that story was. She'd have no reason to ever see him again.

'I guess not all shrinks are bad,' Baz allowed, disgruntled.

Kit patted his hand. 'I'm sorry, Baz. I'm sure we'll come across another narcissistic shrink who you can legitimately hate on sight.'

He scowled for a moment, then laughed. 'Fine.' Then he sobered, and she braced herself for what he'd say next. 'Will you see him again?'

'No. Why would I? Like you keep saying, this case is closed. I might ask Navarro to write him a formal thank-you letter in case his arrest causes him any future trouble.' A psychologist who made his living from clients referred by the courts had to maintain a clean reputation. 'But other than that, I'd have no cause to see him again.'

He gave her a knowing look. 'You can just call him, you know. Ask him out. It is the twenty-first century. Women do that kind of thing.'

The thought was not an unpleasant one.

Which might have bothered her even more than her doubts about Colton Driscoll's confession note.

'I won't,' she said quietly. She might regret not seeing the man again, but that was as far as she'd let it go. 'I have a very full life. The life I want. I'm good, Baz.'

He looked like he'd say more, but he only shook his head. 'Message received. Ix-nay on the ink-shray.'

'Thank you. Look. It's been a long twenty-four hours. Let's check in with Navarro and then I'm going home to give the rest of the treats in my pocket to Snickerdoodle before I take a nap.'

She held a hand out to Baz, pulling him to his feet. He groaned as he stretched his back.

'You're going to take a nap, and you're young. Imagine how I feel. I'm too old to go all night long.'

Kit snickered, then let herself laugh. It rolled from her belly, making her shake as Baz shook his head in amusement.

'I didn't mean it that way,' he said when her laughter had come to a wheezing end.

'I'm so telling Marian you said that. I'm telling *everyone* you said that.'

He narrowed his eyes. 'I'll tell everyone that you *smiled* at the shrink and gave him a biscuit for his dog.'

That shut her up. 'You're an asshole.'

He smiled. 'And don't you forget it.'

SDPD, San Diego, California
Saturday, 9 April, 12.10 P.M.

Kit's heart sank when she walked into the bullpen. Navarro and his boss were in his office, both smiling jovially.

'Don't you dare,' Baz muttered.

She looked at him, more than a little hurt. 'Dare what?'

'Tell them you think that it's a mistake. We found the confession. We found the cuffs and the paint. He's dead. He did it and he's dead.'

She drew a quiet breath. 'I'll do my goddamn job, Baz. Just like you taught me.' Then she marched up to Navarro's office, Baz sputtering behind her.

'Kit,' Baz hissed.

'I'm going to give him the facts. Then it's his choice. Okay?'

Which wasn't true. If Navarro dismissed her concerns, she'd still have them. She'd still poke around for answers. She rapped on Navarro's door and he waved them in.

'McKittrick, Constantine, come in,' he said with a huge smile. 'This is a good day.'

'Yes, sir,' Kit said respectfully.

Navarro's smile faltered. 'What happened?'

Suddenly both men's gazes were locked on her and Baz.

'Nothing,' Baz stated firmly. 'Colton Driscoll has been transported to the morgue and CSU is finishing up at his home. We've confirmed Dr Reeves's story and he's been released. Just as we told you, sir.'

'Then why do you look like you just sucked a lemon, McKittrick?' Navarro demanded.

Kit squared her shoulders and purposely did not look at Baz. 'There are a few details that don't add up, sir.'

Navarro sat on the corner of his desk. 'Something other than the confession letter saying five and not six victims?'

Kit nodded, because she'd already told him about her concerns, but she needed to be sure that he'd heard her. 'Mainly that. I'm also suspicious of his shoes. They were brand new when most of the shoes in his closet were worn. And they just happen to be the same shoe that made the print we found near Jaelyn Watts's grave.'

'It's a common shoe, Kit,' Navarro said, frowning. 'We've all agreed to that.'

Yes, they had, but she still couldn't shake the fact that they were the same shoes that Sam Reeves had also worn to the park. Was that merely a coincidence?

'What else, Detective?' the captain asked. He was a sharp-eyed man with a near-perpetual scowl. But Kit knew that he was a kind man, deep down.

'Why today? Why did he kill himself today? Did he know that he was about to be caught? And if he did, how did he know? How did he know that we'd found five bodies and not four? Did he visit the crime scene? Is that how he knew? We've kept the discovery of Jaelyn's body under wraps.'

The men looked at each other, then at Baz.

Kit finally glanced at her partner. His jaw was tight and his cheeks flushed, whether from anger, embarrassment, or fatigue, Kit wasn't sure. Probably a combination.

'Enough people knew about the fifth body,' Baz gritted out. 'It might have gotten out. Or maybe he didn't know about Jaelyn, and the fifth victim he referred to was Cecilia Sheppard.'

'Either of those could be true.' Kit hesitated, then asked the question that had been bothering her the most. 'But if Jaelyn's murder was leaked, is it possible that the cuffs and pink spray paint were leaked, too?'

The captain's scowl grew. 'Are you suggesting that Driscoll is innocent?'

'No,' she said firmly. 'He knew about the victims, but according to Dr Reeves, he was a pathological liar, so who knows exactly what he knew and when he knew it? He talked about the final victim –

the *sixth* victim – like she was still alive, even though she went missing eight months ago. I'm not saying that he isn't guilty. I'm saying that a few things don't add up and I'd like to make sure we haven't missed anything before we celebrate.'

'Like?' Navarro asked.

'Like how did he lure his victims? He admitted to five. We know there might have been six, if we include Cecilia Sheppard. He's killed young women for at least seventeen years. Maybe twenty. Four of the five victims we found were accidental discoveries. There *have* to be more. Who are they? Where did he kill them? Where are they buried? Why did he choose the parks? And how did he manage to bury people in parks where so many people walked? I have questions.'

The captain nodded. 'All valid. What does the ME say? Has he confirmed cause of death?'

'She's doing the autopsy this afternoon,' Kit said. 'Dr Batra is on the case.'

'She's good,' the captain said. 'We'll wait to see what she says. If she believes there is any reason to doubt that he hanged himself, we'll act accordingly. And if she concludes that Driscoll killed himself, then we still need to find those answers. Especially if there are more victims. And we need to identify the two bodies that are still Jane Does.'

Navarro had moved his gaze from Kit to Baz. 'What are you thinking, Baz?'

Baz leaned back against the door, scrubbing his palm over his face. 'Right now, I'm thinking I want to go to sleep. But mostly I'm thinking that this guy *confessed*. We've been stymied on this case for fifteen years, ever since we found that first body. For a lot of us, this is the case that keeps us up at night sometimes.' He glanced at Kit, his eyes full of regret. 'One of the cases,' he said, and Kit knew he meant Wren's murder. 'I want this to be true, Reynaldo. It quacks like a duck.'

Kit's chest tightened. All three of these men had worked Homicide for years, were familiar with this investigation. Of course they'd have an emotional component to wanting to solve it. She did on the fresh cases she'd caught for the past four years. She did on the cold cases as well. She gave Baz an understanding smile, the band around her heart loosening when he smiled back. Argument settled. They were good.

Navarro nodded grimly. 'I want this to be true, too. We'll wait to see what Batra says after she's done with the autopsy and then we'll go from there. Go home, both of you. Get some rest, because either way, we need to know what Driscoll was up to. And we need to reopen the investigation into the unidentified victims. We need to give their families closure as well.'

'Yes, sir,' Kit murmured.

Baz simply waved. 'Night, all.'

'Wait,' the captain said. 'This psychologist. Reeves. Are we sure he's on the level?'

Baz nodded. 'His boss confirms his story. Seems like this guy just wanted to do the right thing but was between a rock and a hard place with his personal and professional ethics.'

'In fact, I'd like to request a letter from the department, sir,' Kit added. 'Thanking him. It will also go to show that his arrest was a misunderstanding. Something like that could damage his career and he already risked it to help.'

'I'll draft it up today,' Navarro promised. 'You can look it over before I send it out.'

'Thank you. Come on, old man,' she said to Baz. 'I'll drive you home.'

Six

San Diego, California
Saturday, 9 April, 3.15 P.M.

'Oh my God.' Ann Reeves put a hand to her throat as Sam finished the tale of his overnight adventure. 'They *arrested* you?'

He and Joel had come straight to his parents' apartment after picking up Siggy, and now the four of them were gathered around the dining room table, surrounded by remnants of their late lunch – leftover lasagna from the night before.

'And then they let me go,' Sam assured her. 'It was just a misunderstanding. Everything is fine, Mom.'

'But your face.' His mother stared at the bruise darkening his cheek. 'They *hit* you?'

'Not exactly,' Sam told her. 'They were arresting me and I . . . well, I . . .' He drew a breath. 'They grabbed my arms.'

'Oh,' his parents said together.

'You struggled,' his mother said quietly.

'I did. One of the detectives was maybe a little rougher than she needed to be.'

He wasn't going to mention that the detective in question was six inches shorter and sixty pounds lighter than he was. That was humiliating.

Ann's mouth tightened in fury. 'We should sue them.'

'No,' Sam said quickly. 'I did my duty. I just want to walk away.' *With what's left of my dignity intact.*

Bill Reeves turned to Joel, who was consuming his second plate of lasagna.

'This won't hurt his career?' Bill asked.

'No, sir,' Joel said. 'The detectives dropped all charges and thanked him for aiding them in closing a case.' He gave Sam a sly look. 'I think Detective McKittrick even *liked* him.'

Sam rolled his eyes, wishing he hadn't told Joel about her smiling at him. As the adrenaline rush had faded, the more irritated he'd become. He'd liked and respected McKittrick before this. Now . . . Well, maybe he still respected her, but he didn't *like* her anymore. 'She gave me a dog biscuit for Siggy because they'd scared him.'

'And she *smiled* at him,' Joel told Sam's dad in a conspiratorial whisper. 'Detective McKittrick never smiles. Not even at me and I'm . . . well, I'm me.'

Ann laughed. 'Yes, Joel, dear. You are you, and we're grateful for you every day. Can I get you any more lasagna?'

It seemed his parents had taken Sam's cue and let the subject drop and for that he was profoundly grateful.

'No, ma'am, but thank you for offering. My appetite is depressed.' Joel grimaced in distaste. 'Seeing Laura does that to me.'

Bill scowled at the name. 'Laura? Why did you see that—' He cut himself off before he could finish the sentence. His parents' disgust for Laura Letterman knew no bounds.

Joel rolled his eyes. 'Sam called her to represent him.'

Sam winced when both his parents turned to him, expressions sour. 'She was the only defense attorney I knew offhand.'

His father stared. 'Sam! I can't believe you didn't know another lawyer to call. Her, of all people.'

Sam gave Joel a look that promised retribution. Joel just grinned back at him. He instinctively knew all the buttons to push. That was probably one of the things that made him such a good prosecutor.

'I was in a panic, Dad. If I'd been in my right mind, I'd have just let them get me a public defender.'

Although Laura had been far more helpful than he'd anticipated, keeping him levelheaded. Still, it had been a relief to see her go when they'd finished at the police station.

'Or you could have called us,' Bill grumbled. 'I don't know any defense attorneys but I sure as hell would have found you a better one than that bi—'

'Bill,' Ann said sharply, interrupting him. 'She's an awful woman, but we will not stoop to calling her bad names.'

His mother rarely cursed and lectured Sam and his dad every time they did so.

'I didn't want to worry you,' Sam said. 'I'd have never forgiven myself if this misunderstanding caused you to relapse from the stress.'

Bill rolled his eyes. 'I'm fine. I'm staying on my new diet and everything. I didn't even have any of that lasagna.'

'Because I wouldn't let him,' Ann said archly.

Bill really was doing so much better on the new regimen. He'd accepted that his life had to change after his stroke, but he still loved to care for his family, so he continued making the meals they enjoyed.

'At least we know why you didn't eat much last night,' Bill said. 'I thought I'd added too much salt or something.'

'Nope. It's as delicious as always.' Joel rose, holding his dirty dishes. 'Now that you've fed me, I'm going home to sleep. I didn't get much last night.'

Ann frowned. 'I thought Sam didn't call you until dawn.'

'It was five a.m.,' Joel corrected. 'And I hadn't slept before—' He stopped, looking embarrassed when Sam's mom bit her lip to keep from laughing.

'I see,' she said. 'Who was it this time? Do we know her?'

Joel's reputation as a womanizer was well known. Sam wondered how much of that was Joel trying not to get hurt again. Laura's betrayal had devastated Sam, but it had somehow been worse for Joel when she'd done the same to him.

It was, however, the shared experience that had brought them together. Joel was the best friend he'd ever had, so while Sam wasn't grateful to Laura for cheating on him, he'd accepted it as one of those clouds with a silver lining.

Joel sighed. 'Amber from the records department, and no, you don't know her.'

'Well, if you ever find the one, you bring her home to us,' Ann said. 'We will treat her like a queen.'

'Translated,' Bill said, 'Ann will skewer her with questions to make sure she's good enough for you.'

Joel's smile was shy. 'Thank you, Ann. I appreciate that.'

Joel's parents had died when he was in college and he'd missed having someone care about him like Sam's parents did.

'I'll take your dishes,' Bill said. 'You go on home and sleep. We'll make sure Sam and Siggy get home safely, too.'

'It's three floors up, Dad,' Sam said dryly. 'I think we can make it on our own.'

'We're going with you,' Ann said in a tone that brooked no argument. 'And if anyone stares or whispers, we will give them what for, believe you me.'

Oh, Sam believed it. Normally he bristled when they helicopter-parented. He was thirty-five years old, dammit. But today . . .

Today he'd let them do it.

They saw Joel off, another plate of lasagna in his hands, then set off for Sam's apartment. Luckily there was no one either staring or whispering.

But his apartment . . .

'Fuck,' Sam murmured when they'd entered.

'I'd normally tell you to watch your language,' his mom said, 'but . . . fuck.'

There was black powder on the walls and nearly all the surfaces, left over from whoever had dusted for fingerprints. Drawers were opened and his dishes sat in haphazard stacks on his kitchen counter.

His bedroom was in a similar state, the bedding torn off and the mattress up against a wall. The gauzy bottom of his box spring was gone, cut away to reveal the interior. His clothes were on the floor, the dresser drawers lying on top of them.

The contents of his closet were on the floor as well. It was going to cost a fortune to have his suits dry-cleaned.

Feeling like a zombie, he marched around the piles of clothing to the wooden box on top of his suits. Leaning over, he picked it up and lifted the lid. Then shuddered out a breath of relief.

'They're still here,' he murmured to himself. His childhood treasures were intact – his track medals, the Boy Scout sashes covered with the merit badges he'd earned on his way to Eagle Scout.

He found his class ring and . . . hers. Marley's. But he didn't truly relax until he'd found the simple silver band beneath their senior prom photo. He'd given her a promise ring that night, and she'd cried when he'd slid it on her finger. They were going to get engaged when they were twenty-one. Her father had made him promise that he'd wait that long.

Sam had wanted her buried with the simple ring on her finger, but her parents had put it in his hand, closing his fist around it. *Keep it*, they'd said.

Remember her, they'd said.

As if he could ever forget. She'd been seventeen and the love of his young life. They'd been so sure that they'd have forever. But some things were not to be.

'All there?' Sam's father asked gruffly.

'Yeah. The photo's a little bent, but it's all here.' He was surprised, honestly. He figured they'd have taken the box as evidence, given they'd thought he'd murdered a teenage girl.

Maybe it had been the photo of the two of them together, so very young, that had prompted CSU to leave the box behind. He might never know.

He certainly had no intention of asking Detective McKittrick, no matter how much she'd smiled at him. She'd thought him capable of murder.

She didn't know you. She still doesn't.

And she never would. Now that he'd come down from the euphoria of being released, he was shoving the events of the past twelve hours to the back of his mind.

Because *that* was so healthy. But he didn't care. Not right now.

He tucked the box under his arm, backed out of his bedroom, and headed into the bathroom – where he found another mess. All the toiletries were in the sink, along with the over-the-counter medications he'd had in his medicine cabinet. On top of the pile was an unopened box of condoms that had been in the cabinet for four long years.

That wasn't embarrassing at all. He turned from the sink and stopped cold. There was a crusty residue all over his bathroom wall. It covered the wall next to the shower and continued to the tiled wall of the shower itself.

'What is that?' his mother demanded, only her head sticking in through the door, the rest of her still out in the hall.

'Luminol,' Sam realized.

They'd sprayed his walls with luminol. Looking for blood. Because they thought he'd killed someone. Or several someones, from what McKittrick had said.

'Oh my,' his father said faintly from behind him. 'This is . . . wow.'

His mother took Sam's arm, gently pulling him from the bathroom. 'You can't stay here, honey. Get a change of clothes and bring them back down to our place. I'll get some food for Siggy. You can stay in our guest room until this is cleaned up.'

'It'll take me days,' he mumbled, numb.

'No, it'll take a crime-scene cleaning service days,' his mother said, leading him down the hall to his living room. 'Bill, take him and Siggy back to our place. I'll make some calls.'

Sam had the presence of mind to be surprised. 'Mom, how do you know about crime-scene cleaning services?'

She sniffed. 'From TV.'

'True-crime shows,' his father said mournfully. 'She's gotten addicted to them.'

Sam couldn't help it. He laughed and laughed and laughed until his eyes leaked tears. In his mind, he knew this was normal – a release of endorphins after a traumatic experience. So he let it all out, laughing until his gut hurt. When he finally caught his breath, he found himself sitting on his sofa, his parents hovering, their expressions worried.

He wiped at his eyes. 'Sorry. I guess I have some sh— stuff to work out.'

Ann raised a brow. 'Nice save, son. Now go. You've been up all night. Get some rest and we'll figure all of this out.'

'I have to have a suit for Monday.'

'I'll grab one and call the dry cleaner's for pickup,' she promised. 'Go, Sam. Sleep.'

Heaving a sigh, he lurched to his feet feeling like he was walking through molasses. 'Thanks, Mom.'

Standing up on her toes, she kissed his cheek, then swiped gently with her thumb to remove her lipstick. It was such a familiar, sweet gesture that his eyes stung again.

'I'm glad you're here,' he whispered.

'So am I,' she whispered back.

Blinking hard against a sudden wall of fatigue, he leashed Siggy and followed his father downstairs.

SDPD, San Diego, California
Saturday, 9 April, 8.30 P.M.

Kit tugged on her uniform cuffs as she hurried down the hall toward the bullpen. She hadn't worn her uniform in a long time, but it was clean, so that was a bonus. She caught up with Baz, who was opening the door to Homicide.

'What's going on?' she asked, because Navarro had only told her to come in right away and to wear her uniform.

'I'm assuming some sort of statement from the captain since we're in uniform. Navarro didn't say.'

There were several detectives in the office, none wearing uniforms. All of them looked up when Baz and Kit entered. After a split second of silence, Howard Cook started to clap. The others joined in and Kit knew the story had broken somehow.

'Jig's up,' she murmured to Baz.

'Did you really think we could keep something like catching Driscoll quiet until the autopsy came back? It was bound to get out.' Baz gave their colleagues a dramatic bow, drawing chuckles and snorts. 'Thank you, thank you.'

Connor Robinson poked Howard in the shoulder – harder than he'd needed to if Howard's wince was any indication. Howard was one of their oldest detectives, nearing retirement, and his partner was big, brawny, and brusque. Kit didn't think Connor even realized he was being so rough. 'Howard's just happy you closed a case so we can have cupcakes.'

Because that was how they rolled here in Homicide. Solved murders got cupcakes, and it was Howard's turn to hit the bakery.

Howard shrugged. 'It's true. But congrats, guys. This is a big one. Huge.'

It felt awkward, accepting congratulations when she was still unsure, but for Baz's sake, she smiled. 'Thanks, guys,' she said, then turned to Navarro's office.

He was at his desk, also wearing his uniform. A woman in a lab coat sat in the guest chair, her intricate braids an immediate giveaway. Dr Alicia Batra was here. Hopefully that meant she had a cause of death for Colton Driscoll.

Navarro looked up from what he was reading when they came into his office. 'Detectives.'

'Sir,' Kit said, then turned to Alicia. 'What did you find?'

'Death by asphyxiation,' Alicia said. 'Ligature marks were consistent with the rope he was found hanging from. Shape, size, and placement were consistent with a hanging. The basic tox screen came back negative. Still waiting for the results of the other tests you asked for.'

Kit was . . . disappointed. She'd expected Alicia to find something off in her exam. Something that would reinforce her gut feeling that the crime scene hadn't been right.

'But Dr Batra's initial findings are enough to make a statement,' Navarro said.

'Why today?' Kit asked, her skin feeling too tight over her bones. 'I thought we were going to wait for the full autopsy report.'

Navarro glared, but Kit didn't think it was meant for them. 'Tamsin Kavanaugh.'

'Oh no,' Baz groaned. 'What did she do now?'

'Got a real scoop from Jaelyn Watts's parents,' Navarro said bitterly. 'She followed you to their house when you took them home from the morgue, Kit. Plus, she'd followed you two to Longview Park on Monday.'

'But we had that entire area cordoned off,' Baz protested.

Navarro shrugged. 'She used a long-range telephoto lens to get photos of you at the grave site. Apparently, your reactions were enough to make her realize that this was bigger than an individual murder.'

'We didn't tell the Wattses about the handcuffs,' Kit said. 'Did she get a photo of those, too?'

'No, thankfully. But she knows that Jaelyn was a victim of a serial murderer.'

'That didn't come from us,' Baz said fiercely.

'I know,' Navarro said. 'But Kavanaugh's not stupid and she's apparently been keeping records on our homicides over the years. She showed me her notes when she came by two hours ago with her article, looking for my comment. She did her research and knows we have unsolved murders of girls in the same age group with similar physical characteristics. She's already put together that there were five victims, but that we've only ID'd two – Ricki Emerson and Jaelyn Watts.'

'What doesn't she know?' Kit asked, frustrated.

'She doesn't know about Cecilia Sheppard and she doesn't know about the handcuffs. She also doesn't know that you've ID'd Miranda Crisp as one of the Jane Does. She does know that Driscoll died by suicide – she followed you from the precinct this morning. The neighbors saw him being taken out in a body bag, and apparently someone overheard a first responder mention a rope.'

Baz sighed. 'What a mess.'

'No argument from me,' Navarro agreed. 'She has this story ready to go on the front page of tomorrow's paper. Sunday edition, above the fold. She said it's going up on their website within the hour and asked for SDPD's comment. So we had to decide if we'll get ahead of this or not.'

'And Dr Batra's autopsy findings give you the information you need to do that,' Kit said heavily. 'Dammit. We needed more time.'

'Sometimes you don't get more time,' Navarro said, but not unkindly. 'Sometimes we can dot our *i*'s, but we don't get to cross our *t*'s. It's a balance, but if we let this story run tomorrow on its own, it makes us look like we're hiding something.'

Kit blew out a breath. 'I get it. Does she know about Dr Reeves?' *Please say no.* That would be a nightmare for the man with the sincere green eyes.

Navarro shook his head. 'I don't think so. She didn't say anything about him, and I think she would have.'

Relief hit her harder than it should have. But the man had risked his career to help people he'd never met. 'Good. What do you need from us?'

Navarro shook his head. 'Nothing except to stand next to me while I read a statement prepared by the captain's office.'

'Do you need me to be there?' Dr Batra asked.

'Not at this time,' Navarro said. 'You've done your part, and we thank you for making it a priority. Just prepare your office for the follow-up calls.'

'Will you leave Dr Reeves out of it entirely?' Kit asked.

'Entirely. We won't put his career in any more jeopardy.'

Kit nodded once. 'When do we do this thing?'

Navarro checked his watch. 'Now. Let's go. Thanks again, Dr Batra.'

'No problem. I'll have my official report ready as soon as possible. I still have some tests out to be run.'

Kit gave Alicia's arm a pat. 'Talk to you soon.'

'Counting on it,' Alicia said wryly. 'Don't scowl at the camera.'

'That's her normal face,' Baz said, ducking when Kit swatted at him.

But the three of them sobered as they headed to the conference room, the noise from the gathered media growing louder as they drew closer.

The noise quieted abruptly as they filed in, and Kit was surprised to see the mayor and the district attorney already waiting. The DA was Joel Haley's boss. Kit didn't know him well, but Joel respected him and she respected Joel.

Joel, who was Dr Reeves's best friend. Kit had to push the image of Reeves's green eyes from her mind. He'd been telling the truth.

So at least her gut instincts had been right on that.

Kit caught Tamsin Kavanaugh's eye as she climbed the steps to the platform. Tall and athletic, the reporter wore a satisfied smirk.

Kit wanted to knock it off her face. Representing the dead was hard enough. If she was constantly looking over her shoulder for the damn reporter, she'd never get anything done. And if she was always worrying about long-range telephoto lenses, she wouldn't be able to do her job at all.

She shot the reporter a cold glare. Tamsin's smirk faltered, but then returned, smarmier than before.

Kit followed Baz to stand on Navarro's left. The mayor and the DA stood on his right. Navarro read his statement, which covered Driscoll's suicide and his role in the deaths of 'several local women'. He credited Kit and Baz with the closure of the homicides, which set off a flurry of camera flashes, making Kit's head pound. True to his word, Navarro did not mention Sam Reeves.

As expected, the first question was 'How many women?'

'Our investigation is ongoing,' Navarro stated. 'We'll be able to provide more information after we've talked to the families of the victims.'

'How did you identify him?' another reporter asked.

'A confidential informant tipped us off,' Navarro said with no inflection whatsoever.

'Cause of death?' another reporter shouted.

'Manual asphyxiation,' Navarro replied. 'We'll be providing updates as we uncover new information. Thank you for your time.'

Then the mayor got up and said really nice things about the department and Kit and Baz in particular. Kit managed to stand straight and stoic, avoiding any of the reporters' direct gazes.

Especially Tamsin's. It would be just Kit's luck to have her photo taken while sneering at the nosy bitch. Sure, it was Kavanaugh's job to uncover news, but pouncing on a mourning family was beyond the pale. The Wattses had deserved privacy to grieve.

Finally, the torture was concluded and Kit and Baz were free to go. Baz squeezed her shoulder as they walked to their cars. 'What do you want to do about Kavanaugh?' he asked. 'We could have her pulled over every day for speeding.'

Kit chuckled. 'Tempting. We're just going to have to be more careful.'

'That's a problem for tomorrow. I'm going back home to finish dinner with my wife. Navarro called when we'd just sat down to a roasted chicken.'

Kit's stomach growled at the thought. 'I went to Akiko's for dinner. She smoked some salmon and we were going to eat like kings. I hope she saved me some.'

'She's tiny. How much can she eat?'

'More than you and me put together. I don't know where she puts it.'

Baz paused at his car, his expression serious. 'You still having doubts about Driscoll?'

'I don't know. My head isn't clear right now. I'll let you know on Monday.'

Baz smiled. 'See you then.'

San Diego, California
Saturday, 9 April, 8.45 P.M.

Sam was watching TV with his parents, Siggy lightly snoring on his lap. It was one of the true-crime shows to which his mother had become addicted. His father, too, despite Bill's protests to the contrary.

Sam would rather be alone, but they seemed to need him close by. It wasn't like his life had been in danger today, but after having a son who was such a Boy Scout – as Laura had so helpfully pointed out – having him arrested had been a shock.

Join the club.

He could still feel the bite of the handcuffs, the panic of having his arms restrained. The cold suspicion in McKittrick's eyes. At first, at least. After she'd returned from finding Colton's body, she'd been much warmer.

Colton's body. Visualizing it hanging from a rope made Sam ill. He hadn't been lying when he'd told McKittrick that he was surprised that Colton had killed himself. The man had seemed the type to run, to continue lying his way out of every situation.

And to continue killing young women.

Colton would never be able to do that again, and for that Sam was grateful.

'Sam?'

Sam blinked, focusing on his mother, who looked worried. 'Sorry, Mom. What?'

She pointed to his phone. 'You have a call.'

He dropped his gaze to the lamp table on which his cell phone buzzed. It was Joel. 'Hey,' he said after hitting accept. 'What's up?'

'SDPD's doing a press conference in a few minutes. They're going to announce that Colton Driscoll was a killer and is now dead. Thought you might want to watch. It's likely going to be on all the major affiliates.'

Sam's gut twisted painfully. 'Are they going to mention me?'

Bill muted the TV, he and Ann turning in unison to stare at Sam, the worry they'd been trying to hide now plain on their faces.

'No,' Joel said. 'My boss is going to be there with Navarro – he's McKittrick's lieutenant. The mayor's also going to be there, so it'll be a big deal. They're going to keep it short. They still have some open questions to answer.'

'Then why are they doing this now?'

'A reporter caught wind of the investigation and grilled one of the victims' parents for information. They talked to her.'

'The parents of the girl found in the park?'

'Yeah. The reporter followed them home from the morgue after they'd ID'd their daughter's body. She took advantage of their fragile state of mind.'

'That's . . .' Sam searched for a word bad enough. 'Evil.'

'It is. So SDPD had to get ahead of the coverage. My boss is texting me, so I have to go now. I just wanted to let you know.'

'Thanks.' Sam ended the call and exhaled. 'Dad, can you change the channel to the news? Any of the major ones will do.'

His father complied, his hand trembling slightly. 'What's wrong?'

'Nothing to do with me.' Hopefully. 'But there's going to be a press conference.'

Ann's swallow was audible, her hold on Bill's hand visibly tightening.

The TV screen showed a large conference room in which at least forty people sat in folding chairs. A lectern stood on a raised platform at the front of the room.

A minute later, a large man with gray hair entered the frame, followed by two familiar figures. 'That's Detective McKittrick,' Sam said, 'and her partner, Constantine. The gray-haired guy is the lieutenant.'

Ann scowled. 'That woman put her hands on you?'

'And her partner threatened Siggy?' Bill growled.

Sam loved his parents. 'I think *she* was just doing her job. I think her partner is a jerk.' Who threatened to shoot a helpless dog? 'That's the mayor and Joel's boss beside them. Turn it up, please.'

Together they listened to Lieutenant Navarro give his statement. Sam's breath hitched in his chest when the man stated that several local girls had been victims.

'How many is several?' Ann asked sharply.

'Shh,' Bill hissed.

Sam held his breath when a reporter asked how they'd identified Colton Driscoll, then let it out when the lieutenant said they'd had a confidential informant.

He didn't fool himself into thinking that was the end of it, though. That was a tidbit too juicy to ignore. The reporters would dig. That Sam had been hauled into the police station would soon be common knowledge. He'd have to call Vivian and begin whatever preemptive damage control was possible.

When the mayor and the DA finished speaking, the five people on the platform stepped down and filed out. McKittrick and Constantine hadn't said a word, maintaining stony expressions throughout. *It must be a cop thing*.

'You'd think those two detectives would look happier,' Bill

mused. 'This is a big deal for them. They looked like they were marching to a firing squad.'

'I don't think McKittrick cares for the limelight,' Sam said, remembering the video interview he'd watched. 'I think that look is Constantine's default face.'

'She looks . . . small,' Ann observed. 'How ever did she knock you down?'

Sam rolled his eyes. 'Thanks, Mom.'

'Oh, hush.' She met his eyes. 'I'm proud of you, Sammy. That man won't be able to hurt anyone else.'

'He pretty much solved that problem on his own, by killing himself.' That bothered him, though. Not that the young women of San Diego were safer now, because that was huge. Not even that Colton had killed himself.

The timing bothered him. A lot. Why had Colton hanged himself this morning? Had he known the police were on to him? If he had known, how?

Did he revisit the park and see that the grave had been dug up?

Did he know that I was the one who reported him?

But Sam hadn't given McKittrick Colton's name until dawn. She'd said time of death was between three and seven a.m., so Colton had killed himself before Sam had given his name, or right about the same time.

My information had nothing to do with his decision. Unless Sam's line of questioning during their session had caused him to fear being caught. *And if that's the case, did I even need to call the police?*

'Sam?'

He looked up at his mother's gentle tone. 'Yeah?'

'Your father and I are *proud* of you, son. You did the right thing when it wasn't the easy thing. It doesn't matter that the bastard who killed several girls killed himself first. They would have arrested him and taken him off the street. Driscoll just saved them the trouble.'

'And the taxpayers the expense of keeping him in prison.' Bill frowned. 'Don't tell me that you feel sorry for him.'

'No. I really don't. It's just . . . this has been a lot to absorb.'

'I know.' Then her eyes narrowed speculatively. Sam never liked that expression. His mother was too good at reading him. 'You seem to have forgiven the lady detective, though.'

'She was nice to Siggy.'

'She's not bad looking,' Bill put in. 'If you like women that can knock you down.'

Sam had to laugh. 'Well, I don't.'

Which was kind of a lie. He at least respected her ability to handle herself on the job. It meant that she'd be safer from real criminals with intent to harm her.

Nerdy psychologists who were no threat didn't really count.

Ann was looking at her phone. 'Her first name is Kit. Kit McKittrick. That name sounds familiar. Bill, didn't I buy a doll with that name for your sister's granddaughter?'

Sam laughed again, because he'd had the same thought. 'That doll's name is Kit Kittredge. One of the reporters mentioned it during an interview – asked her if she'd been named for the doll. She didn't look amused.' He shrugged. 'I read another article about her that said she'd grown up in the foster system. She was adopted by a couple named McKittrick. She served in the Coast Guard out of high school, earned her degree while serving, then joined SDPD and worked her way up.'

Ann turned her shrewd glance back at him. 'You *like* her.'

His cheeks grew warm. 'I *respect* her. She's done good work, solving the murders of young women who would have been forgotten.'

She hmmed. 'Like the "several" that Navarro guy mentioned.'

'Exactly. When she got to my place last night, she thought I was involved in harming them. She was representing those young women. I mean, I didn't like getting arrested, but once I was free, I understood her suspicion. Her priority was the victims. I didn't know there were several, though. I thought there were only two.'

'And now there will be no more.' Bill stood up, signaling the end of the conversation, which was honestly a relief. 'Who wants coffee?'

Ann raised her brows. 'Decaf, dear.'

'Of course,' he said in a way that clearly indicated he hadn't meant that at all. 'Sam?'

'Sure. Thanks, Dad.' Sam gave Siggy a gentle stroke down his back. Hopefully they'd be back in his own apartment soon and this whole fiasco would only be a bad memory.

Seven

Carmel Valley, California
Sunday, 10 April, 12.10 P.M.

'Hey, Kitty-Cat,' Harlan murmured, pressing a swift kiss to the top of Kit's head. 'I saw you and your boss on TV last night.'

She'd arrived for the McKittrick family's Sunday dinner only to be mobbed by her many foster brothers and sisters chattering excitedly about Navarro's press conference the evening before.

'I didn't want to be there.' She hated the spotlight. She simply wanted to do her job.

'I know. But let your family be proud of you.'

'I did.' Kit had blushed at their accolades, but she'd let them celebrate. Celebrations were one of the things that the McKittricks did best, offering their foster kids an opportunity to see the good in life after being surrounded by pain.

'I'm proud of you, girl. More than you'll ever know. So is Mom. Those families will get closure. They'll no longer be stuck waiting for their daughters to come home.'

'It's a blow either way,' Kit murmured, warmed by his praise. What the public thought about her wasn't so important. That she'd pleased her boss was good. That Harlan and Betsy McKittrick were proud of her was everything. 'But at least two more families will have bodies to bury.' Jaelyn Watts and Miranda Crisp could be laid to rest. Ricki Emerson's body had been returned to her family years before. 'We haven't found one of the victims and two are still unidentified.'

'You'll follow it through. You'll keep searching for those girls' names.'

Kit had already started the request for funds to consult with DNA databases. It was becoming easier to narrow the search for the Jane Does of the world with genetic genealogy technology. The public's interest in knowing their roots had populated many of these databases, turning them into DNA treasure troves.

'I will,' she vowed. She let herself lean into Harlan, resting her head on his shoulder. It was uncharacteristic of her. She hugged him nowadays, able to accept that level of touch, but rarely did she lean on anyone of her own volition.

Harlan stilled. 'What's wrong?'

'I don't know. My gut's gone all wonky with this case. There was a key witness that was a suspect for a little while, but I didn't want to believe he'd done the crimes. I really didn't want to believe it. Baz was all like, "He did it, the bastard," but I didn't want it to be true.'

'That's not like you,' Harlan said mildly.

'No, it's not. Turns out he really was just a key witness and Baz was wrong.'

'That bothers you?'

'Yeah.'

'That Baz was wrong or that you felt a personal connection?'

Damn, but the man knew her too well. She loved him for it, even as it irritated her. 'The second one. Baz is wrong a lot.'

Harlan chuckled. 'Impudent.'

'Always. But really, Baz is rarely wrong. I was more upset at myself.'

'Why did you feel a personal connection?'

'I don't know. I heard his voice and saw his face and I just thought that he wasn't a killer. Which is not smart.'

'You *are* human. You're allowed to have a logical break every now and then.'

'No, I'm not. People could die if I believe a killer is innocent.'

'Oh, Kitty-Cat,' he sighed. 'You take too much on your shoulders.'

'I can't make mistakes, Pop.'

'You didn't, though, in this case. You said you were right and Baz was wrong.' He studied her. 'Tell me what's bothering you.'

'It's the killer,' she confessed quietly. 'My gut says something is wrong, but the department ran with the man we found dead and told the media that they'd closed the case.'

'You don't think he did it?'

'Well, he definitely did something.' She thought about the handcuffs and pink spray paint. The department had agreed that those details should continue to be need-to-know, or they'd have copycats coming out of the woodwork. 'I think he was a killer, but I don't know if he killed himself.'

'Did you tell your boss this?'

'I did, but the ME ruled he'd really hanged himself, and in the end the brass decided that the man's suicide note was an adequate confession.' Mostly because they didn't want to be accused of hiding key information from the public. 'But I'd already told the ME that I was having doubts. I asked her to do a full drug screen, to look for sedatives, especially ones with short half-lives.' Sedatives that would disappear if one waited too long to check. 'Just in case.'

'In case of what?'

'I don't know.' She sighed. 'I probably *am* overthinking it.'

'You?' Harlan said playfully. 'Overthinking? Say it isn't so.'

'Hush, old man. Can we talk about something else? I need to get out of my own head.'

'Of course.' He pointed at Snickerdoodle, who was lying on her back getting tummy rubs from the newest foster kid, Rita. 'You may have trouble getting your dog back.'

Kit smiled at the sight of the girl playing with her dog. Margarita Mendoza was only thirteen and so distrustful. She reminded Kit a lot of herself at the same age. But a dog broke down barriers and Snick was one of the best at giving love to the kids who needed it the most. 'How is she settling in?'

'About as well as you did.'

'Oh. I'm sorry.'

'On her behalf or yours?'

'Both, I guess. I wasn't an easy kid.'

'No, but you were always worth it.'

Kit's throat closed. 'Don't make me cry, Pop.'

'Wouldn't dream of it,' he said, amused. 'She was sitting with us last night, watching the press conference. She seemed very impressed with you.'

She sighed. 'You want me to go over there and give her a pep talk, don't you?'

'I'm so transparent.'

She squeezed his hand. 'I'm so glad that you are. I never could have trusted you otherwise. Don't blame me if the kid runs screaming. I'm terrible at this.' She let him go and turned for the new kid.

'No, you're not,' he said softly to her back.

No, she really wasn't. She was good with kids, especially teenagers. Rita wouldn't be the first foster she'd given a pep talk to.

Kit approached slowly, giving the girl the opportunity to leave or tell her to go away if she wished. Rita's sandy blond hair was streaked with pink, purple, and blue, her dark eyes fringed with long, dark lashes. She was a strikingly pretty girl, despite the lip that curled in a scowl.

Kit recognized the scowl, too. *So much like me at thirteen.* She pointed to the bench on which Rita sat. 'May I join you?'

'I wasn't hurting her,' Rita said defiantly, meaning Snickerdoodle.

'Oh, I know. She loves kids. She especially loves belly rubs.' Kit waited a beat, then added, 'Dogs are a great judge of character, you know.'

Rita rolled her eyes, such a dark brown that her pupils blended right in. 'Yeah, yeah. Did Mr McK send you over to try to win me over?'

'Yes,' Kit said readily, then laughed. 'And no.'

'You guys never give a straight answer.'

'Pop said that you seemed interested in the press conference last night.'

Rita's hand stilled on Snickerdoodle's belly. Snick gave a little wiggle and a whine and the girl huffed, resuming the belly rub. 'You caught a serial killer.'

'*We* did. Team effort and all that.'

'Pretty white girls,' Rita said bitterly.

Ah. The victims. Rita was right. The murders of pretty white girls tended to get more attention in the press. 'They were. But many of the victims we work for aren't. Everyone deserves justice, you know?'

'I know. I looked you up. You catch a lot of killers.' She kept her gaze fixed on Kit's dog. 'Even killers who kill poor people who don't matter.'

'Everyone matters, Rita. *Everyone*.'

Kit knew she'd said the words a little too forcefully when Rita glanced up at her in surprise. She seemed to gauge Kit's response, then nodded.

'I wish you'd been around for my mom.'

Oh, baby. 'Someone killed your mom?'

'Yeah. Her boyfriend.'

'So the police solved the crime?'

'No. He's still out there. My mom worked for his family. Cleaned their house. He . . .' The girl swallowed hard. 'He . . . you know. Hurt her first.'

Raped her. Kit's heartache intensified and she remembered that Harlan had said the girl had feared him at first. Kit wondered what had been done to her. But she wouldn't ask. At this stage, it wasn't her business and any inquiry would be the fastest way to scare Rita off. 'I'm sorry.'

Rita shrugged thin shoulders. 'But he's rich. Knows some cops. So he got off.'

'That's not fair,' Kit murmured and Rita said nothing, keeping her face averted.

Tears fell to Rita's jeans, and Kit pretended not to see them. She'd leave this girl her dignity. She'd also look into her mother's case first thing the next morning.

'My sister was killed,' Kit said quietly.

Rita swallowed thickly. 'She was?'

'Yeah. We were fifteen. The cops tried, but they never caught her killer.'

'They didn't try hard enough, then.'

'You sound like I did back then. I thought that, too. Pop and I looked for her killer. The detective who handled her case helped us. He tried and we tried, but we've never found the guy who did it.'

'Not all cops are like you.'

She sighed. 'I suppose that's true.'

Rita drew a breath and wiped her eyes with her sleeve. 'Is that why you became a cop?'

'It is. After Wren died, it was all I ever wanted to be.'

'You did it,' she said, sounding a little awed. 'You came from this place, from the system, and now you're . . . important.'

Kit's first reflex was to deny that she was important. Her *job* was important. But this girl needed to know that she could be important, too, so Kit nodded.

'Never could have done it without Mom and Pop. I know the others have already told you this, but you're in a good place, Rita. The McKittricks are the very best people on the planet. So many of us have gone on to have amazing lives and they are the reason. I mean, we've put in the work, but they've given us support all along the way. What do you want to do?'

She shrugged again. 'I like dogs.'

'And cats?'

Her smile was small, but true. 'Cats are pretty cool.'

'Then aim to be a vet. Or a vet tech. Or work in a shelter. That's probably something you can do right now, the shelter bit. I happen to know that one of the teachers at your new school organizes a group of volunteers who work at the animal shelter every Saturday morning.'

Rita's eyes, still a little wet, widened. 'Really? Who?'

'Miss Hubbard.'

'I have her for social studies. She's old.'

Kit leaned in a little closer. 'Spoiler alert: she was my teacher, too, way back in the day. She is getting older, but she's really nice. Five stars. Would totally recommend.'

'I'll ask her.'

'You got a phone?'

Rita pulled an older-model smartphone from her pocket. 'My mom got it for me, but I couldn't use it for a long time after she was gone. No plan. Mr McK helped me get a new plan.' She seemed suspicious of the kindness. Kit understood that, too.

'You want my number? You can call me if you need to talk. If you get my voice mail, I'm probably working, but I'll call you back as soon as I can.'

Rita's eyes narrowed suspiciously. 'You do that for all the strays here?'

Strays. It was what Kit had called herself for years after arriving at the McKittricks' home. 'You sound *so* much like I did at your age. And how old does that make me sound?'

Rita smirked. 'Pretty fuckin' old.'

Kit ignored the profanity. At Rita's age, she'd said so much worse. She mock scowled instead. 'You want my number or not?'

'Sure, why not?'

Rita's careless tone didn't fool her. 'Then let's do the AirDrop thing.'

They exchanged numbers and fell into a comfortable silence, Rita lazily petting Snickerdoodle, who soaked in the attention.

'I like it here,' Rita finally whispered.

'I do, too. It's going to take you time to trust that this is a safe place.' Especially if she'd also been hurt. This was not Rita's first foster placement. Kit knew that much.

'Did it take you a long time?' Rita asked. 'To trust?'

'It did.'

'What changed your mind?'

'Pop. After Wren was killed, I found him crying where he thought no one would hear him. That's when I knew that he was different. It wasn't immediate, like, no lightning strikes or anything. But it wasn't long afterward.'

Not entirely true. It had been another whole year and a lot of therapy.

'I'll try,' Rita said softly.

'That's all anyone can ask. You want some chicken? Mom's is the best. And do you see that tall guy over there with the buzz cut?

That's Mateo. He came through the house before I did, but he comes home for Sunday dinner regularly. He's a chef. Has a little restaurant downtown. His empanadas are *so* good. Let's go get some.'

She wasn't sure if Rita would follow her, but she did. Kit met Harlan's gaze for the briefest moment while they walked to the picnic table sagging with the weight of all the food Mom and the others had prepared. He gave her a grateful nod and she gave him a smile.

She was glad she'd come home today. She'd needed the comfort. Needed the peace. Needed to feel like she was giving back.

Now, if she could just get rid of the nagging feeling in her gut over Colton Driscoll, life would be just great.

San Diego, California
Monday, 11 April, 8.40 A.M.

Sam poked his head into Vivian's office. She had her leg propped up on an ottoman, her crutches within easy reach.

'I got you a coffee,' he said, holding it out. He'd already guzzled his down, needing the caffeine.

'Oh, thank you.' Looking as worn out as he felt, she gestured to the chair beside her. 'Sit down and let me look at you.'

He obeyed and she frowned at the fading bruise on his cheek. 'I didn't know that they hit you.'

'I might have resisted. A little.' She scowled, and he continued. 'It looks worse than it is. It barely hurt.'

She rolled her eyes. 'Right. What are you going to tell your clients?'

'That I tripped over my dog. I might embellish with a sad tale of the ruined ice cream cone that I dropped when I stumbled.'

Her lips twitched. 'You could make it more heroic than that. Say you got hurt by ninjas when you saved a busload of nuns or something.'

'Nuns *and* orphans,' Sam said lightly, and she chuckled.

'Stick to the ice cream.'

'Will do.' He pointed to her cast. 'You're okay? And Richard, too?'

'We're fine. Car's totaled, but it's just stuff. Car full of teenagers ran a stop sign and T-boned us. Thank the Lord that they're all safe, too. You look exhausted, Sam. Maybe you should cancel your appointments today.'

'I almost called in today, but I needed to get out of my parents' apartment.'

She frowned. 'Why are you in your parents' apartment? They released your place from being a crime scene, didn't they?'

'Yeah, but it's a mess. They weren't very tidy when they processed.'

'Oh, for God's sake,' she muttered, annoyed. 'You have to clean all that up?'

'Not me. Mom found one of those crime-scene cleanup companies.'

Her frown deepened. 'You have to pay for that out of your own pocket?'

'Yep. And they're not cheap. They do appear to be discreet, at least. I feel incredibly lucky that none of my neighbors seem to know what happened. I don't want that my apartment was a crime scene leaked all over the place.'

'I don't blame you. What a nightmare.'

'I've had those, too,' he admitted. 'I kept seeing Colton Driscoll hanging from a rope.'

Her eyes widened. 'They showed you a photo? What's wrong with those people?'

'No, they didn't,' he said quickly. 'But my imagination filled in the blanks.'

She leaned over and covered his hand with hers. 'You did the right thing, Sam. You might have saved a young woman's life.'

He swallowed hard. 'No. I mean, not the girl he's been talking about. She went missing eight months ago and is presumed dead.'

Vivian seemed to shrink in on herself. 'Oh no.' A moment of silence hung between them before she cleared her throat. 'Well, he would have done it again. You saved those future victims.'

He nodded unsteadily. 'I keep telling myself that.'

'For what it's worth, I've been a therapist for decades and I've never had a case like this one. You probably never will again.'

'I hope you're right.'

She smiled at him kindly. 'Take some time off, Sam. Take Siggy to the desert and camp for a day or two. You always come back rested and restored when you go there. I don't understand why anyone would want to sleep in a tent to begin with, and in the desert, no less.' She mock shuddered. 'But you do like it. So . . . take some time off.'

'You're not.'

'I was in a car accident. We got off easily with only broken bones and some bruises. You were . . . well, arrested. Roughed up. Hauled downtown and subjected to interrogation.'

'Constantine threatened to shoot Siggy,' he murmured. That had also factored into his nightmares.

Vivian blanched. 'What the hell is *wrong* with them? Did they apologize?'

'Not really. But McKittrick felt bad that Siggy was scared. I think she has a dog, too, because she had a treat in her pocket. Gave it to me for Siggy.'

'Well, at least there's that,' she grumbled. 'Under other circumstances I'd suggest legal action, but that would shine a spotlight on you and we don't want that.'

'No, we don't.' That would make things so much worse.

She glanced at the clock on the wall. 'I hate to take your gift of coffee and tell you to hit the road, but I've got a client coming in fifteen minutes and I have to review my notes. Tell Angeline to reschedule your appointments for today, at least. You're not in any frame of mind to listen to other people's problems.'

He nodded woodenly. She was right. He knew that.

'Sam?' she prodded gently, and he realized that he'd just been staring off into space. 'Where will you go with your day off?'

He gave his head a shake to clear it and considered the question. 'Old folks' home. I haven't visited in a while.'

Her forehead crinkled. 'Who do you know there?'

'Everyone. I play for them a few times a month. Piano,' he added when she looked confused. 'All the old standards.'

Her eyes softened. 'I learn something new about you all the time. That's so sweet. I bet they enjoy that.'

'They do. Sometimes they dance.' He wrinkled his nose. 'Sometimes they get handsy with each other while they're dancing and that part's not so sweet. But this time of the morning it'll be time for arts and crafts, and they like to have background music.'

She smiled. 'Good. Text me when you get there. I'm concerned about you.'

He tried to smile back, but if it looked anything like it felt, it was tight and grim. 'I'll be back tomorrow with my head on straight.'

'Take care of yourself, Sam.'

'You too.'

He made his way out of their office building and walked back to his apartment, making himself notice his surroundings. Grounding himself with the small things – the sun shining on his face, the hot dog vendor at the corner, the coffee shop where the owner always had his order ready by the time he got to the counter, the stray cat that darted across his path. He hoped it belonged to someone.

He almost called Joel to see if he wanted to meet for breakfast before he headed to the retirement home, but his friend had said he'd be in court this morning.

It was then that Sam realized that he didn't have anyone else to call.

I need to make some more friends.

And, of course, McKittrick came to mind. She had smiled at him and, even though he was still annoyed with how they'd treated him, he couldn't forget that smile.

She'd been doing her job. *She doesn't know me. Doesn't know I couldn't even hurt a fly.* And, in hindsight, his behavior *had* been shifty.

He walked out of his building's elevator on his parents' floor just as his dog walker exited their apartment. Skyler swept a lock of hair away from her face, tucking it behind her ear as she jiggled the doorknob to make sure the door was completely closed – Siggy was a little escape artist.

Skyler looked surprised when she turned and saw him approaching. 'Dr Reeves. I thought you were on vacation and your folks were Siggy-sitting.'

'Nope. My apartment had a pipe leak and I'm staying with them while it's being cleaned.' It was the lie he was going with. His parents would spread the same story. Nobody needed to know his business.

She made a face. 'That sucks. I just got done walking Siggy. He found a stick.'

'He always finds a stick,' Sam replied dryly. 'It's kind of his thing.'

'This is a big stick.' Grinning, she spread her hands a foot apart. 'He was so cute carrying it in that I didn't have the heart to tell him no – sorry about that. I put it in his crate with him so that if he chews it up, the mess will be easily cleanable.'

Sam chuckled, his heart feeling a little lighter already. Skyler was a nice young woman and she really loved his dog. She'd been walking Siggy ever since he'd moved in four years before. Then she'd been seventeen years old, saving for college. Now that she was in college and working nights, she'd transitioned most of the dogs to other walkers, but she'd held on to a handful of customers, including Siggy.

'He really is cute,' Sam agreed. 'I'm getting ready to take him to the old folks' home. They love him there.'

'Well, he's good and mellow. We walked about a mile.' She pressed the elevator button. 'I'll see you later. Take care!'

'You too, Skyler.' He found Siggy in his crate, chewing on what really was an impressively sized stick. 'Come on, boy. Let's go to Shady Oaks.'

Siggy perked up, recognizing the name.

Sam would play some quiet music to soothe himself and the residents. Win–win. Then he'd get back to work. People needed him and . . . well, he liked that.

It was good to be needed.

San Diego Medical Examiner's Office, San Diego, California
Monday, 11 April, 1.45 P.M.

Kit silently slid a piece of cake onto the ME's desk, waiting for her to look up from the email she was typing. Only a few years older than Kit, Alicia Batra was her favorite of the MEs, mostly because she was intelligent and kind. But also because she could be bribed with baked goods.

Alicia's gaze didn't leave her computer screen, but when Kit moved to take the cake back, the ME lightly smacked her hand. 'No take-backs,' Alicia said tartly.

Kit chuckled despite the tightness in her gut. Alicia hadn't had the results on Colton Driscoll's drug screen first thing that morning and had said to call her after lunch.

Kit had tried not to worry on it while she and Baz went to empty Driscoll's locker at his workplace, hoping to find something to tie him to the murders. Unfortunately, it had been empty.

His coworkers had agreed that Driscoll being a killer was no surprise because he'd had a hair-trigger temper. But they *had* been surprised that he'd killed himself, saying they hadn't thought he'd have the guts to do such a thing.

This intensified Kit's feeling that something wasn't right with the suicide, but she hadn't wanted to make another call to Batra from her desk with so many listening ears in the homicide bullpen. So she'd snuck away as soon as she could, a plate of cake in hand.

'Give me another minute to finish this,' Alicia said, 'and you'll have my undivided attention. Because you brought me cake.'

A minute later, Alicia hit send, then turned to Kit. 'To what do I owe this fine bribe, Detective?'

'Well, first, it's more like half bribe and half thank-you.'

Alicia raised a brow. 'Really?'

'No,' Kit admitted. 'More like seventy–thirty.'

'So mostly a bribe.' Alicia shrugged. 'I think your offerings taste better when they're bribes.'

Kit chuckled again. 'This cake is pretty tasty on its own. One of the guys in Homicide made it.' To celebrate closing the serial murders of six women. Not five, as Colton had written in his suicide note. *Six*. 'Normally we just buy cupcakes from a bakery for celebrations, but it was Howard Cook's turn and he's taking a baking class.'

'So he can meet more women?' Alicia guessed.

Kit nodded, because this was Howard's fifth class, all for the same reason. 'Sadly, yes.'

Alicia sighed. 'At least we get cake out of this class.'

'True.' Howard's last class had been painting stills of fruit. 'He's a nice guy. It's a shame he has to take classes to meet dates.'

'Hard to meet people when you're working all the time,' Alicia observed.

Again, true. Alicia was married and already had a kid, but Kit hadn't had an actual date in nearly two years. She hadn't met anyone she really wanted to spend time with.

You liked Sam Reeves, the little voice in her head said slyly.

You shut the heck up.

Alicia was studying her as she took her first bite of cake, eyes narrowing with interest. 'You got something to share with the class, Kit?'

'Nope.' Kit leaned against Alicia's desk. 'I do have a favor to ask, though. Or two.'

'So now we get to the bribes. Hit me. I figure it's got to be big if you drove all the way down here.'

'It only took fifteen minutes.'

'Fifteen minutes you could have used a number of other ways. Did you need to get out of the bullpen that badly?'

'Kind of,' Kit admitted. The air of celebration wafting through the precinct had been grating on her nerves. 'First, this case.' She put a file on Alicia's desk. 'It's from two years ago. Maria Mendoza.'

Alicia blinked in surprise. 'Not the Driscoll case?'

'Yes, but this first.'

Alicia opened the file and sighed wearily once she'd read the first page. 'I remember this one. The victim was beaten to death. The case went cold, didn't it?'

Kit had looked up Rita's mother's file as soon as she'd sat down at her desk that morning – and Rita was right. There was reason to suspect that her mother's wealthy boss was involved in her death. Yet the man had never been a suspect.

The detective who'd caught the case had retired the following month and no one else had picked up the investigation.

Including me.

Kit would correct that mistake if she could. 'It did go cold, but I think we should look at it again.' She pulled a photograph from the very thin file. 'There's something on the victim's skin, right here.' She pointed to a mark on the woman's cheek. 'It looks like an indentation, maybe from a ring or something. But the photo is blurry. I was wondering if you'd taken any other pictures.'

Alicia was frowning. 'This wasn't among the photos I submitted.'

Kit's brows went up. 'What do you mean?'

'I mean that I'd chosen half a dozen clean photos of the victim's face to be uploaded with this report. The mark on her cheek did look like the indentation of a ring.' Alicia looked troubled. 'Let me go back into my own files and see what I can find. It wasn't that long ago. I keep copies of all the photos I take. I'll let you know.'

Whoa. It could have been a simple mistake. Someone could have accidentally uploaded the wrong photo, but Batra was meticulous to the point of being obsessive about it.

'Who did the uploading?'

'One of the clerks. I'll have to check to see who.'

Kit exhaled quietly, wondering if this was a simple error or if there had been a cover-up because Maria Mendoza's boss was wealthy and well connected. If so, that would be her boss's responsibility to sort. 'Thank you. Full disclosure – I met the victim's daughter over the weekend. Navarro probably won't let me take the case, but I'm hoping he'll assign it to someone else if there's new evidence. Or old evidence that was somehow . . . missed.'

'Missed,' Alicia repeated flatly. 'I have a bad feeling about this, Kit.'

'So do I. Let's figure out what's what before we gloom and doom, though.'

'You know me so well.' Alicia closed the file and took another big bite of cake. When she'd swallowed, she asked, 'What's the second favor?'

'The drug screen for Colton Driscoll.'

Alicia turned to her computer screen. 'I don't get to look for fast-acting sedatives too often. Either too much time has passed when the body's discovered, or the detectives don't suspect the victim's been sedated until well after the drug's worked its way out of their system. Your results weren't back when I checked first thing this morning, but they might be now.' She glanced up at Kit. 'If you're right, you're not going to be Navarro's favorite child. Not after he went public with the news of Driscoll's suicide.'

'I know,' Kit said with a sigh. 'But if Driscoll didn't hang himself, that means someone else did it. Doesn't mean that Driscoll didn't kill those girls, but it does mean that someone else wanted him dead. So there could be other players involved.'

'Well, your results are back, and here comes trouble.' Alicia printed a page and handed it to Kit.

'What is zaleplon?' Because Colton Driscoll had apparently taken a shit ton of it.

'It's a sleeping pill. I see it occasionally in victims who've slit their wrists in a bathtub, but never with a hanging.'

'What does this level mean? How out of it would he have been?'

'Give me a minute or two to do some calculations.'

Kit watched as Alicia did her thing, typing the numbers into some sort of computer software along with Driscoll's height and weight. Finally, she looked up, her expression grim.

'Your guy had taken enough that I sincerely doubt that he would have been able to climb up on the stool he used to reach the noose.'

'Can you translate "sincerely doubt" into percentages?'

'Ninety to ninety-eight percent sure that he didn't climb up on it alone. I'm basing this on the level that remained in his blood at the time we took the sample.'

'It has a short half-life.'

'Exactly. So I ran the numbers at both ends of the time-of-death estimate.'

'As early as three a.m. and as late as seven.'

'Yes. If he died at three, there would have been even more of the drug in his system at that time, and I'd put my guess at ninety-eight percent. But even if he died at seven, there would still have been more than enough to render him non-ambulatory.'

'That's the ninety percent. Got it.'

Coupled with Driscoll citing only five victims in his confession note instead of six and that his shoes were brand new and the footprint was that of a worn shoe . . .

This case was shaping up to be not as straightforward as they'd hoped.

Shit. Kit was going to have to tell Navarro right away. He was not going to be happy.

Eight

SDPD, San Diego, California
Monday, 11 April, 3.15 P.M.

Navarro leaned his head back, his eyes closed. 'Are you fucking kidding me?'

Baz sat silently, rubbing his temples. He'd been so happy eating cake and celebrating their 'win' that Kit had hated telling him what the ME had found. But he'd squared his shoulders and sat at her side when she'd delivered the news to Navarro.

'No, sir. Not kidding.' Her boss had reacted to the ME's report exactly as she'd anticipated. 'It doesn't mean Driscoll's not guilty of murder.'

'The fuck it doesn't,' Navarro grumbled. 'If there's even the smallest chance that this was homicide instead of suicide, the confession he left behind isn't worth the paper it was printed on.' Then he sighed. 'Go ahead. Say it. You told me so. We should have waited.'

'Oh, I don't think so, sir,' Kit said firmly.

One side of Navarro's mouth lifted. 'Smart.'

'Or maybe I just have a very well-developed sense of self-preservation.'

Navarro sighed again. 'Or that. Fuck. Well, what are we going to do next?'

Kit exchanged a glance with Baz, startled to see him looking so . . . old. It was as if he'd aged ten years in the last ten minutes. His shoulders were slumped, his eyes closed. His cheeks were pale and he seemed defeated.

Kit hadn't been in Homicide when any of the earlier victims had been discovered, but Baz had been around for all of them. Being unable to solve their murders for years had affected him as much as Wren's murder had. Closing this case had rolled a weight off his shoulders. A weight that had now visibly returned.

But Baz straightened in his chair, drawing a breath. 'We're going to keep investigating. We'll reexamine Driscoll's house as the scene of his murder rather than only the home of a murderer.'

'I asked CSU to collect evidence as if it weren't a suicide,' Kit added. 'We'll start with what they found. Although I want to repeat that Driscoll could still be our serial killer. He may have been killed for something entirely unrelated. He wasn't well liked from what we understand.'

'You're such a ray of sunshine,' Navarro muttered. 'You really think he did it? That Driscoll killed five women? Maybe six?'

'I don't know,' she said honestly. 'If he didn't, then someone went to a lot of trouble to make us think he did. Batra said it wouldn't have been categorically impossible for him to have climbed up on that stool to stick his head in a noose. Just very difficult.'

'Meaning the two to ten percent chance she gave.'

'Yes, sir. I think that the brand-new Top-Siders on his feet are more problematic if he was killed, because they would have been part of the setup.'

Navarro scowled. 'Which means that someone knew you'd found that print at Jaelyn Watts's grave in Longview Park.'

That had been worrying her since finding Driscoll's body. 'Best case, Driscoll is our serial and he killed himself, just like we thought. Next-best case, he was murdered but whoever killed him had nothing to do with the murders and was maybe mad at his lies. We'll check out the neighbor he assaulted, see if this was a revenge tactic. Medium-best case, Driscoll is our serial and he had a partner who wanted to pin it all on him and/or keep him quiet. Worst case, Driscoll only knew about it, and the real killer is still out there.'

Navarro nodded wearily. 'Is the shrink a suspect again?'

'No,' Kit said – too quickly if the look her boss shot her was any indication. Baz's brows were also lifted. 'The body was still warmish when we arrived at the scene,' she added, keeping her tone logical. Not emotional. 'Batra put TOD between three and seven a.m. Dr Reeves was in an interview room all that time. He couldn't have killed Colton Driscoll.'

'But he could still be involved,' Baz countered.

No, Kit wanted to say again, because she didn't *want* Reeves to be involved. But she forced herself to nod levelly. 'It's possible. We'll check him out. But we're going to dig into every aspect of Driscoll's life. If he did kill those teenagers, we'll find the connection.'

'Then get to work and let me make some tough phone calls,' Navarro said, his gaze dropping to his phone, his dread palpable.

Kit glanced at Baz. She'd told him about the Maria Mendoza murder and he'd been supportive of reopening the case, but right now, he shook his head slightly.

'What?' Navarro barked. 'What else?'

Kit hesitated, then exhaled. Better to get it all over with at once. 'One more thing, sir. Not related to the Driscoll case.' She laid the Mendoza file on Navarro's desk and told him about her conversations with Rita Mendoza yesterday and with Alicia Batra that afternoon.

Navarro's lips thinned. 'Seriously? Someone changed an official autopsy report?'

'Dr Batra isn't certain yet if it was a simple error or something more malicious, but she was sure that she hadn't submitted the single photo in this file. She's investigating. The victim was eight weeks pregnant, sir. That's included in the autopsy report. They took tissue samples from the fetus but never had any suspect to compare DNA. It doesn't appear that anyone even questioned her employer, and definitely no one asked him for a DNA sample. I'm hoping you'll reopen the case. I know I can't work on it because of my connection to the victim's daughter, but . . . what if Maria Mendoza's employer did kill her?'

Navarro stared at the file like it was a poisonous snake. 'You realize that in the two years since this investigation, the employer in question has become a city councilman.'

Kit had to force herself not to wince. 'Yeah. I saw that.'

Navarro pinched the bridge of his nose. 'I'll look into it. I may not reopen until Batra knows what happened to the damn autopsy report, but I will look into it.'

'Thank you, sir.'

Navarro waved at the door. 'Go.'

Kit didn't dawdle, following Baz out the door. She slumped into the chair at her desk. 'That was fun.' She looked into the windows of Navarro's office. He was still staring at his phone. 'I shouldn't feel guilty. Why am I feeling guilty?'

Baz shrugged. 'I'm not. That's why they pay him the big bucks. What first?'

'Let's go back to Driscoll's house and look harder for pills. On the chance that he did dose himself with sleeping pills and hang himself, he had to have gotten the pills somewhere. Our lives will be so much simpler if he had a prescription for them.'

'But there was nothing in his medicine cabinet on Saturday.'

'Not even Tylenol,' Kit murmured. 'That's also been bothering me.'

'You mean that if someone helped him into the noose, they cleaned out his medicine cabinet.'

Yes. 'Maybe. We also need to find some connection between Driscoll and high school drama clubs. These young women crossed their killer's path somewhere, and right now the drama angle is all we have. Knowing this, we can go back and talk to the victims' families and friends. There has to be some commonality with how he lured them.'

'What about Dr Reeves?'

Thinking about the man's earnest green eyes, Kit shook her head. 'I still don't think he's involved, but I'll talk to him again.'

Baz frowned. '*We'll* talk to him.'

'*We* can try. I think he's going to be angry enough at us as it is. But you threatened to shoot his dog. I don't think you're on his favorites list.'

'I don't care.' Baz shot her a pointed look. 'You shouldn't, either.'

'I don't,' she insisted.

Except . . . she did care. A little.

Which was still too much.

Baz sighed. 'Dammit, Kit.'

She didn't want to meet his eyes. 'Let's just go.'

Mira Mesa, California
Monday, 11 April, 6.30 P.M.

Kit met Baz in Colton Driscoll's living room. 'There's nothing here.'

'I know. I mean, the normal stuff is here, but not a single personal item. No cell phone, no photos on the walls, no bills to be paid, no take-out menus or stuff in a junk drawer.'

'It's like the house was staged by a real estate agent or something,' she murmured. She glanced up at the beam in the foyer. It was where Driscoll had looped his rope. 'How did he get the rope up there? There's no ladder in the garage and that beam's too high for him to have reached it, even standing on the tallest chair in the house.'

'I suppose he could have tossed the rope up and over,' Baz said, but sounded doubtful. 'The more we look at this place, the less likely it seems that Driscoll's suicide was unaided.'

'I think whoever killed him wanted us to be happy that he was dead and not come back for a second look.'

'We wouldn't have had cause to if you hadn't thought to ask for the rapid half-life sedative check.'

Baz sounded pleased with her, and that was always an ego stroke. 'It was the five victims, not six,' she said. 'We didn't know about the sixth victim until Friday evening, when Dr Reeves called again and mentioned a lacrosse player. Whoever wrote that confession didn't know that we knew.'

'Well, CSU found only Driscoll's fingerprints on all of the cabinet doors, but his killer went to a lot of trouble. I'm sure he wore gloves. I'm assuming it's a man. Driscoll was too heavy for most women to have dragged him up on a stool to put his head in a noose.'

Kit nodded. 'I agree. CSU vacuumed all the carpets, so maybe the killer dropped a hair we can use. Were any hairs found on the first four victims? In their clothes?'

'No. DNA was a regular tool by the time we found the first victim. The most rapid tests still took twenty-four to forty-eight hours, but we would have definitely tested a hair if one had been found.'

Kit sighed. 'I figured as much. I think we should talk to the neighbors again.'

'Which neighbor was assaulted by Driscoll?'

'David Epstein. He lives across the street. We didn't talk to him on Saturday. He wasn't home.'

'Fine. We'll talk to him and the other neighbors, and then we'll go have another chat with Dr Reeves.' Baz held up his hand like a traffic cop. 'To see if he can recall anything else Driscoll said that might help us.'

'You need to apologize for threatening his dog. He'll be more likely to cooperate.'

Baz rolled his eyes. 'I'll stop at the store and bring his pooch a dog bone.'

'I have dog treats. No need to stop at a store. A simple apology might be enough, Baz.'

'Fine,' he huffed. 'But that dog was snarling at you, Kit. I was worried.'

She smiled at him. 'Tell him that. Come on, let's talk to Mr Epstein.'

They stopped on the front porch to tell the uniform on guard duty that they were finished for now. There had been a constant stream of gawkers driving down the street, and a few had even tried to sneak a souvenir from the house. The overgrown backyard was fenced in and SDPD had put a lock on the gate, but that wouldn't keep out determined true-crime buffs.

The neighbors had kept to themselves, not engaging with the curious public. Hopefully they hadn't engaged with any curious reporters, either, but Kit wasn't too hopeful. She'd bet that at least one neighbor had given the media an earful.

Kit was petty enough to hope that Tamsin Kavanaugh had come up empty, though.

Baz knocked on the Epsteins' front door and it was answered by a forty-something woman with a toddler on her hip. 'If you're reporters, go away,' she snapped.

Kit held out her badge. 'SDPD Homicide, ma'am. I'm Detective McKittrick and this is my partner, Detective Constantine. We'd like to ask you a few questions about Colton Driscoll. Are you Gemma Epstein?'

The woman nodded, her eyes narrowing. 'I am.'

'May we come in?' Baz asked. 'We'd really like to avoid the media.'

'Like vultures,' Gemma muttered. 'They've been bothering us all day long.' She opened the door wider. 'I suppose we should just get this over with. David! Cops are here.'

A man came down the stairs slowly, his gait unsteady. His hair was buzzed, military-style. A framed photo on a side table showed a much younger Mr Epstein in his navy uniform.

'I figured you'd be coming by sooner or later,' he said. 'I'm David Epstein.'

Kit introduced them, then gestured to the living room. 'Can we sit?'

'Please,' Gemma said, looking flustered. 'Let me take care of the baby. Maureen!'

A teenage girl came in from the kitchen, drying her hands on a towel. Her gaze darted toward Kit and Baz and her eyes flickered wildly before she looked away. For a moment, Kit thought it was fear, but the girl had looked away too quickly for her to be sure. 'You need me to take her, Mom?'

'If you would. Thank you, honey.' Gemma handed the baby over. 'Put her in her high chair and give her some Cheerios. Nadine will be by soon to pick her up.' She sat on the sofa next to her husband, gesturing to a love seat. 'Please, Detectives.'

Kit studied the family photos on the walls as she and Baz sat. 'You have a lovely family. Two daughters?'

David nodded. 'Yes, and one granddaughter. Our girls are

Nadine and Maureen. I read the article in the paper. Said Driscoll liked small blond girls. Like mine.'

At least Tamsin Kavanaugh hadn't known about the pink handcuffs.

'That had to have come as a shock,' Baz said quietly. 'I have a daughter, and I can't imagine having lived so close to a predator.'

'Yeah,' David said shortly. 'I know I shouldn't say it, but I'm so glad he killed himself. I don't know how many girls make up the "several," but it was several too many.'

Kit nodded. 'We agree. We're trying to fill in the gaps. He obviously couldn't be questioned and we have so many unanswered questions. Can you tell me about your interaction with him? We know he assaulted you.'

David nodded stiffly. 'My jaw was wired shut until last week. At least I lost thirty pounds.' His attempt at a smile fell flat and his wife made a hurt noise.

'Driscoll was unhinged,' Gemma said. 'He just attacked my David. For a moment, the people who were there just stared. We were all shocked. Then two of the neighbors pulled him off David, and Driscoll stomped off. We called 911 for David and figured the cops could go after Driscoll because none of us were willing to go near him.'

'Makes sense to me,' Kit said. 'What happened next?'

Gemma shook her head as if still unable to believe it. 'He got in his car and tried to run David over.'

'The two neighbors who'd come to help pulled me into the garage,' David added, 'then Driscoll drove away. He got *probation* and *therapy*.' He spat the two words. 'Fucking judges.'

'Did you see him again after that?' Baz asked.

'No,' David said. 'He kept to himself. He lost his driver's license, so he ended up taking the bus. Maureen used to take the local city bus to school. My wife's been driving her there and picking her up. I'm glad, too. With as much as he hated me . . . Well, I've been horrified since last night, knowing he was even worse than we thought he was.'

'Again, that makes sense to me,' Kit said. 'What caused him to lose his temper that day?'

'He's a liar. Lies about everything. He claimed he was a Navy SEAL, for God's sake. That man was no SEAL. He never served anyone or anything but himself.'

'Stolen valor,' Kit murmured. 'I served, too. Coast Guard. People who lie about service make me upset, too.'

'I didn't attack him,' David said. 'I just told him that he needed to knock off the lies or I'd report him. It's a misdemeanor, you know.'

'He wouldn't have gotten any time for it,' Mrs Epstein said, her body rigid with rage. 'Just like he didn't get any time for attacking my husband.'

Kit understood her rage. 'Did you ever see him with any young women?'

David shook his head. 'No sixteen-year-olds. Driscoll's lived here for about ten years. Had two wives in that time – both just barely legal. He liked to come to our block parties and tell his stories. We'd try to time them for when he was on vacation, but he never went anywhere. It got to the point where we'd rotate responsibility for keeping him talking and away from everyone else. The last block party was my turn.'

'And when the fight broke out?' Baz asked.

'Wasn't really a fight,' David said dryly. 'I was injured in combat twenty years ago. I don't have full use of my right hand and I still limp on that side. I didn't swing back.'

Kit sighed. 'What a nightmare for you all.'

David's newly healed jaw tightened. 'Would have been worse if he'd touched my girls. I asked them both and they both said he never did. I haven't talked to many of the others on the block, but the few I did talk to say their daughters said the same.'

'Got it.' Kit glanced at Baz, and he nodded once. They'd gotten all they could from the parents. 'Could we maybe talk to your daughter?' Because if that had been fear in her reaction, Kit wanted to know why. 'She might have heard something in school. She's at the age of the other victims.'

David shuddered. 'I'll stay with the baby. My wife will stay with Maureen.'

'Of course,' Baz murmured. 'We just want to ask her what else she might know. We'll be gentle. I promise.'

With another nod, David went into the kitchen and Maureen came out, looking like she'd rather be anywhere else. Warily she sat next to her mother.

Kit smiled at her. 'You're not in trouble, Maureen. We just wanted to ask if you'd heard any of the girls in school mention Colton Driscoll.'

Her shoulders sagged in unmistakable relief. 'No. Some of the girls on the block would say how weird he was, especially after a block party. The dads would team up to keep him away from everyone. Just talking to him,' she raced to add. 'Nobody did anything bad.'

'So the girls thought he was weird?'

'Well, yeah. He was always talking about knowing Beyoncé and Jay-Z. Or even Meghan Markle. It was like he'd read *People* magazine and just spewed it all out.'

Baz smiled. 'That's pretty accurate, from what we've heard. If you do hear anything at school, can you have your mom call us?'

She looked at her mother uncertainly. 'Sure.'

Kit thought about the way that Driscoll was dressed. 'Did you see him go out Friday night?'

The teenager flinched, but before Kit could probe the reaction, Gemma spoke. 'We did. He left in his car, even though his license was suspended after he tried to run over my husband.' The older woman's cheeks heated. 'We debated calling the police about it, but we didn't want any more trouble from that man. My husband is just now able to work again. We couldn't afford another attack – from a mental, physical, or financial standpoint. And it wasn't like the law was going to do anything to Driscoll. He got probation for breaking David's jaw. They'd just smack his hands if we reported he was driving, and he'd be free to hurt us.'

Unfortunately, the woman had a valid concern. Kit tried to

soothe. 'It wasn't your job to report his infractions. Do you remember what time he left?'

'About eight o'clock,' Gemma said. 'Why?'

'We're trying to establish his movements right before he died,' Baz said. 'Did you see him return?'

Gemma shook her head, but her daughter became even twitchier.

'Maureen?' Kit asked softly. 'Did you see him return?'

Gemma turned to her daughter. 'It's okay, Maureen. If you know, tell them.'

Maureen swallowed. 'I did. My bedroom window faces the street and I saw the headlights. It was about eleven, maybe? He put his car in the garage.'

'Did he leave again after that?' Baz asked.

'No,' she said, a little too quickly. 'Mom, can I go now? I don't like talking about him. He was awful.'

'Of course, honey.'

'Thank you,' Kit said, giving the girl a smile as she scurried up the stairs.

'I'm sorry,' Gemma said with a weary sigh. 'She saw David getting beaten and . . . well, therapy has helped, but she still wakes up with nightmares.'

'We get that,' Baz assured her. 'Thank you for your time.'

Kit and Baz gave her their business cards in case the family remembered anything else and took their leave. Kit chanced a look over her shoulder as they walked to the street. Sure enough, a pair of eyes peered out between the curtains in an upstairs window.

'Don't look up,' Kit murmured.

'She's watching us?' Baz asked, just as quietly.

'From her bedroom window.'

'She knows something.'

'She sure does. And it scares her.' Kit pointed to the house two doors down. 'The lights are on, so they're home. Let's chat with a few more neighbors and go. We can come back to talk to Maureen again tomorrow.'

'That's fine. As long as we talk to Dr Reeves again today.'

Kit wanted to say no, that they should leave the man alone. But her reluctance to bother the man wasn't helping them fill in the blanks left by Driscoll's death – however it transpired. 'Let's ask him to meet us in a neutral place instead of going to his apartment. Being seen with us so close to the presser might lead his neighbors to put two and two together and guess he was our confidential informant.'

Baz's gaze rested on her face for a long moment before he nodded. 'That's fair.'

Fair. That was all she wanted to be. That was what Dr Reeves deserved.

San Diego, California
Monday, 11 April, 8.15 P.M.

Sam watched the two detectives approaching with growing unease. It felt like a troupe of Irish folk dancers was performing in his stomach. He repositioned himself behind the wheel of his RAV4, scared shitless because he had no idea why McKittrick and Constantine had asked to see him again.

They'd asked to meet him in a 'neutral place' of his choosing so that they didn't clue his neighbors in to the fact that he was their CI.

Which he appreciated. He figured it was McKittrick's idea versus her partner's. She seemed the type to think about things like that. It didn't really matter, though. Maybe this was standard operating procedure for confidential informants.

Maybe I should watch more true crime with Mom.

No, that was a terrible idea. He already had enough fodder for his nightmares from his client sessions, thank you very much. The few episodes he'd watched with Ann over the weekend had added detail to his nightmares that he really could have lived without.

McKittrick tapped on his front passenger window. 'Can we get in?'

Sam unlocked the doors and the two climbed in, McKittrick in the front and Constantine in the back.

Sam hadn't vacuumed since the last time he'd taken Siggy to the dog park, so the back seat was probably dirty. Hopefully Constantine's suit would be ruined.

The older detective cleared his throat. 'I wanted to apologize for threatening your dog the other night. He was growling at my partner and I was concerned for her safety.'

Sam blinked. 'Oh. Well, he wouldn't have hurt her.' Probably. 'But I accept your apology.'

McKittrick twisted in the seat so that she was looking at Sam directly. 'We had a few more questions about Colton Driscoll. Trying to tie up some loose ends.'

Sam stiffened. Her words sounded right, but her body language was off. Something was wrong.

'Okay,' he said warily. 'What do you want to know?'

'You told us about what he said concerning the young women – the lacrosse games, the color lilac, the grave site. What did he say about himself?'

'Not a lot. Like I told you, he was a pathological liar. Some liars are unaware that they're lying. Their brains confabulate images or situations, which tumble out of the individual's mouth. But I think Colton Driscoll used lies as a crutch. He wasn't comfortable in social situations, and being someone else allowed him to be charming and sociable. He also used his lies as deflection. He didn't want to be in therapy and was basically punching a time clock.' He had a sudden recollection. 'Oh, wait. Punching. He had abrasions on his knuckles on Friday afternoon. They looked fresh.'

McKittrick nodded. 'We saw those. What did he say about them?'

'I thought maybe he'd hit someone. He claimed that one of his coworkers was giving him a bad time, trying to get him in trouble so that the other guy could have his job.'

'I thought he worked in a mail room,' Constantine said.

'He did. I thought the same thing – what job is lower than the mail room that the coworker could have had? But Colton claimed he took out his anger on a wall. The abrasions seemed to match that story. I offered to teach him ways to deal with his anger that wouldn't hurt him and he seemed receptive for the first time since we'd started sessions.'

'So his coworkers knew about his arrest for assault?' McKittrick asked.

'They at least knew he had an anger management problem. They might have found out about his arrest and probation or they might have heard that he'd lost his IT job because he got mad and punched someone. How much do you know about him?'

'Not a lot,' she admitted. 'We're just getting started digging into his past.'

'Well, he lost at least four IT jobs in the last twenty years because of his temper. Or his lying. Or both. He was a rather . . . unpleasant man.'

Constantine snorted. 'Yeah. We figured. Murdering young girls usually takes an unpleasant person.'

Sam narrowed his eyes at the man and started to bite out a retort, then shook his head. It wasn't worth it.

Constantine made a face. 'Sorry. I worked on these murders over the years.'

'Oh.' Sam hadn't considered that. There had been several victims. 'That must have been disheartening, not being able to get justice for the victims.'

Constantine's expression grew pained. 'It was. Still is. Because those girls didn't get justice. Their families didn't get to face Driscoll in court. He took the coward's way out. So . . . yeah. "Disheartening" is as good a word as any.'

McKittrick gave her partner a sympathetic look before returning her attention to Sam. 'Did he have any friends? Anyone he would have confided in?'

'No. He was very lonely, I think. He could be very charming on the surface. I assume that's how he was married four times. But none of his marriages lasted that long because he couldn't keep up the facade. His wives were only eighteen but figured out that he couldn't be trusted to tell the truth about anything. His longest marriage lasted a year. The shortest was four and a half months. This is according to the court records that came with the referral.

By his own account, his wives were "cheating whores" and he left all of them. Of course, after our first session I knew whatever details he'd provided had to be taken with a grain of salt.'

'Like his home address,' McKittrick said.

Sam's cheeks heated as he remembered that stupid crime board, including the map he'd made of the two potential victims' homes and Colton's real address. 'Yeah.'

'I would have made the same kind of crime board,' she said softly. 'You just had the misfortune of having two suspicious cops see yours at a very bad time.'

One side of his mouth lifted. 'Thanks, but it was stupid.'

She shook her head. 'You cared, Dr Reeves. That's never stupid.' Then she seemed to realize that she'd strayed from the topic. 'We know he had four ex-wives and no children.'

'Thankfully,' Constantine muttered and Sam had to agree with that.

'Definitely,' McKittrick said. 'His parents are deceased and we didn't see any brothers or sisters in his background check. Did he ever mention any other family?'

'No. He was fascinated with famous people almost to the point of obsession. He knew about their affairs, divorces, and their children. He claimed to be buddy-buddy with them, teaching them new skills and partying hard with them.'

'He also claimed to have been a Navy SEAL,' McKittrick said.

Sam sighed. 'Yes, he did. I never confronted his lies, though. There was no point. But we did discuss the difference between lies and illegal lies. He seemed to be surprised that claiming to be in the military was a crime. He blustered about it, saying his neighbor was too thin-skinned and couldn't take a joke.'

McKittrick scowled. 'His neighbor served and was permanently disabled after a combat injury.'

Sam hadn't known that. 'What Colton did to him is even worse, then.'

'Did he ever threaten you?'

'Yes, once. During our last session on Friday.' Was that really only three days ago? 'He said he wanted to skip a session to go to a party in London. I told him that his probation officer would have to approve it and he came at me. I have to admit, for a few seconds I was . . . alarmed.' Scared shitless was more like it, but whatever.

'I guess so, knowing what he'd done to his neighbor,' McKittrick said with a commiserating smile. 'Was he on any kind of medication?'

Sam hesitated, because that was protected information, even though Colton was dead. 'Not according to him.'

McKittrick tilted her head. 'But you know that he was?'

'I can't say.'

She sighed. 'Right. HIPAA and all that. Okay. Can you tell us if he was seeing a psychiatrist who might have prescribed something?'

'Like what?'

It was McKittrick's turn to hesitate, but she met his eyes directly. 'Sleeping pills.'

Sam considered his options because there had to be a good reason she was asking. Finally, he shook his head in an exaggerated fashion while saying, 'I can't say.'

Her smile was quick. 'Got it. So we should be checking for other medications. Thank you. Did he ever mention driving anywhere?'

'No. His license was suspended. Although I don't suppose that would have stopped him. If he drove to any of our sessions, I wouldn't know, but he was supposed to be taking a city bus or the trolley.'

'Did he mention that he had weekend plans?' Constantine asked. 'Maybe meeting someone that evening?'

Sam started to reply, then closed his mouth. This was important. Why were they asking? Colton was dead, his murders ending with him. *Unless . . .*

Holy shit. 'Did Colton have a partner?'

Both detectives flinched, although it was minute. 'Why do you ask that?' Constantine asked, his tone appearing easy, but there was an underlying belligerence that couldn't be ignored.

'Because you asked if he was meeting someone and if he had friends. He's dead, so that shouldn't matter unless he had a partner or an accomplice.'

Constantine's expression darkened. 'Fucking shrinks.'

Sam shrugged. 'Sorry. Did he?'

'We don't know,' McKittrick said, and Sam almost believed her.

Except . . . *Sleeping pills. Partners. Accomplices.* Sam sucked in a breath at an unwelcome thought. 'I've got to stop watching true crime with my mother.'

McKittrick's lips twitched. 'Why?'

'Because now I'm wondering if he really killed himself, and that's just ridiculous.'

He thought they'd laugh at him, but . . . they didn't. They both looked sucker-punched.

'Oh fuck,' Sam whispered, his pulse going from normal to stratospheric. 'You're kidding. Please say I'm ridiculous.'

'Fucking shrinks,' Constantine muttered again, but with less heat this time.

Well, hell. 'Am I in any danger from this partner?' Sam asked, wishing they weren't in his car so that he could escape.

'We don't know that one exists,' Constantine deflected.

That was a lie. Sam could see it in the man's eyes. 'Right. Goddammit.'

'We really don't know,' McKittrick said levelly. 'We don't know much right now, to be honest. We'll keep you updated as it pertains to your personal safety.'

'Wow.' Sam wanted to say something cutting in response to that, but he couldn't think of a single remark that made any sense. He settled for a sarcastic 'Gee, thanks.'

She sighed again. 'I'm sorry, Dr Reeves. This situation sucks and I wish you'd never been involved. But you are. Be aware of your surroundings and call 911 if you feel threatened.'

'That is so not helpful, Detective,' he spat. But it wasn't her fault. He knew that. 'I'm sorry. I don't mean to be rude.'

'It's okay. I get it.'

'What about that reporter? The one who got the scoop on Colton being the killer? Will she find out about me and put my name in the paper?'

'How do you know about her?' Constantine demanded.

'Joel told me.' He winced. 'Dammit. Now Joel's going to be pissed at me, too.' He shook his head. 'Never mind. Will she? Will my name be publicized?'

'She hasn't published it yet,' McKittrick said. 'And I don't think she'd keep something like that to herself if she knew.'

Sam nearly snarled that that wasn't good enough, but she was just doing her job. 'All right.'

'If your name is publicized, we can look at police protection, but it's not likely.' She grimaced. 'Budget cuts.'

Sam closed his eyes, trying to control his temper. 'So I'm on my own.'

'You have a gun,' Constantine said sardonically.

Sam glared at the man. 'You are an asshole.'

Constantine had the grace to look a little ashamed. 'You're right. That was uncalled for. I'm not a fan of shrinks.'

'I figured that out for myself,' Sam said with as much malice as he could channel. 'This is a nightmare.'

'I'm sorry you're going through this,' McKittrick said quietly. 'Can you take a vacation? Go away for a while?'

'I have clients. I can't just up and go.' Although he did have vacation time saved up and Vivian had offered. 'I'll consider it,' he amended.

'Let us know if you leave town,' Constantine warned.

Sam gave him a dirty look, opened his mouth, then thought of something even worse. 'My parents live in my building. I'm staying with them right now. Are they in danger?'

'I don't think so,' McKittrick said and this time he believed her.

'Why aren't you staying in your own apartment?' Constantine asked.

Sam sneered. 'Because your CSU team left my apartment a fucking mess, that's why. There's fingerprint dust on the walls, the contents of every drawer were dumped, and there's luminol on my bathroom wall. I've had to hire a crime-scene cleaner at my own expense.'

Constantine flinched. 'Oh.'

'Yeah,' Sam scoffed. 'Oh. I'm going to tell my parents to go home to Scottsdale. They'll probably fight me on it. What am I allowed to tell them?'

'Nothing,' Constantine snapped.

McKittrick held up a hand. 'Can you go to Scottsdale with them? Maybe make it sound like you need to get away? You can even tell them that you don't want to be around if the media catches wind that you were involved.'

Sam scrubbed his palms over his face. 'Yeah. I can do that.' He glared at Constantine. 'She has good ideas. Be like her.'

Constantine looked momentarily shocked, then he laughed, a loud, rolling belly laugh. 'I'll try. She's the better of the two of us, for sure.'

'She's nicer,' Sam grumbled. 'Especially to my dog.'

'I apologized,' Constantine said, still chuckling. 'You accepted.'

Sam rolled his eyes. 'I should have held out for a treat for Siggy.'

Constantine gave McKittrick a triumphant look. 'Told you I should have stopped for a dog bone.'

McKittrick dug in her jacket pocket and pulled out a bone-shaped treat half the size of her palm. 'There's a bakery near the precinct that makes them. They're good for dogs. My poodle Snickerdoodle loves them. Siggy will like it, too. Give it to him, compliments of SDPD.'

Sam took the treat, charmed despite himself. 'Thank you.'

She smiled at him gently. 'Take care, Dr Reeves. If you think about anything that Driscoll said in session that would be helpful, please contact us. And if you do go to Scottsdale, I'd appreciate it if you'd shoot me a text letting me know.' She drew a card from another pocket and scribbled on the back. 'This is my cell phone and my partner's as well. If you run into any trouble, let us know. We'll do what we can to help.'

He took the card, believing she was telling the truth. Or, more correctly, he believed that *she* believed she was telling the truth. 'Thank you, Detective.'

Hoping he wouldn't need to call, Sam slipped the card into his wallet as they got out of his vehicle and walked away. And then later, when this was all a distant, bad memory, he could call her number and ask her out for coffee.

Dream on, Sammy. Dream on.

Nine

Balboa Park, San Diego, California
Sunday, 17 April, 4.35 P.M.

Kit was supposed to be having Sunday family dinner with Mom and Pop and all the others, but a call from Navarro had sent her speeding toward another park. A teenager with a metal detector had found a human hand. A female's hand, her nails neatly trimmed.

The teen had called 911 right away and Navarro had been informed.

Now she and Baz stood shoulder to shoulder under the tent CSU had erected to keep reporters with long-range lenses from spying on their recovery effort. They waited silently, watching as CSU patiently removed dirt from the body.

Just don't have pink handcuffs. Please.

CSU's Sergeant Ryland was working on the victim's midsection while his assistant removed dirt from her face. Sergeant Ryland would brush the dirt away from the young female victim's joined hands any minute now.

Kit gripped the little cat-bird in her pocket while she watched, holding her breath. And then . . . *No.*

Sparkly pink handcuffs.

'No,' Baz whispered, the one word filled with anger and devastation in equal parts.

'Yes,' Kit whispered back, horrified.

Another one.

Kit gave herself a shake. *Get your head in the game. Details. Notice them.*

This victim was blond but appeared to be older than the others by a few years. A little taller, too, if the length of her torso was any indication. Maybe five-five or five-six.

She hadn't been in the ground long at all. Days, if that long.

Ryland looked up at Kit, his eyes filled with the same despair she felt. He turned to his assistant. 'Call the ME.'

Wide-eyed, the woman nodded and walked a few feet away, making the call.

'I've got to call Navarro,' Kit said, because Baz seemed frozen in place.

'Not yet,' Ryland said. 'Give me one minute. She's got a medical alert necklace.'

Kit sucked in a breath. 'He left an ID on her?'

Baz just shook his head and said nothing.

'No name,' Ryland said, 'but she's given an ICE name and a number.'

Her contact in case of emergency. That was nearly as good as her own name.

Kit opened the Notes app on her phone. 'Ready.'

'Joe slash Denise, 619-555-2540,' Ryland read. 'I took a photo of the ID and sent it to your phones.'

Kit's phone dinged with the incoming photo. The victim had a peanut allergy and carried an EpiPen. 'Does she have ligature marks on her throat?'

'Yeah,' Ryland said bitterly. 'She does.'

'Thanks.' Kit patted Baz's arm. 'I'll call Navarro.'

He nodded, still silent.

Shoving her worry for her partner aside, Kit dialed Navarro. 'Pink handcuffs,' she said when he answered.

'Mother of God,' he whispered. 'And we're no closer to finding out who killed Driscoll.'

It was true. Kit and Baz had interviewed every neighbor, but none of them had been of any real help. They'd even returned twice to interview Maureen Epstein and her mother. Maureen continued to claim she knew nothing. The same was true of Driscoll's co-workers and his four ex-wives.

They'd dug through his financials and his phone records.

Nothing.

'This time he left her medical alert necklace on. No name, but it's got ICE names and number listed.' She ran a reverse lookup on the number. 'Joe and Denise Carville. Can you check the missing-person data—' She froze, her stomach in free fall. 'What the hell?' she whispered, unable to draw enough breath to say the words at a normal volume.

'What?' Navarro demanded.

'Their address. It's Dr Reeves's building. His floor. They're his neighbors.'

Navarro was silent.

'Did you hear me?' she asked.

'I heard you,' he said, his tone clipped. 'The parents filed a missing-person report this morning. Their daughter Skyler was last seen Friday night. She went to work and never came home.'

'What do you want us to do?' Kit asked, unable to keep her voice from shaking. Not a coincidence. But . . . not Dr Reeves. She still couldn't believe it.

She didn't want to believe it.

Dammit, Doc. What have you done?

'Should we do the notification now?' she asked when Navarro didn't answer. 'Or wait until we get the body fully uncovered?'

'I just sent you the missing-person report along with the photo the parents included. Do a visual ID for now.'

Her phone dinged again with the young woman's photo and her knees wobbled. It was her.

Skyler Carville, twenty-one. According to the report she was a student at UC San Diego and worked at a bar. And walked dogs part time.

Kit remembered the conversation with Dr Reeves in the interrogation room, right before she'd told him that they'd found a body. He'd said he had a dog walker, but she wouldn't be awake yet. Because she worked late in a bar and slept in on Saturdays.

Skyler Carville was Sam Reeves's dog walker.

'Well?' Navarro snapped. 'Is it her?'

'Yes.' But the word came out raspy. Kit cleared her throat. 'Yes,' she repeated. 'It's her. She walked Dr Reeves's dog.'

'Where is he?' Navarro growled.

'He went to stay with his parents in Scottsdale. They left on Tuesday. He texted that he'd be back tonight because he couldn't take off any more work.'

'Then wait at his apartment and bring him in as soon as he arrives.'

'This . . .' *Feels wrong*. But she couldn't make herself say the words. 'Okay.'

Navarro made an impatient noise. 'Speak, McKittrick.'

'It's . . . convenient. It feels wrong. Another metal detector? A day after she goes missing?'

He sighed. 'I agree. But we follow the evidence. If he can prove where he was every minute of this weekend . . . Well, we'll see when you get him in here.'

'Driscoll's killer put brand-new Top-Siders on his feet.'

'I know, Kit,' Navarro said, more gently than he'd spoken before. 'It feels like someone is manipulating us. Let's follow the evidence, okay?'

'Okay, sir. We'll do the notification and wait for Dr Reeves. But I won't tell the girl's parents that we plan to talk to him.'

'That's wise. Tell Baz I said not to do so, either.'

'Baz just got to the point where he doesn't hiss every time he says Reeves's name.'

Navarro sighed again. 'I know. Tell him to call me.'

Baz hadn't moved. Not one inch. He looked like he was in shock. 'I'm a little worried about him, boss. He's really not okay right now.'

'Neither am I.'

'No. I mean he's pale and sweating. He isn't speaking, isn't moving. He just keeps staring at the body.'

'He'll be okay. Get him into a car and feed him. Let him rant and rage for a little while. He'll be okay.'

'All right.' Kit ended the call, hoping that Navarro was right as she turned back to look at her partner.

But he's not okay.

The thought barely registered through a fog of instant panic as her body began to move, running frantically toward Baz, whose knees were buckling, his body collapsing to the ground. His face was gray, his eyes terrified.

Kit? He mouthed the word, unable to even whisper.

She dialed 911 as she gripped his hand in hers, her pulse racing in fear because his eyes were now fluttering shut. 'I'm here, Baz. Just hold on.'

San Diego, California
Sunday, 17 April, 8.15 P.M.

Sam grimaced apologetically at the woman who stepped off the elevator on the floor below his. After camping for three days, he was dirty and he smelled awful, but nothing a shower couldn't fix.

He'd stayed with his parents in Scottsdale for three days, wondering all that time if it was safe to come home. Finally, he'd had no choice. He needed to get back to work. Vivian and Angeline had been so good about rescheduling all of his clients after his impromptu escape from the city on Tuesday morning, but they couldn't do that again. Not if it wasn't an emergency.

His parents had stayed in Scottsdale, thankfully, and his apartment was now clean. It was time to come home.

But he'd needed some quiet time after all that anxiety. Needed to get his head back on straight. So, he'd left Scottsdale early on Friday for Joshua Tree National Park. He'd hiked with Siggy all day Friday, Saturday, and most of Sunday, and spent the nights staring up at the stars.

He felt better now. Not a hundred percent, but better.

He made his way to his apartment, Siggy panting happily. The place smelled good. Fresh. He did a slow turn, checking out his living room.

There was no sign of fingerprint dust and nothing was on the floor. His bathroom positively gleamed. Five stars to the cleaning company his mother had hired. His apartment was cleaner than it had ever been.

Time to fix that. He tossed his dirty clothes into the hamper and stepped into the shower, washing off three days of grime and sweat. It hadn't been terribly hot in the park, but the sun had been direct and he'd hiked as hard as he'd dared. There'd been Siggy to think of, of course. His dog was young but there were limits, and Sam had needed to make sure they stopped often so that Siggy could drink water and rest.

Clean and dressed in a worn pair of sweats, he fed Siggy and opened his freezer. Then sighed. It was empty and too late he remembered why. The cleaning company had told his mother that the freezer door had been left open and everything was spoiled. His mother had instructed them to throw everything away, so he didn't have a speck of food to his name.

Delivery it was. He picked up his phone to order something and paused. He had a new text. From McKittrick.

You get home okay?

It made him wary and happy, all at once, because he wasn't sure what had motivated her to ask. More questions, maybe.

Or maybe she just cares. And that was thinking that would get him into trouble.

Just got home, he texted back. ***All okay?***

There was no reply, so he ordered from the Chinese restaurant down the street and sat down to wait. Five minutes later, there was a sharp knock on his door and he frowned.

There was no way that was the delivery guy.

Dread crept up his spine as he checked his peephole.

McKittrick. Only McKittrick, her sidekick nowhere to be seen. She looked grim.

For a moment he debated not opening his door, but she knew he was home.

Fell right into that one.

Cursing his own stupidity, he opened the door a sliver. 'Yes, Detective?'

She threw a look over her shoulder, then met his eyes. 'Dr

Reeves. I need to talk to you. May I come in?'

'Do I have a choice?' he asked, proud that his voice didn't waver.

She lifted one slim shoulder. 'Sure. But that means I'd have to bring you down to the station to talk. It's important.'

'Do I need my attorney?'

She hesitated. 'Not right now.'

The dread settled in his gut like a lump of lead, but he opened the door. 'I've got to be the stupidest man alive,' he muttered.

She exhaled quietly. 'I'm sorry.'

He didn't ask her to sit, choosing to stand in front of her, fists on his hips. It forced her to look up at him, and he needed that small symbol of control, as empty as it was. She held all the power in this situation.

Because you let her in without calling Laura to represent you.

'For what?' he asked tightly.

'Skyler Carville is dead.'

Sam took a step back, shocked. 'What?' he whispered.

Skyler . . . dead? And McKittrick was here so that meant . . . homicide.

He covered his mouth, trying to keep his roiling gut from churning up and out.

'We found her body in a park this afternoon,' McKittrick said in a tone barely louder than his had been. 'Not the one where you found Jaelyn. The mode of death is consistent with the other victims.'

Sam looked around frantically for the nearest place to sit, but the sofa and chairs were too far away. 'No.' He reached for the nearest wall and slid to the floor, hanging his head. '*No.*'

She crouched beside him. 'Where were you this weekend? We need to document your location from Saturday morning at midnight to Sunday morning at dawn.'

He opened his mouth but no words came out.

She remained beside him, her face expressionless. But her eyes were worried and that scared him to death.

'I need to call my lawyer.'

She nodded but made no move to stand. 'Okay. Will you come to the station with me?'

'No. I'll meet you there. I'm calling my attorney first.' He closed his eyes, trying to think. 'Did he hurt her? Rape her?' He opened his eyes when she said nothing, and he could see the truth in her eyes.

He had. Whoever had killed Skyler had raped her before ending her life.

His eyes burned and he didn't even try to stop his tears. 'She was so sweet. Why would anyone target her?' Then realization hit. 'Because of me? Was this because of me?'

'I don't know,' McKittrick said. 'That's the truth. Can you document your whereabouts this weekend?'

He pursed his lips. 'I was camping. In Joshua Tree. From Friday until five o'clock today. Alone.'

She exhaled slowly. 'Okay. Call Ms Letterman. Have her pick you up. I'll wait downstairs in the lobby and escort the two of you into the station.'

'Meaning you don't trust me not to run,' he said bitterly.

Once again she said nothing, but she didn't need to speak.

'Fucking hell,' he whispered.

'Yeah,' she whispered back. 'I'll wait downstairs. Please don't make me chase you. I'm supposed to bring you in – in cuffs if I have to – but I don't want to have to do that.'

Sam remained on the floor as she let herself out. He wasn't sure how many minutes passed, but he finally fished his phone from his pocket to call Laura.

He hesitated, though, calling Joel first. The phone rang and rang, but Joel finally answered. 'Hey, man. What's up?'

'McKittrick was here.'

'Oh? Why?'

'To tell me that my neighbor was murdered this weekend in a way that is consistent with the other murders. And I was camping all weekend, Joel.' His voice hitched, tinged with a note of hysteria. Which was fair, because his heart was beating like a jackhammer. 'I have no alibi this time. Why is this happening?'

'For fuck's sake,' Joel growled. 'Surely they don't think . . . Hell, who knows what they're thinking? Do you have proof that you were camping?'

'I posted a photo to Facebook, just like I always do when I go camping. For my folks, so they know I'm okay.' He'd considered not posting the photo, but the detectives had told him that he was no longer a suspect. He wanted to get on with his life, and resuming his normal habits seemed a good way to do that. *I guess I was wrong.*

Joel's brief silence screamed that a Facebook photo wasn't going to be enough. 'Are you still at your place?'

'Yes. She's waiting in the lobby for me to come down. I said I wasn't coming down without my lawyer.'

'Good. I'm coming over. You want me to call you a lawyer? Or do you want to call Laura again?'

Sam bit the inside of his cheek. 'Laura knows the background. And she's good. I trust her. In this, anyway.'

'She is good,' Joel admitted. 'I hate going up against her in court. Call her. And do not leave your apartment until I get there. What about Siggy?'

'I don't know.' His breath hitched again. 'My folks are back in Scottsdale.' And he didn't have anyone else to call.

'Call Vivian. She knows Siggy. She'll come.'

'She's in a leg cast, but her husband might be able to take him. Why would SDPD think I did this?'

'I don't know, but I'll try to find out.'

'McKittrick and Constantine think that Colton didn't kill himself.'

Joel was quiet for a moment. 'They told you that?'

So he knew, too. It made sense that he would. 'No. I figured it out myself. Why didn't you tell me?'

'You were relaxing with your parents.'

Sam snorted derisively. 'No, I was worried sick the whole time. That's why I went back with my folks.'

'I thought it was to avoid the media.'

'That was McKittrick's idea, to keep my parents from worrying.'

Joel sighed. 'Sounds like her. How did she seem?'

Sam frowned. 'What do you mean?'

'Constantine is in the hospital. He had a heart attack. He'll be okay, but he's out of commission for a while.'

That was why she was alone. Sam hadn't even wondered, too filled with fear. *Justified fear*, he reminded himself. 'She seemed sad,' he said. 'And worried. About me, I think.'

'Well, *that's* not at all upsetting.'

'Are you coming over or not?' Sam snapped.

'Already in my car. Figured you might need to keep talking so you don't freak out.'

Joel knew him well.

'I need to call Laura.'

'Fine. If she doesn't answer right away, I'll get you someone else.'

'Thanks, Joel.'

'We'll figure this out, Sammy.'

Sam ended the call, hoping that Joel was right.

SDPD, San Diego, California
Sunday, 17 April, 9.15 P.M.

Kit was unsurprised to see Joel Haley leaning against the wall outside the interview room in which Sam Reeves waited with his attorney.

'Joel.'

He nodded once. 'I tried to call you but got your voice mail.'

She'd known why he was calling and had purposely let it go to voice mail. 'I've been a little busy.'

He lifted an auburn eyebrow. 'Please. If you don't want to talk to me, just say so.'

She dropped her chin for a moment, trusting him enough to let him see her looking less than strong. Not weak, but not terribly strong right now.

'I heard about Constantine,' he murmured. 'He'll be okay, right?'

She glanced up, found his expression a mix of compassion and anxiety. Which made sense, considering his friend was in interview again. 'Yeah, Baz'll be okay. It was a little scary for a while, though.'

The image of her partner's knees buckling as he collapsed to the ground had been on constant replay in her mind.

'I bet it was.' Joel was quiet for a few beats. 'He's innocent, you know. Sam. He's a good guy. He'd never hurt anyone.'

She drew in a breath, let it out. Decided to be straightforward with the prosecutor, because Joel was a good guy, too. 'I know. At least I believe.' She shrugged. 'I want to believe. But I have to follow the evidence.'

'What evidence do you have?'

She pursed her lips, debating. But Joel would find out one way or another. 'Skyler's parents got a text from her late Friday night. Said she was meeting Dr Reeves for a drink after work.'

Joel winced. 'That's . . . not good. But it's a setup, Kit. You have to know that.'

'Like I said, I want to believe. That's the best I can give you right now. I have to be thorough. I owe it to those girls.'

He nodded, his jaw gone tight. 'Can I observe?'

She shrugged. 'If Navarro says it's okay, I don't have a problem with it. He's back there.'

'I'll ask him. Just . . . dammit, Kit. He's my best friend and he's scared to death. He didn't do anything wrong.'

Kit sighed. 'I need to get in there.'

Joel stepped back. 'Tell Constantine that I hope he's back on the job being a pain in my ass soon.'

'I will.' She started to go into the interview room but stopped. 'Hey, Joel? What's the deal with you two and the defense attorney?'

Joel barked out a harsh laugh. 'She cheated on Sam. With me. That's how we met.'

Kit's mouth fell open. 'What the fuck?'

'Right? I was pissed off because I didn't know about Sam and he clearly didn't know about me. His first look at me was my bare ass. But . . . he's a good guy, Kit. He didn't hold anything against me. He supported me, even though he was devastated. They'd been together for four years. I was only a repeat hookup, but all he could think of was how it had impacted me.'

'He called her when he needed an attorney.'

'He did. He has a great capacity for forgiveness.'

Kit hoped that was true, because she had the feeling that she'd be asking him to forgive her for what was to come. 'Thanks for telling me.'

He nodded once and, gathering her wits about her, she walked into the interview room. Sam Reeves sat at the table in the same chair he'd used the last time they'd brought him in.

Laura Letterman was glaring daggers at Kit. 'Can we get this started? You're causing my client undue distress.'

Kit could see that. Sam had looked almost relaxed when he'd first opened his door that evening. Wary, but not defeated. Now he looked devastated.

His eyes were red and puffy. He'd been crying.

About Skyler? Or about his own predicament? Or was it a clever ruse?

She sat across from Sam, ignoring his attorney's continued glare. 'So . . . can you prove your whereabouts this weekend or not?'

She'd meant the question to come out harsh and snappish, but her voice did not obey her wishes. She sounded soft and concerned.

Navarro was going to lose his shit if she didn't get hers together.

Laura Letterman leaned forward, her gaze as sharp as Kit had intended her words to be. 'My client was camping all weekend. Alone. Given enough time, he can find witnesses to corroborate. He spoke with a park ranger several times over the weekend.'

'I'll need the ranger's name,' Kit said, then turned her attention to Sam. 'If you camped in the park, you'll be on the park's registration list. Right?'

He winced. 'I didn't camp in the park. The campgrounds were filled, but I never use them anyway. I have a friend with property bordering the park. He Airbnbs his house but lets his friends camp on the land, away from the house.'

Kit wanted to sigh, because that was more bad news for him. 'You posted a photo to Facebook on Friday night.' It was a selfie with his dog, his tent in the background. He'd looked at peace in the photo.

He nodded, his eyes haunted. 'Yeah. I did.'

'Was that in the park or on your friend's land?'

'My friend's land. I left the park at five on Friday afternoon. There was a ranger at the gate, so there should be a record of that.'

That was even worse. It meant he'd had opportunity. Still, she found herself trying to help him. 'Do you protect your Facebook settings?' she asked.

He blinked, looking confused. 'What?'

'Do you control who sees your posts?'

Sam shook his head slowly. 'No. I mainly post the photos so my parents can see them. I also chat online with a few other hikers who do the desert parks.'

'So anyone could have known that he was there alone,' Laura said, swooping in on the detail.

'Yes. It's possible. It's also possible that he drove to San Diego after taking that photo and met up with Skyler Carville for drinks after her shift at the bar.' Kit kept her focus on Sam even though she spoke to his attorney.

He frowned. 'Why would I do that?'

'Sam,' Letterman cautioned. 'But that's an excellent question, Detective. Please answer it.'

Kit tilted her head, still watching him. 'Because Skyler texted her parents to say she'd be late getting home. Because Dr Reeves had texted her, asking her to meet for a drink.'

Sam's mouth fell open. 'I didn't.'

'Sam,' Letterman snapped. 'Say nothing.'

He looked at Letterman. 'But I didn't. They can check my phone.'

'We've already initiated a warrant for your cell phone records, Dr Reeves,' Kit said calmly, but she wanted to sigh with relief. He was telling the truth. She was sure of it. *But you'd already made up your mind, hadn't you?* She ignored the little voice in her head and added, 'But it would go a lot faster if you'd grant us access.'

'No,' Letterman barked. 'Absolutely not.'

Sam looked frustrated. 'Laura.'

Letterman leveled him with narrowed eyes. 'Let me do my job, Sam.'

Kit didn't blame the attorney. She was doing her job as well as Sam was allowing her.

Letterman turned on Kit. 'Her killer could have sent that text to her parents, spoofing my client's number. Or sent the text to Skyler. Or both. My client's being set up.'

'Possibly,' Kit agreed. Probably, even. 'We can eliminate Dr Reeves as a suspect if he can prove he was where he says he was.' She held up a hand when the attorney started to say no once again. 'Do you have location services on your phone turned on, Dr Reeves?'

'I don't know.' But there was a glint of hope in his eyes.

If Kit could get him to just let them check, they could settle this quickly and the man could go on with his life.

And I can start looking for the real killer.

Sam's face was the picture of indecision. Maybe one more little push.

'It seems convenient that this happened the weekend you were alone with no alibi, Dr Reeves,' Kit said softly. 'We can make this go away with a quick check.'

'It's not a quick check,' Letterman said with an angry glare at Kit. 'They'll need access to your phone. It's not just letting the detective see your location. Her CSU team will have to check your whole phone.'

Sam's shoulders slumped. 'I can't let you do that. I have a portal that accesses patient records on my phone.'

'We can have a court-appointed special master,' Kit said. 'Someone who isn't SDPD and who will keep your client files confidential.'

Sam looked at Letterman. 'Is that true?'

'It is,' she conceded. 'Although it will take some time.'

'I can call in some favors and speed it up,' Kit said. 'Look, if this is a setup and Dr Reeves is being framed in some way, I need to know immediately because that means there's still a killer out there.'

Sam looked at Kit then, his gaze assessing. Whatever he saw must have satisfied him, because he nodded. 'Do it. But this doesn't make everything "go away". Skyler is still dead. And that is because someone wants to make me look like a killer. She was a good person. She had big dreams.' He swallowed hard. 'Now she's gone and I have to look her parents in the eye, knowing that she was targeted because of me, even if I didn't do anything wrong. And even if you clear me – *when* you clear me – they might always have doubts about me. And that's . . . well, that's . . .'

Kit could feel his anguish. He was right. 'Homicides are always terrible situations. The actions of a killer cause ripples that affect the lives of the people left behind. I can't change that. But I can check your alibi. Also give me the name of that park ranger. I'll contact him – or her?'

'Him,' Sam said. 'His name is Herman Rymer. I don't have his contact info, though.'

'I'll find him,' Kit promised. 'Probably not until tomorrow, though.'

Sam stiffened. 'I don't have to stay here all night, do I?'

'No,' Kit and Letterman said at the same time. 'We will need to keep your phone, though,' Kit added. 'It's evidence now. But it's locked and will remain so until we get the special master assigned.'

Sam pressed his fingertips to his temples. 'But even if you establish that my phone was at Joshua Tree, it doesn't mean that I was.'

Kit hid her wince, but just barely. He was right, but she'd hoped to allay his anxiety for a little while at least.

Letterman shook her head in consternation. 'Sam.'

'It's true, though,' he said to her. 'Isn't it?'

Letterman nodded reluctantly. 'But it's better than nothing.'

'That's why I'll also find the ranger,' Kit added.

'But it won't completely clear me,' he said bitterly, closing his eyes. 'You might be able to convince a jury, but people will always wonder.'

'Dr Reeves, I want to put the right killer away so that he can never hurt anyone else. Clearing your name, if that's where the evidence leads, will be a happy by-product. But my duty is to the victims. I won't rest until they get justice.'

'I know.' But he still sounded defeated and Kit couldn't fix that.

'Is my client free to go?' Letterman asked sharply.

Kit nodded. 'Yes. Where will you go, Dr Reeves?'

He didn't open his eyes. 'Not home. If the Carvilles think that I met Skyler for drinks after her shift, they'll . . .' He opened his eyes and they were filled with such sadness that Kit's heart hurt. 'Well, I don't know what they'll do, but I don't want to find out. I might go to a hotel.'

'You aren't owed his location,' Letterman said to Kit. 'I'm taking my client to wherever he wishes to go. Now.'

Kit forced her expression to blank because the slump of Sam's shoulders was painful to witness. 'I'll contact you, Ms Letterman, when the court has assigned a special master to review your client's phone.'

Kit left without another word to Sam, finding Navarro standing in the observation room alone. Apparently, he'd said no to Joel Haley.

She waited for him to tell her that she'd been too soft on Sam Reeves, but he surprised her.

'He's either very, very good or he's not guilty,' Navarro said, watching Sam with his attorney through the glass. Letterman had her arm around his shoulders and was speaking close to his ear. It was an intimate pose, one that made sense after hearing that they'd been together for four years.

Sam Reeves did indeed have a great capacity for forgiveness.

'I agree,' she murmured.

Navarro turned to meet her eyes, his gaze piercing. 'Find out which he is. Find out who killed Skyler Carville.'

'I will.'

'Work alone for now, but I'll assign you a temporary partner as soon as I can. Until Baz comes back.'

Kit nodded, too tired to argue. She didn't want another partner, even a temporary one. Baz would be coming back and that was all there was to it. 'Yes, sir.'

Hillcrest, California
Monday, 18 April, 7.30 A.M.

Sam locked his jaw and stared Joel down across Joel's kitchen table. His best friend's expression was one of shock mixed with disapproval.

'You're going to do *what*?' Joel asked, squinting over his coffee mug.

Joel had insisted Sam stay with him after they'd picked up Siggy from Vivian's house the night before. Joel's home was a large Victorian on a busy residential street. He had plenty of room, and Sam had been too exhausted to argue. So here he was.

He was still exhausted, having not slept a wink, but he'd been turning this idea around in his mind all night long, and he was sure.

'I'm going to do my own investigation. I've got the time,' he added bitterly.

Because he and Vivian had – albeit reluctantly – agreed that he should take a leave of absence until SDPD cleared his name. Vivian had made sure he knew that it wasn't about her trust in him. It was about the clinic's liability and providing the best and least disruptive care for their clients.

So. Time. He had it, in abundance.

'That's a bad idea, Sam.'

'I disagree. It's my life. My livelihood. My freedom. And if I sit around with nothing to do, I'm going to go crazy.'

Joel sighed. 'How do you plan to do the investigating?'

Sam had thought this through as well, making notes during the night as new ideas occurred to him. 'I figure that Colton either participated in the murders with his partner, who killed him, or Colton was the partner or even the hanger-on. The last one would be more consistent with what I saw in session. Colton was always inserting himself into the lives of other people, so him being the groupie of a murderer makes sense.'

'Okay. I'm with you so far. But what are you going to do specifically?'

'I'm going to look into Colton's background to figure out where the two crossed paths and joined up. I'm going to start with his ex-wives.'

'The police already interviewed his wives.'

'I'm not the police. And not to toot my own horn, but people talk to me.'

'True. But if they say no, you have to walk away.'

Sam rolled his eyes. 'I know that. I'm not going to get myself arrested.'

'Again.'

'Again,' Sam conceded. 'I also want to know how many victims this guy has killed. The police only said "several". Do you know?'

Joel hesitated. 'Yeah.' Then he shrugged. 'Fuck it. This is your life we're talking about. So far there are six, including Skyler Carville. Maybe seven if the girl with the lilac uniform was a victim and not just missing.'

'She was,' Sam said quietly.

Joel nodded. 'I think so, too. So does McKittrick. The girl's name was—'

'Cecilia Sheppard,' Sam interrupted. 'It was a quick google, once I knew what to look for. A missing teenage girl from Tomlinson High School eight months ago. What about the others?'

'They've only ID'd two of the other four. Miranda Crisp and Ricki Emerson.'

Sam noted the names on his phone. The disposable phone Joel had picked up for him last night, since his had been taken by SDPD as evidence. 'Are they sure that these are the only victims?'

'No. Considering all the victims except for Jaelyn Watts were found by accident, most people believe there are more still buried.'

'In unmarked graves,' Sam murmured, remembering Jaelyn's small grave. 'How were they found by accident?'

'Dudes with metal detectors mostly.'

Sam frowned. 'Like the kid who found Skyler's body?'

'Exactly.'

'That seems convenient.'

Joel nodded. 'Extremely convenient, and McKittrick already agrees. That's why she thinks you were set up. But she has to be able to prove it.'

'And that's not possible right now. Not unless she finds who actually did it. How far back do the murders go?'

Joel stared into his mug, then sighed. 'Nearly twenty years.'

Sam's mouth fell open. 'Twenty years?'

'The first victim was found fifteen years ago, but she'd been in the ground for a few years.'

'Oh my God.'

They sat in silence for a few minutes while Sam processed this information. *Twenty years?* No wonder Constantine had been so emotional that night in Sam's SUV. He'd been chasing the killer for twenty years.

And wasn't that depressing? The cops hadn't been able to catch this guy in *twenty years*? And Sam was hoping that they'd clear him soon?

He respected McKittrick, but he wasn't going to sit around for another twenty years while young women died and his own life was ruined. 'Are the missing-person reports public information?'

'Not as a blanket download. You'd have to request specific reports. Why?'

'Because there have to be other victims, and finding out who they are may tell us where they crossed paths with this bastard. The victims so far have been petite blondes who liked theater.' The theater detail had been included in Tamsin Kavanaugh's article about Jaelyn Watts's murder. 'There are other resources for missing kids if I can't get the missing-person reports. The National Center for Missing and Exploited Children or the California clearinghouse for runaways. Someone at New Horizons might even be able to help me.' He'd been volunteering at the teen shelter for four years. One of the shelter's full-time staff would assist him.

Joel hesitated. 'I can make a request for the reports, but they'll probably say no since you're my friend.'

'I don't want you to even try. I won't put you or your job in danger, Joel.'

'I know.' Joel clapped a hand on Sam's shoulder. 'I have to run. I have court this morning. Text me if anything new comes up.'

'I will.' Sam locked the door behind Joel and went back to the kitchen to wash the breakfast dishes. At least he could be a good guest.

Then he opened his laptop and started searching for petite blondes who'd gone missing in the last twenty years.

There were so many. So many shattered lives. The victims and their families.

'So get to work,' Sam told himself and poured himself another cup of coffee.

Ten

SDPD, San Diego, California
Monday, 18 April, 8.45 A.M.

'Talk to me,' Kit muttered as she stared at the murder board she'd set up in the bullpen, at the photos of the known victims of their killer – and at the dozen new photos she'd posted during the night. They were possible victims – missing young women who fit the profile.

But the photos remained silent, of course. She normally didn't talk to photos, but she was growing more desperate than she cared to admit.

'Kit?'

She looked over her shoulder to see Navarro standing behind her, looking concerned. 'Yeah, boss?'

'I've been standing here for over a minute. You never knew I was here.'

Maybe it was because she was so absorbed in the faces of the victims. Maybe it was because she felt safe here in the station and didn't have her guard up.

Or maybe it was because she was mentally exhausted.

The last one wouldn't matter, even if it were true. She had a job to do, and so far she'd failed in a spectacular fashion.

Skyler Carville was dead because they hadn't suspected the right man. Or because they had and he'd fooled them into thinking he was just a nice guy with a cute dog.

She'd gone back and forth during the night, watching the recordings of the two interviews she'd done with Sam Reeves. She still didn't think he was guilty.

And she still didn't trust her judgment because of it.

'Sorry,' she said quietly. 'I've been busy.'

He pulled up a chair and pointed to it. 'Sit down before you fall down. For God's sake, McKittrick, you'd better not collapse on me, too.'

She rolled her eyes but sat in the chair. 'I'm not a fifty-something-year-old man who's been ignoring his doctor about eating better and reducing his stress,' she muttered.

That little factoid had been blurted out by Baz's wife, Marian, after he'd been declared 'out of the woods' by the cardiologist. Luckily it had only been Kit and Navarro standing in Baz's room at the time. They'd keep it confidential, but Baz had been very upset that they'd heard to begin with.

'Still.' Navarro dropped into a chair next to her. 'Who are all of these girls?' He pointed to the dozen new photos grouped to one side of the board.

'I went through the missing-person reports again last night and pulled out every petite blonde between fourteen and eighteen who attended high school in San Diego County and who's gone missing and/or been declared a runaway in the past ten years.'

Navarro frowned at the dozen photos. 'That's all of them?'

'Oh, no. There are a lot more, but I narrowed it down to these twelve. They all either had ties to the drama department at their school or had expressed a wish to become an actress. I kept the ones I set aside in another file because they might also be drama students, but that wasn't included in the report. I'll go through them in depth later, and then tackle the reports from eleven to twenty years ago.'

'I'm getting you some help with that. I should be able to make the announcement by lunchtime. I do have good news for you right now, though.'

'*Please*. I need some good news today.'

He smiled. 'I reopened the Maria Mendoza case last week after seeing the photos that Dr Batra had intended to upload.'

Kit had nearly forgotten about Rita's mother's murder. 'And?'

'And the mark against the victim's cheek was the impression of a signet ring. And two years later, the suspect's wife is ready to cooperate. Seems she's tired of his cheating. She allowed us to search their home and guess what we found?'

Excitement had her leaning forward. 'The ring?'

'Yep. Found it in his sock drawer. It was apparently an heirloom, so he didn't want to get rid of it. He'd cleaned it, but there were traces of Maria Mendoza's skin in the crevices. DNA came back yesterday and it's hers. We're going to arrest him today. That will allow us to take a DNA swab from him to compare to the child the victim was carrying.'

Kit drew a deep breath, her eyes suddenly burning. 'Thank you. Hopefully this will allow my little foster sister to have some hope in the system. She's too young to be so jaded.'

His smile was gentle. 'Thank you for following it up. He might get a good lawyer, but the evidence is pretty damning.'

'Can I tell Rita?'

'Once we've arrested him, yes. I don't know if the girl knows that her mother was pregnant, so tread softly there.'

'Yes, sir. I'll go by Mom and Pop's tonight after work.'

'Good.' Navarro pointed to her board. 'Now, tell me what you're going to do with these dozen possible victims.'

'I need to figure out how he's targeting these girls. The more recent ones have the drama connection, but that doesn't tell us where they crossed paths with him. Or Driscoll. Or both. I've talked to everyone associated with Driscoll and none of them had anything useful other than "He was a creep. I'm glad he's dead." I couldn't find a single person with anything nice to say about him, but all the negative stuff was a big zero in terms of leads. So I went back to the victims.' She turned back to the board. 'I need to develop a better profile of this killer. I've made an appointment with Dr Levinson for one o'clock this afternoon. He's been helpful in the past and he developed the original profile on this case.'

The criminal psychologist was very good at developing personality profiles and suggesting defining characteristics that had been instrumental in catching other killers.

'He's good,' Navarro agreed. 'Is he coming here?'

'He is. I've got a meeting room reserved for one o'clock.'

'Then we can meet with him together. Since I investigated the earlier victims, I might end up remembering something useful. What else?'

She sighed. 'I still think the Epstein kid knows something she's afraid to tell.'

'Should we bring her in?'

'No. I think that would make things worse. I've popped back a few times in the last week. I plan to try again this afternoon when she gets home from school. Although her parents are starting to get aggravated with me. I'm also going to visit the families of these dozen girls. I want to know everything about them.'

'Watch out for that Tamsin Kavanaugh,' Navarro warned. 'I don't want her focusing on any more families of the victims.'

'I've been watching my rearview mirror for the past week. Caught her following once, but Baz lost her.' Her throat tightened at the thought of her partner lying in a hospital bed. He'd looked so gray. Old. And tired. 'He's good at losing pursuers.'

'He'll come back,' Navarro said and it sounded like a vow. 'I'm not ready to see him retire just yet. He's younger than I am.'

She had to push the thought of Baz's retirement from her mind because she wasn't ready for that, either. 'I hope so. This case has me feeling a little . . . desperate.'

'How so?'

'I think he killed Skyler Carville to make Dr Reeves look guilty. So if we don't arrest Dr Reeves, how many more girls will the killer murder to continue making him look guilty?'

'A valid question. What about the boy who found the body with his metal detector? Are we buying that?'

'It's damn good timing,' she said, looking at the photo of Skyler Carville. 'Kid's name is Daryl Chesney. He claimed he got the metal detector for his birthday.'

'Kind of an odd present for a teenager. How old is he?'

'Fifteen. I asked him how he picked that site to search with his metal detector. He said it looked "dug up". He thought maybe someone had buried something useful.'

'Like?'

'"Stuff".' She used air quotes. 'Baz was like, "What stuff, kid?" He became uncooperative when we pressed that question. I thought he might have been looking for drugs or guns, but he denied that with gusto.'

'Was the area dug up?'

'It was. I mean, Skyler had been buried there less than forty-eight hours before. The question I have is why her killer picked that spot. Was it already dug up? I've got a call in to the park's groundskeeper to ask if they'd been doing any digging there before. This killer – or killers – is picking parks and he's never been caught burying any of his victims.'

'He knows it's safe to dig wherever he's digging, then,' Navarro said, sitting up straighter. 'That could be key.'

'I know. I made a few calls to park people after we found Jaelyn two weeks ago, but it was the weekend and no one was in. Then Driscoll happened and I haven't followed up. I will, though. But back to the kid. He didn't act guilty. He was . . .' She closed her eyes, trying to remember everything that had transpired when she and Baz had first arrived at the crime scene. Before Baz collapsed. 'Preening. Like he'd done something important. I mean, he's fifteen, so finding a buried hand is a big deal. Watching CSU erect a tent around the scene had him practically buzzing. I had one of the uniforms take him home so he wouldn't be underfoot. He was filming with his phone.'

Navarro grimaced. 'Wonderful.'

'So I didn't talk to him again after that because Baz . . .' She gave herself a shake. 'I'll follow up with the kid today.'

'You've got a full day planned. Make a list of all the things that need to be followed up on. You and your support can divvy it up.'

She saluted. 'Yes, sir.'

'And no more sleeping at your desk, McKittrick.'

She winced because she'd taken pains to make it look like she hadn't spent all night at her desk, even changing into the spare clothes she kept in her locker. 'Who narced on me?'

'Housekeeping. None of us got our trash cans emptied because they didn't want to wake you up. Said you were sleeping like an angel.'

'I'm no angel,' she muttered.

His chuckle held a note of unmistakable affection. 'Ain't *that* the truth? Work today and then go home. Get some real sleep.'

She sighed. 'Fine.'

He gave her a look that was both stern and kind. 'I'm worried about you. You've been working on this case nonstop and before that, you worked the last case nonstop and the one before that. Baz's heart attack was a wake-up call for all of us. If you don't take some downtime on your own – at least to sleep – I'll have to force you to take some leave. Or order you to see Dr Scott more than once a week.'

Kit's eyes widened in genuine horror. 'You wouldn't.'

Dr Levinson helped them catch criminals and was completely approachable. Dr Scott asked them about their feelings and Kit hated sessions with him.

'Yes, I would. And Scott's not *that* bad.'

She shuddered. 'He really is. He *looks* at you with those *eyes* of his.' Dark, piercing eyes that saw far too much.

Navarro's lips twitched. 'Most people have eyes, Kit.'

'But he sees things,' she murmured. Dr Scott was far too good at ferreting out what she most wanted to keep hidden.

Navarro's expression softened. 'Kit. This job will wring you dry if you let it. Allowing someone to *see things* can help you stay sane.'

Something in his tone caught her attention. 'Do you talk to him?' she asked, then immediately winced. 'I'm sorry, sir. That was personal.'

'It's all right. I brought it up. Yes. I do talk to him from time to time when things get overwhelming. He's helped me keep my sanity more than once over the years. Helped me maintain my sobriety, too.'

She was stunned. She hadn't known that Navarro had chemical dependency issues. That did put Scott in a far different light. 'You trust him?'

Navarro nodded. 'I do. We're lucky to have him on call.'

Kit sighed, having heard this before. 'I know. He could be making a lot more money doing LawTV.' Scott had gotten network attention as an expert witness in a murder several years before and had gone on to have a modest side career appearing as an expert on LawTV specials. He had a good face for television.

'He could,' Navarro agreed. 'But cops are his calling. See him. Let him see you. Or I will order you to.'

'But not if I sleep.'

'Not making any promises. Try the sleeping thing first. You're fraying at the edges and I don't want it to become worse. You're too good a detective for me to lose, and I'll do what I have to so that doesn't happen.' He stood, taking a final look at the new photos. 'I'll see you at one with Dr Levinson.'

SDPD, San Diego, California
Monday, 18 April, 1.00 P.M.

'Detective McKittrick. What a pleasure to see you again.'

Kit sat across from the criminal psychologist at the meeting room table. 'Thank you for seeing us, sir.'

Dr Alvin Levinson looked like a stereotypical professor. In his late sixties, he sported a neatly trimmed goatee that, along with his hair, was mostly salt with very little pepper remaining. He wore a tweed jacket with elbow patches, a bow tie, and round spectacles over eyes that always seemed to be happy. Unless he was talking about killers. Then he was very serious.

He turned to Navarro. 'Reynaldo. It's been a while.'

'Too long,' Navarro agreed.

'And Detective Constantine?' Levinson asked.

'Cranky,' Kit said. 'I visited him at the hospital over lunch and he's already trying to strong-arm the doctors into letting him go home.'

'That's good to hear. Give him my best, will you?' Levinson tilted his head, his expression sobering. 'So. We're back to the pink handcuffs. Again.'

Navarro sighed. 'Again.'

Kit had read the profiles of the killer who had eluded law enforcement for at least fifteen years. The details were sparse. Hopefully, they could fix that.

'I thought that we might be able to take a fresh look at the profile,' Kit said. 'Since I'm new on the case.'

'Fresh look from fresh eyes,' Levinson agreed. 'It's your meeting, Detective.'

For a moment it hit her, how huge this was. A department full of seasoned detectives had worked on this case for fifteen years, and they were no closer to apprehending the killer. What could she add?

You know about Colton. And you know the identities of more of the victims than before.

Straightening her shoulders, Kit opened the folder she'd brought with her. 'We don't have any real leads as to the killer's identity,' she said baldly. 'Except that he either worked with or at least knew Colton Driscoll on some level. So I compiled a list of what we've learned from his victims.'

'How many do we have now?' Levinson asked.

'Six, maybe seven,' Navarro answered.

'Actually,' Kit said, 'six, maybe eight. I combed through the runaway reports and came up with a dozen possibilities, but one stuck out.' She produced a photo from the folder and turned it so that the men could see. 'Her name is – was – Naomi Beckham. When I was interviewing Dr Reeves, he said—'

Levinson held up a hand. 'Wait. Dr Reeves?'

'Sorry. I got ahead of myself.' She explained about Sam Reeves, from his initial phone calls to their interview the day they'd discovered Skyler Carville's body.

He nodded periodically as she spoke, then scratched at his goatee absently. 'I know Sam Reeves. He's dedicated to the community, especially its most underserved.'

Kit remembered Baz thinking that Reeves was covering up bad behavior with good works. 'He volunteers with the elderly and with homeless teens.'

'Yes. We serve together on the board of New Horizons and we both do pro bono therapy for the teens there.'

'I know the place,' Kit murmured. She'd visited the teen homeless shelter several times over the years working cases, and every time she was yanked back to her own childhood. Had it not been for Harlan and Betsy McKittrick . . . *I might have ended up there, too.* 'How long has Dr Reeves volunteered at New Horizons?'

'Four years.'

So when he'd first come to the city. That spoke well of him. Unless Baz was right, but the more she learned about Sam Reeves, the more certain she was that she was right about him.

'Do you think he's capable of being involved in this case in a way other than what he's claimed?' Navarro asked.

Levinson blinked owlishly behind his glasses. 'Are you asking if he's capable of lying? Not about this. But again, I only know what I've seen. His actions speak of a principled individual. He's . . . gentle. I don't think he's capable of hurting anyone, much less killing them.'

Relief washed over Kit, her shoulders relaxing. She hadn't realized she'd stiffened, but she'd been holding her breath, hoping she'd been right about Sam.

'What about his boss?' Navarro asked. 'Vivian Carlisle? We cleared him based on her corroboration of his story.'

'I know Vivian *very* well. We went to college together at UCLA and we both came back to the city to practice when we got licensed. We're friends.' He lifted his brows. 'I'm her daughter's godfather. If Viv says Sam is telling the truth, you can take that to the bank.'

'That's something of a relief,' Navarro said. 'Thank you.'

'Glad I could put your minds at ease. Sounds like poor Sam was caught between a rock and a hard place that we psychologists hope to never encounter. Vivian should have come to me. I would have made sure the information was passed to you all in a way that didn't endanger anyone's career.'

'The trouble is,' Kit said, 'we can't prove that Reeves didn't kill his dog walker. We can potentially show that his phone was in Joshua Tree all weekend, but he had opportunity.'

'I see that,' Levinson said grimly. 'So . . . you were saying something about another victim.'

Kit nodded. 'Right. When I was interviewing Dr Reeves and mentioned the victim he believed was Driscoll's newest target, he asked, "Did she like *Avondale*?" It's a TV show. Driscoll told Reeves that he and the young woman watched the show together. One of the runaways – Naomi Beckham – was last seen while wearing an *Avondale* T-shirt, according to her parents. I haven't spoken to them yet, but they still live in the city. She disappeared three years ago, in February. She's one of two victims to disappear in February, by the way. Jaelyn Watts is the other, of course. The other two we've ID'd disappeared in October – Ricki Emerson and Miranda Crisp. We have a potential third victim – Cecilia Sheppard – who disappeared in September.'

Navarro smiled with satisfaction. 'Another pattern. Nice job, Detective.'

'Thank you, sir. That might go hand in hand with the park connection. Some of the planting happens then.'

'Then we need to follow up on the parks ASAP,' Navarro said.

'I will. Skyler Carville was killed in April, so not part of the pattern. I assume her murder was intended to frame Dr Reeves.'

'Fair,' Levinson said.

'We have Cecilia Sheppard, who disappeared eight months ago; Jaelyn Watts, who disappeared fourteen months ago; Naomi Beckham three years ago; Miranda Crisp seven years ago; and Ricki Emerson ten years ago. We don't have solid dates of disappearance for the two unidentified victims, but their time of death was estimated at seventeen to twenty years and fifteen years respectively. There are either a lot of victims we haven't discovered yet, or he's speeding up his frequency in recent years.'

'Lovely,' Levinson murmured. 'What else?'

'Well,' Kit continued, 'we know Driscoll knew about at least three of the victims, as he mentioned them indirectly to Dr Reeves with references to Cecilia's lacrosse, Jaelyn's grave, and Naomi's love of *Avondale*. Driscoll might not have killed them himself, but Dr Reeves mentioned that he was making strangling motions with his hands while talking about one of the victims in their session.'

'So we don't know in what way Driscoll was involved,' Levinson said.

Kit nodded. 'Right. Driscoll's killer either duplicated Driscoll's MO or he had a hand in killing some or all the others, because Skyler Carville's murder followed the same MO. If this is true, it means that Driscoll and his killer crossed paths at least three years ago because that was when Naomi disappeared. Maybe even before that.'

'Who do you think killed the women, Detective?' Levinson asked. 'Driscoll or his partner?'

Kit had been thinking of very little but this question. 'I think his partner did the murders. According to Dr Reeves, Colton Driscoll was a pathological liar with an anger management issue. I've spoken with the man who Driscoll assaulted. Driscoll lost control and beat the man nearly senseless. It took two other neighbors to pull Driscoll off Mr Epstein. Driscoll nearly hit Dr Reeves in session as well. He held himself back because he knew that Reeves could have his probation revoked. The victims showed no sign of any kind of pummeling. They were raped and strangled. Every single one. I don't think that Driscoll could have kept from hitting them if they fought back at all. He had the cuffs and spray paint in his house, but those could have been planted. Or he was the assistant. I don't think he's the main perp.'

'I agree,' Levinson said. 'So let's assume that the murders were all done by the partner. He's been active for at least seventeen years, maybe twenty. I think it's still correct to assume he's male.'

'Because he sexually assaulted them,' Kit said. 'But it could have been a woman. Using objects.'

Navarro shook his head. 'Possibly, but the strength used to strangle them was more in line with a male.'

'And getting Driscoll into that noose would have required more strength,' Kit said thoughtfully.

'Exactly.' Navarro crossed his arms as he thought. 'We figured he was educated or at least very smart. Probably white. When we found the first victim, we guessed he might have been twenty to thirty years old at the time of her murder.'

'Which put him at twenty-three to thirty-three years old at the time her body was discovered,' Levinson said, 'so he'd be thirty-eight to forty-eight now. Add physically fit to the profile. He's not young anymore, but he could still hoist Driscoll up.'

Kit noted it, then moved on to the next detail of the old profile. 'You figured that the pink handcuffs were a snub to law enforcement. Is that still true?'

'Even more so,' Levinson said. 'It's not an open taunt. He never intended anyone to see his victims. They've all been discovered more or less by accident, except for the body that Dr Reeves reported.'

'And possibly Skyler Carville, Dr Reeves's dog walker,' Kit said. 'I was going to pay the kid a visit at home after school to find out why he was there at Balboa Park.'

'You think someone sent him?' Levinson asked.

She nodded. 'The killer wanted her found. I think he wanted Sam Reeves to be a suspect. Which raises another point. He knew about Reeves. He knew that framing him would distract us.'

Both Levinson and Navarro stilled. 'How did he know about him?' Navarro asked.

Kit shrugged. 'Driscoll might have mentioned Reeves to his partner. Or Driscoll's killer might have found out that we brought Dr Reeves in for questioning. Or both those things. There would be a record of Reeves's arrest for resisting, even though we dropped it.'

'Find out if anyone requested access to those records,' Navarro instructed.

Kit wrote it down on her growing to-do list. 'Yes, sir. But going back to Skyler Carville, it was important that she be killed – and found – this past weekend because Reeves was camping alone with no alibi.'

Levinson nodded. 'Okay. But the other victims were not meant to be found. The pink handcuffs could be his signature flourish. He is into theater, after all. He was setting a scene.'

'And giving a fuck-you to the cops,' Navarro murmured.

'But they *were* found,' Kit said with a frown. 'Again, I'm assuming the man who's been killing for twenty years killed Driscoll and left that "confession" note. He said he'd killed five young women. So he knew we'd found others.'

'He could have been watching the news all this time,' Levinson suggested. 'He knows where he's buried them. When he sees an article about a body being discovered, he would note it. Or maybe he revisits the scenes to check. It seems like someone like him would keep track of his kills. He's arrogant and confident.'

'Hopefully too confident,' Navarro muttered.

'Well, yeah,' Kit said, 'but what I meant to say was that he's known about us finding the first four bodies all this time. He knew we'd seen the handcuffs. Why didn't he stop using them? Then we'd just have a Jane Doe in an unmarked grave. It's the pink cuffs that tie them together. We've always thought that the three victims found with metal detectors were a coincidence, because they were spaced out over so many years. But what if they weren't a coincidence?'

'You think he *wanted* them to be found?' Levinson asked.

'Maybe. At least some of them. We'd have to interview the people who found the first four victims, and at least one of them is dead. But this killer is definitely taunting us. He keeps burying them with their jewelry even though he has to *know* we could track it. Especially the class ring Jaelyn wore on a chain around her neck. We haven't caught him yet, so he's gotten even bolder.'

Levinson polished his glasses, lingering over each lens. 'I think you're right. It is a taunt. But he's not crying for help. He might want us to find a few victims, but he doesn't want to be caught. He just doesn't think we're as smart as he is.'

'Then he's going to be disappointed,' Kit said. 'The other thing that the victims have in common is that none of them mentioned they were seeing a man. He would have been an older man, even when he killed the first victim twentyish years ago. Either he took them by surprise or he convinced them not to mention him to anyone. Not family, not best friends. No one.'

Levinson leaned forward. 'This is new information. We'd only ID'd Ricki Emerson before Jaelyn was discovered. Her family said that she hadn't mentioned a boyfriend, but that was a single point. This is important, Detective.' Then he frowned. 'But you said that Driscoll claimed to spend time with the victims. They watched TV together. That seems to indicate a relationship with Driscoll, not with his partner.'

'He was a liar,' Navarro said. 'He could have made all that up.'

'Or they could have worked together,' Kit added.

Levinson nodded. 'Unfortunately, that's true. None of the victims had any defensive wounds?'

'Nope,' Kit said. 'Nothing to indicate that they'd been forcibly taken. He might have drugged them, though. Nothing was found in any of the victims before because they were found months or years after death. But Skyler was found less than forty-eight hours after she went missing. We could get lucky. Give me a minute.'

Taking out her phone, she texted Alicia Batra. ***Did you get tox screen back on Skyler Carville? Looking for something like Rohypnol.***

She set her phone aside. 'Okay, if he is drugging them, he has to get close enough to do so. The lack of defensive wounds still suggests they knew him and allowed him to get close.'

'Important,' Levinson murmured. 'He's someone they trust. Maybe someone in a position of authority.'

'Maybe someone who's posing as an agent or producer,' Navarro said. 'All of the victims expressed an interest in drama and acting.'

'Baz said the same thing,' Kit said. 'That gives me another line of questioning for the victims' close friends. If they were talking to a producer, one of them had to mention it to someone. These are sixteen-year-old girls we're talking about, give or take a year. They tell their friends their secrets.'

'Did you?' Levinson asked, his brows lifted.

Kit shook her head. 'No, but I didn't have many friends then. The only one I would have trusted was murdered when I was fifteen.'

Levinson winced. 'I'm sorry, Detective.'

'It's fine,' she said automatically, even though it really wasn't. 'Next item. Why *pink* handcuffs? Is it simply because they're girls? Or is it another swipe at the police?'

'He definitely holds us in contempt,' Levinson said. 'Thinks he's smarter than we are. He's able to get his victims to trust him. Could he be in law enforcement?'

Navarro flinched. 'God, I hope not. What other professions garner trust?'

Kit wrote *Is he a cop?* in her notes, hoping that wasn't true. 'Doctors, nurses, teachers.'

'Clergy,' Levinson suggested. 'Or someone posing as one of these.'

Kit noted it. 'I'll check with the schools, too. See if anyone fitting that description was hanging around. I'll focus on the schools attended by Cecilia and Jaelyn since they're the most recent.'

'Have we tracked where Skyler went when she left the bar where she worked?' Navarro asked.

'I reviewed the security footage around her workplace last night,' Kit told him. 'It's in Little Italy and close to the interstate. She left at midnight when they closed, got in her car, and drove toward I-5, but the street cams lost her about a block from the on-ramp. I've asked IT to search the interstate cams, but I haven't heard anything from them yet.'

'What's in that area?' Levinson asked.

'Not her car,' Kit said. 'We searched a four-block radius around the interstate entrance. But that was last night. Her parents said that she texted them at around one a.m. Saturday to say she was meeting Dr Reeves for a drink. So either she thought she was meeting him, or the killer had her *and* her phone by then and sent the text himself. We've requested her cell phone records to see if she received any texts that evening, but we haven't gotten them yet.'

'If she parked somewhere in that area, she would have been towed,' Navarro said, looking at the map on his phone. 'Add checking impound for her car to your to-do list, Kit.'

She did so, then startled when her phone buzzed with an incoming text. *Yes.* 'Batra says the urine screen came back positive for Rohypnol. That's why there are no defensive wounds. He gets close enough to roofie them. Or at least he did with Skyler. The question is – where did he dose her?'

'Add to your list canvassing all the local bars open after midnight with her photo,' Navarro said.

'Done.' Kit had come to the end of her prepared questions. 'To summarize, we've got a forty-something white male who's in good shape. He's smart and cocky and holds law enforcement in contempt. He kills and buries them on a pattern – early fall and late winter. He's trustworthy to his victims – enough to be able to drug them and enough to get them not to tell a soul about him.'

'That's a little more fleshed out than we had before,' Levinson said. 'Good work, Detective.'

'Thanks, Doc. I've got a million things to do, so I'm heading out.'

'Wait,' Navarro said, looking up from his phone. 'I just got confirmation that Cook and Robinson will be free to work with you starting tomorrow morning. They're tying up loose ends on another homicide. They know to report to your desk in the morning, first thing.'

Her brows shot up. 'Howard and Connor? Okay. Sounds good.' Half good, anyway. She liked Howard. Connor was kind of abrasive. 'Will Howard bring more cake?'

Navarro chuckled. 'I'll mention it. Call me when you learn anything new.'

'Will do.'

Eleven

Clairemont, California
Monday, 18 April, 5.30 P.M.

'You're going to get arrested again,' Sam muttered to himself. He'd been sitting in front of the Beckhams' home for thirty minutes, trying to talk himself into going in. He'd gotten himself into trouble the last time he'd tried to play detective, the memory of his stupid crime board still making him flush with embarrassment.

But he thought he'd found another victim and he owed it to Skyler to at least try to find out who'd killed them.

He'd spent hours combing through the missing-person databases available online, then, on a whim, had googled 'missing teenager', 'San Diego', and '*Avondale*'. McKittrick had said that the family of Cecilia Sheppard, the lilac-wearing lacrosse player, had never mentioned the show. He'd begun wondering if Colton had mixed up the details in his mind.

He hadn't gotten a hit right away but had kept digging into the many Facebook shares of missing kids who were suspected to be runaways and had finally found one who had been wearing an *Avondale* T-shirt the day she'd disappeared.

Naomi Beckham had been blond, five foot one, and fifteen at the time of her disappearance three years ago. She'd been declared a runaway because she'd already run once before, following a band she liked.

The post about Naomi's disappearance had several hundred messages from her family and friends. In the beginning, they'd begged her to come home. And then weeks later, they'd begged whoever had taken her to tell them where she was. And, months after that, her parents begged to know where her body had been hidden.

They knew she wasn't coming home. *How their hearts must have been broken.*

He could help find out what had happened to their daughter. He had to.

There were risks, of course. Especially now that he was considered a suspect. But his current reality was very different now. In the past he wouldn't have considered interfering with a police investigation, but everything had changed with Skyler's murder. His life would never be his own again if whoever killed her wasn't found.

So he'd gotten into his RAV4, driving across town to where the Beckhams lived – stopping for gas even though he had three-quarters of a tank. He'd be on the gas station's security camera. In case he needed an alibi.

He also kept the receipt, because those were good for alibis, too, right?

And now here he sat, in front of the Beckhams' modest home. He could have been inside already, talking to them. But this was not so simple.

Should he give his real name? He'd considered an alias. It wasn't illegal, per se, but it was dishonest. Should he simply be honest with them as to why he was asking questions?

If he did, he could ruin his career. Although if he wasn't cleared without equivocation soon, he wouldn't have a career.

And in the end, what mattered more? Stopping a murderer? Or his career?

He knew the right answer, but he was selfish enough to hesitate over the possibility of losing the career he'd worked so hard to build.

But what if he could save his livelihood *and* help this family?

So walk up to the door and knock. Help these parents.

Bracing himself, he got out of his vehicle and walked to the front door. A gangly teenage boy stood there uncertainly, his eyes red-rimmed, like he'd been crying. He looked to be about fifteen. The same age his sister had been when she disappeared, because this boy resembled Naomi too much to be anything but her brother. Nathan, Sam remembered, from the online messages to Naomi. He was three years younger than his sister.

'What do you want?' Nathan asked, voice husky. He wasn't rude, but he didn't open the door wide enough for Sam to see inside. 'Didn't you hurt my mom enough already?'

'Who?' Sam asked gently.

'You cops,' the boy spat. 'You stir up everything but you don't fix anything. You—' He broke off, shaking his head. 'My mom can't talk to you anymore. She's asleep now.'

Cops? 'Did Detective McKittrick come by?'

The boy nodded, his eyes narrowing. 'Yeah. Two hours ago.'

Sam knew that he shouldn't be surprised that McKittrick was also following leads. He'd mentioned Avondale when she'd had him in that interrogation room the morning after she'd arrested him.

This explained the boy's tears. So many memories dredged up.

Any and all thoughts of disguising his name fled right out of his head. 'I'm not a cop. My name is Dr Reeves. I'm a psychologist.'

Nathan recoiled. 'A shrink?'

Sam sighed and shrugged self-deprecatingly. ''Fraid so. Sorry.'

'What do you want?' Nathan demanded.

'A few answers. I've been drawn into this case. Not my idea,' he added when the boy scowled. 'I was being a Good Samaritan, but everything's gone upside down and now I'm involved. I know this doesn't make any sense.'

'No, it really doesn't. Why are you here?'

Sam hesitated, but . . . *In for a penny, in for a pound*. This boy had lost his sister, and his mother was hurting. So he'd be honest. 'Did you hear about the young woman who was killed last night?'

Nathan shook his head. 'I wasn't home from school when the cop came by. I got here in time to pick up the pieces of my mom she left behind,' he added bitterly.

Such pain. Sam's gaze dropped to his feet for a moment before lifting to meet the boy's angry eyes. 'A woman was killed this weekend. The cops think the same person might be responsible for your sister's disappearance. The woman was my friend. She walked my dog. Her killer made it look like I did it.'

Nathan took a step back, nostrils flaring. 'How?'

'A text on her phone to her parents, saying she was meeting me. I was camping and . . .' He shrugged. 'No alibi.'

Nathan scoffed. 'Anyone could have sent a text. They could have spoofed it.'

'I know. And the cops know this, too.'

'Give 'em your phone, man. Have 'em track it.'

'I did. But that just shows my phone was at the campsite. Not me.'

'So you're basically screwed.'

'Basically. So I decided that I didn't have anything to lose by asking questions. I'm not a cop, but . . . Skyler was my friend. I want her killer punished.'

'And you want your life back,' Nathan murmured.

'Yeah. You don't get yours back, though, do you? Not like it was before. I wish I could change that.'

Nathan swallowed hard, new tears filling his eyes. 'I miss her.'

Sam exhaled, his own eyes burning. He understood this boy's pain. 'My friend is gone, too. Not the same as a sister, but still . . .'

'It hurts,' Nathan whispered. 'And makes me so mad.'

'Me too. Look, if your mom can't talk to me, I can come back. I don't want to put either of you in a bad position.'

'She's not really asleep,' Nathan said. 'I only said that to make you go away.' He turned slightly. 'Mom? Can he come in?'

A muted voice said, 'Yes. But tell him I have a gun. In case he gets any ideas.'

Sam's eyes widened. 'I heard her. No ideas. I swear.'

'Then come in,' Nathan said, opening the door wider.

Questioning his life choices, Sam followed the boy into a living room that had been nice once. It was dark now, the drapes drawn. An inch of dust had gathered on all the surfaces and there was a fist-sized hole in one of the walls. Beer cans and wine bottles littered the furniture and, expression embarrassed, Nathan gathered them as they passed.

'I'll be right back,' Nathan said. 'Sit down, please.'

Sam sat in a wingback chair, facing a thin woman sitting in the corner of the sofa. She wore a thick sweater and had an afghan pulled over her legs. A dachshund sat on her lap, its muzzle gray. A half-drunk bottle of wine was on the lamp table beside her. Not a glass in sight. Either she hadn't started drinking yet or she was guzzling straight from the bottle. Sam would bet the latter, because her eyes were glassy.

On the sofa cushion at her hip was the gun.

All right, then.

'So you're not a cop,' the woman said, her voice raspy.

'No, ma'am.'

'A shrink,' she said, her eyes filled with misery.

'Yes, ma'am. I'm sorry to intrude.'

'Yet here you are.'

'Mom,' Nathan said quietly. He had a plastic grocery store bag in one hand and set about gathering more empty wine bottles.

'Leave them, honey,' Mrs Beckham said with such heavy sadness that Sam had to swallow. 'I'll take care of them later.'

Nathan's small sigh and slumped shoulders suggested that it was an old argument and that his mother would likely not follow through. He sat beside her, his cell phone in his hand.

'I'll call 911 if you cross a line,' Nathan warned.

'I won't,' Sam promised. 'I just want to ask you some questions about Naomi. What you remember about when she disappeared.'

Mrs Beckham gestured impatiently. 'Then ask so this will be done.'

'You don't have to answer anything, Mrs Beckham,' Sam said gently. 'I'm not a cop. They'd probably be furious with me if they knew I was here.'

'*Good*. Ask your questions, Dr . . . Reeves, was it?'

'Yes, ma'am.'

'You look familiar,' she said, studying him.

A shard of panic pierced Sam's chest. Had the papers published his name? But he kept his expression placid. 'I don't think we've ever met.'

'No, but I've seen you.' She studied him a moment longer, then nodded. 'At New Horizons. You were there a few times when I went there looking for Naomi.'

Oh. 'I do therapy with the teens.'

'Cushy job,' she commented, as if daring him to deny it.

'No, ma'am. I don't charge them anything.'

'Why?' she asked.

Sam frowned slightly. 'Why don't I charge them?'

'No. Why do you do it? Counsel them?'

'It started when I was an undergrad,' he said. 'I needed volunteer credits. I realized how good my life had been. How lucky I was. And how alone these kids really are. I kept going even after I had my credits. Now it's just part of my life.'

She stared at him as if testing the truth of his words. 'Naomi didn't run away, did she?'

He swallowed again. *She likes* Avondale, Colton had said. Somehow that man – or his partner or both of them – had gotten their hands on this woman's child. 'I don't think so, ma'am.'

She looked down abruptly, her hand trembling as she petted the old dog. 'I told her to go,' she whispered.

'Mom,' Nathan said heavily. A denial. 'It wasn't your fault.'

She shook her head. 'I told her to go. She was talking back to me that day and I'd had a terrible day at work already. I was tired and . . .' A sob cut off her words, shaking her thin frame. Nathan put an arm around her shoulders, his expression helpless. Hopeless.

This family had suffered.

'We argued,' she said when she'd regained control. 'I'd told her she had to clean her room before going out, but I caught her sneaking out anyway. It was a big fight. Then I told her if she walked out that door, not to come back.'

Oh no. It wasn't the first time he'd heard the words uttered by a parent, but it was never easy to respond. Sam leaned forward, hands clasped between his knees.

'Nathan is right. This wasn't your fault. It was the fault of whoever took her.'

Tears ran down her gaunt cheeks. 'My husband didn't agree with that. He left. Blamed me for everything.'

Oh. Unfortunately, that was all too common as well. Many marriages crumbled under the strain of a missing child. 'I'm sorry.'

'Yeah, well. That's done. I don't know what else I can tell you, Dr Reeves. She was a headstrong girl, but she had a good heart. She liked animals. Volunteered at the humane society. Cried when dogs had to be put down. She hated math. Loved broccoli.' Beside her, Nathan sniffled and she patted his knee. 'She was a good big sister.'

'Did she want to be an actress?'

'Oh yes. She did. She would've made it, too. She sparkled onstage.'

'What production was she in?'

'Several. *Once upon a Mattress* when she was in middle school. She had the voice of an angel, you see. She starred in *The Little Mermaid* the year she . . . well. You know.'

Sam knew.

'It was a big deal,' Mrs Beckham went on. 'She was only fifteen, still a freshman, but she got the lead.'

'You must have been so proud of her.'

Her smile was full of regret. 'I was.'

'Was she seeing anyone? Maybe secretly?'

She shook her head. 'The cop asked me that. She wasn't. My Naomi was a good girl.'

But Nathan flinched. Sam briefly met his gaze, but the boy looked away. But not before Sam saw his panic.

Sam hesitated, then decided to try to get Nathan to tell him when his mother wasn't in the room. 'I read the posts her friends wrote on her Facebook page. She seemed to be a popular girl.'

Mrs Beckham shrugged. 'Most of those posts were from kids she knew at school, but few of them were friends. Not when she disappeared, anyway.'

He hadn't expected that. 'What happened?'

She sighed. 'Normally the kids would tell each other about the open auditions and they'd go together, but Naomi had done that earlier in the year for *Avondale* and one of her friends got called back and Naomi didn't. Naomi was disappointed, of course, but she was happy for her friend. Mostly. She was a teenager, after all.'

'Mixed feelings,' Sam said and Mrs Beckham nodded.

'But the next time . . .' She heaved another sigh. 'When Naomi disappeared, there was a rumor that she'd gone for another audition and hadn't told a soul. Her friends were mad. Turned on her. But when she didn't come home, a few of them felt ashamed, I think. That's when the posts started, begging her to come home.'

Something she was hiding from her friends. That was new.

'Audition for what?'

'I don't know. Nobody seemed to know.'

'Did you mention this to Detective McKittrick?'

Mrs Beckham looked startled. 'No. She didn't ask.'

'Is it okay if I mention it?'

'Dr Reeves, I'd give my own life to get her back.' Beside her, Nathan closed his eyes, his expression so desolate that it broke Sam's heart. From the look of the place, it looked like she'd given up living long ago. *So much suffering*. 'If you think it'll help that detective find out what happened to my baby girl, tell her.' She slumped, clearly fatigued. 'I'm really tired. You should probably go.'

'Yes, ma'am. Ma'am, New Horizons offers help to the families of runaways. Counseling. If you'd ever like to come in, I'd help find you someone to talk to. I do sessions with parents, but it doesn't have to be me.'

Her jaw tightened. 'Thank you, but I don't need it. Please go now.'

'Of course. Thank you for seeing me.' He rose, as did Nathan.

Silently Sam followed Nathan to the front door, but instead of closing it behind Sam, Nathan exited with him and quietly closed the door behind him.

'I'm sorry,' Nathan murmured. 'She's not the same.'

'I know,' Sam said, as comfortingly as he could. 'I guess you're not, either.'

Nathan shook his head. 'No.'

He wanted to ask Nathan why he'd looked so panicked when he'd asked if Naomi had been seeing anyone, but he'd care for the boy first.

Sam softened his voice. 'Sometimes this kind of loss pulls families apart. Makes the children left behind feel . . . lost. Abandoned.'

Nathan's shoulders hunched. 'Yeah.'

'We have group therapy for siblings of runaways, too. They miss their brothers and sisters. Some of them hope their siblings come back. Some know in their hearts that they won't. They'll understand where you are right now. I'd be happy to find you a group to sit with. You don't have to say a word if you don't want to. Just listen. And be.'

Nathan swallowed. 'Is it expensive? Because Mom's not working anymore. She just . . . sits there. Drinking. I . . . I bag groceries on the weekend and Dad pays alimony, but . . .' He trailed off, looking ashamed.

Sam wanted to make things right, but he couldn't. He could, however, get this kid into therapy. 'It's free, Nathan.' He gave the boy his New Horizons card. 'Call this number and tell them that I sent you. They have a shuttle that'll pick you up and bring you home.' It was one of the newer services they offered at New Horizons and one Sam had played a part in organizing. It had been immediately, wildly popular.

Nathan took the card gingerly. 'Thank you.'

Sam waited for a few beats, then said, 'You know who your sister left with.'

Nathan looked up, eyes flaring with panic anew. 'I didn't say that.'

'No. But reading body language goes with the shrink territory. Sorry.'

'I . . .' Nathan closed his eyes. 'I told the cops back then. When she disappeared. I told them I saw a car lurking. But they didn't believe me.'

'Why not?' Sam asked, because he sensed there was more to it.

'Because they said she ran away,' Nathan said bitterly.

'And?'

Nathan seemed to go limp. 'They looked at the cameras from all the houses around us and didn't see the car I described. They said I was making things up.'

'Why didn't the car show up on the cameras?'

Nathan's eyes opened. 'You believe me?'

'I do. Why, Nathan?'

He sighed. 'Because I said I saw it from my bedroom window. But I didn't.'

Sam thought he understood. 'Were you out of the house, too?'

Nathan nodded. 'I was coming back from my friend's house. We were playing video games and I lost track of time. I didn't want to get into trouble, but I saw her – and the car – when I was two blocks away from home.'

'What kind of car?'

'Black Mercedes. New. Tinted windows.'

Sam's heart started to race. 'What time was this?'

'About two thirty. But . . .' Another sigh, this one weary, like the secret he'd kept for three years had worn him down. 'The light came on when she got in. I only saw him for a second, but he was old. Like, older than my parents. His hair was gray and he wore glasses.'

Sam's racing heart went into overdrive. Colton's hair was coal black and he didn't wear glasses. His partner, then. 'Did you see his face?'

'Not really.'

Sam made his voice as gentle as he could. 'Why didn't you tell the police that you weren't in your house? Your parents wouldn't have been angry because you lost track of time, would they?'

Nathan made a wounded sound. 'I snuck out after I was supposed to be in bed. My friend's parents weren't home. We drank their booze and smoked their weed. My father would have been so angry.'

'So you lied,' Sam murmured, hoping there was no judgment in his voice.

Nathan nodded, tears rolling down his face. 'And then she didn't come home. My parents were yelling at each other and I just . . . I wanted to hide. I'm sorry,' he ended in a whisper. 'She wasn't dragged into the car. She went on her own. Even told the guy "Hi," all cheerful and happy when she opened the door. I figured she'd come home. And she never did. This is my fault.'

Sam clasped the boy's bony shoulder and squeezed lightly. 'Hey, look at me, please.' He waited until Nathan met his eyes. 'Like I told your mother, this is the fault of whoever took her. Not yours, Nathan.'

Nathan only shook his head miserably. 'But it is. If I'd said something . . .'

'I hate to say this, but they might have still labeled her as a runaway. She left on her own. She wasn't grabbed and dragged away.'

'She's dead, isn't she?'

'I don't know.'

Nathan's stare was mutinous. 'But you think so.'

'Yes. I think so. I hope I'm wrong.' But he didn't think he was.

'I have to go back inside.'

'Can I tell Detective McKittrick this information?'

A shrug. 'Fine. I don't care anymore.' Nathan opened the door and started to slip inside. 'I just don't care.'

Something in the boy's demeanor had a shiver of dread racing down Sam's spine. 'Nathan, wait.' He took out another card and wrote his new cell phone number on the back. 'Please call me if you feel like you're going to do anything drastic.'

'Nobody would care.'

'I would,' Sam whispered fiercely. 'And your mom would, too. Please.'

'Whatever.' But he took the card before closing the door in Sam's face.

Heart heavy, Sam went to his car, pulled out his phone, and texted McKittrick. ***Sam Reeves here. New number since you have my phone. I have some things to share with you. Please call me as soon as you can.***

Then he drove back to Joel's house, wondering what he was going to do next.

Carmel Valley, California
Monday, 18 April, 5.45 P.M.

Harlan's eyes widened when Kit let herself in the McKittricks' front door, Snickerdoodle at her heels. She'd picked the dog up from her place before heading to the farmhouse, thinking Rita might need some cuddle time after hearing the news. 'Hey, Pop.'

'Kitty-Cat!' Grinning, he gave her a rib-popping hug, letting her go before she grunted this time. 'We didn't expect to see you tonight. And Snick, too.' He petted the dog's head, sending Snick's tail wagging.

Kit lifted on her toes to kiss his cheek, enjoying his pleased smile. 'Is it okay?'

'Of course! Mom!' he shouted. 'Kit is here.'

Betsy appeared from the kitchen, wiping her hands on her apron. 'I'm glad I made pot roast.'

Kit's stomach growled. She'd visited Baz on her lunch break and hadn't stopped to eat. 'With baby carrots?'

Betsy looked offended. 'Of course.' She enveloped Kit in a warm hug and Kit inhaled, loving the smell of home on the woman who'd given her everything. 'Are you all right?' Betsy whispered in her ear.

Kit tightened her hold because she wasn't all right. Baz was in the hospital and the afternoon had been one major disappointment after another as she'd pursued leads on the case. But she'd kept her promise to Navarro and clocked out on time. Once she talked to Rita, she and Snick could go home and sleep. 'I will be.'

'Of course you will.' Betsy let her go and patted her cheek gently. 'You know we're here to listen. And we're the vault.'

They really were. Kit knew she could confide anything to them and it would go no further. She rarely did, though, mostly because she didn't want anyone else to share the mental pictures that haunted her.

'I know. I actually came by to talk to Rita. Is she here?'

'In her room,' Betsy said. 'What's wrong?'

'Nothing bad. Well, I hope she doesn't take it badly. She told me about her mother.'

Harlan's gaze darkened. 'That poor woman. And Rita found her.'

Kit's heart squeezed because she'd read that in the police report. 'I looked into her mother's case again. We found some evidence that hadn't made it into the case file.' Batra's office was still trying to find out what exactly had happened, but it appeared that a clerk had uploaded the wrong photo. The person no longer worked for the ME's office and, at last word, was nowhere to be found.

So . . . not good.

'And?' Harlan pressed. 'Don't keep us hanging.'

'Navarro reopened the case.' She couldn't keep from smiling. 'They arrested Maria Mendoza's boss today.'

'Oh, Kit,' Betsy breathed. 'That's wonderful.'

Harlan grabbed Kit in another hug. 'Thank you,' he whispered into her hair, his voice breaking, his body leaning into hers. 'Thank you.'

Kit hugged him back, happy to give him strength this time, instead of always taking his. 'I only did the background work. Two of the other detectives brought him in.' It was Connor and Howard's collar, which was why they were now freed up to assist her starting tomorrow. 'I'm bringing in the cupcakes tomorrow. The really pricey ones from the bakery near the station.'

'Nonsense,' Betsy tutted. 'I will be baking the cupcakes, Kit McKittrick. There is no way you will be celebrating *this* arrest with store-bought cupcakes.'

Kit smiled at her. 'I will never say no to cupcakes baked by Mom McK.'

Betsy did a little shimmy where she stood. 'Rita will be . . .' She sobered. 'She'll be satisfied, I think. But it took too long.'

Kit sighed. 'I know. I'm sorry.'

'Hush now,' Betsy admonished. 'That was an indictment of the system. Not you. Never you. Go on up and see her. She's in your old room. Tell her that dinner is in fifteen minutes. If she's too overwhelmed to come down, I'll take her a tray.'

'I'll tell her.' Kit reached out and squeezed Betsy's hand, hoping the woman knew how much Kit appreciated her. 'Homicide loves chocolate cupcakes.'

'I know,' Betsy said fondly. 'Not my first rodeo, Kit.'

It wasn't. Betsy had always sent baked goods in with Harlan and Kit when they'd visited Baz, long before Kit became a cop. Every time they'd found a lead or even a whisper of a lead, Betsy had made Baz's favorites.

Kit called to Snickerdoodle, then jogged up the stairs, heading to her old room. It had been updated many times in the past sixteen years. Nearly every occupant had made new curtains because Betsy made sure everyone knew how to sew basic things. She'd made sure they could cook and balance their checkbooks and do all the necessary skills that adults needed to do to survive. Not everyone loved the sewing or the cooking or the math, but no one left McKittrick House unable to fend for themselves.

Kit rapped lightly on the door, pushing it open when she heard a muffled 'Come in.'

Rita was sitting on her bed – Wren's old bed – reading a tattered copy of . . . Kit's throat tightened. *Coraline*. That had been Wren's favorite book.

'Wow,' Kit said, forcing a smile. 'Are they still making you read that for school?'

Rita lit up when she saw Snick, then her expression went abruptly wary as she stared at Kit. Patting the bed for Snickerdoodle to join her, she shook her head, the pink, purple, and blue streaks in her hair sliding against each other. 'No. I read the book for school already. I was reading this for . . . you know. Fun.'

Kit sat on the opposite bed, happy that she'd taken the time to bring her dog because Rita had visibly relaxed, petting her. 'That was my sister Wren's favorite book. She loved the spooky, scary stories.'

Rita went still, then turned the book so that Kit could see it. Inside the front cover was written *WMcK* in a heartbreakingly familiar scrawl.

Kit swallowed hard. 'I didn't know that Mom kept it.'

Rita nodded. 'She told me that it was precious and that I had to promise to take care of it.' Her chin jutted out. 'I will.'

'I know you will.' Kit drew a breath. 'I have some news.'

Rita stiffened. 'I didn't do anything.'

'I know, I know,' Kit soothed. 'Nobody even hinted that you did. This is about your mom, honey.'

Rita carefully set Wren's book aside. 'What happened?'

'I looked into her case and we found some new evidence. Your mom's boss was arrested today.'

Kit hadn't been sure how Rita would react. It could have gone a number of different ways, from rage to tears.

Rita lurched to her feet, looking like she wanted to bolt. 'He was?'

Kit remained very still. 'He was.'

'He'll get a fancy lawyer.'

'He might. But we have good evidence and good prosecutors.' She'd learned that Joel Haley would be first chair. 'I know the man who's going to be prosecuting your mom's boss. He's very skilled. If anyone can get a conviction, it'll be him.'

'What do I have to do?'

'I don't know yet. My boss just gave me clearance to tell you. We wanted to wait until he was booked before we told you in case something fell through.'

Rita breathed hard, her hands clenched into fists at her sides. 'What do I say?'

'To who, honey?'

'To you.'

'You don't have to say a thing. I just wanted you to know that sometimes the system works. And that everyone matters. Everyone deserves justice.'

'You didn't lie,' she whispered.

'No,' Kit said softly. She wouldn't tell her everything, especially that her mother had been pregnant with her killer's child. At least not now. She'd ask Rita's therapist for help on that front.

Kit was startled when Rita threw herself onto her lap, her arms twisting around Kit's neck so tightly that it was difficult to breathe. The girl was shaking. Not crying, just shaking.

Kit carefully wrapped her arms around her. 'It's okay. I've got you. You're okay.'

A wordless nod was all she got in reply, so Kit patiently waited until Rita's body shakes became trembles and finally a great shudder. Then Rita was still.

'Nobody cared,' she whispered. 'My mom was dead and no one cared.'

'I care,' Kit whispered back. 'Mom and Pop care. My boss cared.'

'I miss my mom.' The words were a pitiful whimper that broke Kit's heart again.

'I know, baby. I miss my sister, too.'

Rita's tears started then, soaking into Kit's neck, but Kit didn't move. Didn't stop hugging this thirteen-year-old girl who reminded her so much of herself. She rocked Rita gently, murmuring into her hair.

Just as Betsy and Harlan had tried to do for her when Wren died. But she'd pushed them away for more than a year, even after seeing Harlan crying in the barn. Then one day she'd crumpled under the strain, and their comfort had become a balm rather than a torture to be endured. It was shortly thereafter that she'd asked them if she was still adoptable.

She'd been Kit McKittrick ever since. So she'd pay it forward now, giving this child the comfort she hadn't been ready to accept herself.

Rita's sobs turned to hiccups, then little snores. Snickerdoodle carefully climbed onto the bed beside them, nuzzling into Kit's side. Eventually Betsy came up with a tray but backed out of the room when she saw Rita curled up on Kit's lap.

Later, Betsy mouthed.

Kit edged backward until her back was against the wall. Rita slept on, a warm presence in her arms. Normally she didn't like to hug people for so long, but Rita was different. Rita needed her.

Her phone buzzed in her pocket, but she'd wake the girl if she grabbed it. So she let it go for a few minutes.

Just a few minutes. Then I'll wake her up and get us dinner.

Kit woke with a jerk, stunned to see that it was dark. She was no longer sitting against the wall, but lying down, her head on the pillow of her old bed. Someone had covered her with a blanket and taken off her boots.

Blinking hard, she fumbled for her phone.

Shit. It was eleven o'clock. Kit sat up, rubbing her eyes, irritated with herself, but Rita was sleeping in Wren's old bed, Snickerdoodle cuddled close, so Kit kept her grumbles silent. Plus there was a note on the nightstand in Betsy's looping handwriting.

> *I didn't wake you because you needed to rest. Dinner's in the fridge. Eat before you leave. Cupcakes for tomorrow on the table in a box. Love you. –Mom.*

Kit exhaled, relieved. She wasn't sure what she'd ever done to deserve the McKittricks, but she was so glad she hadn't had to do anything to earn their love. It was the purest thing she knew.

Giving herself a minute to wake up, she scrolled through her texts.

Baz: ***Come and spring me out of this joint. Stat!***

Baz: ***Why aren't you answering? Are you okay? Now I'm worried.***

Baz: ***Called Harlan. Says you're asleep. About time, kid. Call me tomorrow. Marian is taking my phone away now. Won't let me text at night. She is a beast. Don't tell her I said that please.***

Kit smiled. Baz's love for his wife was another pure thing. They were so good together.

She went through another few texts, deleting the spam, then paused at a number she didn't recognize. She clicked on the text and barely restrained a gasp.

Sam Reeves here. New number since you have my phone. I have some things to share with you. Please call me as soon as you can.

He'd sent the text at six fifteen, so it must have been the buzz she'd felt right before she went to sleep. She debated whether it was too late to text back, then thought, *Screw it. This sounds important*.

Apologies. I didn't see your text till now. Too late to call? She hit SEND and waited. A few seconds later he replied.

Still awake. I did something you probably won't like, but I learned important details.

Kit stared at the text for a few hard beats of her heart. What had he done?

Forcing herself to remain calm, she tapped out her reply. ***Give me fifteen minutes. Need to get food and then go somewhere where I don't wake up the house.*** And why she'd explained, she didn't know.

No problem. Will wait for your call.

She started to call for Snick, but her dog looked comfortable in Rita's arms, so she left them to sleep. *Time to work.*

Twelve

Hillcrest, California
Monday, 18 April, 11.15 P.M.

Joel sighed. 'Sam, you're making me crazy. Sit the fuck down.'

Sam glared at him. 'I'm freaking out. I'm allowed to pace.'

After the adrenaline from his visit to the Beckhams' home had passed, he'd panicked. What had he been thinking? McKittrick was going to level him and he'd deserve it.

Visiting the victim of a crime that way.

But you got the goods. She wasn't able to. You did good, Sammy.

His feet stumbled to a stop. 'She can't do anything to me.'

'I wouldn't bet on that. She's pretty vicious if you fuck up her crime scene. I did once by accident and, let me tell you, I will never be so careless again.'

Sam blinked at him. 'What did you do?'

'Walked into a crime scene without putting those footie things over my shoes. Cross-contaminated the scene. I had to surrender my shoes to CSU and everything. Took me a month to get them back and they were my Ferragamos.'

'You poor baby,' Sam said dryly because Joel sounded so outraged. 'If you'd bought normal shoes like normal people, you wouldn't have been so upset at losing them.' Why anyone would pay that much for a pair of shoes was beyond Sam. He'd thought his Top-Siders were expensive. Buying them had been his quarterly splurge and they'd been on sale. Joel's shoes cost ten times as much. *Insanity.*

'I *am* normal people. I just like nice shoes. Anyway, Ryland from CSU told me later that they'd been done with the shoes after two days, but McKittrick had kept them for the rest of the month as petty revenge.' He gave Sam a pitying look. 'And I never even said a word to any witnesses.'

Sam scowled at him. 'I was starting to feel better.'

Joel just grinned. 'You're welcome. Oops, there you go.'

Sam's new phone was ringing. McKittrick. He answered, putting it on speaker.

'Detective,' he said, drawing on his therapist voice.

'What did you do?' she demanded.

He sat down heavily on Joel's sofa. Joel's expression was now one of grim encouragement. 'I had some time today, so I decided to do a little investigating of my own.'

A beat of silence. 'What did you do?' she repeated, more ominously.

'Look, I know you're going to do your best to solve this thing, but if you don't, it's just a disappointment to you. It's my life on the line here, Detective.'

She huffed out an impatient breath. 'What. Did. You. Do?'

'I googled missing teenagers and *Avondale*. Naomi Beckham's name came up.'

'Okay,' she said warily. 'And?'

'I went to her house. Talked to her family.'

Another moment of silence, much longer than before. 'You did *what*?' she hissed.

'I spoke to Naomi Beckham's mother and brother. I arrived shortly after you left.'

'There was no brother there.' Her voice was cold, but he thought he heard a minute thread of curiosity.

'He got home from school after you left. His mother was on her way to getting drunk.'

'I don't think she ever stops being drunk,' McKittrick said, her tone grim. 'The house was littered with empty bottles. So . . . tell me about these important details you learned.'

'Mrs Beckham said that Naomi and her friends had shared open auditions in the past, but the rumor was that she'd kept one secret. That was where her classmates thought she'd gone.'

'Huh. That is useful.'

'That wasn't the bombshell, though. When I asked if she was seeing anyone, the mom said no. But the brother – Nathan – looked panicked and guilty.'

'The missing-person report said he saw a car, but the investigation determined that he was either lying or mistaken.'

'He was lying, but only about where he was when he saw the car. He was coming home from a friend's house. It was late, about two thirty. He'd been drinking and smoking weed, so he was afraid to admit to where he'd been. He saw Naomi getting into a black Mercedes with tinted windows. She got in voluntarily. He got a glimpse of the driver, Detective.'

She sucked in a breath. 'And?'

'He said the man was older than his parents. He had graying hair and wore glasses. He didn't see his face. Just those details.'

'Oh my God,' she whispered. 'That wasn't Colton Driscoll.'

'No,' Sam said simply. 'Nathan figured his sister would come home eventually and his parents were constantly fighting, so he didn't say anything except that he'd seen the car. He's a sensitive kid. He was afraid to come forward with the whole truth because he'd been breaking house rules. But Naomi didn't come home and his parents' fighting got even worse. Dad eventually left. It looks like poor Nathan has been taking care of his mom ever since.'

'I see,' she said quietly. 'Will he tell me this himself?'

'I think he might tell you more easily if you get him away from his mother. He's fragile and I think he feels like his mother is the only parent he has left. He's torn up by guilt, but he's really afraid.'

She blew out a breath. 'Wow. Okay. Well, first of all, you could have really messed everything up, Dr Reeves. You might be thinking that it turned out okay, but you could have ruined a witness's testimony simply by being there. You're a *suspect*.'

Sam bristled. 'You don't believe that, though.'

'No, I don't. But my job is not to make you feel better by believing you. Nor is it my job to make your life easier. I get that you're worried about your job—'

'And my freedom,' he interrupted with a snarl, anger hitting him hard.

'And your freedom,' she said, speaking down to him like he was a recalcitrant child, which only made him angrier. 'But you cannot investigate this on your own. *You can't.*'

Sam found that his chin had risen, his jaw clenching. 'Is it illegal?'

'Maybe,' she snapped, sounding exasperated. 'It could be construed as witness tampering. Which is a federal crime, Dr Reeves.'

Gone was his worry that she'd be mad at him. He didn't give a flying fuck. 'Or people might talk to me.'

He heard her inhale, probably through her nose. She was pissed.

He didn't care. It wasn't his job to make her feel better, either. 'Did you know that I'm on a leave of absence now, Detective?' he demanded bitterly. 'My boss believes in me, but my very presence at my job could risk my clients' mental health and their potential recovery. Did you know that?'

'No,' she admitted. 'That's why you have time?'

'It is,' he bit out. 'The Beckham boy said you'd already been by. I figured I wasn't hurting anything by asking a few questions. I got answers. You're welcome, by the way.' He glanced over his shoulder to find Joel staring at him like he was a stranger.

He felt like a stranger. A more powerful stranger. 'If it pisses you off that I'm asking questions, I'm not sorry. Skyler Carville was my friend!' He was shouting now and couldn't seem to stop. 'Her parents think that I killed her! And you just expect me to sit and wait while you figure all this out?'

Joel had slid closer and now gripped Sam's shoulder. 'Hey,' he murmured. 'Settle down. You're not going to win her over by yelling.'

'Who's there?' McKittrick asked sharply.

'Joel Haley. I'm staying at his house because I can't go back to my apartment.'

'The cleaners are still working?' she asked, sounding sincerely confused.

'For fuck's sake,' Sam snarled. 'Are you stupid or just unfeeling?

Her *parents* are my *neighbors*. They think *I killed her*. And you think I can live there knowing that? What am I going to say when I see them in the hallway? "Sorry for your loss, but I didn't do it"?'

'Yes,' she said so calmly he wanted to hit something.

Which wasn't like him. He didn't hit things. Not even the punching bag at the gym.

'Well, you might be able to separate your feelings, but I can't.'

'You're a mental health professional,' she said, speaking factually as if discussing the weather. 'You should be able to as well.'

His rage left him in a rush. She was right. He should be able to. His eyes burned and he took a deep breath that hurt.

'Did you know that I met Skyler when she was only seventeen?' he asked, his voice breaking. 'Did you know that I helped her draw up her business plan for her dog-walking business? Siggy was her first client. I sat with her parents at their kitchen table and together we helped her with her college applications. I was one of her references. She introduced me to her prom date before they left for the dance. I took a picture and told him that he better take good care of her. I still have the picture on my phone. When she decided to major in psychology, I was so proud. Like I'd touched a life. She was like a younger sister. And now she's *dead*, Detective. Some bastard with gray hair, glasses, and a black Mercedes lured her somewhere because she thought she was meeting me for drinks. He killed her because of me. To make me look guilty.' He shuddered and wiped his face because tears had begun to fall and he didn't even care. 'So forgive me for being human, Detective. Forgive me for not being able to separate my personal and professional personas. *But I can't*. If you need to arrest me for anything else, make sure you contact my attorney because I'm not saying another word to you.'

'Dr Reeves, *wait*. Please don't hang up.'

She'd said please, so he drew another breath. 'What?'

'First, I'm sorry this has turned your life upside down,' she said, her tone no longer like arctic ice. This was the woman who'd patted Siggy's crate and told his dog it would be all right the night she'd arrested him. 'It's the ripples.'

'Ripples,' he repeated flatly.

'Yes, ripples. Murder doesn't just affect the victim. It touches family, friends, colleagues. The person who discovers the body, even if they're a stranger. No one in the victim's circle will ever be the same. You tried to do the right thing, but you got sucked into a case that never should have touched you or Miss Carville or her family. But this is where we are.' She hesitated. 'I'm asking you to trust me to do my job. To stay away from this investigation.'

He wanted to say *Okay, I'll back away*. He wanted to pretend none of this was happening. That her ripples hadn't touched his life. But they had. 'They aren't ripples,' he said instead.

'Excuse me?'

'This isn't a ripple. It's a goddamned rogue wave and it's dragging me under with it.'

'Was that a no?' she asked stiffly.

'It sure as hell's not a yes. Have a good evening, Detective. And when you talk to Nathan Beckham, be gentle. I wasn't exaggerating when I said he was fragile. I think he's at serious risk of self-harm. I wouldn't want you to find another body hanging from a rope, because Nathan's would actually be suicide.'

He ended the call and sat staring at his phone.

Joel still sat beside him, his hand still on his shoulder. The silence between them seemed to go on forever. Then Joel sighed.

'I'm so sorry, Sam,' he murmured.

Sam looked over at him. 'For what?'

'For not realizing how much Skyler's death hurt you. I was thinking of this as a danger to your reputation and your career. I wasn't thinking that you were grieving, too. I'm sorry for that.'

Sam shrugged. 'It's okay. I think the detective is going to make my life a living hell, though, because I'm not going to back away and trust her. I can't.' He expected Joel to try to talk him out of it, but he didn't.

'First, I do understand. I'm not going to tell you to stop, but you have to be careful.'

'I will. What's second?'

'McKittrick isn't stupid or unfeeling. I got a new case today, an arrest of a city councilman who's accused of murdering his former housekeeper.'

'Okay,' Sam said cautiously. 'What does that have to do with me?'

'Nothing, but it does have something to do with McKittrick. The murder happened a few years ago, but the guy wasn't even questioned because he's rich and has connections. But Kit met the victim's daughter. She's being fostered by the McKittricks. When Kit found out that the killer was never caught, she looked into it. Found an issue with the evidence and got her boss to reopen the case. Today they made an arrest. She didn't get involved after handing it off to Lieutenant Navarro even though she had to have wanted to.'

'She trusts the system,' Sam said heavily, because that meant she'd expect him to trust it – and her – too.

'She trusts the system to a point. I think it's more accurate to say that she trusts Navarro. I think if Navarro hadn't reopened the case and taken it seriously, she would have stepped back in. She's by the book, nearly all the time.'

'And?'

'Her investigations are nice and neat. She's a workhorse. She never stops, and when she closes a case, she gets a conviction. A Kit McKittrick case will be as airtight as an Egyptian tomb.'

Sam shook his head, becoming frustrated. '*And?*'

'*And* you're toppling her carefully constructed world. I don't think she blames you, but I'd be shocked if she didn't try to stop you.'

'What can she do?'

'Put you in protective custody, for one.'

Sam's eyes widened. 'She'd do that?'

'I honestly don't know. But I wouldn't be your best friend if I left you unprepared.' He squared his shoulders. 'I also wouldn't be your best friend if I let you go this alone. You need a chaperone, someone to vouch for you if the bastard in a black Mercedes does anything else. That's going to be me. I'll need some time to get my cases handed off and request a few days' vacation. I have plenty since I never use it.'

Overwhelmed, Sam's mouth opened and closed before words would come. 'But your career. I won't jeopardize that.'

'I'll tell my boss what I'm doing. I'll have to recuse myself from this case and anything that comes from it, but it'll be okay. I hope,' he added in a mutter.

'I hear a "but" coming.'

'*But* you need to promise me that you won't make any other visits alone. You made yourself incredibly vulnerable today, Sam. The least awful thing that could have happened is that Nathan kid would realize you were the CI mentioned at the press conference. Did you think about that?'

'Yes. Several times. But this is not just about me anymore. Ripples, right?'

Joel nodded soberly. 'Yeah. Ripples. What was your next step going to be?'

'I want to talk to Colton's ex-wives. I don't plan to reveal that I was his therapist, but knowing who his friends were is important, and his ex-wives might know this.'

'McKittrick's almost certainly interviewed them already.'

'She talked to Mrs Beckham, too, but didn't ask the right questions. Colton never mentioned any in session, but one of his exes might have noticed a man with graying hair and glasses who drove a Mercedes.'

Joel pinched the bridge of his nose. 'All right. And then what?'

'The neighbor who Colton assaulted had called him out on his lie. Colton claimed to be a Navy SEAL. The case file I received from the court said that David Epstein confronted him after checking to make sure that Colton hadn't served anywhere. He might have learned something else of value when he was checking into Colton's background.'

'Okay. Tomorrow morning I'm going into the office to talk to my boss. I'll be home as soon as I can. You will stay here, okay?'

'Okay.' Because Joel was right. He had made himself vulnerable today. But he wasn't sorry about any of it.

'Then tomorrow we pull on our PI hats and go fishing for information.'

'You can change your mind,' Sam offered quietly. 'I won't blame you. There's no reason for both of us to put our careers in danger.'

Joel frowned and Sam could see that this worried him. 'We'll see what my boss has to say.'

'What if I got another chaperone?'

Joel's brows rose. 'Who?'

Sam shrugged. 'Laura.'

Joel made a face. 'Shit, Sam.'

'Her involvement as my defense attorney wouldn't be unheard of.'

Joel looked disgusted. 'Why would she do that for you?'

'Because she owes me. She owes both of us. Let her try to make amends.'

Joel sighed. 'Ask her. I'll also ask my boss. We'll see what happens. Try to get some sleep tonight, okay?'

Sam hadn't gotten any sleep the night before. He didn't expect that to change anytime soon.

Shelter Island Marina, San Diego, California
Tuesday, 19 April, 12.05 A.M.

The light was on in Kit's cabin window when she got to her boat. Akiko was here and Kit was more grateful than she could say, especially since she'd left Snick with Rita.

Akiko was curled up on the small sofa, a glass of wine near her elbow and her tablet in her lap. The laugh track from whatever TV show she was watching grated on Kit's ears as she locked her gun in her safe and dropped her keys and wallet on the kitchen counter. The small wooden figurine of the cat and bird followed. Then Kit leaned against the counter, bracing herself on her palms and letting her head drop low.

'Oh boy,' Akiko said after turning off the television. 'That bad?'

Are you stupid or just unfeeling? The words had cut far deeper than she'd let on.

Kit didn't turn around. *I am not stupid*. Of that she was certain. 'Am I unfeeling?'

Akiko gasped and was at Kit's side in a heartbeat. 'No. Never. Who told you that? I'll smack them into next week.'

And Akiko could do it, too. She was a tiny thing, but scrappy. She'd had to be to survive until she'd finally made it to the McKittricks'. Back then, her self-defense moves had been self-taught, more desperately instinctive. Like a wildcat. Now her skills were properly developed at a dojo and she was elegant. And fierce. Back when she was still a teenager, she'd fought off predatory foster fathers and sometimes their sons. Now, she used her skills to subdue frat boys who got wasted and made drunken advances when they were supposed to be fishing on her boat.

The thought of Akiko smacking Kit's detractors usually made her smile. But not tonight. Not when it was Sam Reeves.

Kit sagged when Akiko's hand tentatively touched her back. 'Okay?' Akiko murmured as she began to rub soothing circles between Kit's shoulder blades.

'Yes,' Kit rasped.

'Who said you were unfeeling?' Akiko asked quietly.

'Sam. I mean Dr Reeves.' She'd started thinking of him as Sam in her mind, and that was not okay.

'Who is he?'

Kind. Sincere. Forgiving. *In pain*. 'My CI.'

'Okay. Sounds like he's a little more than that, though. Normally you let remarks like that roll off like water off a duck's back.'

'No, I don't,' Kit confessed. 'I just have a good poker face.'

'We all know that. We just let you believe that we buy your I'm-a-rock persona.'

Persona. The same word Sam had used tonight. He couldn't separate his personal and professional personas. Kit had never had trouble at least pretending to keep them separate.

Tonight, not so much.

'He's a psychologist. Got sucked into this case.'

'The serial killer case? How did he get sucked in?'

'Being a Good Samaritan. Now the killer is framing him.'

'That sucks,' Akiko said, her tone so matter-of-fact that Kit laughed, surprising herself. But it was a watery laugh, tears too close to the surface.

'He's decided to investigate for himself.'

'Oh,' Akiko said flatly. 'I guess I don't blame him. Do you?'

'No. But he could fuck things up.'

'What did he do?'

'Talked to a victim's family.'

'Did he fuck it up?'

'No. He got information that I couldn't. Or didn't. And now we know details about the killer that we didn't know before.'

'I thought you caught the killer.' Then she made a humming noise. 'You didn't catch them all yet.'

'No, but you don't know that.'

'Know what?' Akiko asked innocently. 'I am but a humble fisherwoman.'

Kit chuckled again. 'Right. And I have oceanfront property in Nevada.'

'So are you mad that he talked to the family or that he got the information that you either couldn't or didn't?'

Kit met Akiko's eyes. 'I don't know,' she said honestly. 'That bothers me.'

'Of course it does. You like your life orderly and this isn't. What are you going to do about him?'

'I don't know,' she said again. 'I should stop him, but . . . what if he *can* get information that I can't? What if the information leads us to this killer and we can take him off the street forever? So he doesn't kill anyone else?'

Like Skyler Carville. Sam's friend.

'That sounds like a positive. Isn't it?'

'But . . . he could get hurt. He's a psychologist, not a cop. He has a cute dog and wears these dorky glasses and he's so . . . sincere. He's not a fighter. He panicked because I grabbed his arms.' And she didn't know why.

His attorney did, however. Laura Letterman had said 'oh' when Sam explained why he'd resisted arrest. Like that made all the sense in the world.

Kit had been wondering what had happened to trigger the man like that.

'Could you work together?'

Kit shook her head. 'He's technically a suspect. That's why he's investigating. To clear his name.'

'That sucks,' Akiko said again.

Kit sighed. 'It does. If I did just let him do his thing . . . would I be using him?'

'Maybe. Would he mind?'

'No, I don't think he'd mind.'

'Then let him.'

'He's a suspect.'

'Did he harass anyone? Trespass anywhere?'

'No.'

'Then he has a right to talk to anyone he pleases. And if he passes on what he's learned, then all the better for you.'

'Unless he gets hurt.'

'His life is on the line, Kit. Desperate people often don't care if they get hurt.'

'That's what I'm afraid of. He's desperate and I'm taking advantage by turning him loose.'

'Does he want this killer off the streets, too?'

'Yes.'

'Does he seem to know his own mind?'

'Yes.'

'Then let him try. As long as he's not breaking the law, you can't really stop him. Can you?'

'No. But I still feel like I should try.'

Akiko was quiet as the seconds ticked by. 'You care what he thinks about you.'

'I think I do.' And she hated that. But it wasn't Sam's fault.

'Look, Mom said you napped at her place, but to make you go back to sleep when you got home. So into bed with you. You get out of these clothes and into your pj's. There's rocky road in the freezer, too. I thought we'd celebrate Rita's mom's killer's arrest, but it'll do for hurt feelings, too.'

'My feelings aren't—' Kit stopped herself because Akiko was shaking her head.

'You're human, Kit. Your feelings can be hurt. You don't have to be all grrr all the time.'

So forgive me for being human, Detective.

She had, of course. Forgiven him. *Maybe forgive yourself, too?*

Obediently Kit changed her clothes and got the rocky road from the freezer, smiling when she saw it was lactose free so Akiko could have some, too. Grabbing two spoons, she crawled into bed where Akiko was already snuggled under the blankets.

'Stay?' Kit asked, holding out a spoon.

'Like you could get rid of me,' Akiko scoffed.

'Rita's in our old room,' Kit said around a mouthful of ice cream.

'In Wren's old bed,' Akiko said with a sad smile.

'Your old bed,' Kit corrected, but Akiko was right. It would always be Wren's old bed. 'Mom gave Rita Wren's copy of *Coraline*.'

'I loved that story.' Akiko grinned. 'Especially because it freaked you out so bad. You could talk about killers and bodies and crime scenes like it was nothing, but the Other Mother with buttons for eyes gave you nightmares.'

Kit shuddered. 'Still does.'

'I know, honey.' Akiko got another spoonful of ice cream and held it up to Kit's spoon. 'To a night without bad dreams.'

Kit touched her spoon to Akiko's. 'To sisters who do double time as best friends.'

Akiko smiled. 'You are not unfeeling, Kit McKittrick. You feel too much.'

Kit sighed. 'Don't tell anyone, okay? I got a rep.'

'My lips are sealed.'

SDPD, San Diego, California
Tuesday, 19 April, 8.30 A.M.

Kit held the box of Betsy's cupcakes out to Howard Cook. 'Congratulations on the Mendoza case. And thank you.'

Howard smiled. 'Just ran with the ball. You threw the pass.'

'Did you make these?' Connor asked suspiciously.

'No, my mom did,' Kit said, not taking offense. 'You're safe.'

'Excellent.' Connor took one, then sat at Kit's desk and began peeling the cupcake wrapper, getting crumbs everywhere. 'Bring us up to speed.'

'I got us a meeting room.' Kit scowled at the mess on her desk. 'Clean that up first, though. God.'

She turned on her heel, Howard following behind her, the cupcake box in his hands.

Grumbling, Connor brushed the crumbs into her wastebasket, then shoved the cupcake into his mouth. A whole cupcake. He was a big guy, but that was still piggish.

'Sorry,' Howard murmured. 'I've been trying to housebreak him, but it's not working.'

Kit had to bite back a laugh while Connor made a grumbling noise in his throat. Howard was in his midfifties and Connor was maybe a year older than Kit. Howard had been Connor's trainer and he'd succeeded at that. They were both good detectives, so Kit would cut Howard a little slack on the failed housebreaking.

They took their seats around the table and Kit briefed them on the case thus far.

'A man with gray hair and glasses who drove a Mercedes?' Connor asked doubtfully. 'That's not a lot to go on.'

'More than we had yesterday,' Kit said, 'but yeah. Not a lot.'

'I think the audition is going to be more helpful,' Howard said. 'So, according to Dr Reeves, Naomi got offered an audition and told no one. We believe that Naomi ended up dead. Are we believing Reeves's account of his conversation with the Beckhams?'

Kit nodded. 'For now, yes.'

'Okay,' Howard said. 'So, again, Naomi ended up dead. I wonder if the other victims had the same experience, being offered an audition.'

'I'm assuming so at this point.' Kit nibbled on a cupcake. 'Which makes me wonder about the ones who did tell.'

Connor made an impatient gesture. 'And?'

'There had to be some who told their friends,' she said. 'He wanted them to keep it secret, but not every girl would have done that. I woke up wondering what happened when they told their friends.'

'You woke up wondering that?' Connor asked, his tone the tiniest bit mocking. 'I'd be pissed if my girlfriend woke up next to me thinking about work.' His lips quirked. 'Not that she ever would be. Thinking about work, that is.'

Kit stared at him. Connor Robinson was a handsome guy and always had a girlfriend. Kit had met a few of them, and they'd seemed nice. Which was why they usually left him.

'Do you mind?' she asked.

At the same time Howard hissed, 'Can it, Connor.'

'Sorry, sorry.' Connor lifted his hands in a conciliatory way, but Kit didn't buy it. He'd wanted to get a reaction from them, and he'd succeeded.

She pulled her mind back to the priority. *Dead girls*. 'I wondered if the girls that told their friends still got an audition – along with all their friends – and none of them were killed? Or did he disappear? Make excuses? Did he actually choose someone for the part? Was there a production at all or was it all a ruse?'

'We could ask the drama teachers,' Howard said. 'And, not to digress, but these are amazing cupcakes. Would your mom give me the recipe?'

'Probably. She taught me to make them. Or tried to. My sister Akiko took to the cooking. I just eat to survive.'

'That's sad, Kit,' Howard said. He leaned back in his chair. 'So . . . drama teachers. How do we want to divvy this up? We could make a list of the area high schools, split it three ways, and man the phones.'

'Then pay visits to the drama teachers who remember something,' Connor added.

'Sounds good. I have a list of other follow-up items.' She handed each of them the to-do lists she'd printed first thing that morning. 'We need to ID any other potential victims from the missing and runaway lists, paying special attention to any girl that fits the profile.'

'Fifteen to seventeen, blond, petite, interested in drama,' Howard murmured.

'Was it always auditions, though?' Connor asked. 'These recent victims have drama in common. Did he lure some of the others with something else?'

'That's a good question,' Kit admitted, hoping she didn't sound too begrudging. From Connor's smirk, she figured she'd been unsuccessful at hiding it. 'I've already gone through the reports up to ten years ago and have been putting anyone who fits the physical profile but without the drama connection into a separate pile.'

'I'll take the older reports,' Howard said. 'How far back? Twenty years?'

Kit nodded. 'For now. We don't know that the first victim we found was his first.'

'That's upbeat,' Connor muttered. 'I'll take the reports you've set aside. Fresh eyes and all.'

Kit handed him the stack. 'Thanks. Next on my list is checking with the high schools attended by our most recent victims to see if there was anyone who fits the killer's profile hanging around. Fortyish, physically fit, gray hair and glasses, in an occupation that inspires trust – doctors, nurses, teachers, clergy. We should focus on Jaelyn Watts, Cecilia Sheppard, and Naomi Beckham. Let's each take a school.'

They decided who would go where and Kit went on.

'We need to find Skyler Carville's car. It may be impounded if she parked on the street Friday night into Saturday morning.'

'I'll take that one,' Howard offered.

'Thanks. I requested Skyler's cell phone records and should have them today. Someone lured her somewhere after her shift Friday night. It was probably a burner or a spoofed number, but we might get lucky.'

'Doubt it,' Connor said.

Kit shrugged. 'Me too, but we need to at least check it out. Next, we need to canvass the bars around the interstate entrance in Little Italy with Skyler's photo. That's where she was headed when the street cams lost her car. She had Rohypnol in her system. If she was lured to a bar thinking she was getting a drink with Dr Reeves, she got roofied by someone. Now that we know that Naomi got into a car with a man with graying hair and glasses, we can ask about him, too.'

'There are only dozens of bars in Little Italy,' Connor grumbled. 'A few are open for lunch, but most of them don't open until later this afternoon, like three or four.'

'I'll make a list,' Howard said. 'We can split them up and cover them quicker that way.'

'Good idea.' Kit started to feel some of her tension melt away. The tasks were manageable when divvied up.

Connor frowned. 'Okay, I'm going to stab the elephant in the room.'

Howard sputtered. 'You don't *stab* the elephant, Connor. You just . . . mention him.'

Connor smirked again. 'So, the elephant – Dr Reeves. How do we know he's legit?'

The tension crept back to her shoulders, even though she'd known the question was coming.

'We don't,' she admitted, irritated at how hard it was to say those words. 'But his boss vouches for him, and Dr Levinson vouched for both of them. Looks like Reeves is one of the true helpers.'

Connor snorted. 'I'm surprised, McKittrick. You're usually the one who paints everyone in the worst light. What's the deal with this guy? Are you *seeing* him?'

Kit bit her tongue until she could control her tone. 'No, Robinson, I am not. He could be lying, but I don't think he is. He's given us his phone so that we can check where he was at the time of Skyler Carville's murder.'

'Which was when?' Howard asked.

'Saturday morning between three a.m. and seven.'

'Same time frame as Colton Driscoll,' Connor observed.

'I saw that,' Kit said levelly. 'Might be serendipity or it might be an important connection. If he met Skyler in a bar a little after midnight, it would have taken time to get her roofied and away from the place. Three a.m. might have been the earliest he could take her to wherever he killed her.'

'And buried her in the park,' Connor murmured. 'What's with the parks?'

'I don't know,' Kit said with a frown because she'd forgotten something. *Parks, parks, parks*. 'Oh! Parks. After we first ID'd Dr Reeves as the anonymous caller, I wanted to check the park maintenance schedules. I wondered how the killer managed to bury someone in a public park without getting caught. I thought maybe he picked places where the ground was already dug up – you know, for planting or maintenance, especially with the disappearances occurring in the early fall and late winter. That's planting season.'

'That is very possible,' Connor said, sounding a bit impressed. 'Who wants the parks?'

'I'll take it,' Kit said.

Connor nodded. 'But back to your shrink. We only have his word that the Beckham kid saw a graying man with glasses in a black Mercedes.'

'I'm going to Nathan Beckham's school this morning,' Kit said. 'I'll ask his guidance counselor to sit in.' Because the thought of Nathan harming himself had kept her awake last night. If his counselor saw what Dr Reeves had seen, maybe Nathan could get some help. 'He's a minor and should have a parent present, but Reeves didn't think he'd talk if his mother was around. I want to give him a chance to open up first before we bring in the mother.'

'Poor kid,' Howard murmured. 'Taking care of his mom like that. What about the Epstein girl? If you're so sure that she knows something, how do we shake it loose?'

'I don't know. I was thinking of taking Dr Levinson with me next time I visit her. Tonight if he's available.'

'Or you could ask the "true helper" to talk to her,' Connor said sarcastically. 'Your shrink has a magic voice or something.'

Kit ignored his snark. 'We won't be doing that.' If Sam Reeves wanted to contact her witnesses, she couldn't stop him. But she wasn't going to solicit his assistance. She checked her list again, squinting at the note she'd scrawled on the paper's margin, trying to read her own handwriting. 'Okay, next. The kid with the metal detector. The one who found Skyler's body.'

'Convenient,' Connor said, back to being serious. 'Did you believe him?'

Kit grimaced. 'I don't know. I thought it was awfully convenient, too, but then Baz . . . Well, I got distracted at the end. I meant to follow up and ask him more questions, but I went to the ER once I'd notified the victim's parents.'

'I'll go,' Connor said, the gentleness of his tone surprising her.

'Thank you,' she murmured. 'His name is Daryl Chesney.' She forwarded the boy's address to Connor, then closed her folder. 'Anything else?'

'No,' Howard said. 'This is a good start, Kit. Should we meet back here this afternoon?'

'Four o'clock,' Kit agreed. 'Thanks.'

She walked out with Howard, leaving Connor to trail behind them.

'Sorry about Connor,' Howard murmured.

'Not your fault,' she murmured back. And it wasn't.

Connor wasn't as bad as many of the men she'd worked with over the years. She'd show him that he couldn't bait her, just like she'd shown the others.

But the man still irritated her.

Calling Sam Reeves *her* shrink. He was no such thing. And he never would be.

She'd ignore Connor's verbal jabs. He was only temporary. Just until Baz got back. And if Connor could help her find this killer faster, she'd put up with him.

She didn't have the time to worry about Connor Robinson, though. She'd made that damned appointment with Dr Scott for eight o'clock that evening, so she only had eleven and a half hours to get three days' worth of work done.

Thirteen

Clairemont, California
Tuesday, 19 April, 2.15 P.M.

'Thank you for seeing me,' Kit said to the principal of Naomi Beckham's high school. Howard had taken Jaelyn Watts's school and Connor was visiting Cecilia Sheppard's.

Principal Larkin's smile was crisp and professional. 'Of course, Detective. Please have a seat.'

Kit took the offered seat and waited for the principal to go behind the desk, but she sat in the guest chair next to Kit's.

'Now.' Larkin folded her hands atop the notebook she held. 'What can I do for you?'

'Did you hear about the serial killer who was identified ten days ago?'

Larkin shuddered. 'It's all any of us were able to think about for days. He targeted teenage girls and that's half my student population.'

The age of the girls had been included in Tamsin Kavanaugh's article. At least that had been a good revelation. Parents and educators would be more vigilant.

Except that they still thought the danger was over because Colton Driscoll was dead. The interviews that she and Howard and Connor would be doing today might tip someone off that this was no longer the case. If that happened, they'd do another press conference.

Navarro already had his script planned. Until then, they'd investigate under cover of as much secrecy as they could.

'We're not sure that we've identified all of his victims,' Kit began, 'so we've gone back through missing-person reports for young women who fit the killer's profile.' *Or killers*'. 'We want to be able to give families the closure they deserve.'

Larkin's face fell. 'Naomi Beckham,' she whispered.

Kit nodded, startled but able to hide it. 'Yes, but how did you know?'

'The teachers and I talked about it after watching the press conference and reading the paper. Naomi was a rather willful girl, and it was easy to believe at the time that she had run away. But when we heard about this Driscoll, we wondered if she'd been targeted by him.'

Kit managed to swallow her irritation. 'Why didn't you call us?'

'We don't have any proof and it was only idle speculation. There really wasn't a lot of information given at the press conference. What do you want to know about Naomi?'

'Well, I talked to her brother this morning.' It had been an emotional interview and Kit had seen exactly what Sam Reeves had. Nathan Beckham was so very fragile. She'd left him in the care of his school counselor, who'd vowed to get him the help he so desperately needed, and had made herself a note to let Reeves know. For his peace of mind.

She owed him that much.

Larkin's brows rose. 'Nathan? I wasn't informed that you'd been here.'

'Because I didn't meet him here at the school. I called the office first and they said that he wasn't here today, that his mother had called him in sick.'

Larkin exhaled carefully, but her expression showed her concern. 'His mother calls him in sick often. We've been watching Nathan for any sign that he's being neglected, but he claims to be well fed and his clothes are always clean. We've called child welfare services a few times, but the social workers never found cause to remove him from the home. The office should have told me that you called.'

'I contacted the school counselor and she met me at the Beckhams' house.' The interview process had taken three times longer than Kit had anticipated. That had delayed the other things on her to-do list, but the boy had needed care.

She'd just have to work later tonight.

Color rose on Larkin's cheekbones. 'I didn't know that, either.'

'The counselor left you a message. I heard her do it.'

Larkin rose, shuffled through the stack of pink message slips on her desk, then sighed. 'Yes, she did. I just hadn't read it yet.' She returned to her seat. 'What happened?'

'The counselor stayed with him when I was finished questioning him. She called social services and was going to try to convince the mother to get him admitted to a facility for treatment right away. The kid's depression was off the charts.' And he'd been clutching Sam Reeves's business card like it was a talisman that could ward off anything bad.

'Thank you for taking such care with him,' Larkin said, her voice thick with emotion. 'That poor boy.'

The principal should be thanking Sam Reeves, Kit thought. If Sam hadn't warned her, she might have inadvertently made things worse for Nathan.

'My parents are foster parents,' Kit said. 'I've seen a lot of children in a lot of emotional pain. I know the drill.' She shifted in her chair, meeting the principal's eyes. 'His mother was sleeping off a drunk episode this morning, but Nathan filled us in on what might be important details. First of all, he told us that there had been rumors floating around at the time of Naomi's disappearance that she'd failed to tell her friends about an upcoming audition. That this was why she'd run away. And that her friends had turned on her afterward.'

Nathan had, in fact, corroborated everything that Sam had told her last night.

Larkin sighed. 'Teenagers do that. Hear a rumor, spread it. Amplify it. Then another student's life is upended and they're suddenly a pariah. Canceled, as they say. That happened to Naomi.'

'Do you know what the audition was for?'

'I don't. I asked at the time because she'd gone missing and her parents were frantic. But the kids closed ranks. Nobody talked. Of course, they made it seem like they were confused and didn't know.' She lifted a shoulder helplessly. 'Teenagers.'

'I get it.' Kit had been a champion deflector back then, able to bat her eyes innocently with the best of them. Only Harlan and Betsy had seen through her charade. 'We're trying to establish this killer's MO. How did he target his victims? How did he communicate with them? We have reason to believe that Naomi went willingly the night she disappeared.'

Larkin's eyes widened. 'You think it was someone from the school? From the drama department?'

Kit might have, had it not been for the fact that every known victim had come from a different school. It still wasn't outside the realm of possibility. 'I didn't say that. What I am saying is that she might have been lured by the promise of this audition.'

'Because the other victims were also into theater?'

Kit nodded. The damn reporter had shared that little fact as well. 'Yes, ma'am. Are any of the students who got Naomi canceled still attending the school?'

'Yes. Naomi disappeared in February of her freshman year. Her classmates are seniors now.' Larkin closed her eyes. 'Naomi should be graduating next month.'

Kit thought the same about Wren every time she saw a high school graduation in the paper or on TV. 'Can you call these seniors into your office? I'd like to ask them what they remember.'

'One at a time or all at once?'

'One at a time, please.'

'We'll start with her best friend, Madison.' Returning to her desk, Larkin called the student to the front office.

Ten minutes later, a perky brunette wearing an outfit that cost more than Kit's whole wardrobe knocked on the door. 'Mrs Larkin? I was told to—' She stopped when she saw Kit. 'What's wrong?' she asked suspiciously.

'This is Detective McKittrick. She's got some questions for you about Naomi Beckham.'

'Like what?'

Larkin pointed to the chair next to Kit. 'Have a seat, Madison.

You're in no trouble. The police have reopened the case of Naomi's disappearance.'

Madison's eyes were bright blue – probably colored contacts – and were extremely wary as she sat. 'Okay.'

Kit had known girls like her when she was younger. Madison gave off a *Mean Girls* vibe. Definitely a queen bee.

Pasting on a tentative smile, Kit hunched her shoulders a little and the girl took the bait, both her smile and her gaze sharpening. Sensing weakness. Blood in the water.

All the better to lower Madison's guard.

'Madison, you were Naomi's best friend back then?'

Madison's chin lifted. 'Not really. She was kind of a wannabe, if I'm being honest. We let her hang out with us because we felt sorry for her.'

'But you left such a lovely message on her Facebook page when she disappeared,' Kit said, feigning confusion. 'You said that you'd love her forever. You begged her to come home.'

Madison shrugged. 'Her mother was hanging around the school all the time, crying, asking us if we'd seen her. It got old. If Naomi had just come home, her mother would have stopped. But now the woman's a drunk. My mom knows her. Mrs Beckham used to be on the flower show committee at the country club, but she's been too drunk to do anything for years. My mother's had to pick up the slack. She's the chair now.'

If there had been any compassion in Madison's voice, Kit might have rethought her original impression, but there was none. Just derision. Which she'd likely heard and learned from her mother, the flower show committee chair.

Rich people could be so very irritating.

'We heard that Naomi did you all dirty before she disappeared,' Kit said, still pretending to be tentative.

'Oh, she did,' Madison said with a haughty nod. 'Selfish bitch.'

Kit glanced at Mrs Larkin, who appeared to be doing her best not to speak. She didn't look happy with Madison.

Kit leaned in a little, lowering her voice to a conspiratorial whisper. 'What did she do?'

'Kept an audition all to herself,' Madison spat. 'That is simply not done. Not if you want to stay on the right side of us.'

'Us?' Kit asked.

Madison rolled her eyes. 'Our group. The drama kids. When she ran away, we figured good riddance. We didn't need a backstabber like her hanging around.'

Kit nodded. 'I can see how that would make you angry with her. Do you remember what the audition was for? Was it a play or a movie maybe?'

Madison shook her head. 'It was for a scholarship.'

Kit barely managed to keep her eyes from widening. Partly because it was unexpected, and partly because she didn't think a girl with Madison's apparent wealth would be that interested in – or eligible for – a scholarship. Maybe Madison's family wasn't as wealthy as they appeared. 'A scholarship to what?'

'The Orion School for the Performing Arts.'

Kit glanced at Larkin because the older woman had sucked in an audible breath. 'The private high school downtown?'

'A very *exclusive* drama school downtown,' Larkin said. 'Very expensive. They accept less than five percent of applicants.'

'More like less than one percent,' Madison corrected bitterly. 'It's nearly impossible to get an audition with their intake committee. They had an opening back then and Naomi heard about it. She should have told us. At least me. But she kept it a secret. None of us got to try out.' She scoffed. 'Like Naomi would have gotten the spot anyway. She wasn't that good.'

'How did you find out about the audition?' Kit asked, because this could be the break they'd been waiting for.

'I saw the form in her backpack.' Madison shrugged. 'I needed her lipstick, so I went through her stuff.'

'Did she know you'd seen it?'

'Yeah, because I was mad. When I yelled at her, she told me that I'd had my chance with *Avondale*. That this was her chance.' Madison sat up straighter. 'I . . . slapped her. I'm not proud of that. But I was angry.'

'What's this about *Avondale*?' Larkin asked.

Nathan had mentioned the *Avondale* audition that morning, but Kit waited to see what Madison would say.

'There was an open audition for *Avondale* three years ago. It was in the fall. Naomi found out about it and told us. We went up to LA – me and Naomi and a few others. We all tried out and *I* got the callback. Not Naomi.' Madison jabbed herself with her finger. '*Me*. Naomi thought she was such a big deal because she got the Ariel role in *Mermaid*.' She scowled. 'She wasn't. And she sang off-key anyway,' she added in a grumble.

Wow, Kit thought, so happy that she was no longer a teenager.

'What happened with the *Avondale* role?' Larkin asked.

Madison's scowl darkened. 'They canceled the show and the opportunity was gone. Getting into the Orion School is huge. You can write your own ticket. Their graduates get Hollywood roles and sing on Broadway. That Naomi kept it to herself was . . .' She shook her head. 'Selfish, like I said before.'

'Did you know who her contact was for the scholarship audition?' Kit asked.

'No. She wouldn't tell me.' Madison drew a breath. 'That was when I slapped her.'

Kit had a tiny bit of sympathy for Madison. That would have been a terrible betrayal. But it was only a tiny bit, because she didn't think that Madison had told anyone this back when it mattered. 'What did she do then?'

'Cried. Like she didn't deserve being slapped. I told her that I'd tell everyone what she did, and her name would be shit around school. That I'd make sure of it.'

'What happened then?'

'She left. It was only lunchtime, but she walked out.'

'And then?' Kit prompted.

'She was gone. The day we fought was Friday and by Sunday, her parents were calling every one of my friends, trying to find her.'

'Did you tell anyone about the scholarship audition at the time?'

A petulant shrug. 'I told her parents that she was talking about going out for a role. That she'd probably be back by Monday with her tail between her legs because she was a talentless hack.'

'But she didn't come back,' Kit said quietly, watching Madison for any spark of empathy, of regret.

'Nope,' Madison said lightly, like it didn't matter. Maybe it did, maybe it didn't.

I bet Sam Reeves could figure her out.

And . . . *Whoa.* Where had that come from? Not only was the thought jarring, it was also wrong. *Because* I'm *figuring her out, all right?*

'When was the audition?' Kit asked.

'The paper she had in her backpack said it would be the next day, first thing in the morning.'

But Naomi had left in the wee hours of Saturday morning, hours too early.

Then Kit remembered a detail. Nathan had said that his mother had yelled at Naomi earlier that evening, at around nine p.m. Right before he'd snuck out to play video games and smoke weed with his friend. Naomi had left the house after her mother had told her to never come back if she walked out. Where had she gone between nine p.m. Friday night and two thirty Saturday morning?

'Did Naomi come by your house that night?' Kit asked.

Madison's mouth fell open. She quickly snapped it shut, but that told Kit what she wanted to know.

'She did, didn't she?' Kit murmured. 'What happened?'

Madison's chin went up. 'She called me after dinner, crying again. Said she wanted to explain. To make it up to me. That my friendship was important to her. So I let her come over, but she wasn't sorry. So I threw her out. At that point, she was dead to me.'

Kit wanted to sigh but didn't. It likely wouldn't have made any difference if Madison had let her stay. Naomi would have still gone with whoever had offered her that audition. But what would Madison do if she knew that Naomi probably was dead?

'Mrs Larkin told you that I'm a detective. She didn't mention that I'm a homicide detective.'

Kit watched as emotions flitted across Madison's face. Shock. Horror. Denial. Then . . . understanding followed by a cool acceptance.

'What happened?' Madison asked.

'I don't exactly know yet. Did she happen to mention an older man?'

'Yeah. He was going to give her a ride to Orion the next morning. She offered to let me come, too.'

Kit's pulse sped up. 'Did she describe this man?'

'No. Said he wanted her to keep their relationship on the down-low. Because he was older and they'd get into trouble. She did say that he had a nice car. That we could ride to her audition in style.'

'Did she say what kind of car?'

'A black Mercedes. Which was not special. Half of the school's parents drive Mercedes.'

'Why didn't you go with her? That was what you wanted, wasn't it?'

'It was only to give her "moral support",' Madison said bitterly, using air quotes. 'I figured it out when she said we'd ride in style to her audition. Not ours. I wasn't going to be able to audition. There was only one slot and she said she'd already taken it. That she'd turned in her paperwork days before. What I saw in her backpack was just a copy. That's when I threw her out.'

'When was this?'

'Around midnight? I don't remember. I guess I was lucky. If I'd been with her, I'd be dead, too.'

Maybe. Especially if the killer had known that Naomi had confided in Madison.

'What was she wearing that night?'

Madison rolled her eyes. 'Her *Avondale* T-shirt, same as she wore to school. She had a dress packed to change into when she did her audition.'

'Did she mention spending time with this older man?'

'Yeah. He'd invited her to his house to practice. He had a baby grand and played for her while she sang. I would have worried that he'd have tried something. You know, in exchange for the audition. I accused her of sleeping with him. She said he'd been a gentleman, that he'd never touched her. That they'd watched *Avondale* reruns together. That he really just wanted to help her.'

She met Kit's eyes and Kit finally saw a spark of sadness. 'I guess that was a lie, huh? There was never an audition?'

Madison wasn't sad about Naomi's disappearance. She was sad that there never had been an audition. *Wow.*

'I don't know. Did she mention where he lived?'

'No.'

'Do you know where she went after you threw her out?'

'Back home, I guess.'

Kit wasn't sure about that. The cops had checked surveillance cameras back then, and that would have been noted. 'Why didn't you mention any of this when her parents started looking for her?'

A final shrug, nonchalant. 'Like I said, Naomi was dead to me. I wasn't going to help her then. Don't get me wrong. I'm not glad she's dead. But she lied to us and karma's a bitch. None of that was my fault.'

Okay. 'Did you ever see a man with gray hair and glasses hanging around Naomi?'

Madison huffed, sounding bored. 'No. But you just described half of our teachers, so . . .'

'One more question. Did you ever audition for the Orion School after that? In the fall when they had regular tryouts?'

Madison's eyes narrowed to angry slits. 'Yes,' she hissed.

That she hadn't been accepted didn't need to be said.

'Thank you for your time, Madison.'

'Can I go back to class now?' Madison asked coldly.

'You may,' Larkin said and gave her a note. 'Here's your hall pass.'

When she was gone, Larkin dropped her head into her hands. 'I need to retire.'

'Do you have a contact at Orion?' Kit asked.

Larkin looked up, her eyes glassy with unshed tears. 'No. It's private and exclusive. We're a public school. Our paths don't cross. I'm sure the school office could set up an appointment, though. I'm . . . devastated. If we'd known, we might have been able to save Naomi.' Larkin frowned. 'Wait. Gray hair and glasses? The man your boss was talking about in the press conference wasn't gray.

And didn't wear glasses.' She abruptly straightened in her chair, her eyes growing wide. 'Is there another killer?'

'Hard to say.' Kit pulled out the answer that Navarro wanted her to give. 'We think there was involvement from another individual. He's a person of interest at the moment. We're still trying to suss out all the victims. Can you think of anyone who meets that description?'

'I hate to agree with Madison, but she's right. Half of the male teachers on this campus are gray with glasses. I mean, none of them drive a Mercedes. We are public school educators, after all.'

'If you see anyone meeting that description who looks suspicious or remember anything, please give me a call.' Kit set a business card on the woman's desk, knowing that it would probably get lost in the stack of pink message slips. 'Thank you for your time, ma'am.'

Mira Mesa, California
Tuesday, 19 April, 3.30 P.M.

'Thank you,' Sam murmured as Laura Letterman parked on the curb outside the Epsteins' home.

'You don't have to keep thanking me, Sam,' Laura said, her tone firm yet somehow tentative at the same time. 'You're in trouble because you tried to do the right thing. I can help you, so I will.'

She'd rearranged her schedule to be free to drive him around town, although their time had been unproductive so far. Colton Driscoll's ex-wives numbers three and four hadn't been home when they'd knocked, probably at work. Ex-wife number two had moved to the East Coast and his first wife had died in a car accident while still in her twenties, a few years after their divorce.

Sam would have to return to the homes of ex-wives three and four later one evening. But not tonight, because he felt guilty using Laura this way. It had seemed so simple at first – he'd be giving her a chance to make amends. She'd jumped at the opportunity so hard that even Joel had been impressed. But now Sam wondered if he'd been fair.

'I appreciate it,' he said sincerely. 'But I can't expect this every day. You have a career and a life. I'll make other arrangements.'

'Or,' she said with a wince, 'and I hate that these words are even coming out of my mouth – you could trust McKittrick to do her job.'

Sam stared up at the house belonging to the man beaten by Colton Driscoll. It was a nice house with a tidy lawn and a whimsical mailbox built to look like a ship. After his medical discharge from the navy after being wounded in the line of duty, David Epstein now worked for a military contractor.

Epstein was just one of many who'd been hurt by Colton Driscoll, but at least he was still alive. There were at least eight young women who would never grow up thanks to Colton and his partner, the mysterious man with gray hair, glasses, and a black Mercedes.

Sam had considered backing away several times that day, but . . . he kept thinking about the victims. That small grave in Longview Park.

Nathan Beckham and his mother, their world torn utterly asunder.

About poor, sweet Skyler's family, who thought that he'd lured her to her death.

'She called them ripples,' Sam murmured. 'McKittrick. She called the victims' families and friends "ripples". Consequences of the murder that went on and on. But they're not ripples. They're tsunamis.'

Laura sighed. 'I don't like McKittrick on principle, but she's never made a wrong step. None of her cases get thrown out on a technicality or a bad search. She's focused, dedicated, and a straight arrow. But she does care, too. I don't think she meant that the ripples were small, gentle things. I think she meant that they spread, touching many other people. I think it's because of her own loss.'

Sam turned to look at his ex with a frown. 'What loss?'

Laura's eyes widened. 'You don't know? I thought you researched her.'

'I did. I read about the cases she's closed and watched a video interview. Why? What am I missing?'

'Oh. Well. You haven't watched the right interviews. You knew she grew up in foster care?'

'Yes. She was adopted by the McKittricks.'

'Before that, her foster sister was murdered. They were fifteen.'

Sam stared in horror. 'Oh my God.'

Are you stupid or just unfeeling? Never had he wished words back with such intensity.

'Yeah. From what I heard, it was awful. She and her foster father followed up leads for years. That's how she met Baz Constantine. He was the lead detective on her sister's case. I don't think Constantine got over it, either. He helped her and Harlan McKittrick run down leads until the leads dried up. From what I heard, Kit practically lived in the precinct as a teen. Now understand, McKittrick and I are not besties, so all this came from the rumor mill, and the one interview where this topic was brought up, she walked out. But that's why she became a cop – again, rumor mill. But it tracks. She's a machine. Works all the time. Takes on other people's cold cases on her own time. Closes them, too.'

'You admire her.'

'I do, as dirty as that makes me feel. She's not rude, either. In court, I mean. A lot of the cops get vindictive and foul-mouthed to defense attorneys, blaming us for freeing the criminals they arrest, but I've never heard of McKittrick doing that. But she's not soft. She *will* put you down like a rabid dog if she thinks you had anything to do with these murders. Joel knows that, too. That's why he didn't want you to leave yourself vulnerable.'

'I said something terrible to her last night,' Sam murmured.

'You don't say terrible things to people, Sam. Not even when they deserve them.'

Like me, went unsaid. Sam had never yelled or cursed at her when he'd discovered her in bed with Joel. He'd simply turned and walked away.

'I accused her of being unfeeling.'

Laura winced. 'She's heard worse, I'm sure.'

But not from me. Guilt lodged in his throat, making him swallow hard.

'I'll have to fix that later. Let's go talk to the Epsteins.' Because his life was still on the line, regardless of what a good person McKittrick was.

'Okay,' Laura said quietly.

They walked to the Epsteins' front door in silence, Sam trying to get control of his racing heart. He'd apologize to McKittrick later. That was all he could do. Now he had to concentrate.

He'd rehearsed what he planned to say, how he'd explain his interest in Colton Driscoll, but his words disappeared like mist in the sun when the door opened. A teenage girl stood there, her face so pale that Sam worried she'd faint.

'Are you all right?' Sam asked.

The girl gulped audibly. 'Yes. I'm fine. Who are you?'

'My name is Sam Reeves. I'm investigating Colton Driscoll. I was hoping to talk to your father.'

'He isn't here. He's still at work.' She went even paler. 'I wasn't supposed to tell you that.'

Sam smiled, hoping to put her at ease. She clutched the door so hard that her knuckles were white. 'It's okay. I'm only here to ask questions. What about your mom? Is she home?'

The girl hesitated. 'Yeah. Mom!' she called over her shoulder. 'More cops.'

'I'm not a cop,' Sam hastened to say. 'Just a psychologist.'

The girl blinked. 'Not a cop?'

And she relaxed. Visibly. Laura had noticed as well, her expression going cautiously curious.

'Not a cop,' Sam confirmed.

'What about her?'

'I'm a defense attorney,' Laura said. She gave the girl a card.

'Huh.' The girl looked up. 'You can have anything printed on a card, though.'

Laura's lips twitched. 'You can, but I didn't. You can google me.'

'Maureen?' An older woman came to the door, holding a toddler. Gemma Epstein, David's wife. She blinked when she saw Sam and Laura. 'You're not McKittrick.'

That McKittrick had already been here was no surprise.

'No, ma'am,' Sam said respectfully.

'He's a shrink named Reeves and she's a lawyer named Letterman,' Maureen supplied.

Sam had to keep himself from wincing at the disparaging look that crossed the teenager's face when she said *shrink*. 'Mrs Epstein, do you have a few minutes to answer some questions about Colton Driscoll?'

Gemma's eyes narrowed. 'Why?'

Because I'm researching serial killers. That was what he'd planned to say. But he didn't. 'He hurt people I care about.'

This was true. Colton hadn't killed Skyler, but his partner had.

Sam had never met Jaelyn Watts, Cecilia Sheppard, or Naomi Beckham. But he still cared about them.

Gemma glanced at her daughter, who was looking at her phone.

'She's really a lawyer,' Maureen said, showing her mother the screen. 'Totally legit.'

'Then I guess it's okay.' Gemma opened the door. 'Please come in.' She led them to the living room. 'Pardon the mess. Toddlers.'

Sam sat next to Laura on the sofa and Gemma held the child out to Maureen. 'Take her in the kitchen, please.'

'No, Mom,' Maureen said. She took the baby and sat in one of the chairs. 'I'm not leaving you alone with them.'

Her mother sighed, exasperated. 'You said she was legit.'

'She is, but I'm still not leaving.'

Gemma sat down, shaking her head. 'Then let's make this quick. She's going to need a bottle soon. What do you want to know about Driscoll and why? Who did he hurt that you care about?'

'Did you hear about the young woman who was killed this weekend?' Sam asked.

Both Epsteins nodded warily. 'And?' Maureen asked, a little too belligerently. She'd gone pale again. 'It wasn't Driscoll. He's dead.'

'The police think that he had a partner,' Laura said. 'Or an accomplice.'

Maureen's mouth fell open and she looked sick. Her mother swooped in to grab the baby before Maureen dropped her. 'Mo? What's wrong?'

Maureen closed her eyes and covered her mouth with her hands. 'Oh my God,' she whispered. 'Oh my God.'

Sam slid from the sofa, dropping to one knee next to her. 'Head between your knees, Maureen,' he said soothingly, placing a hand on her back to urge her forward. 'Breathe with me. In and out.'

He'd had to do this several times in sessions when clients became overwhelmed. He gave Gemma a questioning look, but she was staring at her daughter in horror, clutching the baby so hard that the child squirmed.

Laura came to the rescue, taking the child and settling her in a playpen before returning to the sofa. 'What can I do?' she asked helplessly.

'That was good,' Sam said, using his calmest voice. 'Maureen's going to be fine. She just needs to breathe.'

'My fault,' Maureen whispered. 'All my fault.'

'Just breathe,' Sam said, waiting until the girl lifted her tear-streaked face.

'I thought it was over because he was dead.'

Laura placed a box of tissues on the arm of the chair where Maureen sat, and Sam gave her a grateful smile before turning back to the teenager.

'Maureen,' he murmured. 'If you know something, you need to tell someone.'

'McKittrick will arrest me,' she whispered.

Her mother gasped. 'What?'

Sam's mind raced as he wondered what she knew. 'Tell us and we'll figure it out together, okay?'

She nodded, new tears pooling in her eyes. 'I'm sorry, Mom.'

Gemma moved to sit on the arm of Maureen's chair, her arm going around her daughter's shoulders protectively. 'Hold on, Mo. You need to wait until we get you a lawyer.'

'I'm a lawyer,' Laura said. 'If she needs one, I'll act on her behalf.'

Gemma looked Laura up and down, no doubt noting her expensive suit and designer shoes. 'We can't afford you. My husband was out of work after Driscoll beat him up. We're barely making ends meet.'

'Pro bono,' Laura said quietly. 'Sam's my friend and I want to help him. If your daughter knows something that could help him, I'll help her.'

Sam's throat tightened with emotion. 'Thank you.'

Laura's smile was sad. 'Like you said this morning, I owe you. Tell us what you did, Maureen. And what you know.'

Maureen was looking between him and Laura, then her mother, who nodded.

'You've been troubled by something for weeks, honey. I thought it was just what happened to Dad. Tell them, and we can get past this.'

'I was so mad at him. Driscoll. He hurt my dad. My dad is a good person and that man . . . he hurt him. I wanted him to go to jail, but they gave him probation and sent him to a shrink.'

Sam managed not to react to that. He'd been appalled as well at the slap on Colton's wrist. He could only imagine how furious this girl must have been.

'What did you do?' he asked gently.

'I wanted to catch him doing something. Something the cops would actually put him away for.' She looked down at the tissues in her hand. 'So I put cameras in his house.'

Gemma gasped once again. 'Maureen!'

Cameras. In Colton's house. Sam had to remember to breathe. This could be huge. 'What did you see, honey?'

'A man in black. He wore a mask. It was one of those ones that goes over the head with only space for the eyes, so I didn't see his face.'

'A balaclava,' Laura supplied.

Maureen shrugged. 'I guess. I put four cameras in Driscoll's living room. One pointed at the wall with the door to the garage and one pointed at the kitchen. The other two were on the other two walls, so I got a view of everything going on in the living room. The man dragged Driscoll into his house and made him show him his safe.'

The partner. Of course, they still couldn't ID his face, but it was more than he'd had. More than McKittrick had, too, because Maureen hadn't told her about this.

'What did he say to Driscoll?' Sam asked.

'I don't know. It was an old security system with no audio. I bought it off a kid at school. The man pointed a gun at Driscoll's head and Driscoll opened his safe.'

Sam hadn't heard that Colton had a safe. But it wasn't like McKittrick had shared much with him, after all. 'What was in the safe?'

'Not exactly sure. They looked like external hard drives. Maybe ten of them? The block ones that hold, like, a terabyte. Then the man made Driscoll go past the kitchen, to the back of his house. I think it was to his bedroom, because a few minutes later they came back and Driscoll had changed his clothes. He'd been wearing all black, but he'd changed into a jacket and pants.'

'That's odd,' Sam said. 'Then what?'

'He kept holding the gun at Driscoll's head and made him take some pills. Then waited until he went to sleep. He cleaned out all of Driscoll's DVDs and took his DVD player and laptop and put them all in a box. Took it to the garage. Took his safe, too. It wasn't bolted down. I think that surprised him because he gave it a yank, then stumbled back when the safe just . . . came at him. He took the safe to the garage, then emptied his kitchen drawers. He took a bag into the bedroom and didn't have the bag when he came out.' She grimaced. 'I didn't put cameras in his bedroom, so I don't know what he did with the bag. Sorry.'

'That's fine,' Sam said, still on one knee in front of her. He was afraid to move, afraid she'd stop talking. 'What happened then?'

'He, um . . .' She blew out a breath. 'He had a rope. Two ropes, actually. He tied one into a noose and brought a stepladder in from the garage. He set it by the front door and climbed it. The angle wasn't right to show what he was doing, but the noose dropped down for a minute before he pulled it up and out of the picture. Then he made kind of a sling with the second rope. Used it to pull Driscoll up higher. I couldn't see Driscoll's face anymore, but his legs . . .' She closed her eyes. 'They . . . dangled. Swinging.'

Driscoll's killer had used the second rope to lift him into the noose because Driscoll was too sedated at that point to climb up himself. McKittrick and Constantine had asked about sleeping pills the night they'd talked in Sam's RAV4. This was why.

'Oh, baby,' Gemma breathed, pulling her daughter closer.

At least Maureen hadn't seen Driscoll's face as he'd died. Small comfort.

'Then what, Maureen?' Laura asked. 'Just finish it.'

'He took the second rope away and then he changed Driscoll's shoes. Then took the second rope and the stepladder into the garage. He came back in and did a final sweep, I guess.' Maureen shuddered. 'That's when he found my cameras.'

Her mother made a sound between a gasp and a moan. 'Mo.'

Maureen was so pale that Sam almost urged her to put her head between her knees again, but the teenager squared her shoulders. 'He pulled the first camera from in between the books on the shelf where I'd hidden it and he looked straight into the camera. Then he found the others and the videos all ended. I thought maybe the man was someone else Driscoll had hurt.' She looked away, ashamed. 'I was kind of glad he was dead. Then I found out that he'd killed all those girls, and I thought the man might be one of their parents. But when the detectives came, I was afraid to tell. I'm sorry.'

'Oh, honey,' Sam murmured. 'Anyone would be afraid.'

'I'm going to jail, aren't I?' Maureen was crying again. 'I broke into his house.'

'You're not going to jail,' Laura said firmly. 'The worst that will happen is community service and I can get that waived, too. If you tell the detective this, you'll be a hero.'

'But if the man finds out it was Maureen's camera?' Gemma whispered. 'My daughter will be in danger.'

'Safe house,' Laura said simply.

'We have to hide?' Maureen cried. 'I'm sorry, Mom. I'm so sorry.'

'Could he trace the cameras to this house?' Sam asked, trying to keep his tone logical.

Maureen shrugged miserably. 'I don't know. I used a proxy server, so probably not, but I hooked it into our Wi-Fi, so I don't know.'

'Well,' Laura said. 'The first thing you're going to do is tell McKittrick. I will not leave you. If it looks like she's going to do anything not in your best interest, I'll shut her down.'

Maureen lifted her chin. 'Promise?'

Laura smiled. 'I promise.'

'Then okay. Should we wait for Dad?'

'I think so.' Gemma startled when the baby began to cry. 'I need to feed her.'

'We'll wait here,' Laura said, turning to Maureen when her mother hurried to the kitchen. 'I'll record your interview with McKittrick for your protection. But let's go over what you saw again. I don't want you to miss anything.'

Maureen frowned. 'I have the video, if that's easier.'

Sam's eyes widened. 'What?'

'The cameras,' Maureen said slowly, like she was talking to a child. 'I have the video.'

Sam pushed to his feet. 'I'll call McKittrick.'

Fourteen

SDPD, San Diego, California
Tuesday, 19 April, 4.00 P.M.

Howard Cook sat across the meeting room table from Kit and handed her a sandwich from the deli down the street. 'They had a twofer sale.'

Connor Robinson rolled his eyes. 'They did not.'

Howard threw his partner an irritated look. 'Hush, Connor. Everyone knows she doesn't stop for lunch.'

Kit hadn't, but it kind of bothered her that her colleagues talked about it. Cops were the worst gossips. 'Thank you. I grabbed a granola bar, but that was a while ago.' She plucked the receipt from the bag where it was stapled. 'I'll pay you back.'

Howard shrugged. 'Fine. I don't know about you guys, but my day was mostly unproductive. I went through the runaway lists up to twenty years ago and separated out the petite blondes between fourteen and eighteen, but not a single report mentioned drama club. I went forward a year and found that Ricki Emerson's report listed drama club, but we already knew about her.'

'Ricki Emerson's body was discovered eight years ago, right?' Connor asked.

Kit nodded. 'Yes, but she'd gone missing two years before that. Baz and I reinterviewed the family, but no one knew anything about any auditions back then. She might have kept it secret, though, like Naomi Beckham did.'

She told them about her visit with Naomi's brother and the follow-up with the principal of her high school.

Connor was shaking his head by the time she finished. 'Teenage girls are such bitches. I do not miss that about high school.'

'I think we remember the bitches,' Howard said quietly. 'There were plenty of quiet, nice girls in school. But the bitches tended to be the loudest. And most popular.'

'I was popular,' Connor said, and it surprisingly didn't sound like he was bragging. Just stating a fact. 'Was homecoming king, even. I kept checking my back at the dance to make sure the queen hadn't stuck a shiv in my back. She was brutal.'

Kit had hated the popular crowd in high school. Of course, she'd been focused on finding Wren's murderer and hadn't joined in on any school activities. Harlan and Betsy never pushed her to, either. One more reason she loved them.

'Madison was like that,' she said. 'Very arrogant. I'd be totally shocked if she wasn't prom queen. But she did give us something important. The Orion School.'

Connor whistled quietly. 'I've heard of that place. Posh as fuck. One of my girlfriends went there.'

Kit blinked at him. 'Really? How did you meet her?'

'She lived in our neighborhood when we were in high school. Met her at the country club when I went with my folks. I was captain of the football team and she liked muscles.' He shrugged. 'She was shallow. But so was I, so we were good for about two months. Then we graduated. I went on to UCSD and she went to Juilliard. She's on Broadway now. I see her from time to time, though, when she's home visiting her family.' He smirked. 'She still likes muscles.'

Kit almost laughed but swallowed it so that she didn't encourage him. He was impossible. But maybe useful. 'Do you think she'd have any insider info on Orion? Because I called them on my way from seeing Principal Larkin and asked to speak to the director. I couldn't get past the front desk. The director is supposed to call me back tomorrow or when they "get a free moment". I'm going to have to go in person and flash my badge. It would be great if we could get some background information about the staff, because I'm betting they put me off today so that they can call in the lawyers before they call me back.'

'I'll call her when we're done. She's in a show now, so I might not talk to her until tomorrow.'

'Thank you, Connor,' Kit said sincerely.

Connor looked pleased. 'You're welcome. Do you think the gray-haired man actually worked at the Orion School?'

Kit had spent most of her drive back to the station considering this very question. 'I don't know. It's certainly possible.'

'I'll ask my friend about scholarships,' Connor said. 'Who got them, who gave them, and what the decision process was. If she can give us the name of a scholarship recipient, we can ask questions before going to the hallowed halls of Orion. I don't think Orion would be too receptive to a fishing expedition, but if you already knew exactly what to ask, it'd go better.'

Kit had been thinking the same thing. 'Excellent.' She noted it in her file. 'What else?'

'I found Skyler Carville's car,' Howard said. 'It had been towed to a city impound lot. She'd parked on the street on a yellow curb.'

The yellow curbs were commercial loading zones. Parking was prohibited in the daytime but allowed at night.

'She only meant to meet for drinks,' she murmured. 'I'm sure she figured she'd be back well before sunrise. Where's her car now?'

'Had CSU pick it up,' Howard said. 'They're going over it. I doubt they'll find anything, but we could be surprised. My visit to Jaelyn's school yielded nothing. No one knew about any auditions nor had they seen a gray-haired man with glasses unless you want to count half the male teachers on the faculty.'

'That's what Principal Larkin said,' Kit said.

'About a quarter of the male teachers at Cecilia's school,' Connor added. 'But no one caught anyone's notice. Like none of the gray-haired men were creepy or hovering or anything. Nobody knew anything about any audition, secret or otherwise. Cecilia had played lacrosse the year before but was also in the drama club. She'd starred in *Oklahoma* in her freshman year.'

'Like Naomi played the lead in *The Little Mermaid*,' Kit said.

'Oh!' Howard looked excited. 'Jaelyn played Golde in *Fiddler* in her freshman year.'

Kit shared his excitement. 'Maybe that's how he found victims. He saw them onstage. We'll have to explore who attended their plays.'

Connor held up a hand. 'Before you go that direction, I have more. I talked to Cecilia's lacrosse coach, too. They'd been looking at her getting an athletic scholarship, but she'd gotten hurt over the summer. ACL. It was a bad injury.'

Kit winced. 'That could've dashed any athletic scholarship dreams.'

Connor nodded. 'Her coach said she wasn't devastated, though. That her parents were the ones pushing the athletic scholarships. Cecilia wanted to go to acting school.'

Kit's breath caught. 'Did the coach mention Orion School?'

'No, but she did say that Cecilia was looking at her ACL as a gift.'

'Did her parents know this?' Howard asked.

'Her coach didn't think so. She said that she'd offered to talk to Cecilia's parents with her, but then Cecilia disappeared and her coach didn't want to hurt the folks any more than they already were.'

'So she might have been lured by an acting scholarship the same way that Naomi was,' Kit said thoughtfully. 'Did Jaelyn's school mention anything about Orion School?'

Howard shook his head. 'Maybe we should pay another visit to her family. Ask any of them if she mentioned an acting scholarship.'

'He might have used a different lure,' Connor said.

'Quite possible,' Kit agreed. 'Howard, please contact the Wattses again and ask them. But be gentle with them. They fell apart when they identified Jaelyn's body at the morgue. And then Tamsin Kavanaugh swooped in on them like they were prey, just so she could get a story.'

Howard winced. 'They didn't deserve that.'

Kit sighed. 'No, they didn't.' She turned to Connor. 'Did you find Daryl Chesney? The metal detector kid?'

'Yes and no.' Connor took out his phone and brought up a photo. 'Is this the kid you talked to?'

Kit studied the photo. 'That's him, but he's a little younger and neater in this picture. His hair was longer when I saw him and his eyes were slyer. This kid in the picture looks happy, but on Sunday he looked more . . . opportunistic, I think. I figured he'd try selling his story to the paper. I'm surprised Kavanaugh hasn't interviewed him already. What did he say?'

'I didn't talk to him. I went to the address you gave me, but Daryl Chesney's gone missing.'

Kit gaped at him. 'You should have led with this,' she snapped.

Connor looked genuinely taken aback. 'You were going down your list in order. You like things in order. I figured we'd get to it.'

Kit felt bad. 'I apologize. I shouldn't have bitten your head off. What do you mean, he's missing? Since when and from where?'

'He didn't come home Sunday night. His mother's been worried sick and she filed a missing-person report yesterday evening. She thought she had to wait twenty-four hours.'

'So, Daryl Chesney leads us very conveniently to a body and then he disappears?' She didn't like the sound of that. 'Does he disappear often?'

'Not according to the mother. But she also said he'd gotten mixed up with some kids that hang on the corner. I talked to them, too, and they claim that he'd bragged about earning some cash but wouldn't tell them from where. He didn't want to have to share it with them.'

Kit rubbed her temples. 'Shit.'

'He's probably dead,' Howard murmured.

Connor nodded. 'I mean, I hope we're wrong, but I don't think we are.'

'Let's check his records to see who contacted him,' Howard said.

'Cheap pay-as-you-go cell,' Connor said. 'I asked. His friends were cagey about their phones. Said none of them had nice phones, that they all used cheap ones from Walmart. Nobody could afford a plan. I think they were dealing and using burners. I got surveillance video from the grocery store across the street and it showed a mud-splattered black Mercedes slowing down to talk to the boys Sunday morning. Daryl was with them.'

Kit's smile was so big that her cheeks hurt. 'Bingo. Plates?'

Connor made a face. 'Covered in mud. Couldn't see the numbers.'

Her smile dimmed but didn't disappear. 'But we know that he's still driving a Mercedes.'

Connor nodded. 'And that he's bold AF. It was a low-risk way to hide his plates. If he got stopped by a cop, he'd just promise to wash his plates and no one would be the wiser.'

'This is coming together,' she said with satisfaction.

'We still need to canvass the Little Italy bars to find out where Skyler Carville was taken from,' Howard said, sliding pieces of paper to her and Connor. 'This is the list of bars in the vicinity of where her car was towed from. I split the places into three groups of five bars. We can all take a group and message back if we find one that remembers Skyler.'

'Good work,' Kit told him. 'I'll take the first five—' She was cut off by her cell phone's ringtone and her heart stuttered before beginning to pound.

Sam Reeves was calling.

'McKittrick,' she answered, not putting it on speaker.

'Detective. I've got some information that you need to see.'

He'd said that he was never telling her anything again. She wondered what had changed. 'What is it?' she asked, conscious of Howard and Connor watching her.

'I've been talking to Maureen Epstein.'

Anger pulsed up from Kit's gut. '*What?*'

'She talked to me. She has video. Of Colton.' He sighed. 'Getting killed.'

Kit was stunned into speechlessness for a few seconds. 'Did you say that Maureen Epstein has video of Colton Driscoll's murder?'

Both men stared at her, openmouthed.

'I did,' Sam confirmed. 'She's scared, Detective. And she has legal representation. Laura Letterman is with me.'

'I see.' Although she didn't see at all. How the hell did Maureen Epstein get video of Driscoll's murder? And why was Letterman with him? Maybe they were reconnecting, although Kit had given

Sam more credit than to crawl back to the woman who'd cheated on him. But that didn't matter. What did matter was that Maureen had talked to him. Maybe he did have a miracle voice. 'I'll be there as soon as I can.' She ended the call.

'Maureen Epstein has video of Driscoll's murder?' Connor asked, still looking as stunned as she felt.

'I guess so. You guys get started on canvassing these bars for Skyler. I'll check out my five bars when I'm done with the Epsteins.' She had hours before her appointment with Dr Scott. 'But I'm telling Navarro first. I'll be in touch.'

Gathering her papers, she rushed from the room.

'Kit,' Howard called and she paused, looking over her shoulder. 'Your sandwich.'

With a grateful smile she grabbed it and practically ran to Navarro's office.

Mira Mesa, California
Tuesday, 19 April, 5.05 P.M.

Eyes wide, Kit watched Driscoll being murdered, Navarro at her side at the Epsteins' kitchen table. She hadn't quite believed Sam until she'd watched Maureen's video – four simultaneous views on the screen, one from each camera – with her own eyes.

When the screen went dark, Kit looked down the table where Maureen huddled, her eyes swollen and red. Her parents stood on either side of her like an honor guard.

Sam Reeves and his attorney sat beside her. Letterman had informed them that she was representing the girl.

For trespassing. As if that paltry offense even registered on the radar compared to what the girl had captured. The illegal recording was a bigger deal, but still not even close to what they'd gained.

She glanced at Navarro, who tilted his head as if to say *Go for it*.

'Let's get the big issue dealt with. Maureen, you know what you did was wrong, right? Breaking and entering and illegal recording are serious.'

Maureen swallowed. 'Yes,' she whispered.

Laura Letterman started to open her mouth, but Kit stayed her with a raised hand. 'Please, Ms Letterman. Let me finish before you jump in. So, Maureen, I have to write this up, but you have a good lawyer and I'll make sure the prosecutor has all the facts. It will be all right.'

'What does that mean?' David asked stiffly, his hand gripping his daughter's shoulder.

'It means,' Kit said as kindly as she could, 'worst case, she'll have a misdemeanor on her record, but she's a juvenile and we can have it sealed. Best case, charges will be dropped because of her contribution to this case. I think we can work with Ms Letterman to keep this from having any long-term detrimental effects on Maureen's life.'

Kit saw Sam Reeves's shoulders lower a few inches. He'd been worried about what she'd do. He noticed her attention and gave her a slight nod. *Thank you,* he mouthed.

Maureen's parents also relaxed, David's grip on Maureen's shoulder loosening to a gentle squeeze.

'Thank God,' Gemma whispered.

'We'll push for a total drop of charges,' Letterman said briskly.

'I figured you would, Ms Letterman. That'll be up to whichever prosecutor you draw. But I'll put in a good word for Maureen.' Kit lifted her brows, keeping her tone mild as she addressed the still-pale teenager. 'I would have put in an even better word if you'd told me the first three times I asked you, but I understand why you were scared.'

Maureen nodded timidly. 'I'm sorry.'

'I know,' Kit said. 'How did you even get into Driscoll's house? Didn't he have an alarm?'

'If he did, it didn't go off. I waited for him to go to work, then I went in through his garage door. It was a flimsy lock. There's a YouTube video on how to pick them.'

Of course there is. 'Just . . . stay out of people's houses, okay? And no more recording people without consent.'

'I won't,' Maureen promised.

'Thank you. Now, to the video. It answers a lot of questions.' It also confirmed that the Top-Siders on Driscoll's feet had been an attempt to connect him to Jaelyn Watts's grave near the pond in the park. How Driscoll's killer had known about the footprint was currently unknown. She'd put it on her follow-up list, because it was a critical point. Tamsin Kavanaugh hadn't included that detail in her article.

Kit would also bet that the bag the masked man carried had held brand-new handcuffs and a can of sparkly pink spray paint. It was all planted.

So what had Driscoll actually done?

He'd known about at least three of the victims – Jaelyn's grave in Longview Park, Cecilia's lacrosse, and Naomi's love of *Avondale* – but had he been involved in killing them?

And what was on those hard drives his killer had taken from his safe?

'But it also threatens my daughter,' David said. 'If Driscoll's partner finds out that she made the video, her life is in danger.'

'We can ask for a safe house,' Kit said, 'but it might be better if you all went out of town for a little while. Maybe visit out-of-state family?'

Maureen looked at Laura Letterman. 'What do you think I should do?'

'I think going away sounds like a good idea,' the lawyer said. 'But I'll make the arrangements and get you a rental car. I'll pick you up and take you to the rental car. Pay for gas with cash. That way no one can track you.' She smiled at Maureen. 'Just in case.'

'We'll go,' David said. 'But for how long? I can't take off work forever and Maureen has school.'

'Get your wife and daughter settled wherever you decide to go,' Laura said. 'Then you can come back. I can find a place for you to stay until it's safe for Maureen to return. Tell her teachers that you have a family emergency and have to go away. Ask if Maureen can do her subjects virtually. If you run into issues, let me know. Plan on leaving tonight.'

Kit chanced a glance at Sam, expecting him to be focused on his ex-girlfriend. His lawyer. Whatever. But he was watching Kit, his expression kind of sad, and she spared a second to wonder why before turning back to Maureen.

'Do you have any copies of the video?' Kit asked.

The girl shook her head. 'I don't. That's the original, on my laptop. Do you need to take it?'

'Afraid so. At least until we download the video onto our server. We'll scrub it from your laptop afterward.'

That Maureen had obtained the evidence illegally wasn't likely to be a problem. There was precedent for police to use evidence obtained by private citizens, even if illegally obtained. The citizen had to face the consequences for however they'd gotten the evidence, but Maureen would do that.

Kit would keep her promise to do everything possible to keep this from ruining Maureen's life, because she understood the need to do something to avenge her family. Luckily Harlan had kept Kit from doing anything stupid back then.

Navarro touched Kit's shoulder. 'I'll be going. I can take the laptop with me.'

'Thank you. I'll ask CSU to go over that beam in Driscoll's house again. Hopefully the rope he used to haul Driscoll up left some trace evidence. See you back at the office.'

Navarro pointedly looked at his watch. 'Remember.'

She wanted to forget that she had an appointment with Dr Scott tonight, but Navarro would follow through on his threat and make her go more often.

But if this killer suspected they were getting closer, would he kill another Skyler Carville to further incriminate Sam Reeves, trying to throw them off his scent? They needed to solve this case soon.

But it was just one hour out of her life, so she nodded. 'Of course.'

Navarro shifted his pointed gaze to Reeves. 'Dr Reeves, thank you for this information. Please don't do it again.'

'Of course,' Sam said mildly.

Kit didn't need to be a shrink to know that meant Sam was totally doing it again.

Scowling, Navarro left with the laptop, and Kit returned her attention to Maureen. 'So, seeing a murder is a big deal. I see bodies often and it still bothers me. Nightmares, y'know.'

Maureen nodded, her eyes haunted. 'Yeah. Me too.'

'Maybe Dr Reeves can recommend someone for you to talk to,' she suggested gently. Kit herself wasn't going to therapy voluntarily, but this girl was so young, her life touched by the ripples.

Sam looked surprised. 'Yes, of course. Ms Letterman can tell me where you'll be, and I'll find you someone. Or I can recommend a therapist who does virtual appointments. Not the same thing as in-person therapy, but it can be useful nonetheless.'

Maureen nodded. 'Okay. I just don't want anyone else to die.'

Kit's gaze flew to Sam and her mouth opened, then closed. *What did you tell her? Did you tell her that there was another killer?*

Although it really didn't matter. The fact that they were asking folks about a man with gray hair, glasses, and a black Mercedes would tip someone off sooner rather than later. Principal Larkin from Naomi's school had already figured it out.

Sam didn't look away, meeting her eyes with polite defiance.

Kit pushed away from the table. 'Okay. We won't process any paperwork on Maureen's offenses until she's safe. Then we'll talk consequences and the prosecutor can work the deal.'

Letterman nodded. 'Thank you, Detective.'

The Epsteins echoed the thanks and Kit made her way to the front door. She was almost to her car when Sam's voice stopped her.

'Detective McKittrick.'

She turned, watching him approach. The evening sun had turned the sky pink, picking up reddish highlights in his hair, surprising her. She'd thought it was nearly black.

He pushed his glasses up on his nose. 'I'm sorry.'

She tilted her head. 'For what?'

'For saying you were unfeeling. I shouldn't have said that.'

Kit shrugged, uncomfortable with the apology because she hadn't blamed him. 'But you're sticking with the stupid part?'

He huffed. 'Not that part, either. I was upset and I took it out on you.'

'I understand. I really do, more than you know.'

He swallowed and she caught herself staring at his throat. She jerked her gaze back to his face, only to be blindsided by his next words.

'I didn't know about your sister. Laura told me.'

Kit stiffened. It was one thing if she brought Wren up, and she really didn't do that very often. She had with Rita because the girl had needed to know that she wasn't alone.

Maybe Sam is trying to say the same thing.

She drew a breath. 'Not a good time in my life,' she said and hoped he'd leave it there. She was grateful when he did.

'Thank you for helping Maureen.'

'You're welcome. Please, don't do it again.'

He shrugged. 'No promises.'

Her mouth curved before she could stop it. 'Where are you going next?'

'Colton's ex-wives.'

'They wouldn't talk.'

He didn't say a word, simply lifting his brows.

Kit sighed. 'I know, Maureen didn't talk to me, either, but she talked to you.'

'Maybe you wore her down so that she was ready when I came by.'

Kit laughed quietly. 'Very gentlemanly of you. Oh, I wanted to tell you that I saw Nathan Beckham this morning. I had his school counselor with me, and she called a social worker. They're referring him for therapy. I hope it helps him.'

'Thank you. That was . . . good of you to do.'

She took a step back, mainly because she wanted to stay and talk to him some more and that wasn't okay. 'Well, thank you for calling me tonight, especially after you said you'd never tell me anything again.'

'I've become better informed. Joel and Laura both speak highly of you.'

Joel's approval didn't surprise her, but Letterman's did, and that made Kit more than a little disgruntled. She didn't want to like the woman.

The woman who'd lived with Sam Reeves for four years before cheating on him.

But that did not matter. It did not. It could not.

But she wanted it to. *It can't.* I *can't.*

'That's good to hear. I have an appointment that I need to get to, so I have to go. Have a good evening,' she said, waving over her shoulder as she turned and all but ran to her car. She had two hours before her appointment with Dr Scott, but if she'd stayed, she might have started making small talk with Sam. And that wouldn't do at all. He was technically still a suspect. And a shrink to boot.

If she ever found herself in a relationship, it would be with a man who wasn't trying to psychoanalyze her every time she opened her mouth.

She'd get some dinner and then she'd see Baz. And forget all about Sam Reeves and how nice he was. How smart. How . . . cute.

Stop it.

When she got to the end of the street, she looked in her rearview mirror. He was still standing in the Epsteins' driveway, watching as she drove away.

Chollas Creek, California
Tuesday, 19 April, 7.00 P.M.

'Thank you,' Sam said quietly as Laura pulled into a parking place in front of Colton's fourth wife's apartment building. Sam had told her to take him back to Joel's house after they'd finished at the Epsteins', but she'd shaken her head, making travel arrangements for the family on her cell phone while she drove. After she'd finished, they'd driven the rest of the way in silence, but it hadn't been awkward.

If nothing else, he and Laura could get some closure on the ending of their relationship.

'I told you that I'd stick with you,' she said. 'Today was the only day I could free up completely, so we need to make the most of it. Tomorrow I can't pick you up until the afternoon, so arrange who you want to see by priority.'

'That's not necessary, Laura. I don't want to take advantage of you.'

'Stop. First, you're worth it. Second, I want to do the right thing here. So many people I defend are guilty as sin. Don't get me wrong – I don't feel bad for defending them. It's their right under the law, but it doesn't mean that I don't like to feel like a hero every now and then.'

Sam exhaled. 'Thank you.'

She smiled wistfully. 'Third, I truly want to make amends. Thank you for giving me the chance. I don't kid myself that you're ever going to forgive me. I was an idiot and . . . Well, I lost a good thing with you. You deserve good things, Sammy.'

'Forgiveness and trust are two different things,' he murmured. Because he might be able to forgive her, but he'd never trust her again. Not with his heart anyway. Apparently, he trusted her enough to safeguard his freedom.

Laura nodded in understanding before she looked away, watching some little kids playing on a set of swings. 'You were really good with her.'

'Maureen? She was ready to talk.'

Laura's lips curved sadly. 'I meant McKittrick.'

Sam startled. 'When?'

She shrugged. 'I might have followed you when you followed her out of the Epsteins' place. I wanted to be sure she didn't try to coerce you into anything.'

'I thought you admired her.'

'Admiration and trust are two different things,' she said lightly. 'Especially when it comes to your freedom. But she did surprise the hell out of me by agreeing to hold processing of any charges against Maureen until she's no longer in danger. That could be a long time.'

Sam's heart sank, because that meant his life would be on hold for a long time, too. 'Hopefully not, especially if she's as good at her job as you and Joel seem to think.'

Her nod was brisk. 'Here's hoping. Are you ready for wife number four? She's home.' Laura pointed at an older Ford with rusted fenders. 'That's her car.'

Sam hadn't even noticed. 'Then let's go talk to her.'

When they knocked on Veronica Gadd's door, she opened it with a frown. She was very young, having married Colton when she was only eighteen – just like his other three wives. They'd been divorced for two years and married for less than one, so Veronica was barely old enough to buy alcohol. 'I'm not interested.'

'Please,' Sam said. 'I'm not selling anything. I wanted to talk to you about Colton.'

Veronica's expression shut down. 'No comment.'

Sam started to put his hand on the door, then dropped it to his side. 'I'm not a reporter or a cop. I'm a psychologist. My name is Dr Reeves. One of the victims was my friend.' Not Colton's victim, but he didn't feel bad for the obfuscation.

Veronica's shoulders sagged. 'I'm so sorry for your loss, but I was only married to Colton for a year. I don't know anything about him. Nothing that could help you, anyway.'

Sam looked over his shoulder. One of Veronica's neighbors was peeking around her slightly open door. 'May we come in, Ms Gadd? I'd really rather not have this conversation in front of your neighbors.'

Veronica scowled at the neighbor. 'Mind your own business, Gertie.' She rolled her eyes. 'That woman lives to spy. Look, my place is a mess. I wasn't ready for company.'

She was nervous about allowing him in and Sam got that. 'Could we take a walk, maybe?'

Veronica eyed Laura. 'Who's she?'

Sam glanced at Laura. 'She's my ex. But she's generously helping me out.'

He'd snagged Veronica's interest with that tidbit. 'Okay. Fine. Let me get my jacket.'

They walked with her down the apartment stairs, waiting until they were outside before Sam spoke again. 'This is Laura Letterman. She's also my attorney.'

Veronica gave Laura a curious look. 'There's a picnic area down the way. It'll be mostly empty this time of day.'

There was a picnic table near the swing set that they'd seen from the parking lot. The children were gone and it was quiet.

Veronica sat on one of the benches and Sam and Laura sat on the other side. 'Thank you,' Sam said. 'We won't take much of your time. As you know, Colton is accused of killing several young women. I was trying to be a Good Samaritan and help the police, and now I'm also a suspect.'

Veronica's eyes widened. 'How?'

'He had a partner,' Sam said bluntly. Kit would probably be angry that he'd disclosed this, but he was growing desperate, a sick urgency twisting his gut. He didn't want anyone else to die. Plus, Kit's holding back information hadn't helped her get these folks to talk. Time for a different approach. 'And that man killed my friend over the weekend. I was camping all alone.'

'No alibi,' Veronica murmured. 'He set you up to take the fall.'

'Exactly. So, I'm trying to find out who his partner might have been. I was hoping you might know someone Colton was close to. Maybe someone he spent time with.'

Veronica scoffed. 'Like Brad Pitt or Prince William?'

Sam sighed. 'So, he's been doing that for a while, huh?'

'I was so stupid. Naive. Maybe I still am, because I'm sitting here talking to you. I should go.'

Laura pulled out her phone, tapped the screen, then handed it to Veronica. 'This is an article about Dr Reeves. He is a psychologist who volunteers with homeless youth at New Horizons. He's not lying to you. He's a good man and doesn't deserve what's happening to him.'

Sam looked at Laura in surprise, but Veronica said nothing, reading the article carefully before returning Laura's phone to her outstretched hand.

'Thank you,' Veronica said to Laura. 'This does make me feel a bit better. Ask your questions, Dr Reeves. I'll answer what I'm able.'

'Did Colton have friends?'

'Not that I knew. He talked about a few of his high school buddies, but they never gave him the time of day. One of those buddies – Brian – finally called me after Colton had seen him in a bar and bragged about how he'd "bagged a pretty young thing". Brian warned me that I'd married a pathological liar, but I wasn't ready to hear it then. He's an attorney, too. Helped me get a divorce when I finally was ready to admit I'd fucked up. I've started a new life since then, and I'm getting past Colton and his mind games.'

Pretty young thing. Sam couldn't quite stifle his shudder. 'What kind of mind games?'

'Telling me that he knew a Hollywood agent who'd make me a star. That was the big one. The one that hooked me in. I was only seventeen at the time and humiliatingly gullible. He didn't start with the celebrity lies until after we were married. He was so good to me at the beginning, buying me things and taking me to dinner. Saying sweet things. I thought I'd met a Prince Charming, but he turned out to be far worse than anything I could have imagined – again, after we got married. Then he'd get so angry.'

'Did he hit you?' Laura asked softly.

Veronica nodded. 'That's why Brian helped me. He saw me in the grocery store one day and I hadn't quite been able to cover the bruise with concealer and big sunglasses. He was so sad. Because I wasn't the first wife who'd left Colton. He and his wife took me in when I finally walked away from Colton because I didn't have anywhere else to go after I'd moved in with him. They helped me go to college. I'm working on my BSN in nursing. It's taking me a while because I'm working full time, but I'm getting there. I'm just grateful I got away before Colton killed me.'

'He beat up his neighbor, too,' Sam said, and Veronica's eyes widened.

'Who?'

'David Epstein.'

Veronica's hand flew to cover her mouth. 'He was so nice to me. Is he okay?'

Sam nodded. 'He's mostly recovered now, but after meeting

him, I'm not surprised to hear that Colton hit you, too. But I promised I wouldn't take much of your time. He really had no friends? No one he worked with that he was close to?'

'No. I'm sorry, but for the year I lived with him, the only people he talked to were the guys he played video games with online.' She tilted her head. 'I was shocked to hear that he'd committed suicide. I didn't think he had it in him. He whined about getting a splinter in his pinkie finger.'

Sam wasn't going to tell her that Colton had been murdered. That would be McKittrick's job. 'Did he get splinters often?'

'Oh no. He didn't like physical labor. I was the one who had to keep up the house, mow the lawn.'

Which explained why the lawn was so overgrown. Colton had lost his full-time laborer. 'I heard that he was an IT guru a while back. I guess he was more used to working on computers.'

'Yeah, he'd talk about the time he used to work for a big company. Sometimes it was Apple and sometimes it was Microsoft. He'd say he was the one who really thought of all the technology, and the famous guys just took credit for his work and forced him out, so he started his own consulting company. He told me that he had an office in this high-rise downtown. I went to visit him once. Only once.'

'What happened?' Sam asked, although he suspected what was coming.

She laughed, but it was a bitter sound. 'I asked the front desk which office was his and the receptionist told me that he worked in the mail room. I didn't believe it, so she walked me to the mail room to show me. He turned around and saw me standing in the doorway with my mouth hanging open and he was so embarrassed.'

'How bad was it that time?' Laura asked, her normally sharp tone incredibly gentle.

'I couldn't move for hours after he was through with me. Just curled up on the floor in my own blood.' She grimaced. 'That's when I called Brian, who helped me. He and his wife came over because Colton would always leave after he hit me. I don't know where he went, but he was usually even madder when he came back. I didn't want to be there when he came back, so Brian and Beth helped me pack my things and got me out of there. I'm sure Colton told everyone that it was my fault. That I'd done him wrong. That's what he said about his other wives. He was a liar, through and through. I think he even believed the lies sometimes.'

Sam sighed. 'He might have. Did you report him to the police?'

'No. Brian and Beth wanted me to, but I just wanted to be gone. I thought about it later, but I'd just freeze up, so I put it off. And now he's dead, so it doesn't matter.' She smiled crookedly. 'Sorry. You came to ask me questions about Colton's acquaintances and I've gone off about other things.'

'It's okay,' Sam assured her. 'But I would like to ask about his computers.' He thought of the hard drives that Colton's killer had forced him to remove from his safe and wondered what he'd saved to them. 'Did he have a lot of them?'

'No. Just a laptop. But he was obsessive about it. I wasn't allowed to touch it. Not even to dust it. I did once and . . .' She touched her right eye. 'Swelled so bad that I couldn't see out of it for a week.'

Sam exhaled. 'I'm sorry you went through that.'

She shrugged. 'I know what kind of man not to fall for now. So something good came of it.'

Sam nodded, hoping that was true. He'd seen too many people – male, female, and nonbinary – who kept choosing the same kind of partners. It was a savage cycle.

'What do you mean, obsessive about his computers?' he asked.

'Oh, he was always backing his laptop up.' She rolled her eyes. 'He had this stack of hard drives and they might have been gold bars for how he guarded them.'

Yes. 'What was on them?' Sam asked, wanting to sound only interested, not desperate. He wasn't sure he'd succeeded because she grew very serious.

'I have no idea, but he had a lot of them. I only saw inside the safe once, from across the room, but it was filled up. Had to have been twenty or thirty of those drives. Maybe more. The big ones, like a deck of cards. I once asked if they were movies and he laughed and said that they were better than movies. I still don't know what he meant.'

Now all those hard drives were gone, confiscated by Colton's killer, and—

Wait. Twenty or thirty? There were only ten in the safe when Colton had been forced to empty it. Assuming that Veronica was right, what had happened to the others?

'Did he have any other hiding places?' Sam asked.

Veronica paled. 'Oh my God. What was on them? Please say it wasn't kiddie porn. Please.'

'I don't know,' Sam said honestly. 'But why did you ask that?'

'Because he likes his "pretty young things".' She pointed to herself. 'I looked a lot younger than eighteen when he met me. I looked fifteen, tops. He really liked that.'

Sam had to swallow back the bile that burned his throat. 'You think he was into child pornography?' Sam asked.

'Honestly? Yeah. I mean, I don't think he was actively out there abusing kids. He was too scared of getting caught. But he had proxies and these VPNs so he could do untraceable searches. But I didn't ask questions. By then I was afraid of him.'

'I don't blame you,' Sam murmured.

She shook her head. 'I look back at that year and wonder how I even survived. One time, he hit me with a shovel.'

Laura blanched, then drew a breath. 'A shovel? I thought you said he didn't do manual labor.'

Veronica looked a little startled. 'I-I don't know, he must have been doing manual labor that day. I blacked out after he hit me and I had horrible headaches after, so I didn't give any more thought as to what he'd been doing with the shovel. I had a concussion for sure. He was a real bastard. I can't say that I'm sorry he's dead.'

'I don't blame you for that, either.' Sam leaned on the picnic table, bracing himself on his forearms. 'Did you notice anything different outside when you were able to think again?'

She paled even further. 'Did he bury someone in the backyard? Oh my God.'

Sam thought that was entirely possible. 'Tell me about the backyard.'

She closed her eyes, trembling. Sam hated that he was making her relive this, but Colton's partner – whoever he was – would keep killing unless he was stopped. If there was any chance Colton had buried evidence, McKittrick needed to know about it.

'He changed the backyard,' Veronica said slowly. 'Yeah, he did. Before the shovel, we had some lawn chairs and a crappy old table. But then later, it was nice. And he had a firepit, but not dug into the ground. It was movable, with a propane tank. Had these pretty rocks. He said he'd made the yard pretty because he was sorry that he'd accidentally hit me with the shovel. But it wasn't an accident.'

'No, it wasn't.' Sam's heart was racing. Whatever – or whoever – Colton had buried, it had to be important. 'I'm so sorry you've had to remember all this.'

She smiled sadly. 'It's okay. I never really forgot. I just blocked out the most painful stuff. He was . . . really rough, you know?'

'Sex?' Laura asked gently.

Veronica nodded. 'Especially when he'd come back from wherever he went to blow off steam. Like I said, he'd be worse when he came back – and always horny.' She touched her throat. 'He was into breath play. Strangling me, you know. Thought he'd kill me a few times.'

Sam remembered Colton's hands twisting, *strangling* that bottle in his office. Maybe Colton had just come back from killing someone the night Veronica was remembering. Like Jaelyn or Cecilia or Naomi.

Sam was glad he hadn't had dinner yet.

'Do you remember when this was?' he asked.

She shook her head. 'No. All the times just kind of blended together. The only time anyone ever saw the abuse was when Brian saw me at the grocery store and when he and Beth helped me get away. I can ask him when those times were, if that would be helpful.'

'It might be,' Sam said truthfully. He gave her his business card, writing his cell phone number on the back. 'Give me a call if you remember anything.'

She took the card. 'I will.'

'Can I ask why you didn't tell the police any of this when they came by last week?' Laura asked.

Veronica looked embarrassed. 'I was worried that they'd think I did something wrong. The lady detective asked me about Colton's friends, and I told her the same thing I told you – he didn't have any. I should have told her the rest, but I was exhausted. I'd just worked a double shift and had been up all night finishing a term paper. I was afraid I'd say something wrong and get myself into trouble, especially since I didn't report his abuse.'

'You weren't obligated to report anything,' Laura said firmly.

Veronica looked only partially relieved. 'I still should have. I was just scared of him. Men like him who get arrested for beating their wives are often back home a few hours later. I can talk to her now.'

'I'll let her know,' Sam promised. He held out his hand and she shook it. 'Thank you. You might have saved some lives.'

Her smile was brilliant. 'Then it was worth reliving it all. I hope you get this settled, Dr Reeves, so that you can go back to helping homeless kids. I volunteer at New Horizons and it's a good place. I don't think I would have been as comfortable talking to you if I hadn't known you volunteered there, too.'

Sam gave Laura a grateful look before returning his gaze to Veronica. 'Maybe I'll see you there. Good luck with your studies.'

'Thank you. You guys have a good night. I think I'm going to take the long way back to my place. It's a pretty night for a walk.'

Sam looked over his shoulder as he and Laura walked back to her car. Veronica was walking slowly, her face lifted to the twilight sky, her expression peaceful. Serene, as if the weight of her secrecy had been lifted from her shoulders.

'I need to call Kit,' Sam said quietly. Veronica's recollections could be even more important than Maureen's video.

Fifteen

Hillcrest, California
Tuesday, 19 April, 8.00 P.M.

Joel stared up at Sam from the weight bench in his home gym, hands gripping the barbell still in its rack. 'You think Driscoll buried shit in his backyard? What did McKittrick say?'

Sam frowned at his phone. 'I've been calling her ever since we left Veronica Gadd's apartment. She's not picking up.'

Laura had dropped Sam off a few minutes before, waiting until he was in Joel's house before heading back to the Epsteins' house to take them to their rental car.

'That's not like Kit,' Joel said. 'Did you text her, too?'

'Several times.' His frown deepened. 'Do you think she's okay?'

Joel snorted. 'McKittrick can take care of herself. Trust me.'

Sam remembered how easily she'd swept him off his feet – literally. It was embarrassing. 'Oh, I know.'

Joel grinned. 'I guess you do.' Then he slid out from under the barbell and grabbed his phone. 'She might have gone to visit Baz in the hospital. Don't they make you turn your phone off in the hospital?'

'Only in the ICU, but I didn't think Constantine's heart attack was that bad.'

'I didn't think so, either.' Joel dialed a number and listened before hanging up. 'Voice mail. I'll call the hospital and ask for his room. Did you try calling Navarro?'

'I left a message on his office voice mail. I didn't have his cell phone number.'

Within another minute, Joel was asking for Baz Constantine's room, and then he put it on speaker. 'Hey, Baz,' he said when the detective answered. 'It's Joel Haley. I'm trying to reach Kit. Is she there?'

'She was, but she left about twenty minutes ago. Said she was going home.'

'To her boat?'

She lives on a boat? Sam fought a shudder. Boats were not his favorite. All that water. One wrong step off a boat and a person could drown. Give him a desert any day of the week.

'No,' Baz was saying. 'She said she was going to see her folks. Is everything okay?'

'It is,' Joel assured him. 'I have some info for her on one of her cases.'

'She said you caught the Mendoza murder case.'

'I did. Robinson and Cook did a good job on that case. It's not a slam dunk because the asshole already has a team of expensive lawyers, but it's solid.'

'Good. But it was Kit who got the case reopened.' The man's pride was clear and softened Sam's remaining resentment. 'You take care of little Rita,' Baz went on, his voice gruff. 'She found her mama. Kids never get over something like that, no matter how good the McKittricks are to them.'

'I know,' Joel said quietly. 'I'll do my very best. Take care, Baz.' Joel ended the call and stood up. 'Give me two minutes to change my clothes and we'll go.'

Sam followed him, standing outside Joel's closet as his friend's exercise clothes came flying out the door, hitting the floor. 'Go where?'

'To the McKittricks' house. I have their phone numbers in Rita's mother's case file, but I don't have that with me. I do, however, know where they live.'

'How?' Sam asked warily.

Joel left the closet wearing a pair of dress slacks and buttoning up a shirt. 'I go there for holiday dinners sometimes. Kit invited me when she found out that my folks were gone.'

'Oh.' Sam wasn't sure how he felt about that. 'I thought she said no to dating.'

'She did, but she said that friends didn't let other friends spend Thanksgiving alone. You were in Scottsdale with your parents or I'd have tried to get you an invite, too. That was a few years ago.' He pulled on his socks and shoved his feet into another pair of very expensive shoes. 'Since then, I have an open invitation to their house. You can talk to Kit and I'll chat with Harlan. I need to arrange for them to bring Rita to my office so I can get her statement.'

'Rita's the girl whose mother was murdered.'

Joel grabbed his wallet and keys. 'Yeah. Thirteen years old now, but she was only eleven when she found her mother's body.'

Sam's heart clenched. 'Poor kid.'

'Yeah, but at this point there's no better place for her than the McKittricks'.'

Sam followed Joel to his car, waiting until they were on the interstate before asking the question that wouldn't leave his mind.

'You're sure you're just friends?'

Joel smirked. 'Why, Sammy? You got plans you want to share?'

'No.' But he knew that he'd said it too quickly and with too much force because Joel's smirk widened into a knowing grin. *Dammit.* But he'd replayed that moment in front of the Epsteins' house a thousand times since it had happened. She'd blushed.

And fled.

He'd felt a spark and he thought she had, too. He'd caught her staring at him before she'd run away. There had been interest in her eyes. He was sure of it.

'Sam?' Joel prompted.

'I don't know,' he said honestly. 'I don't think she trusts me.'

'Give her time. But if she says no, don't take it personally. I mean, she resisted me, after all.'

Sam laughed. 'She must have a will of steel.'

'What else could it be? We'll be at the McKittricks' in about twenty. Go over what you found out today again. In detail.'

So Sam did, and if he took special care to remember the route to the McKittricks' house, he was only filing it away for future reference. In case he came across a kid who needed a good foster home.

It was a nice place, he thought as Joel drove them up the country road leading to the family farm. It looked like a farmhouse out of a painting, warm and inviting, with lights burning in most of the windows and a lit porch light. There was a barn a short distance from the house and fenced pastures, clear and sharp in the moonlight.

'This seems like a perfect place for kids,' Sam murmured.

'It is. And Harlan and Betsy are the whole package. But be careful of Betsy. She'll mother you with food.'

Sam smiled. 'As long as she cooks better than my mother, that's cool.'

Joel grimaced. 'She couldn't cook much worse.'

'True.' Sam followed Joel up to the front door, looking around. 'Do you see Kit's car?'

Joel's gaze swept from side to side. 'Huh. I don't actually. She drives a Subaru Outback.'

Sam looked at the four vehicles parked in the driveway. 'They're all Subaru Outbacks, Joel.' Which was odd, wasn't it?

'Yeah. One of the McKittricks' former foster sons owns a Subaru dealership and gets them discounts. Hers is blue, though. I wonder if she's left already.'

'Maybe we should leave,' Sam said doubtfully.

'Nah. I can still talk to Harlan about Rita.' Joel knocked on the front door. 'I bet we can even wrangle some pie from Betsy. She always has pie.'

But Sam wasn't so sure. This was Kit's family. Her safe place. He was intruding. He'd taken a step back when the door opened to a very large man. He had to be six-two with broad shoulders and eyes with prominent laugh lines.

'Joel Haley! What are you doing here, son?'

This must be Harlan McKittrick.

'Came looking for Kit, actually,' Joel said, shaking the man's hand. 'But I was hoping I could have a moment to talk to you about Rita as well.'

'Heard you got the case. I was relieved.' Harlan opened the door wider. 'Come in. Who's your friend?'

'This is Sam Reeves.' Joel waved a hand between them. 'He's working a case with Kit.'

Sam could see the moment Harlan figured it out. 'The CI,' he murmured, as if to himself. Then he smiled again. 'Welcome, Dr Reeves. Please, come in.'

'Harlan?' a woman called. 'Who's at the door?'

'Joel and his friend, Sam Reeves,' Harlan called back.

'Kit's Sam?'

Sam's eyes popped wide. *What?*

Joel was looking like he was trying not to smile, and Harlan's lips twitched. 'One and the same,' Harlan said.

'Well, don't dally,' she said. 'Bring them into the kitchen.'

And that was how Sam found himself at a large kitchen table that appeared to be hand carved. A plump woman with a smile as big as Harlan's was bustling around, grabbing plates and mugs.

'You'll want some coffee,' she said. 'Please sit.'

'You don't have to do that, Betsy,' Joel said.

She threw an amused look over her shoulder. 'But you won't say no, will you?'

Joel grinned. 'Never, ma'am.' He sat and pointed to an empty chair. 'Sam.'

Sam sat, feeling overwhelmed. 'Thank you,' he said when Betsy put a steaming mug of coffee in front of him, followed by a slab of pie that smelled so good that his mouth watered. 'Apple pie is my favorite.'

'Good,' she said and, after serving everyone else, she joined them. 'What's up, boys?'

'We were looking for Kit,' Joel said around a mouthful of pie. 'Baz said she was coming home to see you tonight.'

The McKittricks shared a worried glance. 'She's not here,' Harlan said. 'Haven't seen her since last night. I was up when she left, but she was in a hurry and we didn't get a chance to talk.'

Because she was rushing to call me, Sam thought.

Joel nodded. 'Can you call her, Harlan? She might be screening her calls if she's working, but she'll answer for you.'

Harlan nodded slowly, then turned his gaze to Sam. 'He's okay?' he asked Joel.

'He is, sir. I vouch for him personally. He's my best friend.'

'All right, then.'

'Mrs McK?' a small voice asked.

They all turned to find a girl standing in the doorway. Her sandy blond hair was streaked with a rainbow of colors, but her eyes were swollen and red-rimmed. She'd been crying and Sam's heart hurt to see it.

'Rita,' Betsy said, getting up to put her arm around the girl. 'Did you have a good nap?'

'Yeah,' Rita mumbled. 'But I missed dinner.'

Betsy kissed the top of the girl's head. 'I saved you some. Have a seat, sweetie. I'll warm up your plate. What about you boys? Dr Reeves, you're looking a little peaked, if I might be so bold.'

'He hasn't eaten,' Joel said.

Sam opened his mouth to argue, but Betsy was already fixing him a plate, too.

Rita sat, eyeing Sam and Joel cautiously.

'I'm Joel Haley,' Joel said, extending his hand over the table.

Rita shook it, still wary. 'The prosecutor on my mom's case?'

'Yes. I was hoping to set up some time that you can come to my office. We'll get your formal statement.'

Rita glanced at Harlan, who nodded. 'Okay,' she said. 'When?'

'Tomorrow, if you can swing it. When are you done with school?'

Rita sucked in a harsh breath, her expression closing. 'Today.'

Harlan sighed. 'We might be in a homeschool situation. We'll see.'

Rita had dropped her gaze to her hands. At some point she'd pulled a small carving from a pocket because she was holding it in one hand and stroking it with the other. It was an oyster, wide open with a pearl inside.

'That's a pretty carving,' Sam commented quietly. 'I've never seen one like it.'

Again the girl's gaze shifted to Harlan. 'Mr McK made it for me. My name means "pearl".'

Sam smiled at her. 'Then it's a priceless gift.'

Harlan stroked a big hand over the girl's hair. 'Just like our Rita.'

Rita dropped her gaze again, and Harlan's eyes grew sad. This child's pain was palpable, and Sam wanted to help her but wasn't sure what to say.

'Let me call Kit and we'll sort this out.' Harlan excused himself into the living room, leaving the table quiet.

Rita started in on the plate Betsy put in front of her, pausing when a standard poodle sauntered in like it owned the place. 'Snick,' Rita said reprovingly. 'You're not supposed to be in the kitchen.'

'Only when I'm cooking,' Betsy said. 'She can come in when you're eating unless you don't want her to.'

Rita's free hand found the dog's curly head. 'No. She can stay.'

'Snick?' Sam asked.

'Short for Snickerdoodle,' Betsy said. 'Kit's dog. Left her here last night because Snick had fallen asleep with Rita.'

'She hogs the bed,' Rita muttered, but a tiny smile curved her lips.

'The famous Snickerdoodle,' Sam said, then dug in his pocket for a treat. 'My dog, Siggy, got one of her treats, so maybe she'd like one of Siggy's.'

Rita's eyes widened as she took the treat. 'You know about Snickerdoodle?'

'We've never met, but yes. I know of her.' He held his hand under the table for the poodle to sniff and was rewarded with a delicate lick. 'She's a real lady.'

'She is,' Rita said fondly, then snuck a bite of her dinner to the dog.

Betsy just shook her head as she put a plate of something wonderful in front of Sam. 'Eat this first, Dr Reeves. Then you can have some apple pie.'

His stomach growled. 'Chicken pot pie? One of my favorites.'

'Mine too,' Rita said.

Betsy sat with them, hiding a smile behind her coffee mug. 'No more of the people food to Snick, Rita. Or you'll be cleaning up the aftereffects.'

Rita made a face. 'Okay, Mrs McK.' She eyed Sam again, less warily this time. 'Do you have a picture of Siggy?'

Sam scoffed. 'Only a million. Most of them are on my other phone, though. But you can look at the ones I've taken in the past few days.' He offered Rita his phone, opened his photo app, and dug into his own dinner as she smiled at Siggy's antics.

'He's got a stick in his mouth in every picture,' she said.

'That's why he's named Siggy. Short for Sigmund, like the famous psychologist. He smoked cigars.'

Rita chuckled softly. 'It does look like your dog's got a cigar. That's so cute.' She pulled out her own phone to the pictures she'd taken of Snickerdoodle and Sam oohed and aahed over them while Betsy looked on approvingly.

Joel put his plate in the sink. 'I'll go talk to Harlan and leave you guys to talk dogs. Sam can talk about Siggy for hours.'

When he was gone, Rita gave Betsy an anxious look. 'Is he a good lawyer?'

Betsy nodded. 'He is.'

'Definitely,' Sam agreed, giving the girl her phone. 'He's my best friend so I'm probably biased, but your mom's case is in good hands, Rita.'

'Won't bring her back,' she muttered.

Sam swallowed hard, his eyes stinging. 'No, but he can get her justice.'

She met his eyes, hers grim and far older than they should have been. Ripples, he thought. Ripples that had become rogue waves. This child had been swamped by them, her life overturned.

'I want him to pay.'

'So do I,' Sam said and had never meant anything more.

SDPD, San Diego, California
Tuesday, 19 April, 8.00 P.M.

'Detective, please have a seat.' Dr John Scott waved Kit to a chair in the office he kept in the SDPD headquarters. He was about Baz's age, so midfifties, even though he looked a lot younger, his hair still dark and the skin around his eyes devoid of wrinkles. He was a handsome man, his face now recognizable by millions thanks to his appearances on the legal TV shows. He made a very credible expert witness and audiences loved him. Cops, not so much. Mostly because they were forced to bare their souls to him. It was humiliating.

She sat, forcing a smile to her face. 'Thank you for seeing me so late.'

He sat behind his desk, his smile calm, putting her instantly on high alert.

No, she'd been on high alert ever since she'd driven away from Sam Reeves. It had been all she could do not to blurt the whole thing to Baz when she'd visited him in the hospital before this appointment. He'd known something was up, but he hadn't pressed her on it, for which she was grateful.

He had pushed when she'd gotten up to leave, pouting because she couldn't stay longer. She hadn't wanted to tell him that she was coming to see Scott, because Baz would have worried. Or been annoyed on her behalf, because Baz didn't like coming to see him, either. So she'd lied for the first time ever to her partner, saying that she was going home to McKittrick House.

'It's no problem,' Dr Scott said affably. 'My assistant told me that you seemed surprised when she told you I was available so late. Almost like you'd thrown out a time that you thought I'd refuse.'

Kit's cheeks heated, but she didn't look away. *Do not show weakness. Do not let him in.*

She always said that to herself, but then he always seemed to be able to weasel around her best intentions, dragging details out of her mouth that she hadn't wanted to share.

'Maybe,' she allowed. 'I'm really busy right now.'

'I heard. I think everyone's heard that you're working the serial killer case – a case that a *lot* of other detectives have worked on over the years.' He smiled sadly. 'I've been around a long time. You're not the first detective to sit in my office after finding the body of a teenage blonde buried in a park.'

Navarro, she thought. That Homicide hadn't caught this killer weighed heavily on him. 'I suppose not.'

Dr Scott waited for her to say more, but she kept her mouth firmly shut. His lips quirked up. 'You have to talk to me, Detective,' he said, sounding mildly amused, 'or our time doesn't count.' He tilted his head. 'How do you feel, knowing so many detectives before you have tried to solve this case but have been unable to?'

She considered his question carefully. 'It's a huge responsibility and I'm feeling that.'

He nodded, seeming satisfied with the answer. 'I wouldn't have expected anything less. How are you sleeping?'

She held his gaze, having expected that question. 'Okay.'

He held up a finger, wagging it. 'Honesty, Detective.'

She huffed. 'Fine. Not well. Is that what you want to hear?'

'No, because I don't want you to be losing sleep. But if it's the truth, I'm glad to get it out there. What do you do when you can't sleep?'

She eyed him suspiciously. 'Is this a trick question?'

'No.'

She huffed again. 'I work.'

He smiled. 'Now *that* I believe.'

'I'm not the only one.' She winced because that sounded whiny.

He must have thought the same thing because he rolled his eyes. 'No, you're not. I mean, it's job security for me, I suppose, but it's genuinely painful to watch you all work yourselves into an early grave. How is Baz, by the way?'

This time she flinched. 'That's not fair.'

'Is anything fair?'

She drew a breath because she wanted to scream. She hated shrinks who asked questions like that. *No. Nothing is fair. Life is not fair, but we all just push forward*. That was all she could do. 'He's doing well. I saw him at the hospital before I came here. He wants to go home.'

'Where he'll probably work. Or try to.'

'Probably. Marian won't let him, though.'

Dr Scott shifted in his seat, studying her. 'Who's going to stop you?'

'From doing what?' she asked, pretending to misunderstand.

'From working yourself into an early grave, Kit,' he said softly.

Her eyes burned and that made her mad. 'Nobody,' she snapped. 'I don't need anyone to—' She cut herself off because he'd lifted a brow.

'To what? Stop you?' he asked when she pursed her lips. 'Help you? Protect you?'

'I don't need protecting.' She said the words quietly, but even she could hear the anger roiling beneath.

'That's not true. You have a big heart, Detective, and you want to fix everyone's problems. But you can't. You work too much. Plain and simple. You're going to burn yourself out before you're forty, and that will be a damn shame. SDPD needs more detectives like you. But you'll be gone. Whether dead or retired early, I don't know. But you will not last. Not at this pace.'

She clenched her jaw and deliberately checked her watch.

'We're not even close to time,' he said.

He was right, damn him. 'This is a big case. And it's urgent.'

'But it's *not* urgent, Kit. It's a *cold case*. Those victims and their families have been waiting for years. Some of them a lot more years than others. A few more days – or even weeks – won't make a difference in the long run. They'll still grieve. Their lives will still be traumatized. But slowing down could make a big difference to you.'

'But it *is* urgent. It stopped being a cold case when Skyler Carville was killed over the weekend.'

He frowned. 'What? But . . .' He shook his head. 'Wait. You arrested the killer. Colton Driscoll. I saw the press conference.'

'Driscoll had a partner,' she said, taking satisfaction from seeing his mouth fall open.

'How? Who?'

'We don't know. Still working on that.'

He puffed out his cheeks as he struggled to regain his composure. 'Well, I suppose that is urgent, but you still have to sleep. When was the last time you actually slept?'

'Last night. I fell asleep at my parents' house. I got five hours.' Almost.

'That's a lot for you,' Scott said dryly. 'Did your mother drug you?'

Surprised, Kit laughed. 'No. I was tired and . . .' She sighed. 'The new foster at my parents' house lost her mother to a killer. The man was arrested yesterday, and it was all over the news. I wanted to be the one to tell her before a stranger on TV did, so I stopped by the house.'

Dr Scott's brow furrowed. 'The city councilman?'

She nodded, remembering the way Rita had launched herself at her. How Rita had sobbed in her arms. And how good it had felt to know she'd given the girl closure.

'*That*,' Scott said abruptly, and she blinked at him. 'What was that?' he asked. 'You went all soft for a moment. Relaxed. Not a bad look on you, if I'm being honest.'

'Rita,' she admitted. 'When I told her about her mother, she jumped on my lap and cried herself to sleep.'

Scott's smile was gentle. 'You let her?'

Kit bristled. 'I wasn't gonna dump her on her ass. She was crying.'

He still smiled. 'You let her.'

Kit exhaled. 'Yeah, I let her. And it felt . . . good. Like I'd fixed something.'

He lifted his brows in a classic told-you-so expression.

She shook her head, smiling ruefully. 'So I'm a fixer. Not a crime.'

'No, it's not. What would be a crime is burning yourself out too soon and making the Ritas of the world miss out. Who's going to fix their lives if you're not here?'

She crossed her arms over her chest, disgruntled. 'You *may* have a point,' she conceded.

He threw up his hands. 'Hallelujah! Can I record you saying that?'

'No,' she said grumpily.

He chuckled. 'Fine, fine. So what's next, Detective?'

'What do you mean?'

'What are you going to do when you leave here?'

'Go home,' she said dutifully. 'And sleep.'

He rolled his eyes. 'Right. And here I was thinking we might have made a little progress. My bad.'

'I *will* go home and sleep,' she insisted. Eventually.

'This is a hard time for you,' he said, sober once more. 'This time of year. It's a pattern and it keeps continuing. Spring rolls around, the daffodils come up, and you start working yourself into the ground again. It was the same last year and the year before, which was why Navarro asked you to see me this year. To cut it off at the pass.'

'Sorry.'

'No, you're not. That's the problem.'

'I know my body. I know what it can do. I know how much sleep I need.' Which came out sounding defensive, like the teenagers she'd been talking to for the past few days.

'Now, yes. You're what, thirty-five?'

She scowled. 'Thirty-one.'

'A veritable child.' His sarcasm game was strong. 'I bet Baz said that he knew his body, too. Right up until he had a heart attack.'

She narrowed her eyes. 'Leave Baz out of this.'

'Okay, fine. What about Snickerdoodle?'

She blinked again. 'What about her?'

'When was the last time you spent a full day with your dog?'

She opened her mouth and closed it again. A while. Too long. 'My sister takes care of her when I'm working.'

'That wasn't an answer. Maybe it's been so long that you can't remember.'

She lifted her chin at the deliberate taunt. 'A week and a half ago. We went to Mom and Pop's for Sunday dinner.'

'That's good. Did you work while you were there?'

'No.' She had talked about the case to Harlan and she had talked to Rita about her mother's murder, but that didn't really count.

'Uh-huh.' He clearly didn't believe her. 'How about when you got home?'

'Not much. Some light reading.' It had been everything she could find online about Rita's mother's boss. So not very light at all. But, ultimately, it had been worthwhile.

'Uh-huh,' he said again. 'Light reading.' He sighed. 'What—'

Kit startled where she sat when her phone rang in her pocket.

He frowned, seriously displeased. 'Detective, you know the protocol. Phones silenced when you're in my office.'

'I know.' She pulled her phone from her pocket, showing him the screen. 'But I have my dad on a special ringtone.'

Scott waved his hand. 'Answer it, then. We're nearly done anyway. I'll work on my notes.'

She answered, putting the phone to her ear. 'Pop? Everything okay?'

'I think so,' Harlan said warily. 'Two men stopped by to see you. Seemed to think you were here. They say that Baz told them so.'

Damn. The one time she told a lie, she got caught. 'I was planning to come out to see you,' she added a little lamely. 'I left Snick there, after all.'

'Are you okay?' Harlan asked urgently.

'I'm fine. Just needed a little quiet time.'

'Oh?' Harlan asked slyly and she nearly choked. He thought she was on a date.

'I'm *working*, Pop. But wait.' They'd gotten sidetracked. 'Who's there?'

'Joel Haley and his friend Sam Reeves.' The way he said Sam's name was the same as how he'd said *Oh?*, but she wasn't going to touch that with a ten-foot pole. Harlan could always tell when she was avoiding a truth.

Kit pulled the phone from her ear long enough to glance at her messages. She had several from both Joel and Sam and a few from Baz. 'Are they causing you any trouble?'

Dr Scott turned to give her a concerned look, but she shook her head. *It's fine,* she mouthed and he dropped his eyes back to his notes.

'Oh, they're no trouble at all,' Harlan said. 'Your mother is feeding them pie. Says Dr Reeves looks a little peaked.'

Kit snorted. 'He does not.' Sam Reeves looked very healthy, his body toned and his skin lightly tanned from camping in the freaking desert.

'Oh?' Harlan repeated, back to sly.

'Pop. Tell Joel I'll call him in a few minutes.'

'Or you could come out for pie, too.'

'Yes!' Betsy called in the background. 'I didn't get to talk to her last time. She fell asleep. Tell her to come and see her mother.'

Kit wanted to be irritated but could never find it in her when the McKittricks were involved. 'Tell her I'll be back soon. Is Rita okay?'

'She's sitting at the table with them.' He lowered his voice. 'Asking questions about her mother's case. She knows, Kitty-Cat. About her mother's pregnancy.'

'Dammit. Did Joel tell her?'

'No. She heard it at school. Some reporter – not Tamsin Kavanaugh this time – was digging into the arrest of a city councilman and saw the pregnancy on Maria Mendoza's autopsy report.'

Regret cut deep. 'I should have told her. I would have,' she added helplessly, 'but she fell asleep.' And then she'd had to leave. To work.

Maybe Dr Scott really did have a point. She did work too much. Especially this time of year. *Dammit*. She hated admitting the shrink was right.

'I think she knows you would have. You can tell her when you see her.'

'I'll come by tomorrow. Can you put Joel on the phone?'

A few seconds later Joel was there. 'Hey, Kit.'

'I'm at the station. By the time I get to Mom and Pop's, it'll be close to ten and then we'll both have to drive south. Can we meet at my place to talk?'

'Sure. Did you eat dinner? Your mother is asking.'

Kit chuckled. 'Tell her that I'd love anything she gives me.'

'I will. We'll meet you at your place. Still on the marina?'

We. He was with Sam. Who Kit really didn't want to see again so soon.

For reasons she didn't want to dissect.

'Yep,' she said, managing to keep from sounding awkward. She hoped. 'Same slip. I need to talk to my dad again.'

Harlan's voice came through the phone again. 'Kitty-Cat. We hoped you'd come by, but it is late. You'll be going to sleep soon, right?' He sounded so hopeful.

'Of course.' It was only a small fib. Probably. 'Can you keep Snick till tomorrow? She can sleep with Rita again.'

'Rita will like that,' he said gruffly.

'See you tomorrow.' Kit ended the call. 'Sorry, Dr Scott.'

'It's fine, Kit. Family is important. I'm glad you have such a good one.'

'So am I.'

Scott smiled at her, glancing at the clock. 'Same time next week?'

She sighed. 'Yeah, sure. See you then.'

Sixteen

Shelter Island Marina, San Diego, California
Tuesday, 19 April, 9.30 P.M.

Kit had brought a little work home. Just a little. She'd received both Dr Reeves's and Skyler Carville's cell phone records in her email that afternoon, so she'd go through them tonight. She still had to check out the five bars in Little Italy to do her part of the recon, but she could do that after Joel and Sam left.

Because Joel and Sam were coming *here*. What in blue blazes had prompted her to suggest they meet her here? Why hadn't she just demanded they tell her over the phone? She couldn't think of a single reason why.

Sessions with Dr Scott messed with her head. That had to be it.

She wasn't going to overthink it. Sam would give her the information and then he and Joel would leave her alone.

Which was how she liked it.

Liar.

Shut up and work.

She'd just sent the cell phone records to her home printer when she heard the footsteps up on deck. She made sure there was enough paper in the printer tray, then smoothed her slacks nervously.

Which was stupid. She didn't get nervous. Not about stuff like this.

Not about men.

Not about Joel, for sure. Telling him they'd only be friends hadn't been a chore at all. But Sam? There had been something there the first time she'd seen his photo. Hell, the first time she'd heard his voice on that initial anonymous call.

He was so damn *nice*.

And he was here.

She opened the door and stepped back to let the two men through. Both had to duck their heads as the doorway was just shy of six feet. Joel had a football player's bulk, much like Connor Robinson, but Sam Reeves had the lean build of a runner.

'Hi,' she said, wanting to wince. *Awkward* was an understatement.

'Hi.' Sam looked around, seeming both curious and ill at ease. But he said nothing in the way of explanation, so Kit let him be.

Joel handed her two covered plates. 'Can you warm these? I ate hours ago, so Betsy made me one, too.'

She went to the microwave, grateful for something to do. 'Sit, please. Did you not want any, Dr Reeves?'

'Your mother fed me,' Sam said wryly. 'I don't think I had much of a choice.'

She laughed. 'That's my mom.'

She'd said all of that without turning around, busying herself in the galley kitchen, gathering bottles of water and cutlery while the food warmed. Finally, the microwave dinged a second time and she was forced to face them, plates in hand. Both men sat on her sofa, Sam still looking around as if he'd never seen the inside of a boat before.

Maybe he hadn't.

'Is this your first time on a boat, Dr Reeves?'

'Not on a boat, but in a cabin like this, yes. I've done a whale-watching cruise or two.'

And what he'd thought about the experience was plain on his face.

'Didn't care for them?' she asked lightly, handing Joel his dinner.

Sam grimaced. 'I never got sea legs. And there was a lot of water.'

She laughed again. 'It is a boat. On the ocean. Gotta expect some water.'

Sam shuddered. 'I like dry land. But this is nice. Cozy. I've never met anyone with their own boat before. I grew up in the desert.'

'My older brother's boat,' she said, taking a bite of pot pie and suppressing a groan. She was starving. She'd taken a few bites of the sandwich Howard had brought her, then had forgotten to eat the rest. 'Arthur's in the navy and currently stationed on a ship in the South Pacific. I'm renting until he gets back.'

'That's nice,' Sam said, his damn sincerity front and center.

'So. What brings you by? I saw your texts, Dr Reeves. Sorry, I wasn't in a place where I could answer my phone.' She hadn't looked at her phone before heading into Dr Scott's office, not wanting to distract herself. She needed to be on guard when she saw the department shrink.

Sam's a shrink, too. But somehow, she didn't feel the need to be on guard. At least not for the same reason.

Sam rubbed his palms over his face. 'Laura Letterman and I saw Veronica Gadd after we left the Epsteins'.'

Kit wasn't surprised. He'd told her that was his next stop, but that he was here told her that, once again, he'd been more successful than she'd been with getting a witness to talk. 'You must have found something.'

'Yeah, we did.'

She resumed eating her dinner as Sam related the events of his visit with Driscoll's fourth wife, her eyes widening more with each detail he revealed. That Driscoll had beaten his young wife wasn't a shock, although Kit was sad that Veronica hadn't been comfortable sharing that with her as well.

'*Wait*. You think he buried something in the backyard?' she asked, interrupting when Sam got to that part.

'He had a shovel,' Sam said grimly. 'Hit her with it, too. Then used a new outdoor living area as an apology gift.'

'And she saw a lot more hard drives in his safe than we saw on camera,' she murmured. 'Okay, this changes my evening.'

'What will you do?' Joel asked.

'Get someone out there with a GPR. Ground-penetrating radar,' she added when Sam looked confused. 'We'll get a picture of what's underground before we start digging.'

'She mentioned a movable firepit,' Sam said. 'The whole outdoor area seems odd to me. He never mentioned entertaining and Veronica confirmed that he had no friends.'

'Except for whoever he went to see to let off steam.' That had been new information as well. 'I need to get additional uniforms out to Driscoll's house to cover the backyard. Just in case whoever cleaned his house finds out there's buried treasure out back.'

'Possibly,' Sam said nervously. 'There may be nothing.'

She gave him her kindest smile, because she thought she understood the source of his concern. 'Don't worry, Doc. If we don't find anything, nobody's going to blame you. Will Ms Letterman be available to give a statement as well?'

Sam nodded. 'That's why she went with me. She and Joel didn't want me caught without a reliable alibi again.'

'Yeah, not a bad plan unfortunately. Hopefully you'll get your life back soon.'

Sam swallowed, his green eyes haunted. 'I'd be satisfied knowing that Skyler's parents don't believe that I'm a murderer.'

Kit put her plate on the side table with a sigh. 'I considered telling them that you weren't a credible suspect, but then whoever really killed Skyler would find out.'

'And maybe kill someone else,' Sam finished. 'I thought of that. That's why I'm not staying at my apartment. Her parents would confront me, and I'd feel compelled to defend myself. I don't want her killer to know you're looking at anyone other than me. I don't want anyone else to die.'

Her heart squeezed. She had no trouble believing that he'd sacrificed his good name to save other people. He'd already done so before.

'When this is over, I'll make sure the Carvilles know the truth.'

'But it won't bring Skyler back,' Sam said thickly.

'No,' she murmured. 'But we'll prove who did it and get your friend the justice she deserves.'

Something settled in his eyes as he nodded. 'I'm going to see the other ex-wife tomorrow. The one that still lives here in San Diego.'

'You're going with Ms Letterman?' Kit asked, wishing her dislike for the lawyer were only due to her chosen occupation. But she'd cheated on Sam and still expected to be a part of his life.

But that was Sam's business. *Not mine.*

'When she's finished with work, yes.'

She wasn't going to bother telling him not to make the visit. 'Please keep me up to speed, and I promise I'll return your calls more promptly.'

'I will.' Sam looked at Joel. 'Was that it?'

'It was,' Joel said. 'We didn't have Navarro's number, or we would have told him straightaway. And I didn't think Baz should be involved. He's supposed to be recuperating.'

'Thank you for that,' Kit said. 'Although he's going to be pissed off that we didn't involve him. Which doesn't matter because I'm far more scared of Marian than I am of Baz.'

Joel chuckled and stood with his empty plate. 'Smart. Where do I put this?'

'I'll take it.' Scrambling to her feet, she took both plates, holding them in front of her like armor when Sam rose as well. Her living room was minuscule, and he was too close. 'Um, Dr Reeves, how did Rita look when you saw her?'

'Sad,' he said. 'She'd been crying.'

'Harlan said it was because she found out that her mother had been pregnant,' Joel said darkly. 'Some kid at school saw it online and made sure to tell her.'

'The punk bastard,' Sam growled. 'Damned reporters make life hard for anyone associated with a victim. Rita's had enough shocks in her life for a lifetime.'

That he was worried about Rita and not himself was not lost on Kit. 'I know. We've protected your role in this, Sam. None of the damned reporters should find out that you were our CI.' She hoped.

Sam shrugged. 'I've told a few people that I'm a suspect, so it might get out on its own, without any of the reporters' help.'

Kit almost dropped the plates. 'You did *what*? We were trying to protect you by not letting that out and you just *told* people?' She looked at Joel. 'Did you know about this?'

'He's a grown-up, Kit, and a damn smart one at that. I figure that he knew the risk.'

'I don't know if people would have talked to me otherwise,' Sam said. 'Revealing the truth made me vulnerable and . . . people want to help other people in trouble.'

She blinked at him. 'Are you for real? Like, you *do* work with criminals, right?'

Sam's lips twitched up. 'A lot of criminals. That's my area of specialization, in fact. But I talk to a lot of victims, too. Sharing a vulnerability helps level the field. Helps them open up. It worked for me.'

She sighed, because it had. 'What time are you going to see Driscoll's third ex-wife?'

'Probably not until tomorrow night. We went by her place during the day today and she wasn't home, so she must have been at work.'

'Call me. I might be able to join you.' She lifted a brow when he stiffened. 'Unless you don't want me to.'

'No,' he said slowly. 'But . . . you're a cop. Veronica was afraid you'd think she was involved with whatever Colton was doing. I think they talk to me because I'm not a cop.'

'He's got a point, Kit,' Joel said.

Unfortunately, he did. 'I'll think on it. Hopefully we will have unearthed something in Colton's backyard that will help us know the questions to ask.'

She followed them to the door, her gaze settling on Sam's shoes. And she had absolutely *not* checked him out on her way down to his feet. 'Wait. That is a brand-new pair of Top-Siders, Dr Reeves. The shoes you wore to the park were also Top-Siders. Why did you pick that shoe if you don't like boats? It's a boating shoe.'

Joel snickered, nudging Sam with his elbow. 'Tell her, Sammy.'

Sam's sigh was aggrieved. 'They were on clearance, so I bought several pairs. Unlike my friend here, I'm unwilling to spend a month's salary on a pair of shoes. And I've broken in those Top-Siders you took, so they're comfortable. I'd like to get them back someday.'

Because they'd held on to his shoes as evidence. 'You will eventually. Thank you for coming all this way to tell me about Ms Gadd.'

He turned to meet her eyes. So damn *nice*. 'You're welcome, Detective.'

She waited until their footsteps trailed up the dock before releasing the breath she'd been holding, then closed the door with her foot. Stepping back to the galley, she washed the dishes as she called Navarro.

His response was equally explosive. 'Driscoll buried something in the backyard?'

'I think so. I should have looked.'

'We did a cursory check, but yeah. We should have had the GPR guys out already. Did you call them?'

'My next phone call. I'll call Sergeant Ryland and have him set up spotlights so they can do their scans.' Finished with the dishes, she turned to her printer and scanned the pages, quickly finding what she'd already expected. 'Also, I've just reviewed the cell phone records for both Dr Reeves and Skyler Carville on the night she was killed. She got a text from Dr Reeves's phone number, but there was no outgoing text from Reeves's cell. The killer spoofed Reeves's number.'

'Sloppy on the killer's part,' Navarro said.

'Maybe. I'm betting he didn't think that Sam would give us access to his phone so readily.'

'Sam?' Navarro asked quietly.

Kit cursed silently. 'Sorry. Dr Reeves.'

'Are you going to shadow him on his next call? Because I'm guessing that asking him to stop talking to our witnesses isn't going to work.'

'I said I would, but he's worried they won't open up to me.'

'Nonsense. People open up for you. That's why you're such a good closer.'

His confidence made her feel better. 'Thank you. This case has me—' *Doubting myself*. She'd barely stopped herself from saying it. 'Off balance.'

'I know. And I also know that I've been preaching at you not to burn the candle at both ends, but tonight is an exception. The sooner we find out what Driscoll buried – if anything – the sooner we can put a killer down for good.' He hesitated. 'Did you go to your appointment tonight?'

'I did. And it might have helped. A little.'

He snorted. 'A glowing recommendation from you. All right. Call CSU. I'll meet you over there in an hour or so. I'm not in the city right now.'

Not for the first time she wondered what Navarro got up to when he wasn't in the office, but it wasn't her place to ask. Maybe he was on a date.

The notion made her happy. Which was how Harlan must have felt tonight when he thought she'd been on a date.

She hated disappointing the man she loved most in the world, but Harlan was going to have to wait for her to date. She had far too much to accomplish first.

Starting with digging up Colton Driscoll's backyard.

SDPD, San Diego, California
Wednesday, 20 April, 3.15 A.M.

'Is he almost done?' Navarro muttered.

Sergeant Ryland glared at them over his shoulder as he processed the evidence they'd found in Colton Driscoll's backyard. The GPR had found the mother lode – thirty hard drives buried in a small vault under the firepit. When CSU had moved the firepit aside, the GPR had given them a readout of dozens of bricklike items.

Kit shushed Navarro. 'He'll go slower if he's stressed out.'

'I can hear you,' Ryland snapped. 'Go get some coffee. I'm not rushing this.'

'I've had way too much caffeine,' Kit said. 'I'll bust out of my skin if I have another cup of coffee.'

'Sounds like a you problem,' Ryland snarked.

'Very much so,' Kit murmured. She was tired, but her brain was far too wired to even attempt to rest. Reaching in her pants pocket, she stroked her thumb over the cat-bird carving, hoping she wasn't rubbing off the detail. Carefully she pulled it out and held it up to the light.

It was unblemished. Harlan must have treated it so that she couldn't hurt it. He knew her too well, after all.

'What's that?' Navarro asked.

'Pop made it.' She held out her hand, the cat-bird nestled in her palm.

'I don't know how Harlan gets them so detailed.'

'He's a master. He made a heart for Baz,' she added, thinking about the affection on Baz's face as he'd held it in his hand when she'd visited him in the hospital hours before. 'An anatomically correct heart.'

Navarro chuckled. 'I like your father.'

She returned the cat-bird to her pocket. 'Everybody does.'

'Okay,' Ryland called. 'I've got the first hard drive copied. No booby traps and no encryption, which surprises me.'

Kit's jitters returned. 'He probably figured he'd never get caught. What's on it?'

'Videos,' Ryland said. 'It's crammed full of movie files.'

Kit stood next to Navarro behind Ryland's chair, trying not to beg the man to hurry. Ryland was notoriously methodical. Evidence he processed usually held up in court, so Kit didn't complain.

Ryland tapped his keyboard and a video file filled his monitor.

Kit sucked in a harsh breath. The camera had captured a sofa from the back. A teenage girl sat on the sofa in a nicely decorated living room – not Driscoll's living room. There was a wingback chair to the side of the sofa. The walls were decorated with several framed posters from Broadway musicals, including *West Side Story*, *Wicked*, and *Phantom of the Opera*.

'He likes musical theater,' Navarro murmured. 'There's the connection.'

Then the girl on the sofa turned around to look at the camera, her smile nervous.

Oh my God. 'That's Jaelyn Watts,' Kit rasped out.

Navarro was vibrating like a plucked string. 'And a man. Not Driscoll.'

'Not built the same,' Kit agreed. Her heart was pounding, because the man had just walked in front of the camera, his back filling the frame. But then he was moving again, away from the camera. He was leaner than Driscoll and not as tall. Maybe five-eight, five-nine. Driscoll was six feet tall.

'Driscoll's killer?' Navarro whispered.

'Same body type as the guy in Maureen's video,' Kit whispered back. A sharp pain in her hand made her realize that she was gripping the cat-bird again. She withdrew her hand from her pocket, crossing her arms over her chest.

They'd see the man's face any minute. Any second now.

The man walked toward the sofa, a glass tumbler in one hand. He sat next to Jaelyn, then turned his face toward the camera.

Kit leaned forward, shocked. 'What the fuck?'

Because the face was Colton Driscoll's.

'That's . . .' Navarro sputtered. 'What is this? His body type is all wrong.'

But the face was Driscoll's, and the voice was Driscoll's, too. He was smiling as he gave Jaelyn a glass of something dark and carbonated.

Kit had to remember to breathe. 'What do you wanna bet he's just roofied her?'

'Sucker bet,' Navarro said grimly.

The video rolled on and Jaelyn's eyes drooped, then closed, her head lolling on the sofa's back cushion.

Then the man with Driscoll's face pulled a set of sparkly pink handcuffs from his back pocket. He snapped them on Jaelyn's wrists and lowered her to the sofa.

Kit didn't want to watch what happened next, but she kept her gaze on the screen as she bore witness to Jaelyn's assault. *So she won't be alone*, she thought, even though she knew that was foolish.

Tears burned Kit's eyes and she blinked them away. Most of what was happening was being blocked by the back of the sofa, which was a small mercy. But they could see the man moving.

'Sonofabitch,' Navarro whispered, his voice breaking.

Kit nodded wordlessly, squeezing Ryland's shoulder when the CSU leader shuddered out a ragged breath of his own.

The man arched his back as he finished, then shifted his body, sitting on the sofa at Jaelyn's feet. Kit guessed he was zipping his pants back up from the way he moved. Leaving Jaelyn where she lay, he rose and approached the camera again, his body blocking the shot. Then he moved to the window, a martini glass in his hand.

The shot ended, abruptly shifting to the next clip. It was the same living room, but the shadows had changed. It was later in the day.

On the sofa, Jaelyn was stirring but appeared groggy and disoriented.

The man with Driscoll's face reappeared, sitting on the sofa where he lifted Jaelyn so that she sat upright. He pulled the tie from his shirt collar and wrapped it around her throat while she struggled sluggishly.

Jaelyn was awake enough for him to see her fear, but not enough for her to have the strength to put up any kind of a fight. Not that she'd have been able to overpower the man. She was too small.

'Coward,' Kit whispered.

The man pulled the tie tight, holding until she finally stopped struggling.

He'd killed her.

Releasing the tie, he removed it from her neck and neatly retied it around his own, snugging up the knot. Driscoll's face broke into a pleased grin that made Kit want to throw up.

She sat, breathing through the nausea. 'Goddammit.'

He'd waited until Jaelyn had woken up to kill her. He could have done it while she was unconscious, but he hadn't. He'd wanted to see her fear.

Ryland grabbed some tissues from the box on his desk and blew his nose before passing the box back to Kit. She wiped her own eyes and passed the box to Navarro, who did the same.

'What did we just watch?' she asked hoarsely. 'It's Driscoll's face and voice, but that man is at least three inches shorter than Driscoll. Maybe four. Is the video faked?'

'I don't know about all of it,' Ryland said, 'but at least part of it – the man's face – is definitely a deepfake.'

Shit. They were seeing 'deepfakes' more and more frequently – videos in which one person's face was superimposed on another person's body. The technology was increasingly accurate, some of the fake videos nearly impossible to distinguish from the originals. The software was free and many deepfake producers needed only a fast computer and editing time to get the look they wanted.

The dangers presented by a well-done deepfake video could be disastrous. A husband seeing his wife having sex with another man? A politician saying something career-ending? A police official making a catastrophic announcement that was untrue? They could induce mass panic and violence.

It appeared that this deepfake was the commission of a real murder as well as an element of Driscoll's fabricated life.

'How can you tell?' Navarro asked.

Ryland paused the video, the frame showing the fake Driscoll face. 'Aside from the fact that this man is four inches shorter than Driscoll, the shadows on his face are all wrong. They don't match the shadows in the room.'

Kit hadn't even noticed. 'But the rest?'

'I'd have to analyze it,' Ryland said. 'The voice is dubbed, but the mouth movements match the words. I think the rest is real.'

'So Driscoll somehow obtained this video,' Kit said, 'then superimposed his face on the killer's and dubbed the audio?'

Ryland nodded. 'That'd be my guess.'

'Can you see what's underneath his face?' Navarro asked. 'The real face?'

Ryland's expression was both grim and full of regret. 'No. We'd have to have the original, and this clearly isn't it.'

Onscreen, the man with Driscoll's face had hefted Jaelyn over his shoulder, her blond hair trailing down his back.

There were a few seconds of empty living room, then the video ended.

Kit pinched the bridge of her nose. 'Driscoll used to be an IT person for a big firm in town before his temper got him fired. Could he have had the kind of expertise to do this?'

'Sure.' Ryland grabbed a bottle of ibuprofen from his desk drawer. 'It's easy for anyone familiar with photo editing to do. Time consuming, but not difficult. This is an excellent execution, though. Excepting the shadows, the head looks right on the body.'

'How did Driscoll get this video?' Kit asked. 'Did he plant the cameras? Did he steal them from the killer? Did the killer record his kills for kicks? Did Driscoll do any of the murders or did he just claim this guy's kills?'

'Good questions,' Navarro said wearily. 'Let's find out. Unfortunately, we're going to have to watch the rest of the videos. Maybe some of them are originals.'

Ryland squared his shoulders. 'Okay.'

Kit exhaled. It was going to be a very long night.

SDPD, San Diego, California
Wednesday, 20 April, 8.45 A.M.

Kit looked up from her computer screen blearily as Connor Robinson sank into the chair beside her. He looked like shit. Just like everyone else looked after watching Colton Driscoll's videos for nearly five hours.

'You okay?' she asked. She'd called Connor and Howard in to help sort through the video evidence and they'd divided the task with the CSU techs.

'Not really. This is some seriously sick shit.'

So far, they'd witnessed the rape and murder of seven teenage girls, all appearing to have been killed within the last five years. Cecilia Sheppard was the most recent, having gone missing eight months before. They'd identified Jaelyn Watts, of course, and Naomi Beckham as well. There were three victims between Jaelyn and Naomi, all tentatively identified using their photos in the missing-person reports.

The oldest video – so far – showed the assault and murder of

Rochelle Hamilton, who'd gone missing five years ago. Miranda Crisp and Ricki Emerson, who'd disappeared seven and ten years before respectively, were not in any of the videos, nor were the two Jane Does discovered thirteen and fifteen years before. This led them to believe that Driscoll had begun recording the murders five years ago. Or, if the killer had made the recordings, Driscoll hadn't gained access until five years ago.

Of the new victims they'd discovered this night, none had drama club included in their missing-person reports, but they'd follow up with the families to find out. There were no bodies for these victims, though, and that meant that the families still wouldn't have complete closure.

'I know,' Kit said, trying to shove the images she'd viewed into a box in her mind, but it was hard. They'd all been so young. So hopeful. Until they'd accepted a drink from their killer.

It broke her heart.

'I had to stop,' Connor said raggedly. 'I'll watch more later. Driscoll was one sick SOB.'

'Yeah.' Kit rubbed her sore eyes. She'd cried a lot, and she hadn't been the only one. Connor had cried, too, which had softened the edges of his frat boy persona. 'Where's Howard?'

'He went home for a little while. Said he needed to recharge, but he'd be back soon to finish watching.'

Because although they'd reviewed seven of the hard drives, they still had the contents of eight hard drives to view. Half of the thirty they'd found were duplicates, and that had been a relief. Having to watch the suffering of seven victims had been devastating. Watching thirty . . . Kit didn't want to think about it.

Colton hadn't only spliced his own face onto the killer's body. In the other videos on the hard drives they'd searched so far, he'd replaced the victims' faces with those of his favorite celebrities.

He'd been able to watch himself doing unspeakable things to the famous people he'd bragged about knowing during his sessions with Sam Reeves.

Sam. He'd be wondering about what they'd found. Kit owed him an update. She'd find time today to tell him.

'Do you want to head home for some sleep?' Kit asked Connor.

'No. I'm too wired to sleep. What're you looking at?'

Kit returned her attention to her screen. 'The Orion School's website. I need to have my ducks in a row in case your friend isn't able to tell us anything.'

'She texted me back,' Connor said. 'Said she'd call me this morning. She wanted to check with the scholarship recipient to make sure it was okay to give me her number. Do you want to listen in on the call?'

'If I can, yes. If I'm not around, don't wait for me.'

He nodded, rolling his chair sideways to see her screen. 'What did you find so far about Orion?'

'Nothing yet. I'd just clicked on it when you sat down.' She explored the menu, checking the admissions tab. 'Auditions happen in front of a committee.' She noted the committee members' names. 'We'll need to run background checks on them before we head to the school.' She glanced at him. 'You up for a trip to high school?'

He grinned. 'Hell yeah. This time the principal will have to listen to me and not the other way around.'

She chuckled. 'I stayed far away from the principal's office. Kept my head down. Just wanted to pass my classes and get out.' She moved from the admissions tab to the one labeled *About Us*. 'These private schools have their own boards. This one has a board of trustees.' She clicked on it and gasped as one name stood out. 'What the hell?'

'Oh,' Connor murmured. 'That could be very good or very bad.'

Dr Alvin Levinson. Their criminal profiler was on the board of the Orion School. 'He never mentioned it when I talked to him Monday.'

'You didn't know about Orion School on Monday.'

'True,' she said. 'But if he knew about the drama world, he should have said something, shouldn't he?'

Connor frowned. 'You don't seriously think he's involved, do you?'

No. But the response was knee-jerk. *Levinson's one of us*. He wouldn't hurt anyone.

But was she sure about that? The man in the horrific videos with Driscoll's face had the same build as Levinson. And he had gray hair and glasses. She swallowed hard, bile rising in her throat at the thought that he could be involved in any way. 'No, I don't think so,' she said uncertainly, 'but I have to ask him what he knows about Orion scholarships.'

'Ask who about Orion scholarships?' Navarro asked, leaning on one corner of Kit's desk. He'd been in the commander's office for the past hour, updating the brass. They were going to have to do another press conference soon, admit that Colton Driscoll had been murdered and that he hadn't acted alone. That a murderer was still out there, targeting young women. And that they had leads, but no suspects.

What they did have, though, was a mental health professional who had the same body type as their killer with a solid connection to the school at least one of their victims was so determined to attend.

Kit met her boss's sharp gaze. 'Dr Levinson.'

Navarro's brows nearly shot up off his forehead. 'Al Levinson? What are you talking about?'

She pointed to her screen and Navarro came around to look, flinching in shock. 'Why didn't he mention he had a tie to a drama school on Monday?' he demanded.

'I don't know,' Kit murmured. 'But we're going to ask.'

'You bet your ass we will. I've known Al for twenty years. There is no way he is involved in anything like this.'

'Same body type,' Kit said quietly.

Navarro shook his head. 'He's pushing seventy, Kit. There's no way he'd have been able to get Colton Driscoll into that noose.'

'Driscoll's killer created a pulley system with one of those ropes,' she pointed out reluctantly. 'He didn't need to bear Driscoll's entire weight.'

'That's ridiculous. There's got to be a good reason he didn't mention Orion,' Navarro said while dialing on his cell phone. 'Hey, Al. Can you come into the office again this morning? It's important.' He was quiet for a moment, then said, 'See you then. We can meet in my office.' After saying goodbye, he slid his phone back into his pocket. 'He'll be here in half an hour. Run background checks on the rest of Orion's board and the staff in the meantime.'

Kit hoped he was right. She liked Dr Levinson. 'Yes, sir.'

Navarro had started to walk away when Connor said, 'Hey, boss. Wait.'

Navarro looked back at them, visibly bracing himself, because Connor's tone was ominous. 'Yes?'

Connor grimaced. 'Another article by Tamsin Kavanaugh. She says that we've got a second killer and that Orion School is suspected of involvement in victim recruitment.'

'Motherfucker,' Navarro snarled. 'Who's her source?'

'Unnamed,' Connor said.

Kit took Connor's phone and skimmed the article. 'Her source could be Madison, the girl at Naomi Beckham's school. She's the one who wanted the audition for herself. She's the only one who knows about the link between Naomi and the Orion School, other than the school principal and us.'

Navarro's expression was one of tightly controlled fury. 'Did Dr Reeves know about Madison? Did he talk to her, too?'

Kit shook her head. 'I'm sure I didn't mention it. We only talked about Veronica Gadd, Driscoll's fourth ex-wife.' And she'd asked him about Rita, but that wasn't important to this conversation.

'Shit,' Connor hissed. 'This is a disaster, boss. Orion's never going to talk to us now. We'll have to break through a wall of lawyers. We have to get in front of this.'

Navarro raked his hands through his hair. 'You tried to call yesterday, right, Kit?'

'I did. Left a message with the front desk for the principal.'

'Then we've attempted to get their statement. Let's get Levinson's take on the school before you head over there.'

'And talk to Connor's old friend,' Kit added. 'She's supposed to call him soon.'

Navarro nodded. 'Good. Let's gather what information we can before we go in.' He pointed to the two of them. 'You two go together.' Then he went into his office to deal with what was sure to be angry brass.

'Could Kavanaugh have followed you again?' Connor asked quietly. 'Or put a tracking device on you?'

Kit shook her head. 'I mean, it's possible. But I checked a car out of the garage. It wasn't my car. She'd have had to know which one I was taking, and *I* didn't even know.' She rubbed her temples. 'We don't have time for her shit.'

'We have to make time,' Connor said grimly. 'Because she keeps getting the jump on places you've been and people you've talked to.'

He was right. *Dammit*. 'She had to have followed me to Naomi's school, just like she followed me to Driscoll's house. Tamsin would have put two and two together, knowing I was working on the serial killer case.'

'Your psychologist also knew about Driscoll.'

She blinked. 'Dr Scott?'

Connor shook his head impatiently. 'Reeves,' he snapped. 'He's known about Driscoll from the beginning. He went to Naomi Beckham's house after you left there. What if he's following you? What if he followed you to Naomi Beckham's school and asked questions there, then told the press?'

She started to say that Sam would have no reason to reveal the information as it spotlighted him as the confidential informant, but stopped herself. Sam had told people that he was a suspect. She didn't think he cared if anyone knew at this point. 'Yes, he knew about Driscoll and Naomi Beckham. I don't believe he'd go to the press, though.'

'I'm not so sure. I don't know him like you do.'

There was something accusatory in his tone, and Kit frowned. 'What's that supposed to mean?'

'Just that you've trusted him with a lot of information, Kit.' He shook his head before she could comment. 'Who else knew about Orion?'

'Principal Larkin was there when Madison was talking about the school, but I doubt she'd talk to a reporter, either. The more I think about it, the more I think that Madison called Tamsin Kavanaugh to get her fifteen minutes of fame.'

Connor's scowl deepened. 'You just did it again. You dismissed the possibility that your shrink is involved. That he could be orchestrating all of this.'

'Because it's not true,' Kit snapped.

Connor's expression grew smugly arrogant. 'Whether you want to admit it or not, your shrink has come up with the evidence that has us where we are on this case. He's the one who talked to Naomi's family and found out about the secret audition. That led you to Naomi's high school, which led you to Orion. Your shrink's the one who talked to Maureen Epstein and got her to admit to spying on Driscoll. That gave us confirmation that Driscoll was murdered and that he had hard drives. Your shrink's the one who talked to Driscoll's ex-wife and told us that Driscoll buried something in his backyard. He's given us practically all the information we have now.'

Kit swallowed, not wanting to admit that Connor had a point. But he did. 'All that is true. It doesn't make him guilty.'

Connor glared at her. 'No, but it makes him a fucking suspect. What is *wrong* with you?'

'Nothing is *wrong* with me.'

He cocked his head. 'Then why are you seeing Dr Scott?'

Kit had to bite back so many swear words. 'That is none of your business.'

He folded his arms over his chest. 'You're right. It's not. I apologize for that. But Reeves got information out of all the people you'd already interviewed. He got blood from all the stones. And he could be legit. But he could be manipulating us every step of the way. Doesn't that make you a little bit concerned?'

Yes. Yes, it did. That it was impossible to consider made her even more concerned. 'Let's run the background checks for Orion's staff and board.'

Rolling his eyes, Connor returned to his desk. 'Fine.'

Sam Reeves was not guilty. She was sure of that – and she really shouldn't be.

'I'll do backgrounds on the board of trustees,' she said stiffly, 'if you'll start on the staff.'

His nod was clipped. 'Fine.'

But she couldn't focus. All she could see was Sam Reeves with his green eyes and his sincerity. All she could hear were Connor's very practical arguments.

She cleared her throat. 'What would eliminate Dr Reeves as a suspect in your mind?'

Connor's expression softened from outright hostility to grudging respect. 'I don't know yet. Let me think about it.'

'Okay.' She opened the background check software and began her search.

Seventeen

Hillcrest, California
Wednesday, 20 April, 9.00 A.M.

'Siggy, stop barking. Please.' Sam pulled his growling dog away from Joel's front window, where Siggy had burrowed underneath the drawn drapes so that he could look out onto the street. Siggy spent his days in an apartment, so he wasn't used to watching the world go by. Everything in the neighborhood was making him bark.

Siggy went right back to his post under the drapes, but at least he'd stopped barking. Sam got some pain reliever for his headache and downed it with a gulp of coffee. And checked his phone. Again.

He'd been watching his phone since dawn, hoping for at least a text from Kit telling him what – if anything – they'd found in Colton's backyard. Surely they would have started digging by now.

And, of course, with every minute that passed, he became more convinced that something had gone horribly wrong and that she suspected him again. Which was stupid.

'You're being paranoid,' he muttered to himself. 'It's all the coffee.'

Which was part of it, for sure. But it was mostly the stress of the entire situation. He'd heard from Vivian that morning. She'd asked if SDPD had confirmed his alibi for the time that Skyler was killed. If they'd established that he'd been in Joshua Tree all weekend. When they did – '*When*, not if, Sam,' she'd said – then he could return to work. She still believed in him, at least.

The problem was, he didn't know the status of his alibi. Kit had promised she'd locate the park ranger. Had she done that? Was the special master finished reviewing the location tracking on his phone?

Would he ever get his phone back? Would he ever get his shoes back?

Would he ever get his *life* back?

He was going crazy. He couldn't leave the house unless he had a babysitter.

Relax. It's not like you've been trapped inside for a year. It's been less than twelve hours.

He needed to *do* something.

So he gathered the runaway reports he'd downloaded from the California clearinghouse for missing persons. He knew Kit would continue to search for the victims of Colton and his partner, but she wasn't infallible.

After all, Sam had gotten a lot of information that Kit hadn't been able to extract. It was a small comfort to his battered ego.

There were so many runaways. He wasn't sure staring at the photos of missing teenagers was going to improve his mental health, but this was the task he could do until it was time for Laura to take him to Colton's third ex-wife.

He made another pot of coffee and spread the reports over Joel's kitchen table. Time to make himself useful.

SDPD, San Diego, California
Wednesday, 20 April, 9.15 A.M.

Connor's ringing phone distracted Kit from the background checks she was running. So far, no one on Orion's board of trustees seemed to have any skeletons in their closets.

Connor beckoned her to his desk. 'It's the call I was waiting for. Remember, Parker thinks I'm asking about scholarships for a friend. She doesn't know you're here.'

Kit mimed zipping her lips. He handed her the headphones he'd plugged into the receiver so that she could also listen, then set the recorder to run.

'Hey, Parker,' Connor answered warmly. 'How are you?'

'Cold. You have sun in San Diego, but we had freezing rain last night.'

'In New York?' Connor asked, as if he had all the time in the world.

Kit wanted him to hurry along but contained herself. This was his call, and she'd let him play it the way he felt best.

'I'm doing a traveling show right now. We're in Toronto. Look, I got in touch with the woman who was the scholarship student in my class at Orion. She enrolled in our sophomore year.'

Only one per year? Kit thought.

'They only gave out one scholarship a year?' Connor asked.

Good. They were on the same wavelength.

'That's it. I texted her last night and she said we could call, so I'll loop her in. Is it okay if I sit in? She doesn't know you.'

'Of course,' Connor said smoothly, but he grimaced because that might limit what they could ask.

After thirty seconds, another voice spoke. 'I'm here.' It was resonant and familiar somehow. Kit frowned, trying to place where she'd heard it.

'Okay,' Parker said. 'Tanya, this is Connor Robinson. Connor, Tanya Westbrook. Connor has a friend whose kid wants to get into Orion on a scholarship.'

'Good luck to her. Or him?' Tanya asked.

'Her,' Connor said. 'My girlfriend's daughter. She's just finishing her freshman year in high school, and all she can talk about is Orion School. What can you tell me?'

'Well, she has an uphill climb ahead of her,' Tanya said. 'But it's worth it if she's persistent. Orion opens so many doors. It's how I met my agent.'

'Tanya has three gold records,' Parker said proudly.

Kit and Connor shared a puzzled glance. 'I'm sorry,' Connor said, apologetic. 'But I haven't heard anything you've recorded.'

Parker laughed. 'That's because Tanya is her real name. She records as Sybil Tucker.'

Kit's mouth fell open. *Sybil Tucker?* Her songs were all over the radio. No wonder she sounded familiar.

Connor was having a similar reaction. 'Wow. You're really good. I have two of your albums downloaded.'

'Why, thank you! So. Orion. It's hard to get into, but even harder to excel once you're there. It's kind of a viper's nest. Present company excluded. Parker was the only one who sat with me at lunch on my first day of school.'

Connor's smile was warm. 'Doesn't surprise me at all. So what was the application process?'

'Well, students can apply starting the summer before their freshman year of high school and if they don't get in, they can keep applying until they graduate from their home district school. If they get in – and if they can pay the tuition – they start that fall. Applicants send an audition tape first. Orion gets hundreds during the summer. A team of incoming seniors review and submit the top hundred to the admissions director. He narrows it down to twenty-five. Those twenty-five come in and audition live for the committee. Gotta say, that was the most nervous I have *ever* been.'

'Sounds brutal,' Connor said. 'How much is the scholarship worth?'

'Full year's tuition,' Tanya replied. 'A cool forty grand.'

Kit covered her mouth with her hand to keep the gasp from jumping out of her mouth. Eyes wide, she stared at Connor.

'For high school?' he asked, equally shocked. 'That's what a lot of universities cost.'

'Exactly,' Parker said. 'That's why the scholarships are fought over.'

'I guess so.' Connor shook his head. 'So is this a full scholarship until graduation, or do you have to try out every year?'

'Once you're in,' Tanya said, 'tuition is covered for the duration. You can get kicked out, but hardly anyone does.'

'Okay.' Connor still looked shell-shocked. 'My girlfriend's daughter heard a rumor that there were other ways to get in. Not that she's going to do them, but some of the other girls were talking. You know. Like girls do.'

'And boys,' Parker said dryly. 'Check your misogyny at the door, Connor.'

Connor blinked. 'What? I'm not misogynistic.'

Kit gave him a look. *Seriously?*

Connor looked a little hurt and Kit wondered if no one had ever confronted him before.

'I'm sorry,' he said quietly. 'Boys gossip, too. I think the topics are different, though.'

Both Parker and Tanya laughed. 'I wouldn't be so sure,' Tanya said. 'So this rumor. Is it that there's a guy who knows someone who can get them a private audition, which is code for sex?'

'Yeah. Any truth to it? My girlfriend's daughter was worried she'd lose out because she wasn't willing to do that.'

'Good for her,' Tanya said fervently. 'That she knows her personal limits so young is good to hear. I heard that rumor when I was in school, but I attributed it to people who were angry that my tuition was free. You know, she only got in because she slept with someone. Sick people.'

'There is that other scam, though,' Parker said. 'Which is probably worse, because so many kids get disappointed.'

'Yeah,' Tanya agreed. 'It's fake, but nobody can ever figure out what the scammer gets out of it other than humiliating some high school kids.'

Kit and Connor shared a glance. *This could be it.*

'What's the scam?' Connor asked. 'So I can warn my girlfriend's kid about it.'

Parker sighed. 'A high school kid – always a girl – would get an email from someone claiming to be on the admissions committee. They always said they'd seen her in her high school production and thought she was super talented. You know, the flattery that we all like to hear. Then they say that Orion is doing an audition for an extra scholarship.'

'First red flag,' Tanya cut in. 'They only do extra admission auditions for kids who've transferred into the district during the school year. And never for scholarships.'

'He sends a form and has her fill it out and says she can invite her friends,' Parker continued. 'She tells her friends and they all show up at Orion for this audition, only to find locked doors and a grumpy security guard telling them to go away.'

Yes, Kit mouthed, and Connor grinned at her, triumphant.

'And there's never another email from this asshole?' Connor asked.

'Nope,' Parker said. 'It's really sad. I was at the school for a weekend rehearsal once when a group of kids showed up for the fake audition, and there were tears. *Buckets* of tears. Girls and boys, crying their eyes out. And then they ganged up on the girl who was the scam recipient. It was ugly. They screamed in her face, and when they left, they didn't take her with them.'

And yet that girl's probably still alive, Kit thought. Unlike Cecilia, Jaelyn, Naomi, and the others.

'You called her a cab,' Tanya recalled fondly. 'You even gave her cab fare.'

'I felt so sorry for her,' Parker said. 'She couldn't afford the cab home. Her parents didn't have the money for things like that. And certainly not for Orion's tuition. I think whoever was targeting these girls knew they were financially desperate.'

Good to know. Financial need was a detail they hadn't yet considered. But who paid forty thousand dollars a year for a private high school?

Apparently, all but the one scholarship kid in every Orion graduating class.

'So basically, there are no shortcuts,' Connor said. 'My girlfriend's daughter has to go the distance.'

'She does,' Tanya said. 'Tell her to make sure her audition tape is flawless. It doesn't matter how many takes she needs to do, there cannot be a single mistake.'

'And the admissions director?' Connor pressed. 'He's fair?'

'He is,' Tanya said. 'And he's been there *forever*.'

Parker hummed her agreement. 'He was old when we were in school.'

'Old and gray, huh?' Connor fished. *He's clean,* he mouthed to Kit, bringing the man's background check up on his screen. There was nothing suspicious.

Tanya chuckled. 'He'd be gray if he had hair. He's been bald forever, too. Look, I have to run, but tell your girlfriend's daughter that I wish her all the luck.'

Kit wished they could come clean about the real reason for their call. Rita would love an autograph from Sybil Tucker, a.k.a. Tanya Westbrook.

'Thank you both,' Connor said sincerely. 'Break a leg, ladies.' He ended the call and turned off the recorder.

'So that's how he does it,' Kit murmured.

'It's like you thought. The girls that don't share the good news with their friends are his victims.' He fidgeted with his computer's keyboard before meeting Kit's eyes. 'I'm sorry.'

Kit tilted her head. 'For what?'

'If I've said things that were . . . y'know. Misogynistic.'

She smiled at him. 'You have, actually, but I accept your apology.'

'Feel free to tell me when I'm out of line. I don't want to hurt anyone, even by accident.'

'I will.' She looked up when the door to the bullpen opened. 'It's Levinson. You want to come with?'

'Sure.' Connor stood. 'I'll probably still be a dick sometimes. Just so you know. Old habits being hard to break and all.'

'I'll consider myself warned.'

She might even miss him once Baz came back. She'd miss Howard more, though. He brought cake.

SDPD, San Diego, California
Wednesday, 20 April, 9.45 A.M.

Kit and Connor followed Dr Levinson into Navarro's office.

'Detective,' Dr Levinson said. 'You're joining us?'

'I am,' Kit said. 'Do you know Detective Robinson?'

'We've met,' Levinson said. He sat at the conference table, cleaning his glasses once again.

Older. Gray hair. Glasses. A drama connection.

When the four of them were seated, Navarro started. 'Al, we told you that the thing the victims had in common was an interest in acting. But we've made another connection.'

Levinson sighed. 'Orion School. I read it online this morning. I already had my coffee in a travel mug when you called, Reynaldo. I was coming in to see you. I figured you saw my name on the board of trustees list.'

'We did,' Kit said. 'Why didn't you mention it when we talked on Monday?'

'Because you weren't talking about Orion School,' Levinson said simply. 'You were talking about auditions in LA for TV shows. In hindsight, I probably should have suggested that you talk to the folks at Orion, but they're not the most welcoming group. They wouldn't have given you any information voluntarily. They're . . .' He shrugged. 'Stuck-up.'

'What's your role on the board?' Conner asked.

'Fundraising only. There's another psychologist on the board who actually deals with student issues. I offered my services to the student body because those kids are high-strung, but the principal became indignant. Said their students were not *criminals*.' He rolled his eyes. 'Little does she know. Some of them are. Not murderers,' he added. 'Mostly drug use and dealing.'

'We need to talk to Orion today,' Kit said. 'Any tips?'

'Have a warrant ready,' he advised. 'Half of the board of trustees are lawyers.'

She grimaced. 'That'll take a while. We might go in asking for information as lowly public servants first. Why you? Are you a fundraising guru or something?'

His smile was self-effacing. 'Kind of. It's a side hobby. Maybe I learned from all the scam artists I've interviewed over the years, but I am a little better at getting rich people to part with their money than the average bear. I'm on four boards right now. I used to be on six boards, but I've cut back in the past few years. Semi-retirement, after all. I'd do it full time if I could. Profiling criminals has become rather exhausting.'

'What boards are you on?' Kit asked.

'Orion School and New Horizons, but you already knew those.'

'Dr Reeves also serves on the New Horizons board,' Kit told Connor.

'That's how you knew to vouch for him?' Connor asked.

Levinson nodded. 'Indeed. I also serve on the boards of a shelter for domestic violence survivors and an organization that provides help to homeless people going for job interviews.'

Navarro's expression had gone politely flat, and that didn't bode well. 'What were the two you pulled out of?'

'Skateboards for All. My son was a skateboarder. I joined for him because he was sad that some of his school friends couldn't afford decent equipment. The other was a model railroad society, which is purely because I love model railroads. Supporting nonprofits is kind of my jam. Once I'm fully retired, I'll be rejoining the railroad board.'

'What do you know about the admissions director at Orion?' Kit asked.

'He's dedicated. Grumpy because he hates paperwork. My opinion is that he's not involved in anything like this. He could be a good actor, of course. It is a drama school, after all, but I don't see him being violent.'

Kit thought about the videos they'd seen. 'Does he wear ties?'

Levinson frowned. 'Why? Oh, is that the murder weapon?'

'We believe so,' Navarro said before either Kit or Connor could reply.

Navarro's deflection bothered Kit. Navarro normally would have been one hundred percent up front with Levinson, telling him all the details.

Levinson's frown deepened and she wondered if the psychologist thought the same thing. 'He hates ties. I've never seen him wear one. Says it constricts his throat and damages his voice. Are we finished, Lieutenant?'

Kit bit back her wince. It had been *Reynaldo* when they'd first sat down. Yeah, Levinson knew that Navarro was now uncomfortable with him.

She wanted to sigh, but bit that back, too.

'For now, yes. Detectives, you may go. Can you stay for a few minutes, Dr Levinson?'

Levinson's expression was impassive. 'Of course. Best of luck breaking into the hallowed halls of Orion School, Detectives.'

'Thank you, sir,' Kit murmured respectfully, then followed Connor out.

'That was awkward,' Connor said when they were back at their desks.

'Yeah.' She glanced at Navarro's office, but the window blinds had been pulled. 'Navarro didn't buy his story.'

'I didn't think so, either. Did you?'

She shrugged. 'He fits the body type of the man we saw in the video.'

'He has a goatee, though, and Driscoll didn't.'

Kit frowned. 'What does that have to do with it?'

'In deepfakes, the person with the replacement face starts out making a video of himself. Or herself. Fifteen, twenty minutes of mugging different expressions. That video is broken down into individual frames – thousands of frames. Those frames are analyzed by the software and matched to the face in the destination video. In our case that would have been the killer murdering our victims.'

'Okay. That's a really good explanation, by the way, but what does that have to do with Levinson's goatee?'

'The closer the facial details of the source – the faker – are to those of the face in the destination video, the better the result. Driscoll's videos were good. If he was pasting his face over Levinson's, he might have grown a goatee of the same shape.'

'But he didn't. Driscoll was clean shaven.' She exhaled. 'Okay, that makes me feel better. Thank you. How close are you to getting the background checks run?'

'Give me another half hour and I'll have them done.'

'Same. Then we can sign out a car and pay a visit to the stuck-up folks at Orion School. I'm hoping they might have more insight on this scam artist than your friend did. If I had someone luring students to my door with any regularity, I'd work hard to identify the perpetrator.'

The door to Navarro's office opened and Levinson emerged. He gave Kit and Connor a small wave, his smile tight as he departed.

Navarro closed his door and didn't come out.

Kit let her sigh loose. Navarro hadn't let his emotions dictate his investigation with respect to Levinson. That was how she should be treating Dr Reeves.

Not Sam. He can't be Sam anymore, even in your mind.

She looked at Connor to find him studying her carefully. 'I know what we can do to try to eliminate your shrink as a suspect,' he said.

Hillcrest, California
Wednesday, 20 April, 11.00 A.M.

Sam had finished his second pot of coffee and had compiled a list of five new possible victims when Siggy started growling and barking again. He'd been growling all morning, so Sam had started to dismiss it as background noise.

But this time, the growling was followed by a knock at his door.

The knock startled him, and he nearly knocked his mug over.

No more coffee for me, for real. His jitters had progressed to the shakes.

Reading dozens of missing-person reports wasn't helping, either. Even if the runaways hadn't been murdered, it was unlikely that many of them had landed in a safe place. His work at New Horizons made that all too clear.

Going cautiously to Joel's front door, Sam checked the peephole and straightened abruptly. Kit McKittrick. With a man he didn't recognize. They looked tense.

Foreboding shivered down his back as he opened the door. 'Detective? How can I help you?'

She smiled at him tightly and the sense of foreboding rose to suffocate him.

'Can we come in?' she asked.

Wordlessly he stepped back, closing the door when she and the man were in Joel's living room.

'Dr Reeves, this is my partner, Detective Robinson.'

Oh right. Because Constantine had had a heart attack.

Robinson was a big, beefy man who wore an I-don't-trust-you expression that gave Sam serious pause. It was like they were back to square one.

Sam wondered if he should hide Siggy, because his dog was still growling low in his throat. But that was ridiculous. He hoped.

'How can I help you?' he asked again.

Kit sighed and she sounded exhausted. Looked it, too. 'May we sit down?'

He gestured to the sofa. 'Go ahead.' He took the recliner but sat upright, his stomach twisted into a knot. He'd observed her for a few weeks now and something was not right. Something other than all the other shit that wasn't right, anyway.

'I wanted to let you know what we found last night in Driscoll's backyard,' she said.

She stopped talking, as if waiting for him to comment, but Sam could hear Laura's voice in his head, warning him. So he kept his mouth shut.

Finally, she went on. 'We found a number of hard drives. They contained videos.'

Now Sam could hear Veronica Gadd's voice in his mind. *Oh my God. What was on them? Please say it wasn't kiddie porn. Please.*

'What kind?' he asked, unable to keep the dread from his voice.

'Like this.' Kit handed him her phone on which a video was cued to begin.

Sam glanced at Detective Robinson. His eyes were suspicious and . . . waiting. Sam got the impression that this was a test of some kind.

Call Laura! Make them either arrest you or leave.

But he didn't. Because part of him still trusted Kit McKittrick.

I'll probably regret that later, he thought as he hit play, aware that both detectives were watching him like hawks.

This was not going to be good.

It started with a living room he'd never seen before, decorated in soft blues and grays. Broadway musical posters covered the visible walls. The camera was focused on the back of a leather sofa.

Then a man came into the room. Colton Driscoll. And then . . .

'Oh God,' Sam whispered. Because Naomi Beckham had been lying on that sofa. And now she was being murdered. By Colton. With a necktie.

Memories came flooding back, filling his mind with the images that only came out in his worst nightmares. Because he'd already seen something like this before. It had ended in death.

Just as it was ending in death for Naomi, who was fighting Colton, but slowly. Weakly.

Colton smiled when her body had gone limp.

'Dr Reeves? Dr Reeves? *Sam?*'

He looked up to find both detectives staring at him. Kit had leaned forward, her hand outstretched. Like she was about to shake him but had hesitated. Numbly, he wondered how many times she'd called his name.

'Why?' he whispered, his voice breaking. 'Why did you make me watch this?'

He'd never be able to unsee this. Never. He knew that from experience.

This was what had happened to all those poor girls. It had happened to Skyler.

It had happened to his Marley.

He dropped the phone on Joel's carpet and ran to the bathroom, throwing up everything he'd eaten that morning.

When his stomach was empty, he hung over the toilet. Shaking. And angry.

With Colton for being a sadistic monster who really had killed those girls.

With Kit for tormenting him this way.

With his own mind for holding so tightly to the memories he wished he could forget.

'Sam?' Kit said quietly from the doorway.

Something cold touched his shoulder. A bottle of water.

Furiously, he snatched it from her hand and rinsed his mouth out.

'Satisfied?' he demanded.

'No,' she said sadly. 'I'm sorry. I needed to see your reaction. I needed to know.'

Sam twisted his body, landing on his ass, his back against the tub. 'So now you do. Please leave.'

She crouched a few feet away and he noticed the dark circles under her eyes. He shoved away the flash of compassion. Because she didn't deserve it. She still didn't believe him. Still didn't trust him.

I should have listened to Laura and kept my mouth shut.

'You've been conveniently present for a lot of important revelations on this case,' she said.

'Not because I wanted to be,' he said through gritted teeth.

'I know.'

'No, you don't,' he said bitterly. 'Otherwise you never would have done that dog-and-pony show out there. Were you trying to prove something to your new partner or to yourself?' A shadow moved in the hallway. Her partner was there listening. *Goddammit.* Sam was sick and tired of being a suspect.

He shoved himself to his feet. 'You know what? It doesn't matter. I don't care what you believe. Get out. You can call my lawyer. And you, Robinson, you can stop lurking in the hallway. You want to see my reaction, too? Come and look at it.'

The partner came into view, his expression still grim. But there was a softening around his eyes. He'd been suspicious before, but now? He looked more unsure.

And I don't fucking care.

Kit rose slowly. 'Okay, but first I need you to know that the killer on this recording wasn't Colton Driscoll.'

'What?' Were they still playing with him? 'Of course it was. I just *saw* him strangle Naomi Beckham. Thank you for that, by the way. It's not like I don't have enough shit in my head.'

She shook her head. 'Driscoll's face was faked. Deepfakes, they call them.'

Well, damn. Now he was interested again, despite his better judgment. 'I've heard of that,' he said warily. 'Saw it online. So who was it really?'

'We don't know. Someone shorter than Driscoll, but still strong enough to carry a teenage girl out of the room over his shoulder. Did anything in the video look familiar to you? Like, did Driscoll say anything in session to make you think he'd been to this place?'

He went to the sink and splashed cold water on his face while he contemplated his answer. Or *if* he even should answer. He should make them talk to Laura.

But he wanted to help them. Help Kit.

He wanted this nightmare to end. For himself and for the girls.

He dried his face and turned to face her and the hulking detective who stood behind her, watching him.

'No. Unless they were watching *Avondale* on the TV before the clip started. That was the only thing he said.' He folded the towel and rehung it on the bar, trying to calm his mind and remember if there really was anything else. 'He said that he watched her do her homework. Geometry, maybe? Yeah, I think it was geometry because that was the first thing that had me thinking he was abusing a minor. Geometry isn't usually a college course.'

Detective Robinson flinched and Sam wondered if he'd seen a video of a girl studying geometry before she'd been killed, whichever girl it had been.

'You're right,' Robinson murmured, his eyes growing haunted. 'It's usually a high school course.'

Robinson's haunted look made Sam wonder what they'd seen. 'Did you watch all of the murders?' Sam asked, feeling compassion that was, once again, unwelcome.

Because if they had, he couldn't blame them for being upset. He could blame them for making him see it, too, but he knew what it was like to have to watch helplessly.

'Not all,' she said. 'But enough. One working theory is that Colton somehow got cameras in the killer's home and had been watching him. Spying on him.'

'And incorporating what he saw into the lies he told you,' Robinson added.

Spying on him. Another memory surfaced from the static still filling Sam's mind. 'He said his coworkers in the mail room gave him a hard time. I asked him if he'd informed his boss. He said his boss was basically useless because he spent all day spying on the building's residents.'

'Through the security cameras?' Robinson asked.

'Those are usually in hallways,' Kit said thoughtfully. 'Not much interesting happening there.'

Robinson tilted his head. 'I wonder if they have cameras in the offices.'

Sam shrugged. 'All I know is that he said his boss watched the people in the building. I didn't ask him if he watched, too. I didn't think about it. Didn't think I needed to. I was more worried about his pretty young things at the time.'

And if the words came out with a bitter edge, he wasn't going to blame himself.

Kit looked away for a moment before returning her gaze to meet Sam's. 'I am sorry. I've had a few shocks on this case. It's been hard to know who to trust.'

He didn't look away. 'Yeah. I kind of know how that feels.'

She winced. 'We'll go now.'

'I'll lock the door behind you.' He followed them to the living room, where Siggy had curled up in his doggy bed and gone to sleep. So much for being a protection dog.

'At least I have an alibi for the last twenty minutes,' he added acidly as he opened the front door.

Kit pursed her lips, then nodded once. 'Stay safe, Dr Reeves.'

Detective Robinson gave Sam a considering look as he walked through the door ahead of her. 'She believed you,' he said quietly. 'I didn't. The video was to convince me.'

'Doesn't matter,' Sam snapped, even though Robinson had said *didn't*. Like now he *did* believe Sam. *Doesn't matter*. 'You're cops. You see this shit all the time.' *I only saw it happen once*. 'I'm a psychologist.' *I only saw it once but it changed me forever*. 'I hear about the aftereffects. I visualize in my mind what every victim has endured as they tell me their stories, but now I have this real-life footage to add to my nightmares.'

Kit's throat was working frantically as she looked up at him, and he was taken aback to see tears in her eyes. 'We don't,' she whispered brokenly. 'We don't see this all the time. We come in after it's happened. We see the bodies. But we had to watch it, Sam. All of it. All of them. So much more than we showed you. I'm sorry I made you watch that. I'm sorry I put things in your head that you can't unsee. But my duty is to the girls. The ones that are dead and the ones he plans to kill.'

Sam closed his eyes, so damn weary. 'I know,' he murmured.

'You're collateral damage,' Robinson said from Joel's front porch. 'Sucks to be you, man.' But the words didn't sound crass and unfeeling. Maybe tentatively regretful. 'Thanks for the tip on the backyard. It's going to be a game-changer. Once we figure out where it is that he lives, we'll be one step closer to IDing him.' He turned and walked down Joel's steps toward the black sedan parked in Joel's driveway, leaving Sam standing alone with Kit.

'You okay?' Sam asked gruffly.

She rolled her eyes, drying her wet cheeks with the sleeve of her jacket. 'No. But I am sorry.'

'I know,' he said sadly, because now that his anger had faded, he really did know. 'Just . . . hurry, okay? I don't want anyone else to die.'

Her shoulders slumped. 'Me either.' Then, straightening her spine, she dug in her pocket and pulled out another one of the treats she'd given him that night in the car, when she'd told him to leave town. To return to Scottsdale.

Sam now wished he'd stayed there.

He also wished he could give this woman comfort. *Which makes me a fool.*

'For Siggy,' she said, handing him the treat.

'Thank you.'

Then she left and he locked the door behind her. Returning to the kitchen, he put the dog treat on the table, sank into a chair, and dropped his head into his hands, the images of Naomi's murder replaying in his mind. It all mixed with memories of Marley and he wanted to go back to bed and pretend none of this had ever happened.

No time for self-pity. Get back to work.

He looked at the photos of the runaways he'd thought might have been potential victims, now wondering if Kit had seen them die, too.

Eighteen

Hillcrest, California
Wednesday, 20 April, 11.35 A.M.

'I'm sorry,' Connor said when both he and Kit were in the department sedan.

In the passenger seat, Kit leaned her head back and closed her eyes, blocking out Joel's tidy Victorian house. 'We needed to know. Dr Reeves has been conveniently in the middle of all the major discoveries on this case.'

'You called him Sam in there.'

She winced. But she wasn't going to apologize. 'Yeah, I did.'

Connor sighed and started the engine. 'I believed him, too.'

'I have since the beginning,' she confessed.

'You've got a good gut, Kit. Everyone knows it.'

She turned to look at him, wondering who this man really was. Sometimes she wanted to smack his face. Other times, like now, he could be gentle and kind. 'Thank you.'

He backed out of Joel's driveway and into the street. 'We need a warrant for the mail room where Driscoll worked.'

'I'll call it in. Maybe Howard can do the search while we're at the school.' Connor grunted his agreement and Kit dialed Navarro, putting the call on speaker. 'Connor and I just left Dr Reeves,' she said when her boss answered.

'Why?' Navarro asked sharply.

Maybe he was still smarting over whatever he and Levinson said to each other. Kit was almost too tired to care.

'We needed to know if Reeves knew what was on those hard

drives. We showed him about twenty seconds of the one with Naomi Beckham.'

There was a long, long pause and Kit thought he'd be angry with her, but he only asked, 'And?'

'He threw up. Both Connor and I believed his reaction was real.'

'Okay, then,' he said brusquely. 'You checked off that box. You on your way to Orion now?'

'Yes, but we need a warrant for the mail room where Driscoll worked.' She told him about the spying that Driscoll claimed his boss was doing.

'That building has apartments, too,' Navarro said. 'Swanky ones on the top floors. Maybe he lives there.'

Connor shook his head. 'He would have had to get the dead girls out of the building somehow. I think someone would have noticed a dead body over his shoulder.'

'Could have transported them in a big suitcase,' Navarro said. 'I'll request the mail room warrant and keep you updated on the status. It's not a lot to go on, but we might get lucky. Wealthy people have apartments in that building. I imagine they'd want to know if someone was spying on them. May give me a little extra convincing power with the judge.'

'I hope so,' Kit said fervently. 'We need some luck. We've been playing catch-up to this bastard for years. He's been several steps ahead of us the whole time.'

Navarro heaved a sigh. 'We actually did have some luck. Or at least Levinson did us a favor. He gave me the name of the head attorney at the school. I talked to the man, told him that the reporter is publishing an unsubstantiated rumor. That we want to talk to them as witnesses versus suspects.'

'That's true,' Kit said. 'None of our background reports came back with any smoking guns. Doesn't mean there aren't any, but if we get bad vibes from anyone at the school, we can dig further. Who are we going to see?'

'The headmaster, the admissions director, a shit ton of lawyers, and their IT guy. They should have them all gathered by the time you get there. I'll send you a list.'

'We'll review their backgrounds again while we drive. Thanks, boss. Did Howard come back yet?'

'No. He called in, said he was taking a personal day.'

Kit felt a flicker of irritation at that. She and Connor had watched more of the videos than Howard had, and they were still working. From the way Connor was muttering under his breath, he appeared to be thinking the same thing.

'What about CSU?' she asked. 'Have they examined the remaining hard drives?'

'Almost. Sergeant Ryland says there are no more murder victims so far, but Driscoll had a lot of child porn on the other hard drives. Preteens mainly, but some younger. We've called in ICAC to take custody of those videos. They say that they've seen them online before, that Driscoll probably didn't make them.'

The Internet Crimes Against Children department dealt with sick bastards day in and day out. 'I don't think I could do that job,' she murmured.

'Me either,' Navarro agreed, his voice heavy. 'Ryland says they still have a few hard drives to go. I'll text you when I know more. Good luck with Orion.'

'Thanks.' Kit ended the call. 'Let's review the files for the people we're going to meet.'

The Orion School, San Diego, California
Wednesday, 20 April, 1.00 P.M.

Kit studied the stony faces around the table in the lavishly decorated conference room at the Orion School. The carpet was thick under her boots and the paintings on the walls looked like museum pieces. The table itself was a solid piece of wood that appeared to be mahogany.

Forty thousand dollars a year tuition.

Right.

There were ten people at the table, not counting her and Connor. Just one of the ties the men wore cost more than the monthly rent on her boat slip.

Kit had expected wealth but had honestly expected a more laid-back, creative vibe. It was an art school, for heaven's sake. Where were the kids dancing in the hallways singing show tunes?

She felt betrayed by *Glee* and *Fame*. This place was like an ice castle.

Kit met each of the gazes currently glaring at her. Lawyer with a blue tie; lawyer with a red tie; lawyer with a rainbow tie, so at least he had some personality. The principal – wait, so sorry, she was the *headmaster* – looked very stern. More lawyers. And one IT guy who looked only slightly posh.

He must be the misfit of the Orion School staff.

The admissions director was noticeably absent. She and Connor would need to find out why that was.

Two of the attorneys had the same body type as the killer on the videos, and Kit noted their names. They'd do more in-depth background checks on them later.

'So,' Kit began. 'I'm Detective McKittrick and this is my partner, Detective Robinson. I tried to call yesterday. Gave the woman at the front desk my name and badge number. Told her it was urgent that I speak with the headmaster.'

'I've spoken with the receptionist,' the headmaster said. She was Headmaster Worthington, because of course she was. Her suit was clearly designer and very expensive, because of course it was. 'She is being reprimanded. Had I known you'd called, I would have answered immediately.'

That might even have been true. It didn't really matter now.

'The department regrets that this story made it to the media,' Connor said sincerely, just as they'd agreed as they were en route. He was to be the good cop today, which was fine because Kit rather enjoyed the bad cop role. 'But the reporter didn't cross-check her facts. She was incorrect.'

'We'll be dealing with the media outlet,' one of the lawyers said grimly. 'This is unacceptable. The very idea that someone in our school was involved.'

The very idea.

'Someone is hunting and killing teenage girls, sir. We've

identified twelve victims and are confident there are more that we don't yet know about.' Kit let the statement hover for a moment, waiting until their expressions began to change from stony to something more human. 'It is unfortunate that a reporter included your school in her article without fact-checking, but your reputation, while important, is by far the least of our concerns. We need to stop this man before he kills again.'

It was Kit's fear that their killer would soon feel cornered and kill again to throw suspicion back on Sam Reeves.

It was just a matter of time.

The lawyer had the good sense to look chagrined, but it was the headmaster who spoke. 'Of course, Detective. You're quite right. Justice for the lives of these young women is the most important thing. How can we help you?'

'Thank you.' Kit opened the folder she'd brought and selected a photo of Naomi. 'One of our victims, a fifteen-year-old named Naomi Beckham, told a classmate that she was coming here for a scholarship audition. That her benefactor was an older man with a black Mercedes.'

'None of us drive a black Mercedes,' another lawyer said. 'Other colors, yes, but not black.'

Kit's smile was tight. 'We know. We checked before we came. The young woman who thought she was getting an audition disappeared that night. We now know that she's dead. She likely died that same night.'

We saw him kill her. The killer's living room had been lit by lamps when Naomi was killed. She hadn't lived to see the sunrise.

'Many of our victims,' she continued, 'participated in drama club or expressed an interest in acting. Along with basic physical characteristics, it is the only commonality.'

Connor offered a sad smile. 'We know that you've been harassed by a scammer who's offered teenagers auditions over the years. Naomi's experience seems to fit with this.'

'Your lieutenant said as much. How did you learn of the scam?' the headmaster asked.

'Unlike the reporter,' Connor said, 'we do our homework before we charge in. What we'd like to know is how often these scams occurred, what times of the year, and what you did to track the perpetrator. Because we're assuming you tried to stop him.'

It was a nice deflection and redirection, Kit thought. *Good job, Connor.*

The headmaster nodded once. 'We did. Your lieutenant gave us an idea of what you wanted, so I invited Ted Bolin, our IT professional, to the meeting. Mr Bolin, please tell them what we know.'

The IT guy smiled nervously. 'The first time this scam occurred was fifteen years ago. I wasn't here at the time, but my predecessor kept track. There was always a scholarship dangled as a prize, and the target of the email was always female.'

'Blond and under five-three?' Kit asked.

Ted nodded. 'Yes.'

'Did they occur in specific months?' Connor asked.

'Yes,' Ted said again. 'September and February.'

'The September occurrences always puzzled us,' the headmaster inserted. 'We open the application process in the late summer, both for regular admission and the scholarship award. We've never done an audition in the fall.' She frowned. 'Did some of the victims go missing in the fall?'

'Yes, ma'am,' Connor said sincerely. 'February as well.'

'It didn't happen every year,' Ted said. He handed them a sheet of paper with several dates. 'These are the reported occurrences of the scam.'

The pattern was immediately identifiable, at least for the last five years. Every time a scam occurred, there'd been no video of a murder, including this past February, two months ago.

Kit had been right. The girls who kept the secret ended up dead.

The list of occurrences was short – only four in the fifteen years they'd been happening. Which meant that the majority of the girls kept the secret.

The killer had to have a good feeling who he could trust not to tell. *Add that to the profile.* But how had he lured his earliest victims if not using the scholarship scheme? Their first Jane Doe was murdered between seventeen and twenty years before – two to five years before the first occurrence of the scam.

And why had the 'scam' begun only fifteen years ago? The Orion School had been operating for nearly thirty years.

Oh. 'When did you start offering scholarships?' Kit asked.

'Seventeen years ago,' the headmaster said. 'Why? Is that important?'

Kit glanced at Connor before answering. 'Most probably, yes.'

The headmaster paled. 'He's been using our school to lure his victims all the time?'

'He may have had other lures,' Connor said. 'We don't know. It's a puzzle and we're just starting to see the major pieces.'

Because Sam Reeves had needed to do the right thing. *Thank you, Sam.*

Kit hoped he was okay. She'd hated leaving him so torn up. *I never should have put him in that position.*

But she'd needed to know. For the girls.

'Ted, did you or your predecessor try to trace the emails?' she asked.

'Yes, of course. We even brought in consultants to help. But whoever is doing this knows what he's doing. He uses VPNs and routes his communications through servers all over the world.'

'We figured as much,' Connor said. 'Would you be able to show our CSU team the analyses you've done? They may have forensic tools that look a little deeper.'

Kit didn't hold much hope for that. Finding the living room in the videos would be a better use of their time. It had to be in the city because the girls had been able to easily get there.

'Of course,' the headmaster said. 'Whatever you need.'

Kit gave her a nod of appreciation. 'Thank you. We can't help but notice that your admissions director isn't here. Why is that?'

Worry flickered in the headmaster's eyes. 'When he read that article, he was devastated. He's been with Orion from the very beginning and we're his life. His health is a little frail, so I told him that we'd try to address your questions first. If you still need to see him, he'll be available.'

'We will want to talk to him,' Kit said. 'We need to know if any of the victims reached out to ask questions about the scholarship.'

'He'll give you full access to his email,' the headmaster promised, surprising Kit. She'd figured that the school would require a warrant.

One of the lawyers leaned in to whisper in her ear, but she shook her head. 'I know they officially need a warrant. I'm saying that we are not going to require that. We will be cooperative. We don't want any more girls to die.'

They probably wanted the good press that full cooperation would provide, but that was okay. As long as she and Connor got access to the emails.

'Thank you,' Kit said. 'Who helped start the scholarship program and how was it originally publicized? Was there a press release to all the high schools? Did you run ads on TV, radio, or social media? Who would have known about it from the beginning?'

The headmaster blinked. 'I don't know off the top of my head who started it. It was already in place when I was selected for the position of headmaster. I assume there was a committee. I'll find out for you. As for publicizing, the school has always sent student reps to various high schools in the district to promote. Usually they do a Q&A with the drama clubs.'

'Do you choose the schools at random or is there a schedule?' Connor asked.

'Oh, it's never random.' The headmaster made a note on the tablet she held. 'I'll get you the schedules for as far back as we've had them.'

'That would be very helpful.' Kit slid the list of occurrences into her folder, then turned to Connor. 'Any more questions?'

He nodded. 'Yes, just one. Did you ever ask for law enforcement assistance in dealing with this scam?'

The lawyers looked at each other, then the one with the rainbow tie spoke. 'We did about five years ago. We simply wanted it to stop. We thought that the fact he was offering a forty-thousand-dollar scholarship constituted fraud, so we called SDPD's fraud department. They came out and talked to us, looked at the emails, then said it was a prank. That the "prankster" didn't financially benefit.' He swallowed hard. 'I wish we'd pressed harder.'

'It might not have mattered,' Kit said practically. 'Like my partner said, we're just now gathering the puzzle pieces. We didn't have anything to go on before, and the likelihood of connecting this scam to our Jane Does back then was minimal at best.'

The lawyer nodded. 'Thank you, but I think we'll be second-guessing ourselves for a long time.'

Welcome to a very crowded club, Kit thought as she rose. 'Thank you all for your time.'

Connor stood and handed the staff their business cards. 'If you remember anything else, please call. Ted, CSU will contact you ASAP.'

'We're still filing a formal complaint against that reporter,' the first lawyer said.

Kit let herself smile, just a little. 'Good.'

They were walked out by Ted, who gave them his contact information when they reached the front door. 'We should have tried harder to find him,' he said heavily. 'It happened intermittently, and we'd get complacent when we had a few years off. We'd think, *Great, he stopped*. But now we know what he was doing when we thought he was inactive.'

'Don't beat yourself up,' Connor said quietly. 'Unless you know of anyone here who's too interested in the female students.'

He shook his head emphatically. 'No, and I'm all over the school every day. A computer crashes and I'm the one they call. I've never heard of any staff member doing anything inappropriate. The kids usually talk around me like I'm not there.' He shrugged. 'Mostly it's the really rich kids since they have staff at home. You'd be shocked at some of the things I hear. But abusive teachers have never been one of those things.'

'Good to know.' Kit gave him a smile as they took their leave. 'Take care.'

She and Connor said nothing until they got to the car. 'I don't think they were involved,' Connor said as he started the engine.

'I agree. But knowing who was there at the beginning of the

scholarship program might point us in the right direction. That and identifying the location of that living room are our best leads right now.'

'We didn't find any bartenders who'd seen Skyler Carville on Friday night,' he countered. 'We might still find him that way.'

'That's true,' Kit said. 'I still haven't checked my five bars, what with digging up Driscoll's backyard and all. I'll take care of that.'

Connor restarted the engine. 'Didn't you want to talk to the parks and rec people about maintenance schedules in the parks where we've found bodies?'

'Yes, especially with the September/February pattern. That's fall and spring planting season,' she added when he frowned. 'Farm girl, remember? The ground might have been dug up for him to bury them in.'

'Oh right, you told us that. I'll make the parks and rec calls while you bar-hop.'

'Thank you.' And then she was going to take a nap without even being nagged to do so.

Chula Vista, California
Wednesday, 20 April, 3.15 P.M.

'Thank you for seeing us,' Sam said as he and Laura sat on Rayna Copely's threadbare sofa. He'd been surprised when Colton's third ex-wife had readily opened her apartment door when they'd knocked.

Rayna was only twenty-four years old, but she looked forty. She was thin to the point of being gaunt. Her expression held a bone-deep weariness that trudged hand in hand with desperation.

She sat on an equally threadbare chair. 'I got a call from one of Colton's old "buddies".' She used air quotes. 'He'd gotten a call from wife number four, who asked him to tell me that you might be coming by.'

Sam should have realized that Veronica Gadd would share their discussion with the man she trusted. Who'd saved her from Colton.

'You've stayed in touch with Colton's old friend, Brian?' he asked.

'No. I never met him, but I'd heard plenty about him. Colton used to rag on him, complain that when he needed him, Brian deserted him. I think Brian just didn't want Colton to fuck his life up, too. Anyway, he apologized for not being there to help me when I was married to Colton. He got number four out safely and wished he'd known to do the same for me.' She tilted her head. 'I talked to the cops already. Didn't have much to tell them, though. They asked about Colton's friends, but he didn't have any.'

'That's what we're hearing,' Sam said. 'You weren't married to Colton for very long.'

Laura had found the marriage certificate and divorce decree. The union had lasted only four and a half months.

'I wised up quick. I was a stupid seventeen-year-old when I met him. Married him on my eighteenth birthday. I was in foster care and not lucky enough to have a good home. No abuse, but it was miserable. Colton was going to be my ticket out.'

'But then he abused you,' Sam said.

She nodded. 'The first time he hit me, he was so sorry. Classic story, I know.'

Sam smiled sadly. 'Classic for a reason. But you did leave.'

'After the third time. I went to a women's shelter in the city and they gave me a place to stay while I got my life together.' She waved a hand at the small apartment. 'It's not much and I have to work three jobs to feed myself, but it's mine and I don't have to depend on rats like Colton.' Rayna shrugged. 'For the first month with him, everything was amazing. Or so I thought. I had food, a place to sleep, and a person who said he'd take care of me. Then he lost his job, and everything changed.'

'He worked in IT,' Laura said.

'He did. But he lost his temper and it was, like, his third strike, so he was out. Seemed like everyone knew he had an anger issue but me.'

'Third strike?' Sam asked. 'So he'd had previous altercations at work?'

'Apparently. The office was sending him to therapy for anger management, but that didn't take.'

That was a surprise. 'He was in therapy?' Sam asked.

'For the first month we were married, yes. It had started before that, but I don't know how far back. I didn't know the guy was his therapist at the time – Colton would come home and talk about his "best friend". How they did all these things together. How the guy was famous, richer than God, had box seats at Dodger Stadium, and how they'd be going to the games. Then, after Colton got fired, he lost his insurance. He got a job in a mail room downtown right away, but that job's insurance didn't cover his therapy. His "best friend" cut him loose when he couldn't pay for the sessions, and that's when Colton got violent.'

This was important. This other therapist might have more information about Colton. Although the man hadn't come forward when Colton was declared a serial killer. Then again, he wouldn't have been able to, even if Colton had confessed to old murders.

Duty to warn was the key. If the therapist hadn't felt that there was any imminent danger to a living person, he wouldn't have come forward.

Still, it couldn't hurt to ask.

'Did Colton threaten his therapist?' Sam asked.

'Oh yeah. All the time after the guy dumped him. Colton said he'd get back at him. That he'd make him pay, that he "knew things" about him that would ruin him.' She shrugged. 'He ranted like that about actors and politicians, too, so I didn't pay much attention until he took out a business card and cut it into little pieces. I pulled the pieces out of the trash can and put them back together.' Her expression grew grim with memory. 'Colton caught me. That was beating number three, the same day I walked away with the clothes on my back. I hitchhiked to a church, and they set me up with the women's shelter.'

'Do you remember the therapist's name?' Laura asked, seemingly on the same wavelength as Sam.

Rayna frowned. 'I don't. I might have written it down in my

journal, but I'd have to hunt for the right volume. Is it that important?'

'Maybe,' Sam said. 'Hard to say until we ask the man some questions, but I'd really appreciate it if you were able to find his name.'

'I'll look in my old journals,' she promised, then stood. 'I'm sorry, but I've got to get ready for work.'

Sam and Laura rose and headed for the door. 'One more question,' Sam said as they walked. 'You said he got the job in the mail room right away. Did he look for another IT job?'

Because he'd wondered about that. IT professional to the mail room was quite a downgrade.

'Not that I remember. I figured that he'd burned so many bridges by then that he didn't even try. I remember being surprised that he took the mail room job because he was always saying that it was beneath him. I asked him why and he said it had its perks. That was before his therapist dumped him. I asked him again when he complained about the pay cut and he smacked me into a wall. That was after therapy ended.'

Sam held out his hand. 'Thank you. I hope things get easier for you.'

Rayna smiled as she shook his hand. 'I think they will. One good thing came of this. Brian – the old buddy of Colton's – offered me a job today, working for his legal firm. I'm giving my two weeks' notice tonight.'

Oh? Sam's warning bells went off. Who was this Brian guy who just happened to be there when Colton's ex-wives needed him? They needed to check him out to make sure he was legit. Rayna had been through enough.

'That's wonderful,' Laura said, then gave the woman her card. 'But if it doesn't work out for any reason, call me. I might be able to help.'

Rayna took the card, her eyes filling with tears. 'Thank you. After so long on my own, it's so nice to have support.'

They said their goodbyes, then walked to Laura's car, not speaking until they were inside.

'We should check Brian out,' Laura said. 'I don't like how convenient this was.'

'Same,' Sam said grimly, then checked his phone for the time. 'But I'd like to visit the family of Rochelle Hamilton first.'

'The girl you found in the runaway clearinghouse?'

'Yes. She disappeared five years ago.'

'Which would have been right about the time that Colton lost his job and threatened his therapist,' she noted.

Sam did the mental math based on the date from Rayna's marriage license. 'You're right. But his partner – and maybe Colton, because who knows now? – was killing long before that. Joel told me that the first victim was found fifteen years ago. I figure I'll work my way backward.'

'Then to the Hamilton house we go.' Laura started to pull out of her parking place, then stopped. 'Got a text. Rayna found that therapist's name.' She passed Sam her phone.

The young woman texted that she'd been so appreciative of their kindness that she'd immediately searched for the journal, finding it faster than she'd thought.

Sam cut and pasted the man's name into Google, finding that he had an office in the city.

But before he could click on the phone number, a video thumbnail caught his eye. The therapist had been interviewed, the Broadway show posters in the background behind him frozen in the frame.

Sam knew this room. He'd seen it *today*. Right before he'd thrown up.

Holy shit.

'Sam?' Laura asked, sounding worried. 'What's wrong?'

His heart raced as he stared at his screen. 'I have to call Kit.'

Nineteen

Little Italy, San Diego, California
Wednesday, 20 April, 4.00 P.M.

Kit paused outside the third bar on her list when her phone buzzed in her pocket. Connor's name flashed on her screen.

'Hey,' she said, stepping away from the bar's front door. 'What d'ya got?'

'I've been calling the parks in town, asking about planting schedules. I focused on Longview Park, where Jaelyn Watts was found, since she's the most recent victim, not counting Skyler Carville.'

'Because Skyler wasn't his MO.'

'Right. Longview Park confirmed a scheduled maintenance for two weeks around the day Jaelyn disappeared. They weren't planting, though. It was a new irrigation system. They'd just finished putting it in that morning. The ground had been dug up, leveled, and was sodded over the very next day, covering up the body.'

Yes. 'Who had access to that information?'

Connor blew out a breath. 'Who didn't? The park staff and the volunteers. That part of the park was closed off for a while, so it was on their website.'

'Well, shit.' Anyone in the public would have known that area wasn't going to be accessible. 'I guess we have to start looking at park employees and volunteers.'

'And the board of directors.'

Kit's brows went up. 'They know about maintenance schedules, too?'

'For some maintenance, yes – at least at this park, because it's private and charges for admission. That area is a major draw because of the pond, and schools sometimes use it for picnics. It being closed meant an expected drop in admissions revenue and that, along with the expenditure of the new irrigation system, required approval from the board. I've requested a list of board members.'

Which was exactly what she'd been about to ask. 'Excellent. Maybe get a list of their membership from the public, too? Since this killer exclusively uses parks – at least from what we know so far – it's more likely that he's more involved in the system rather than a random guy who cruises park websites looking for service outages.'

'I already asked the person from Jaelyn's park for their general membership list, but she clammed up. Said she'd need to ask the lawyers.'

'Which means a warrant.'

'Already requested it.'

Kit was impressed. 'Thank you. What about the earlier victims? Any success there?'

'Most of the parks don't keep records that long. Unfortunately, that was the case for the park where the victim before Jaelyn was discovered.'

'Miranda Crisp,' Kit murmured.

'Right. She disappeared seven years ago. I did request maintenance and planting schedules from all the parks for as far back as they had them, though. I've got details for two of the parks already and am waiting for the rest. Hopefully we'll get those soon, because we already got a match. Balboa had scheduled a planting for the week around when Cecilia Sheppard disappeared.'

'He buried Skyler in Balboa as well.'

'Hell, Balboa's so big he could have buried half his victims there and no one would have suspected a thing. I've asked CSU to get a team out to the area where Cecilia might be buried ASAP with a GPR to scan the ground.'

'Wow. You've made so much progress. I should have made

those calls weeks ago, dammit. We could have had all this information earlier.'

'Don't beat yourself up,' he said kindly, surprising her yet again. 'You've been working nonstop on this case. Besides, we didn't have a lot of the details to make sense of the schedules.'

'Thanks,' she said, but was still angry with herself. 'What next?'

'Navarro is working on getting us a search warrant for the mail room where Colton Driscoll worked.'

'So we can hopefully match the living room in his videos.'

'Yep. When that comes through, I'll call you and we can go over together. Until then, I'm going to keep calling the parks. Finding those bodies might not give us any new information about their killer, but we can at least enable their families to bury them.'

Kit's chest tightened. 'Yes. The closure is important.'

'I know,' he murmured, and she wondered what he meant. Was he empathizing with what she and the McKittricks had gone through with Wren, or did he have his own story to tell? 'Where are you?'

'In front of the third bar on the list Howard gave me,' she said. 'I checked the security footage at the first two but didn't see Skyler and no one remembered her. I'll call you as soon as I'm done with the remaining bars.'

'Unless you find him first.'

'Your mouth, God's ears.' She ended the call, pocketed her phone, and pushed through the bar door. It was dark, unlike the first two places she'd checked out, which hadn't yet been open and had the lights on full as they prepped the serving areas.

The bartender, whose name tag read Rosie, gave her an easy smile. 'What can I get you?' she asked.

'Information,' Kit said, returning the smile. Easier to catch flies with honey, after all. She flashed her badge, then produced the photo of Skyler Carville. 'I'm Detective McKittrick. Do you remember seeing this woman last Friday night?'

Rosie immediately put down the glasses she was stacking and took the photo, studying it. 'Yeah. I saw her. I remember carding her because she looked so young. She was twenty-one, though.'

Skyler would never see twenty-two. 'She died that night. I'm trying to retrace her steps.'

Rosie flinched. 'Oh my God. How?'

'Homicide. Do you remember if she met someone here?'

The woman frowned, thinking. 'No, I don't. But I can get you the security vids. They're not the best quality, but you can have a look.'

'I'd appreciate that, thank you.'

Rosie called someone over to cover the bar, then led Kit back to the office, which was filled with boxes of booze and one ancient desk with a newish desktop computer. A few clicks of the keyboard brought up the footage from Friday night. 'You can sit here and watch,' Rosie said. 'I can't leave you here alone, but I'll go over there and do some inventory.'

Kit sat in front of the computer, setting her concentration to the screen, just as she'd done twice already that afternoon. But this time she saw Skyler walk into the bar and look around.

For Sam. Skyler thought she was meeting Sam. Pity sat heavy on Kit's heart as she watched the young woman take a seat at the bar. There was Rosie on the screen, carding her, just like she'd said.

Minutes passed and Skyler waited. She finished the white wine she'd ordered and was getting up to leave when a man with gray hair slid onto the bar stool next to her.

Kit's pulse started to beat faster. Same body type as the man in Driscoll's videos. She couldn't see his face because the camera was only catching his back. She waited impatiently for him to turn around, but he kept his body turned just right. Kit was about to ask Rosie if there was another camera positioned to catch another angle when the man on the screen gestured for the bartender. A male bartender approached and poured another white wine for Skyler.

Kit saw the moment that Skyler's killer added powder to her glass. Skyler had turned to look at something and he slid it in so quickly that Kit would have missed it had she not been specifically watching. He'd clearly had a lot of practice drugging his victims.

The minutes passed and Skyler clearly grew disoriented, but not so much that someone would have noticed. The man put his arm around her waist and turned her around toward the door.

Giving Kit a glimpse of his face before he slid on a pair of sunglasses.

For a moment she stared, disbelieving.

Not possible. No.

No, no, no.

She froze the frame, her movements jerky. She couldn't breathe. *But he doesn't really have gray hair. He doesn't really wear glasses.*

Her cell phone rang, and she answered automatically, bringing her cell to her ear. Her focus was pinned to the screen, her mind racing along with her heart. 'Yeah?'

'It's Sam. I know who he is. It's a psychologist here in the city. He works with cops, Kit. His name is Scott. John Scott.'

Her throat closed, betrayal hitting her like a brick as she stared at her therapist's face, thinking of the secrets she'd revealed to this man. This killer. 'I know,' she mumbled numbly. 'I found him with Skyler.'

'What?' Sam asked. 'I can't hear you. What did you say about Skyler? *Kit?*'

His use of her name knocked her brain back into gear. 'How did you find him?'

'He was Colton's prior therapist. His third ex-wife gave us his name and there's a video interview online. It's the same living room, Kit.'

Kit forced herself to breathe, aware that Rosie the bartender was watching her, wide-eyed. 'Meet me at the station as soon as you can. We need to brief Navarro. Are you with Laura?'

'Yes.'

'Have her call the desk when you arrive. If I'm not back, I'll have Detective Robinson walk you in. I don't want you alone at any time.'

'My alibi,' he said grimly.

'Your *life*,' she corrected tersely. 'If he knows you know, he'll kill you, too.' Rosie gasped, and Kit cleared her throat. 'I need to go.' She ended the call and looked over at Rosie. 'I'll need a copy of this footage.'

'Of course,' Rosie said, and Kit got up to let her sit in front of the computer.

With shaking hands, she texted Connor. ***Go to Navarro's office. I need to update you both ASAP.***

Are you okay? Connor texted back.

No, she was not okay. ***Unhurt. Will call in a few minutes. Wait for me.***

She wasn't going to text them this information and she wasn't going to say another word in front of Rosie. She'd already revealed too much while talking to Sam.

It took only moments for Rosie to download the footage to a thumb drive. She handed it to Kit. 'Be careful,' the bartender said seriously.

Kit nodded, still numb. 'Thank you,' she managed. 'Have a good day.'

Dr Scott. Motherfucking Dr Scott.

He'd had her trust.

Shit. Fucking shit. He'd also had Navarro's trust for how many years? Most of the investigation, that was how long. Navarro would have disclosed details.

All the details.

Scott must have been so goddamn smug.

This was going to destroy Navarro. Kit felt destroyed with the minimal information she'd provided. Navarro had been telling Scott his secrets for *years*.

She ran back to her vehicle, dialing Navarro's number before she'd even closed her door. 'It's Scott,' she said as soon as Navarro picked up.

'What?' Navarro asked. 'Scott who?'

'Dr Scott,' Kit snapped. 'Our. Therapist.'

'What?' Navarro repeated, incredulous. 'Come on, McKittrick. It wasn't Levinson, either. What's gotten into you?'

'I have the video evidence. In my hand.' Kit started the car, her hands still shaking. 'He met Skyler at the Lazy Oyster Bar. I saw him roofie her drink. I saw him lead her out. *I saw him.*'

For a long moment, there was silence.

Then Connor gently asked, 'Where are you now, Kit?'

'On my way back.'

'Okay,' Connor said, still gentle. 'Get yourself back here safely. You hear me?'

'Yeah. Boss?'

'Yeah?' Navarro asked hoarsely, and Kit's heart broke for him.

'Not your fault, boss.'

'I told him *everything*,' Navarro said, his voice cracking. 'Are you sure it's him?'

'Yes. Plus, Sam Reeves found him, too. He's on his way in. If I'm not back yet, please escort him up, Connor.'

'Of course, but how did Reeves find him?'

'Third ex-wife told him that Scott was Colton's therapist. Sam found an interview video Scott did from his living room. It's the same living room in the videos.'

'Let me google Scott,' Connor said, then cursed a minute later. 'Reeves is right. There's a video online and it's the same living room.'

Navarro cleared his throat. 'I'm sending uniforms to his offices and to his house right now to make sure he doesn't leave.'

'Offices?' Connor asked. 'His office is here. In this building.'

'One of them,' Navarro said, sounding like he was barely holding on. 'He has another office. Oh fuck.'

'What?' Kit demanded.

'The address. I hadn't been there in years, not since he got the office here. I wouldn't have recognized it offhand. It's in the building where Driscoll worked.'

'Does he live there, too?' Kit asked. 'In one of those penthouses?'

'No. He has a waterfront place on Mission Beach.'

'All right,' Connor said calmly. 'I'll coordinate uniforms to all the places. Kit, you just get yourself back here in one piece. Do I need to send someone to drive you?'

'No. I'm okay to drive. See you soon.'

She ended the call and rested her head on the steering wheel, trying to catch her breath. Her phone rang again, and she answered it without checking the screen. 'Connor?'

'No, honey, it's Pop.'

'Pop,' she breathed. Just the person she needed to hear right now.

'Where are you, honey? I was waiting outside for an hour, but you guys didn't come out. I'm in the coffee shop now, but you're not here.'

Her racing heart stopped. 'What? What are you talking about, Pop?'

'You texted Rita,' Harlan said, his voice now echoing her anxiety. 'Told her to meet you at the coffee shop near your office. I dropped her off, just like you said in your text. I waited at the curb for an hour, but she never came out. I came in to find her, but she's not here. Neither are you. What's happening?'

'Pop.' Kit gasped for air as the possibilities bounced around her mind. It couldn't be. Scott didn't know about Rita.

But he did.

Because I told him.

'I didn't text Rita.'

'What?' Harlan whispered. 'Kit, *what's happening?'*

'Stay where you are. I'll be there as soon as I can.'

Her hands had only been trembling before. Now they were full-out shaking as she redialed Navarro. Tears clogged her throat and her voice came out thick and raspy. 'Rita Mendoza is gone.'

She heard the echo of the room as Navarro put her on speaker. 'Who? Wait. You mean Maria Mendoza's daughter? Your foster sister? Did she run away?'

Fury exploded within her. She'd heard those words before, when Wren disappeared.

'*No*. She did *not* run away. She was tricked into meeting me. Just like Skyler was tricked into meeting Sam. Scott has her.'

'How does he know about her?' Connor asked.

Kit tried to swallow the sob, but it broke free. 'Because I told him about her in my last session. *I told him.*'

'Fucking hell,' Navarro breathed. 'Come back, Kit.'

'No. I'm meeting my pop at the coffee shop.'

'No,' Connor said sharply. 'You come back here *now*, or I'll send someone to get you. I'll send a car to get your father and get CSU out there. They'll check out the security footage from the shop. You can't touch this case anymore, Kit. You know I'm right.'

She did know. But . . . 'She's just a kid, Connor. She's only thirteen.'

'I know,' he said quietly. 'We'll get everyone out there searching for her. You get back here, okay?'

'Okay,' she whispered. She ended the call and called Harlan. 'My partner's sending a car for you, Pop. They're going to bring you to meet me at the station.'

'Kit,' he barked. 'What is happening?'

'I think Rita's been abducted.'

'Oh my God,' he whispered. 'Not this. Not again.'

'We'll find her, Pop. I have to go. I'll see you at the station.'

She ended the call and put the car into drive.

If that bastard hurt Rita . . . *I will kill you myself.*

Carmel Valley, California
Wednesday, 20 April, 7.30 P.M.

It was a nightmare. Again.

Kit sat in Harlan and Betsy's living room, feeling fifteen all over again. Except it was worse this time. This time she knew exactly what was happening to Rita.

She'd seen it herself.

'Here.' Sam sat beside her on the sofa, holding out a cup of fragrant tea. 'Akiko says it will calm you down.' Because Kit's sister had raced home as soon as Kit had called her. Akiko had put out the word, and now the kitchen was filled with fosters, here to support Mom and Pop. 'She tried to give some to your mom, but Betsy's pounding on bread dough like a prizefighter.'

Betsy always baked bread when she was stressed. She found punching the dough cathartic.

Kit couldn't stand the look on her mother's face. Or her father's. Betsy was attacking bread dough, but Harlan looked shattered. He'd held Kit too tightly when she arrived, but Kit let him without a single protest. He'd looked a breath away from a breakdown.

Because of me. Because I told that bastard about Rita.

Harlan was sitting in the kitchen right now, surrounded by foster kids, looking as brokenhearted as he had the night of Wren's funeral. Kit hadn't been able to stand it, so she'd come out to the living room to blame herself in private.

Except she wasn't in private anymore. Sam was sitting beside her, and she didn't want him to go. He was generosity and forgiveness and kindness, and she needed those things.

Kit wrapped her cold hands around the warm mug. 'Thank you.'

'You're welcome.'

He'd brought her here after Navarro had sent her home. She hadn't wanted to go to the boat. She'd needed to be with Harlan and Betsy, but Sam had taken her car keys, unwilling to let her drive while she was so shaken.

Navarro had already sent Harlan home with a uniformed officer who sat outside in his cruiser. Just in case.

Kit wasn't even sure what that meant. In case of what? In case John Scott came for them? He wouldn't. He only attacked little girls. He'd taken Rita, a thirteen-year-old girl. Yes, he'd killed Driscoll, but only after he'd drugged him.

He'd probably killed Daryl Chesney, too. The boy who'd 'found' Skyler Carville's body with his metal detector. No one had seen him since Sunday afternoon.

'I'm sorry,' Sam murmured.

She turned to stare at him. At his eyes, warm, sad, and so damn *sincere*. 'Why are you sorry? You're the one who's been wronged in all of this. You and Rita and all the others. You have nothing to be sorry for.'

'I wish I'd figured it out sooner.'

'I'm the cop. I should have figured it out sooner. I never should have told Scott about Rita. What was I thinking?'

'That you could trust him,' Sam said gently. 'You should have been able to, Kit. I'm sorry you – and other cops – lost that. This is not on you. It's on him.'

The words were kind. And maybe even true. But it didn't matter.

She clutched the mug tighter. 'I feel so helpless, sitting here like this.'

Because she'd been recused from the case the moment Scott had approached Rita in the parking lot behind that coffee shop. Rita's cell phone records showed several texts from Kit's number. Spoofed, of course. They only knew what the first text said because Rita had shown it to Harlan.

Hey, kiddo, I have a break this afternoon. Wanna meet me for a latte? We can have some girl time. I'll wait for you inside the Never-Empty Cafe. Pop knows where it is. Have him drop you off.

The texts that followed must have asked Rita to come to the back parking lot, because the shop's cameras showed her walking out the rear door of the shop. And then getting into a gray Toyota RAV4.

Sam's SUV.

Or what had appeared to be Sam's SUV. Sam had been able to tell them that his RAV4 had a dent in the left rear fender, but otherwise, it was identical. The glass had been too dark to see the driver.

Kit could only guess that Scott had been holding a gun on Rita. Nothing else would have compelled the girl to get into the car.

Sam's car had been stolen from Joel's driveway, further making it look like Sam had abducted Rita. Except Sam had been with Laura Letterman all day. *Thank God for that.*

Joel had given the police his home security video, which showed a tall young man in a hoodie stealing Sam's RAV4 that afternoon. Connor believed that Dr Scott had recruited another street kid, just like Daryl Chesney. Which made sense.

Connor had put a trace on Sam's GPS, but so far, they hadn't found a hit. The SUV had probably ended up in a chop shop, but Joel had assured them that Siggy was safe, sleeping in his crate. That, at least, had eased Sam's mind a little bit.

A cold nose pressed against Kit's arm and she was suddenly so glad that she'd left Snickerdoodle here, because all she wanted to do was bury her face in the dog's curly coat and cry. Instead, she patted the sofa, sinking her fingers into Snick's curls when she jumped into her lap.

'What *can* you do?' Sam asked.

She glared at him. 'Nothing, apparently.'

He held up his hands. 'I'm not being cruel or sarcastic. I'm being serious. If you were on this case, what would you be doing right now?'

'Searching Scott's house.'

'Your new partner is doing that. Scott's not there.'

He's not my new partner. Baz is coming back. But that wasn't what she should focus on. Connor was at Dr Scott's house with Navarro and half of the homicide squad. Connor had been good about texting her what information he could.

He was pretty good for a temporary partner.

But that wasn't what Sam had asked. *Focus, Kit. Rita's life depends on it.*

If she's still alive.

'I'd be working with Baz, pulling together what we know. Trying to figure out where else Scott would take her.'

'Can you call Baz?'

She wanted to say yes. She wanted that so much. Baz had been her rock for sixteen years, her partner for four. But she couldn't.

She shook her head. 'He has to stay calm. He had a damn heart attack, Sam.'

As soon as the words were out of her mouth, her cell phone buzzed with a FaceTime call, and she blinked at the screen. 'It's Baz.'

But Sam didn't look surprised, and she wondered what he'd done.

'Hey,' she answered, trying to keep her voice level and failing completely. Just the sight of his face made her want to weep.

'Kit,' Baz said softly. 'Talk to me.'

'I can't,' she whispered. 'Marian will kill me.'

'No, she won't,' Marian said from off camera. 'Unless his blood pressure or pulse start climbing. Then I'll end the call. Talk to him, Kit. He needs to help.'

Kit shuddered out a breath. 'How did you know to call me?'

Baz smiled. 'I might have gotten a call from a certain someone who may have finally forgiven me for threatening to shoot his dog.'

Kit's gaze flew to Sam's face. He shrugged. 'The forgiveness part is still up in the air, but I did call him.'

'Thank you,' she said softly, then turned back to her screen. 'It's all fucked up, Baz.'

'Tell me what you know,' Baz said in the no-nonsense way on which she'd come to depend. 'Is Connor keeping you up to speed?'

'He is. He and some of the other detectives are searching Dr Scott's house right now. Rita's not there, and neither is Scott. His black Mercedes is in the garage.' Clean and shiny. No trace of the mud they'd seen in the street cams on the metal detector kid's street. 'They found a gray wig and glasses.'

'He disguised himself,' Baz said. 'Should have been watching for that.'

'They also found the stepladder he used to hang Driscoll and all the stuff he took from Driscoll's house. We think he drove Driscoll home in Driscoll's car, killed him, came back to his place on Mission Beach to dump the stuff, then drove back to Driscoll's to leave the car in the garage. Connor said that one of the other detectives had found the taxi driver who picked up a gray-haired man with glasses about a mile from Driscoll's house, not even twenty minutes before we arrived.'

'We just missed Scott,' Baz said, sounding disgusted. 'What else did Connor find?'

'A drawer full of handcuffs and a case of sparkly pink paint cans. And three dozen photos.'

Baz frowned. 'Of the victims?'

'Not exactly. They're eight-by-ten photos of beautiful parks, framed and hanging on his living room wall.' Ironically, they hung just above where Driscoll's camera had been, so they hadn't been shown in the videos. The camera was no longer there, and Connor didn't yet know when it had been removed. 'Two of the photos they were able to ID – the grave sites of Jaelyn Watts and Skyler Carville.'

'So he didn't keep his victims' jewelry, but he went back and took photos of their grave sites?'

'It looks that way. There were two photos in between the pictures of Jaelyn's and Skyler's graves. Connor said that the photo closest to Jaelyn's is probably Cecilia Sheppard's grave. He identified it this afternoon through Balboa Park maintenance records. The second one was between Cecilia and Skyler's graves.'

'A new kill,' Baz said grimly. 'What else did they find?'

'Driscoll's laptop and the hard drives that Scott took from his safe. The laptop wasn't password protected, so CSU's going through it now. Maureen's video showed Scott making Driscoll sign into his computer. Seems like Scott was cocky enough not to reinstate a password.'

'Bold bastard. But we knew that. What else?'

'Scott had his own cameras around his house. Driscoll came to Scott's house the night he died, skulking in the bushes, trying to see in the windows.'

'Why?'

'We don't know yet.'

'So you followed the lead on the parks,' Baz said. 'Good job, Kit.'

'Connor did it.'

'Because you told him to, right? Right. If Scott's not in his Mercedes, what is he driving?'

'A car that looks like mine,' Sam said. 'Mine was stolen out of Joel Haley's driveway by a tall kid in a hoodie. But it's not my car.'

'So a gray RAV4,' Baz said. 'He had to have acquired it recently. You could check for where he bought it from – or stole it from – and see if there's GPS.'

'That could take a while, though,' she said. 'And Rita doesn't have a while.'

'Okay. Has he tried to go home?'

'Connor says no. Even if Scott wanted to, there are a couple dozen cops there right now. And if his security cameras can be accessed with his phone, he might already know that.'

'Good point.' Baz drew a breath and Kit recognized the movement. It meant she wasn't going to like what came next, so she braced herself.

'I assume his plan is to kill Rita and make it look like Reeves did it.'

She'd been right. She didn't like it. 'Yes.'

'If he had someone steal Reeves's RAV4 out of Joel's driveway, he probably thought Reeves was there. Thought he wouldn't have an alibi again.'

'But I was with my attorney,' Sam said.

'Smart move,' Baz said. 'Someone stole your car, so that's a lead to follow.'

Kit shook her head. 'If Scott did hire someone to steal it, he'll probably kill them, too. The kid who found Skyler's grave apparently went to collect payment and hasn't been seen since.'

'Do you think he'd take Rita to a park?' Sam asked.

To bury her.

Kit's heart began to pound anew because she should have thought of that. 'Yes. If he follows his pattern, he'd take her to one of the parks that has maintenance going on. They dig up the earth for him and there's no one around because the area is cordoned off from park visitors.'

'Where is that happening right now?' Sam asked.

Kit swiped away from the FaceTime screen to scroll through her emails. 'Connor sent me the list he'd compiled of maintenance schedules.' She found the email and clicked on the attachment. '*Please*,' she muttered as she scanned the document. A moment later she sucked in a breath. 'The Simpson Botanical Garden. They had a water main break. It was fixed this afternoon. That's where he is.'

'I know that place,' Sam said. 'It butts up against the Torrey Pines Extension. I hike there with Siggy all the time.'

That was where she was going. She gave Snickerdoodle's head a quick kiss before sliding out from under her.

'Kit,' Baz said sharply. 'Call Connor. Let him go.'

'I'll call him for backup. I'm closer than he is right now. Thank you, Baz.'

'You did it yourself. I just helped you focus. Call me when you get him.'

'I will,' she said. 'Gotta go.' Ending the call, she was at the front door before she realized Sam was on her heels. 'Where are you going?'

'With you. You might need an alibi.'

She stared at him in disbelief for a split second, then opened the door, unwilling to waste time arguing. 'You can drive.' She had calls to make.

'*Kit!*' Harlan shouted as she was about to get into her Subaru. 'Where are you going?'

'I know where Scott is,' she called back. 'I'll bring her home.'

Alive. Please let her be alive.

Twenty

Del Mar, California
Wednesday, 20 April, 8.15 P.M.

Sam drove faster than he ever had before.

It's going to be dangerous. You could get hurt. Killed.

But he wasn't going to leave Kit McKittrick. Not until her backup arrived. She wasn't herself. Which wasn't a surprise. He knew enough of her story to know that she and all the McKittricks were reliving the abduction and murder of Kit's foster sister.

They were less than ten minutes from their destination. For the first few minutes, Kit had been on the phone with her new partner.

Her backup was on its way, and Connor Robinson had been yelling at her to *Stay put* and to *Go home* and to *Think, Kit, think.* She'd told him that she was thinking and that if he wanted to help, to hurry his ass up.

Sam had nearly smiled.

She hadn't said a word in the last ten minutes, so when she spoke, he startled.

'Why don't you like to have your hands restrained?' she asked.

He hadn't expected that question. 'Long story.'

'Give me the abridged version. It was why you resisted arrest, wasn't it?'

It was a story that he didn't tell often. Laura had understood immediately because he'd shared the story with her. His parents knew, of course, as did Joel.

Sam didn't like to share it, but he knew so many things about Kit McKittrick. It seemed only fair. And it might take her mind off her mounting anxiety. She was visibly vibrating in the passenger seat.

'I was beaten up back in high school. Prom night, actually.'

'Did they tie your hands?'

'Yeah.' He could see the scene in his mind as if it were yesterday and not seventeen years ago. 'My car had a flat after the dance. On an isolated road.' He'd taken that route on purpose. He and Marley had wanted to be alone. He'd had the promise ring in his pocket. 'I didn't have a spare. I was with my girlfriend. I'd just proposed.' Because for him it had never been just a promise ring. He'd wanted to marry Marley for two years.

'Oh. You don't need to tell me the rest.'

He shrugged like the memory didn't cut soul deep. 'Not much to tell. Assholes came along. At first, we hoped they were there to help us, but they weren't.'

Her hand was suddenly on his arm. 'Sam.'

'They were going to rape her,' he said, speaking about it as if telling a story that had happened to someone else. It was the advice he gave his clients now because it generally worked. 'They held me down. One of them wanted to see how it felt to strangle someone with his bare hands, so he did that to her first. Killed her by mistake and made the others mad because they'd lost their turn. They were going to slit my throat, but another car came. They dropped the knife and ran.'

'Were they caught?'

'Yeah. Her killer is still in prison. The other two got out a few years ago but were back in a few months later for other crimes.'

'I'm sorry,' she whispered.

'Thank you.' Because what else could he say?

'Your struggle that night makes sense now. I'm sorry I put you through that. And then I showed you the video of Naomi Beckham being killed.' Her voice hitched. 'I'm so sorry.'

'I didn't like it, but I understand why you did it.'

'So you became a psychologist . . . why? To stop evil people from being evil?'

'No. Evil people are always going to be evil.' They were

approaching the turnoff for the park. 'I specialized in criminal psychology because I wanted to help stop them before they hurt anyone. Or anyone else if they already had. I like to keep balance, so I also do therapy with the victims. Help them regain control.'

'And homeless kids, too?'

'Yes. Many of them have been victimized, too, in some way. That's why they're runaways and homeless.'

She was quiet for a moment. 'I'm sorry about the circumstances that made our paths cross, but I'm glad I met you. My first thought when I saw your photo ID was that you seemed sincere. That's the word I still think. Don't ever change.'

Her words were the balm he hadn't realized he'd needed. 'Thank you.'

He slowed the car only enough so that when they turned, they didn't tip over. 'Do you know where they're doing the maintenance?' he asked.

'The rose garden. Park in the lot and I'll walk the rest of the way. You need to stay in the car.'

'Okay,' he said. He'd park in the lot.

He was not staying in the car.

She was out of the Subaru before he put it in park. Closing the door quietly, he followed her.

She was running along the trail, following the signs to the rose garden, using her Maglite to light the way because there were no lamps anywhere around.

They came to an abrupt halt when they saw the vehicle ahead. It must have come through one of the other gates, because there was no sign that it had driven through the park the way they'd come. The vehicle's headlights illuminated a small patch of ground.

Where a man stood, shoveling loose dirt into a pile.

He wasn't standing in a hole, so he must have just started digging. He hadn't buried Rita yet.

Sam knew that Kit wanted the girl to still be alive. So did Sam, but he knew the likelihood was low and he'd tried to prepare himself for that eventuality.

He knew he hadn't, though. He kept seeing Rita's face as she'd shared the photos of Snickerdoodle on her phone.

Don't let her be dead.

He'd prayed the same prayer that night seventeen years ago, but Marley had already been gone.

The universe owed them a boon, him and Kit. And Rita, too.

Kit looked over her shoulder, glaring at him for not staying in the car before extinguishing her Maglite. Together, they crept along the darkened trail, coming up behind the RAV4 that was almost identical to Sam's. *Trying to frame me.*

Sam was so glad he'd listened to Laura and Joel and hadn't gone out by himself.

The man – John Scott – hadn't heard them yet. His face was covered by the same balaclava that he'd worn when he killed Colton Driscoll.

Kit crept to the RAV4 and peeked inside. She glanced back at Sam and shook her head.

Dammit. Rita wasn't in the SUV.

Kit rounded the SUV, staying out of the headlights. If Scott turned around now, he'd be blinded by the light. One fact in their favor.

Sam really wished he had his gun.

At least Kit had hers and she'd drawn it.

Dr Scott froze and Sam's heart stopped. Scott had heard them.

Kit had frozen, too, her head moving side to side as she searched for Rita in the dark.

Scott dropped his shovel and lurched to the right, out of the headlights. 'Stay back!' he shouted. 'I will kill her.'

He hadn't yet. Sam's knees nearly buckled in relief.

His relief evaporated a moment later because he could see Scott in the shadows and he had the girl in his grip, Rita's wrists cuffed in front of her.

He was holding a gun to Rita's head.

'You'll kill her anyway!' Kit shouted back, her gun aimed at Scott.

'Maybe not,' Scott said, no longer shouting. 'Do you want to take the chance?' he continued smoothly in a tone that Sam recognized well. It was Dr Scott's therapist voice. 'Do you want to live with the consequences if I pull the trigger? Her blood would be on your hands, Kit.'

Kit stiffened and Sam wanted to tell her that Scott was bullshitting her. Scott had been Kit's therapist and, while she hadn't revealed to Sam what she'd told the man, guilt over her failings was a given.

It was always a given with cops.

Damn this bastard for using that against her.

Because it was working. Kit was faltering. Sam couldn't see her face well, but he could see the outline of her body and her shoulders were slumping.

He wanted to scream for her not to listen. To follow her instincts. But he was her last resort. Her backup. Right now, he'd hold his tongue because she still had her weapon trained on Scott.

But she rallied, her spine straightening. 'Let her go, Dr Scott,' Kit said with a calm that surprised Sam. This was the McKittrick he'd read about. The detective who got results. 'She's just a child.'

'Just as I like them,' Scott taunted. 'She was good, Kit. Gotta say. Great lay. Thank you for telling me about her.'

Kit was silent for too long and Scott laughed.

'You expected me to deny it?' he asked. 'While I'm holding her in my arms? You thought I wouldn't do to her what I did to all the others?'

'Why?' Kit asked and Sam realized that she was stalling for time. 'Why do you use the pink handcuffs?'

Sam squinted. Were they pink? Had all the victims been handcuffed that way? Sam bet that was the case, that Scott had been taunting the cops for years with those pink cuffs.

Scott laughed. 'You can thank your boss for that.'

Kit's flinch was visible even in the near darkness. 'Navarro?'

Scott chuckled. 'Oh, yes. He was so frustrated that the first two victims he found had no connecting characteristics, even though he was sure it was the same doer. Such a dedicated young detective he was back then. Only a little older than you are now. So I gave him something flashy, just in case he found more of them. I even helped him find a few. The kid who found the dog walker wasn't the first person I paid to play with metal detectors.'

This went so far beyond a betrayal of a client relationship. There were no words to describe how this would affect Dr Scott's clients.

Such a breach of trust.

'There were more?' Kit demanded. 'Before the first body we found with pink handcuffs?'

'So many more. But not your Wren, if that's what you're wondering. I wish I had killed her, though. That would have been the icing on a very delicious cake. But I'll make up for it with this one.' He tightened his hold on Rita.

'Why Rita?' Kit asked, still managing to sound calm. 'She's not your usual victim.'

'Because she's yours. And because Reeves met her.'

What the fuck? How did he know that?

'How did you know that?' Kit demanded.

'Put your gun down, Detective,' Scott said. 'You're trying to stall until your backup arrives, and I'm afraid I can't let you do that.'

Dammit.

'What will it take for you to let her go?' Kit asked.

Rita might not be alive, Sam wanted to scream, but he shifted his body until he could see Rita's face in the shadows at the edge of the area lit by the headlights. Her eyes were open. She looked disoriented, but she was alive.

Kit had to have seen that, too.

Oh, Kit. Sam had no idea of how to help, but he edged closer, coming up behind Scott. *Gotta figure something out. And fast.*

'Drop your weapon, Kit,' Scott said loudly, but pleasantly.

'You'll kill me.'

He shrugged. 'You or her. Your choice.'

'How do I know you won't kill her afterward?'

'You don't. But I *will* kill her if you don't drop your weapon. You're here, Kit, so you know a lot more than I expected you did. I didn't know you'd gotten so close. You don't talk as much in session as Navarro does. He gave me so much information. All these years.'

Her jaw tightened. 'You'll leave her here? Alive? No one else will know.'

'After you're dead?' Scott sounded amused.

No! Sam wanted to scream, then he realized what she'd just said. *No one else will know.*

I would know.

She'd said that for Sam. She wanted him to take care of Rita if Scott killed her.

Dammit, Kit. He crept a little closer, waiting for what, he didn't know.

'If it will save her life, I will,' Kit said.

'She's seen me, Kit,' Scott said mildly. 'She'll tell.'

'She's disoriented. You drugged her. She won't remember your face. Let her go and I won't kill you. You have my word. Do I have yours?'

'Sure,' Scott said, still sounding chuffed. 'But I *am* a liar, you know.'

'A cold-blooded liar,' she agreed. 'I thought that was Colton Driscoll, but I know now that it was you all along. But you did help me once or twice. I'm hoping there's enough decency left in you to let Rita live. She's already been through so much.'

She was still stalling, Sam realized. She really was good at this. Navarro had to be getting close.

'Stop stalling, Kit,' Scott snapped. He tightened his hold on Rita and shoved the gun harder into her head. 'Drop your gun, or she dies in front of you. You want to see that? I didn't think so. Kick the gun away.'

Kit didn't take her eyes off Scott as she placed her gun on the dirt, then kicked it way. 'Now let her go.'

'No.' Scott pulled the gun from Rita's head and pointed it at Kit.

Sam couldn't breathe. And then he saw the shovel that Scott had discarded. Leaping for it, Sam grabbed the handle and swung the thing at Scott's head in one motion, making contact with a sickening thud.

That was for Skyler, you motherfucker. And for all the others.

Scott staggered forward, falling to his knees. He still had both Rita and the gun, but he no longer pointed it at anyone.

So Sam hit him again.

Scott dropped the gun that time.

Sam kicked Scott's gun away and, keeping hold of the shovel, grabbed Rita. Swinging her up into his arms, he carried her to the back of the RAV4, out of the line of fire. Just in case. He laid her gently on the ground, then ran back to Kit, raising his shovel again. Just in case Scott got his gun back.

But Kit had it under control. She'd retrieved her weapon and had Scott flat on his stomach, her knee in his kidney.

Sam had nearly forgotten what that knee had felt like. It had sucked.

That she was doing it to Scott made Sam happy. She slapped her handcuffs on Scott's wrists, restraining his hands behind his back.

'Sorry they're not pink,' she snarled. 'You motherfucker.' She ripped his mask off. 'You coward. Hurting girls. You're disgusting.'

Scott turned his face to glare at her, his hatred apparent. But he said nothing.

Kit looked up and saw Sam. 'Thank you,' she said, her voice breaking. 'Thank you so much. Where is she?'

'Behind the SUV. She's safe.'

She nodded once, rising to point her gun at Scott, as if he could magically get out of the cuffs. Maybe he could. Sam wasn't negating any possibilities at this point. 'Can you wait with her?' she asked. 'She might be in shock.'

Sam should have thought of that. 'Of course.' He hesitated for a moment, contemplating kicking Scott in the head for trying to frame him. But that wouldn't do any good, so he backed away, confident that Kit had it under control.

He lowered himself to the ground next to Rita. 'Hey, honey. You with me?'

Rita stared up at him, blinking dazedly. 'Dr Sam?'

'Yeah. You're going to be okay.'

'Kit came for me.'

'Of course she did. She always will.'

As Sam's heart slowed, he thought about the approaching police. He pulled his cell phone from his pocket and dialed the only cop whose number, other than Kit's, he had stored in his contacts.

'Yeah?' Baz answered, his voice tense.

'She's okay,' Sam said. 'We were in time. Rita's alive and Kit's got the bastard in cuffs.'

'Oh my God,' Baz said on a shuddered exhale. 'Oh my God.'

Sam didn't like the sound of the man's breathing. 'Are you all right, Detective?'

'Yes. I am now. I was so damn scared. Never been so damn scared in my life. She didn't see it when we talked, but I was terrified.'

'You didn't show it.'

'You went with her.'

Sam looked around the RAV4, able to see Kit standing guard, her gun still pointed at Scott. 'Yeah, I did. Helped save the day, too. Hit Scott with a shovel.'

'You're okay, Doc. And I am so sorry for threatening your dog.'

Sam laughed, aware that he sounded more than a little manic. 'You already apologized. Can you call Navarro? I don't have his number in my phone. Tell him we're in the rose garden.'

'I'll do that right now. Thank you, Sam. Thank you.'

Sam ended the call and dialed 911, reporting their location to Dispatch. He sounded pretty damn calm. *Go me.*

Finally, after what seemed like an eternity, sirens began to wail, growing louder. He could see flashing lights in the distance.

And then the beams of a dozen Maglites cutting through the darkness.

Detectives Navarro and Robinson were the first to arrive. Robinson ran to relieve Kit while Navarro dropped to his knees next to Rita and unlocked the cuffs.

'Hey, sweetheart,' Navarro said softly. 'We have an ambulance coming.' He looked at Sam. 'You want a job as a cop?'

He was joking, right? He had to be joking. 'Um, no, thank you.'

Rita tugged on Sam's hand and he bent down to listen. 'He didn't do it,' she whispered.

Sam frowned. 'He didn't do what?'

'Touch me. That way. At least I don't think so. I know how it feels after.'

Sam went cold, his first thought that she shouldn't know what sex – consensual or not – felt like. She was thirteen. Then he realized that Scott had lied again, trying to throw Kit off her game.

The man had been terrified of Kit, even while he'd held the power.

Navarro appeared stricken. 'You do? How, honey?'

'Mom's boss.'

Navarro's jaw tightened. 'We'll talk more when you're feeling better, but I can do something about that legally if you want.'

'Can you call Mom and Pop? I just wanna go home.'

'I don't have their number,' Sam said, but Navarro handed Sam his phone. It was already ringing, Harlan's name on the caller ID. Sam took the phone. 'Rita's fine. We got her,' he said as soon as Harlan answered.

A harsh sob was all that came through the line, but Sam could hear Betsy McKittrick demanding to know what had happened. Then she was on the line.

'Lieutenant Navarro?'

'No, it's Sam Reeves. I have Navarro's phone. Rita is here and she's okay. She wants to come home. Kit's fine, too.'

Betsy choked on a sob of her own. 'Thank you, thank you, thank you,' she said brokenly. 'Where . . .' She cleared her throat. 'Where can we meet them?'

'I'll let you work out the details with Lieutenant Navarro.' Because Kit had come around the SUV. She fell to her knees and gathered Rita in her arms, rocking her. Kit's face was twisted with relief, misery, and residual fear.

There were no tears on Kit's face. She remained strong. Stoic. But brittle, like one more thing would shatter her into a million pieces.

Sam knew how she felt. He hesitated, then gently put his arm around her. He expected her to pull away, but she leaned into him, pressing her face to his neck as she held on to Rita for dear life. He wrapped his other arm around Rita and together they sheltered the girl, denying Scott the last look he sought as the cops dragged him down the trail to a squad car.

But Kit had turned her head, meeting Scott's eyes, and Sam thought she might confront him one last time. But she simply watched Scott until the squad car's taillights disappeared into the night. Sam was sure she'd pull away from him then, but she didn't, instead leaning her head on his shoulder, her body finally relaxing.

She trusts me.

Sam felt ten feet tall, especially when Navarro gave them a disbelieving look as he walked by them. Sam suspected that Kit was not normally touchy-feely and that this behavior was unusual.

An incredible sense of peace washed over him, like this was the place he was supposed to be. Beside the person he was supposed to be with. He'd been certain that she was special from the moment he'd read the first article about her dedication to her job and her compassion for the victims. Everything she'd done since then had cemented that certainty.

That they'd done this thing together, that they'd made a killer pay, that they'd rescued Rita and made life safer for the rest of the girls . . . That made it even better.

But there was sadness, too. Because dozens of young women would never come home. Skyler would never come home. *I'm so sorry.*

His arms tightened when he felt Kit begin to tremble. The night was cool, but not cold. This was more likely an adrenaline crash, he thought. He saw new flashing lights approaching. The EMTs were coming. They'd take care of Rita and Kit. Until then, Sam wasn't letting go.

Navarro appeared again, wordlessly draping a thermal blanket around the three of them before walking away.

Suddenly exhausted himself, Sam rested his cheek on top of Kit's head. 'I've got you,' he murmured. 'It's okay. You did it, Kit. He'll pay for Rita and for all the girls.'

It was over. They'd done the hard part. They'd survived. Now it was time for the next hard part.

Healing.

Carmel Valley, California
Thursday, 21 April, 7.25 A.M.

Kit woke up in her old bed at Mom and Pop's house, feeling completely disoriented. Until she spied a cream-colored poodle with brown flecks on the other twin bed. Snickerdoodle was curled up at the foot of Rita's bed, snuffling softly. Rita was safe.

She was also asleep, thankfully.

That was why Kit had slept over. Rita wouldn't let go of her after her ordeal. Not that Kit could blame her. Rita had been drugged, abducted, handcuffed, and threatened at gunpoint. Who knew how much care and love it would take to get her past this?

But if anyone could, it would be Harlan and Betsy.

Kit and her parents had been up with Rita until about five a.m., giving her hugs. When the girl had finally closed her eyes out of sheer exhaustion, Kit had flopped into bed, still wearing her clothes from the day before. That she'd managed to take off her shoes had been an achievement.

Moving quietly, Kit reached for her phone, wincing at the number of texts she'd received in the few hours she'd managed to sleep. Most were from reporters, ravenous for an exclusive. Not just the local journalists, either. There were requests from all over the world. All the major networks plus the BBC and the CBC.

It was going to be an awful ride for a while. Dr Scott was not only a serial killer; he was a media personality from LawTV. *This is going to suck.* She deleted all the reporters' texts. Any interview she did would have to be arranged by the department, and even then, she'd balk.

The next text was from Connor. ***Checking in. U ok?***

She smiled. If she'd had to have a temporary partner during this case, she was glad it had been Connor. ***Got a few hrs sleep,*** she replied. ***Rita is resting. Thx for everything yesterday.***

There was a text from the captain, congratulating her on closing a case that had stymied an entire generation of homicide detectives. She thanked him politely.

There was nothing from Navarro and that worried her. He'd moved around the crime scene last night like an automaton. Navarro wouldn't agree, but he was a victim of Scott, too. Not like the dead teenagers, but a victim nonetheless.

Normally, she'd think 'ripples'. But Scott's actions directly targeted her boss. Using the pink handcuffs just to taunt Navarro was beyond sick and cruel. After this, they'd probably all need therapy, but she bet that none of them would be trusting a shrink anytime soon.

Of course, the next text was from the one shrink who'd earned her trust. He'd been there for her last night. Had been there for Rita. He hadn't left her when she'd needed him.

How is Rita? Hoping you get some rest. And hoping we can talk for real sometime now that I'm no longer a suspect.

Kit smiled, because a minute later he'd texted: ***I *am* no longer a suspect, RIGHT?*** Followed by the scared emoji.

Right :-), she texted back. ***Let's have a drink sometime.*** She'd need to debrief him. She owed him that much.

His reply was immediate. ***Tomorrow?***

Saturday, she countered.

Sorry, folks here all day Saturday. Golfing w/my dad. Sunday?

Sorry. I have family dinner at noon.

Then coffee? 10 am Sunday?

Coffee worked. ***Sounds good,*** she texted, thinking that would be the end of it.

His reply was, once again, immediate. ***It's a date.***

Her mouth opened and closed as she stared at the three little words on her phone screen. *It's. A. Date.*

Oh my God. What did I just do?

Whatever you did, undo it. Now.

But he'd saved her life last night. She couldn't say *No, it's not a date*. That would hurt his feelings, and she'd done enough of that already.

She wanted to groan, but Rita was still asleep. *Don't panic. You can fix this.*

But do you want to?

That thought hit her like a brick, knocking her out of her panicked spiral. Did she want to fix it? Or did she want to have a date with Sam Reeves? Sweet, kind, sincere Sam Reeves with his green eyes and nerdy Clark Kent glasses? Who was no longer a suspect?

Maybe?

She was still staring at her phone, trying to decide what she wanted to do, when a new text came in from Baz.

We need to talk. It's important. Can I call?

That didn't sound good. New worry for Baz layered over the panic about Sam, which had settled over the fatigue due to Rita.

Give me 5. At Mom and Pop's. Need to go outside.

She rolled out of her old bed and shoved her feet into her shoes. Snick looked up for a moment before settling back onto Rita's bed with a delicate snore.

Kit blew her a kiss.

You need to spend more time with your dog.

She grimaced as she went down the stairs because she'd heard those words in Dr Scott's voice, which had been distasteful even before she'd known he was a raping, murdering monster. It would probably be a long time before she worked him out of her brain. That would probably make him smugly happy.

Asshole.

The kitchen was quiet, maybe for the first time in Kit's memory, which was weird. But Mom needed to sleep, too. Someone was up, because a pot of coffee sat on the coffee maker and it was still warm.

Akiko, probably. Kit poured herself a cup and added a lot of sugar because she needed it this morning. Looking out the window, she saw that Akiko's Subaru was gone. Her sister had a charter today, so she was on her way to the marina.

I should help her more often, too. No more working myself into an early—

Kit closed her eyes. *Early grave.* How many times had Scott said those words to cops while secretly smirking about the grave he'd just dug?

Asshole.

Taking her coffee, she went to the barn and, feeling strangely young again, slid the door open just enough to squeeze through. She drew a deep breath of hay-scented air before sitting on one of the bales.

Baz, you better not be dying, she thought as she dialed him on FaceTime. She'd watch his face while he talked because she could always tell if he was minimizing a problem.

No, you can't. He hid a heart condition from everyone.

Dammit.

'Kit.' His face filled her screen. He was smiling, but tentatively. His eyes were bright, though, even if his skin was a little sallow. 'Good morning.'

His hospital bed was his backdrop, but he had a cup of coffee in his hand. 'Good morning to you, too. Are you drinking coffee, Baz? Really? Did your doctor say that was okay?'

'It's decaf,' he said glumly.

She chuckled, despite her concern. 'I'm sorry. Mine's not.'

'Rub it in, why don't you?'

Her smile faded, because something was not right. 'Okay, so are we done with morning banter? You've got me scared, Baz. What's so important?'

'I wanted you to hear it from me because things are already going up on Facebook.'

Don't panic. 'What things?'

'I'm retiring.'

She stared at his face, hoping to see a twinkle in his eye. He threatened to retire all the time, but it was always a joke. This time, though, he was serious. 'When? Why?' When he didn't answer right away, she blurted, 'Are you dying?'

He smiled at that. 'No, Kit. I'm not dying. But I could have. I've been thinking a lot about the time I have left and how I should be using it. I'm retiring effective May first, but I have vacation to use, so it's really effective immediately.'

Her heart was in her throat. He was retiring.

'Kit?' He leaned into his phone's camera. 'Say something.'

Her mouth worked, but no words would come out and she couldn't stop the tears that filled her eyes.

'Kit, no,' he whispered. 'Don't. Please.'

He was right. She needed to pull herself together. 'Sorry. Just a shock. I guess I should have seen it coming, huh?'

'I didn't,' Baz said honestly. 'I've spent more time with Marian this week than I have in years. It only took a heart attack to make it happen. She deserves better, Kit. So do my daughter and my granddaughter. I want to see Luna grow up.'

'I understand.' And she did. Still . . . She drew a breath and pasted on a smile. 'Gonna take up golfing?'

Baz shuddered. 'Hell, no. But I might call Akiko and set up a fishing trip. Last time we went fishing was when you made detective.'

Akiko had hosted the celebration party on her boat. 'That was a nice day. You deserve all the nice days, Baz.' Her lips trembled and she firmed them. 'So it's on Facebook already?'

He made a face. 'Marian is so excited. She's already planning my retirement party and a cruise.'

'A cruise, too? You jet-setter, you.'

They went silent for a long moment, then Kit sighed. 'You've been in my life for sixteen years, Baz. I'm not sure how to be a cop without you.'

'That's fucking ridiculous,' he stated. 'You are a damn good cop and would have been no matter who trained you. I was lucky it got to be me.' He shrugged awkwardly. 'And I get to go out on a bang. A serial killer is behind bars. I mean, you solved the case, but I trained you, so I get to claim at least partial credit.'

'You were there with me, old man. Full credit.'

'That's not exactly true, but I'll take it. Connor did well, huh?'

'He did.' She narrowed her eyes. 'Is he my new partner?'

Baz looked up at the ceiling. 'I didn't say that.'

She huffed. 'Who did?'

'The captain. He stopped by an hour ago, so I told him my retirement plans. He wanted to check on me and congratulate me on the case.' He hesitated. 'He also wanted to tell me that Navarro's taking a leave of absence.'

Kit gaped. 'What?'

'He's not in a good place, Kit. He's blaming himself for Scott killing those girls. Says that if he hadn't been feeding the bastard information, they might have been able to catch him faster.'

'That's not true.'

'Yeah, but it's how he feels. The captain said he'd be telling you later, too. So act surprised. I wasn't supposed to let that out of the bag.'

'I'll try. So . . . when did you decide on this retirement?'

'A few days ago, but I sat on it until last night.'

'What happened last night?'

'I was able to help you get past your panic, so you'd see what you needed to do. I realized that I've been hanging around because I didn't want to leave you all alone. But, Kit, you're a superstar. You're only going to get better.'

She scowled at the compliment. 'If you're going to say I don't need you, just . . . don't.'

'I wasn't. I was going to say that I consulted with you last night. I can do that anytime you need me. I'll be a phone call away. I don't have to leave you all alone.'

But you are. 'I won't abuse the privilege. I don't want to face Marian's wrath.'

Baz mock shuddered. 'Who does?' His expression softened. 'You did good, Kit. Your gut was spot-on this whole time.'

She rolled her eyes. 'Hardly. Scott fooled me.'

'He fooled everyone. But you believed in the good shrink from day one.'

One side of her mouth lifted. 'The good shrink? Is that what we're calling him now?'

His smile was sweetly paternal. 'You can call him Sam.'

And I have a date with him on Sunday.

I'm not ready for this. Then a thought occurred. 'If Connor's my new partner, what's happening to Howard?'

'He's retiring, too. Captain told me. He's met a lady.'

'In baking class?'

'Yes, actually. She was taking the class with her daughter, but the woman lives on the East Coast and was only visiting.' His smile dimmed. 'I heard that Howard snapped yesterday when he was watching those videos you found in Driscoll's backyard. Said he was done. The lady wanted him to move back east with her, but he was waiting till fifty-five. The videos changed his mind. He submitted his resignation yesterday. Said life was too short.'

Kit sighed. 'Lots of changes, and that means new people. It's gonna suck, Baz.'

'You'll survive. You always do.' His gaze shifted and his face lit up. 'Gotta go. My granddaughter's here. We'll talk soon.'

He ended the call and she sat on the hay bale, staring at her phone.

He was leaving. Really leaving.

'Hey, Kitty-Cat.'

Kit looked up to find Harlan standing in front of her. Hay clung to his work pants and he had a block of wood in one hand, his carving knife in the other. The stall door was open. 'Were you here all along?'

'Sorry. I should have said something.'

'Nah. I would have told you anyway.'

He sat next to her on the bale. 'Big changes,' he murmured. 'You gonna be okay?'

She shrugged. 'I have to be.'

'Change is scary, but it can be good.'

She narrowed her eyes at him. 'What are you driving at, Pop?'

He pulled his phone from his pocket and handed it to her with a wince. 'Best you see it now.'

She stared at a phone screen for the third time in less than an hour. This time at an article. 'Tamsin Kavanaugh,' she seethed. The photo the woman had taken was a little grainy, but Kit and Sam holding Rita was still clear. At least Rita's face couldn't be seen because she and Sam had their arms around her.

But Kit's face was pressed into Sam's neck and they looked cozy together. Intimate.

'Fuck,' she whispered.

And I have a date with him on Sunday.

'You gonna bolt?' Harlan asked mildly. 'Because you look like you're gonna bolt.'

Kit shuddered out a breath. 'I might.' This wasn't okay. 'But if I bolted, I couldn't get revenge on Tamsin Fucking Kavanaugh.'

Harlan pressed a kiss to her temple. 'You should be pitying her. Her mother was awful to give her that middle name.'

Kit laughed, but it came out as a sob. Her life had completely spiraled out of control. Navarro was on leave, Baz was retiring, Connor was her new partner, her damn photo was online looking cozy, and she had a *date* with *sincere* Sam Reeves.

'What am I gonna do, Pop?'

'What you always do, Kit. You're going to live. And I'm going to help you any way I can.'

The tears spilled. 'Pop.'

He put his arm around her. 'It'll be okay, Kitty-Cat. I promise.'

'Don't go anywhere, okay? Please.'

'Not planning on it. Now, let's go put some breakfast on. Mom deserves the morning off.'

'Pancakes?' They were her go-to comfort food.

'Absolutely.'

Twenty-one

San Diego, California
Sunday, 24 April, 10.30 A.M.

Clutching Snickerdoodle's leash tightly in one hand and the gift bag Betsy had prepared in the other, Kit approached the corner café. A kaleidoscope of butterflies fluttered in her stomach and she didn't like the feeling.

She was thirty minutes late. She wondered if he'd still be waiting.

Who was she kidding? Of course he'd be there.

Sam Reeves had promised to meet her for brunch in the café near his apartment. He wouldn't break that promise.

Betsy would be so upset if she'd known that Kit had kept the man waiting, but once she'd parked her Subaru, she'd simply sat there, staring at the passersby.

What am I doing?

She was meeting Sam Reeves for brunch, which was insane. She'd started so many times to break the date but couldn't make herself do it.

He didn't deserve a brush-off. But this was complicated.

I let him hold me. In front of everyone. Everyone in the world because the photo had gone viral. It was a disaster.

But he made you feel safe when you needed it most.

She didn't need anyone to make her feel safe. Well, maybe Harlan and Betsy and Akiko and Baz. But that was all.

Somehow Harlan and Betsy had found out about the date and prepared gifts for the man. She couldn't back out now.

But this was insane. She didn't do relationships.

You hadn't met Sam Reeves yet.

Shut up.

So she'd come up with a plan for this morning. She'd use the time to bring him up to speed on what they now knew about John Scott and Colton Driscoll. Then she'd bid him a cordial goodbye.

And that would be that.

She'd even brought Snickerdoodle with her to be her excuse to leave. Rita was waiting for them to come back. The girl had slept with Snickerdoodle every night since they'd rescued her from John Scott.

They. Kit and Sam. Together.

The butterflies in her stomach became lead weights. There was no *they*.

And then she saw him. He was watching her approach, slowly standing at the table he'd snagged at the very edge of the outdoor eating area, shielded on two sides by a wooden fence. They'd have privacy there.

His expression was serious, his eyes intense behind his dark-framed glasses.

She really liked those glasses. She liked a lot of things about him. That was the problem.

The butterflies were back, dammit.

She forced a smile as she came up on the table. 'Dr Reeves.'

He lifted dark brows, one corner of his mouth bending down in a frown. 'Kit.'

A blush heated her cheeks. He knew exactly what he was doing. She was trying to push him into the friend/colleague zone, and he wasn't having it.

He'd have to deal.

This wasn't a date.

She looked down and noticed the Lab mix at his feet. 'Siggy.'

The dog had been looking adoringly at Sam but turned his gaze on Kit. Or, more correctly, on Snickerdoodle. The two nosed each other, and then Snickerdoodle flopped to the ground beside Siggy with a big doggy sigh.

Sam came around the table to hold her chair and she barely resisted the urge to glare as she sat down. She held the bag out to him. 'From my mom. She made you one of her coffee cakes.'

Sam took the bag with a wary smile. 'It's awfully heavy for a coffee cake.'

'There's an apple pie in there, too. And some cinnamon rolls.'

'Wow. I'll have to thank her.' He set the bag on the extra chair and studied her. 'You look . . . rested.'

She'd been holding her breath, expecting him to say *nice* or *pretty*. *Rested* was better.

Liar.

He smirked a little while pouring her a cup of coffee.

He was smug. She hated that she liked it.

She liked a lot of things about Sam Reeves.

Friends. They could be friends. Couldn't they?

'How's Rita?' he asked, yanking her out of her mental negotiation.

'Peppy when we're watching, withdrawn when she thinks we're not. Pop's already got her scheduled for therapy.'

'I figured as much. Harlan called and asked me for a recommendation.'

Which must have been how he and Betsy had known Kit was meeting Sam this morning. 'Rita's been through so much,' she murmured. 'I hope this person can help her.'

'My boss is good. If anyone can help Rita, she can.'

'Dr Carlisle?' Kit asked in surprise.

'She specializes in counseling victims of crime.'

There was something he wasn't saying, and she suddenly knew what it was. 'She talked to you after what happened to you and your girlfriend.'

His girlfriend, who'd been murdered in front of his eyes.

'Not immediately after. I was in Scottsdale then. But she guest lectured in one of my classes at UCLA. I had follow-up questions and we hit it off. I did an internship with her when I was going for my doctorate and she offered me a place in her practice once I was finished. I think you and I have this in common. We both work with our mentors. Me with Vivian and you with Detective Constantine.'

Kit's heart squeezed painfully at the reminder. 'Not anymore.'

He frowned. 'Is Baz okay?'

She nodded. 'But he's retiring. The heart attack scared him. He said it made him see what was important. His wife and daughter and granddaughter.' *Not me*. Which was selfish and awful, but there it was.

'I'm sorry,' Sam said softly. 'And now you have to break in a new partner.'

'Already did. Connor Robinson.'

'I thought that was just temporary.'

'It was. His partner decided to retire and move out east with his girlfriend.' But she didn't want to think about the upcoming changes, so she looked down at the dogs and remembered the other gift. 'Pop made you something.' She pulled it from her pocket, bringing the cat-bird with it. She separated the two carvings, holding Sam's out to him cupped in her palm.

So that he'll have to touch you to claim it. Just once.

He did, sliding one of his fingers over her palm before bringing the carving closer to his face. He broke into a delighted smile. 'It's Siggy.'

She tried to ignore the shiver that danced across her skin at his touch. 'Pop found a picture of him on Facebook. He and Mom are so grateful to you for your help in bringing Rita home.' She drew a breath that hurt. 'I don't think we could have made it through that again.'

He looked at the cat-bird she held in her other hand. 'Did he make that, too?'

She nodded. 'Every year he makes me a wren.'

'For your sister.'

'Yes. This year he made this one, too.'

Sam gently gripped her wrist, bringing her palm closer so that he could study the carving she held. 'A cat and a bird?' Then recognition filled his eyes. 'Because he calls you Kitty-Cat.'

This man was far too observant. *Get it done and get out of here.*

'Yes.' She tugged her wrist and he immediately let her go. She slid the cat-bird back into her pocket. 'I thought you might like some of the blanks filled in.'

Sam leaned back, seemingly at ease with her subject change. 'That would be nice.'

'First, your phone.' She pulled the evidence bag with his phone from her jacket pocket. 'The special master finally confirmed it was in Joshua Tree.'

He gave her a wry look as he set the phone aside. 'Thank you. And the park ranger?'

'He finally got back to us Thursday afternoon, confirming that he'd seen you. I'm sorry it took so long.' He didn't say *That's okay*, but she hadn't expected him to, because it wasn't. Folding her hands on the table, she pressed forward. 'Dr Scott isn't talking about the victims.'

He lifted his coffee cup to his lips, his gaze fixed to hers. 'Not surprising. You want him to tell you where his victims are all buried, but he'll want something for the information. It's like a dance and, when he thinks he's leading, he'll talk.'

'I agree, but we're matching the photos of the grave sites in his living room to the local parks. It would be easier if he told us, but eventually we'll figure out his burial places. Connor found cell phone videos on Driscoll's laptop of Scott burying some of the victims, so that should help us narrow down at least a few of the locations.'

'I figured that Colton had followed Scott – at least with Jaelyn – since he knew where she was buried. It's good to know for sure, though.'

She sighed. 'We're going to be looking for bodies for a long time.'

'Three dozen bodies.'

She nodded grimly. 'He's been killing for twenty years, two victims a year for most of that time. He likes order and patterns. And gardening, apparently. He was on the board of several private parks and gardens in San Diego County and volunteers with them. He helps them plant in the spring and fall. That's how he knew about which parks he could bury bodies in without raising suspicion. He also knew about the employee-only gates, which was probably how he was able to get the bodies to wherever he buried them. We've heard from parks all over town saying how they were fooled. He was a very charming liar.'

'He's also a narcissist and needed to have the evidence posted on his wall for anyone to see. Made him feel smarter than the rest of us. Did you find out how he was connected to Orion School?'

'He was on their board when they developed the scholarship. He did a bit of community theater in college and acting, along with gardening, were his hobbies.' *Along with killing*, she thought bitterly. 'He was on Orion's first admissions committee.'

'*T*'s crossed, *i*'s dotted.'

'Exactly. We've gotten a lot of information from Colton Driscoll's laptop, too. CSU found it in Scott's apartment. Driscoll had been recording Scott for five years.'

'Ever since he lost his job and when Scott cut him loose as a client.'

'Yes,' she said. 'You were right about that. Driscoll had purposely gotten a job in that mail room because that's where Scott's other office was. Driscoll was the one who installed the cameras in Scott's office and his house. We found the footage on his laptop.' She sighed. 'Rochelle Hamilton, the victim who went missing five years ago, had been in his office. He was her therapist, too.'

Sam flinched. 'Oh my God.'

'Yeah. Looking at the date stamps on the videos on Driscoll's laptop, it appears that Driscoll saw Dr Scott making advances toward Rochelle in his office. She was a troubled girl and had spent time in juvie. She was receptive to his advances and I guess Driscoll was titillated. The recordings in Scott's living room started a few days after that appointment, and that's when Driscoll saw him murder Rochelle.'

Sam looked shaken. 'Which was what Colton meant when he told his third wife that he "knew things" about his therapist.'

'Yes. Dr Scott dropped Driscoll as a client a few days after that, which matches up with when he could no longer pay. I dug into

Driscoll's finances from five years ago and found he'd bounced two checks to Dr Scott. We only looked at three years of Driscoll's finances when we first started digging. If we'd gone deeper then, we would have seen the connection to Dr Scott a lot earlier.' And maybe saved Skyler's life, at least. But that train of thought was unhealthy.

She'd still think it, though, because it was true.

Sam drew a breath, regaining his composure. 'How did he know to frame me?'

'The videos on Driscoll's laptop show that Scott was actively searching for cameras in his apartment starting the day after you first called me.' She exhaled. 'Navarro was so hopeful that we'd had a break on the serial killer case when we found Jaelyn Watts's body, but he didn't want to get his hopes up. He made an appointment with his therapist.'

Sam's face darkened. 'Dr Scott.'

'Yes. So Scott knew that someone had seen him burying Jaelyn. I think he thought that he'd been followed to the grave site. But he's also paranoid, so he started checking his house for cameras and listening devices. Driscoll's cameras caught Scott doing this. CSU found that footage saved to Driscoll's laptop, too. But Scott had security cameras, as well, and he caught Driscoll lurking outside his living room windows Friday evening.'

'That doesn't make sense. Why would Colton go to Scott's house if he knew that Scott had found his cameras?'

Kit sighed. 'Because he saw something in Scott's living room that he couldn't resist.'

Sam's shoulders slumped. 'The victim between Cecilia Sheppard and Skyler?'

He was sharp. 'Yes.'

'Because the scam happened this past February, so his scholarship lure didn't work. How did he lure this girl?'

'He had photos of her in a school play. And texts from his phone telling her that he was an agent and asking her to meet him. She did.'

'Her family didn't know?'

'Another foster kid. His browser history showed that he researched his victims very well before approaching them.'

Sadness filled Sam's green eyes. 'He knew how to pick them, and I guess Colton was addicted to watching Scott kill. Is that why Scott wore a mask when he got to Colton's house the day he killed him? He expected more cameras?'

'That was our guess. Like I said, Scott's not talking. But I got sidetracked. You asked how Scott knew about you. We think that Driscoll told him. Scott's camera shows him holding a gun to Driscoll's head when he caught him lurking outside. Scott's browser history shows that he looked you up late Friday night – before he killed Driscoll – and he started cyberstalking you. Your Facebook post from Joshua Tree was a gift.'

'How did he know that I knew Skyler?'

'She tagged Siggy on her Instagram. He's smart, Sam. He did a search on your dog, on your parents, on Joel. On Dr Carlisle and her family. Even on Laura Letterman. Anyone who was important to you. He saw Siggy's name, googled Skyler, and saw that she had a dog-walking business and that she lived in your building. She'd tagged you a few times over the years. Usually thanking you for helping her set up her business or helping her with her college applications.'

'What about Rita? How did he know I'd met her?'

'He'd bugged his office. He was recording everything we said, and his bugs could pick up cell phone calls. Pop called me when I was in Scott's office and told me you were having apple pie with Rita. Scott figured he'd frame you for her murder, too. That's why he had your car stolen. We think he'd planned to continue the murders and use the RAV4 he bought to frame you for them.'

'Why not just use my RAV4?'

'I think he was afraid it'd be tracked. Your car's been located, by the way. A few pieces of it, anyway. It was at a chop shop and the owners were quick to ID the guy who sold it to them.'

'The guy in the hoodie who stole it from Joel's driveway?'

'Yes. He said a guy with gray hair and glasses in a black Mercedes gave him three hundred dollars to steal the RAV4 and get rid of it. He's lucky, actually. He's still alive. The body of the boy who found Skyler was discovered in an abandoned warehouse yesterday.'

'Shit,' he whispered.

'I know.' The boy hadn't known he was making a deal with the devil. 'How are Skyler's parents?'

'Grieving. But they told me that they never believed I had anything to do with her death. Still, it was kind of you to visit them and tell them in person that I wasn't involved.'

'It was the least I could do.'

They were quiet for a moment, then Sam asked, 'What about that guy Brian who helped Colton's ex-wives? Was he involved?'

'We don't think so. He helps victims of domestic violence divorce their abusers. He seems to be just a nice guy.' *Like you*, she wanted to say, but bit it back.

Sam ran his thumb over the carving of Siggy. 'How is Lieutenant Navarro? I've been worried about him. He's got to be feeling a lot of guilt.'

'That's an understatement. I don't know how he's doing. He's gone on leave. That Scott used him for so long, that Scott went out of his way to use those damn pink handcuffs just to taunt him . . . It was cruel.'

'It was a betrayal of Navarro's trust.'

'All of our trust. Those of us who were Scott's patients are going to have serious trust issues with any therapist.'

Something flickered in Sam's eyes. Sadness? Disappointment, maybe? 'With me, too?'

Kit opened her mouth to deny it, but she couldn't. She wouldn't lie to this man. 'Probably.'

Sam swallowed. 'But you trusted me.'

She wanted to look away, but she couldn't. 'I did, yes.'

'Do you still?'

She hesitated and his sadness grew even stronger.

'I'm sorry,' she whispered.

He didn't smile. Didn't nod. Didn't tell her that everything was fine.

'If I weren't a psychologist, would you have called me Sam when you sat down this morning? Would you have wanted this to be a date?'

Once again, she opened her mouth and closed it again, searching for the right words. Because he was waiting patiently.

'I . . .' She reached down to scratch Snick's head. 'Maybe? But I'm not a good bet. For anyone. But especially for you.'

He flinched and the sight hurt her heart. 'Because I'm a shrink?'

Yes. 'Because you're nice. And kind. And sincere.'

'I think I hate that word,' he murmured. '"Sincere".'

'Don't. It makes you . . . you.'

He still didn't smile. 'What happens next?'

'I go back to work tomorrow and fill out reams of paperwork. You go back to work tomorrow and keep doing good. I figure out how to work with Connor because Baz isn't coming back. Rita goes to therapy.'

And Mom and Pop look at me sadly because I'm telling this nice man to go away.

He was quiet for a long moment. 'So this is goodbye?'

No. No. No. The butterflies were now bees and she felt physically ill. But she said what she needed to say. 'It's best that it is.'

He nodded once. 'Very well. I won't bother you anymore.'

She swallowed, her eyes stinging. 'You didn't bother me before.'

'Well, I'm bothering you now, by being who and what I am. Will you do something for me, though?'

'Depends,' she whispered, her throat too tight.

One side of his mouth lifted, as if he'd expected her to say that. 'Find another therapist. Ninety-nine percent of us aren't like Scott. Your job is stressful, but you do good, Kit. You need someone you can trust.'

I trust you. She'd thought that she might be able to tell this man anything, and he'd be her vault. Like Marian was to Baz.

But that wasn't going to happen. 'I'll try.'

'Okay. Have a good life, Kit. I mean that.'

'I know you do. You do the same. Don't take any more murderers or cold-blooded liars as clients, okay?'

He didn't smile at her light teasing. 'I'll try.'

She stood and waved him back down when he started to stand as well. 'Thank you, Sam.'

Then she turned and all but ran to her Subaru, Snickerdoodle trotting along beside her.

She stopped when she got to the corner, looking back once. He was still watching her.

She could go back. She could have this. She could have someone.

But people left. And the good ones who didn't leave . . . well, they deserved someone better than a woman who worked too many hours because she was running from her own demons.

Huh. I guess I got something from Dr Scott after all.

Deliberately, she turned the corner, walking away.

San Diego, California
Sunday, 24 April, 11.00 A.M.

Sam's heart sank as she walked away.

He'd been afraid that she'd be afraid of him, even after she'd asked him out for coffee. She wouldn't agree that she was afraid. She would say that she wasn't afraid of anyone or anything.

But that wouldn't be true. She was afraid of opening up. Of leaning on someone. Of depending on someone. On me.

But she *had* opened up. She *had* leaned on him. She'd trusted him.

I shouldn't have called this a date. I should have let her think it was just coffee.

But that wouldn't have been honest, and Sam wasn't going to be anything else.

She *was* interested. Sam could see it. She was denying it, though. Or she'd already decided that it would never work. Probably a little bit of both.

He wouldn't push her, even though he wanted to.

She'd told Joel that they could be friends. She totally walked away from me.

That was both frustrating and encouraging. *If she didn't care, she would have just said we could be friends, too.* But she'd walked away.

And you're analyzing her, which is probably the last thing she wants.

'Sam?'

Sam looked up to find his noon appointment standing by the table, studying him with a worried expression. Shaking off his frustration over Kit, Sam stood and shook Alvin Levinson's hand. 'Al. You're really early.'

He'd agreed to see the other psychologist at noon because Kit had said she had Sunday dinner with her family then.

'I'm hungry,' Al said. 'Figured I'd get us a table and have breakfast before you got here. But here you are.'

'Yeah. Here I am. Sit, please. It's been too long.' He hadn't seen the psychologist since the last board meeting at New Horizons.

Sam liked Al Levinson. He was a good man and an excellent therapist. And he had the job that Sam had always dreamed of – consulting with SDPD. It was the kind of job Sam had wanted the whole time he'd been earning his degrees. Now that he'd had a tiny taste of it, he wished for the job even more.

And, because he was honest, he could admit that working with Kit again was a serious factor. Someday, maybe.

Al sat down, glancing at the full cup of coffee at his place. 'For me?'

Sam had poured it for Kit, but she hadn't touched it. 'It's probably cold by now. Let me get you another cup.' He waved to the server, pointing to the cup. She gave him a nod, holding up one finger. 'Elena will be right with us.'

Sam had told her that he'd be seeing a few people this morning and she'd promised to give him privacy. No surprise as Sam was an excellent tipper.

'You must come here often,' Al said.

'Every day. My office isn't far from here. I usually take my coffee to go, though. It's nice to sit and not be in a rush.'

Elena slid up to their table, switching the cup of cold coffee for an empty cup and his empty carafe for a full one. 'What can I get you boys?'

Sam had lost his appetite after watching Kit walk away, but he should eat something. 'Eggs and bacon, please.'

'Same,' Al said, settling into his chair as Elena left them alone. 'Was that Kit McKittrick's coffee?'

Sam frowned. 'How did you know?'

'One, I saw her walking on the other side of the street when I was coming to meet you. I waved, but she had her head down.'

'What's two?' he asked, torn between being sad that Kit was hanging her head and relieved that leaving might have been as difficult for her as it had been watching her do so.

Al pointed to Harlan's carving of Siggy still sitting next to Sam's cup. 'Harlan McKittrick has been making carvings for years. He donates them to fundraisers. Some of them bring hundreds of dollars. I have two of them at home.'

'He made it to thank me for helping with Rita. It's my dog, Siggy.'

Al smiled. 'Cute name. Cute dog, too.'

Sam didn't want to be rude, but the small talk was killing him. 'What's this about, Al? You've never asked me to meet with you outside the boardroom before.'

'The truth is, your name came up a few days ago when I was meeting with Navarro and McKittrick about a case. Well, you know which one.'

Sam nodded warily. 'You know how that ended, right? I'm one of the good guys.'

Al chuckled. 'I know. I know you were a suspect for a little while, but don't feel bad. They suspected me, too.'

Sam's eyes widened. 'I didn't know that.'

Al shrugged. 'Not something I'll publicize, but I can't blame them too much. I'm on the board of directors at Orion School.'

Sam's eyes widened. 'Oh. And you didn't tell them?'

'I didn't think about it. I've always had a peripheral role, mostly fundraising.'

'You're really good at that.'

He smiled self-deprecatingly. 'I am, aren't I? I should have told them when we first started talking about the drama connection, but it truly didn't occur to me. None of the victims went to Orion and . . .' He shrugged. 'But you asked why I asked you to meet me.'

'Not to put me on a leave of absence from the board of New Horizons?'

Al blinked at him. 'Heavens, no.'

'Good. I was on leave this past week. Mutually agreed upon with Vivian, but it sucked. It's hard to be a court-ordered therapist when you've got a murder charge hanging over your head.' Sam grimaced. 'Words I never thought I'd say.'

'And will never say again. So. My business. I'm semi-retired.'

Sam lifted his brows. 'I know. You've been "semi-retired" for as long as I've known you. Which really isn't all that retired, because you put in more hours than I do with all your charitable work *and* the SDPD.'

Al's lips twitched. 'That I do. But I want to slow down, so something's got to give. I don't want to give up my charity work, so the SDPD's got to go.'

Sam stared at him. 'You're quitting? For real?'

'Yes, but not right away. I thought I'd bring someone in to start taking over. Maybe mentor him a bit. Hand over existing cases and consult on new ones until he doesn't need me anymore.'

Sam drew a breath, hardly daring to hope. 'Who were you thinking about?'

Al laughed. 'Sam, are you interested?'

'Yes,' Sam said, his pulse starting to pound. 'But why now? Why me?'

'Why now? Truthfully, Baz's heart attack got me thinking. I'll be seventy next month. My wife is seventy-two. We have children and grandchildren. I've missed a lot of dinners and even a few birthdays because of my job with the SDPD. I want to enjoy my grandchildren and get back into model railroading. It's time.'

'So why me?'

'Why not? I've always liked you, and Vivian can't speak highly enough of you. And now you have a relationship with SDPD. They respect that you risked your career to warn them about Driscoll. Even Baz Constantine likes you.'

Sam chuckled. 'He definitely didn't at first, but I think he's coming around.' Then a thought occurred. 'Wait. If you're seventy, does that mean Vivian is, too? You went to college together, didn't you?'

He'd met Al through Vivian. His boss had introduced them, and Al had brought him into New Horizons.

Al shook his head. 'Oh no. I'm not going there. You want to know how old Vivian is, you ask her yourself.'

Sam recoiled. 'I don't think so.'

'Smart man. You'd work with me at first, but I'd step back when you were comfortable. Doesn't pay a lot and it's not full time. You'd want to keep working with Vivian at least part time – so don't piss her off by asking about her age. Still interested?'

Sam couldn't stop his grin. 'Yes. When do you want me to start?'

'Next week? You and Vivian talk it over. Figure out what makes sense and let me know.'

Sam made himself calm down, think of all the angles. 'What if SDPD says no?'

'They might, but I don't think so. I told Navarro I was going to ask you. He said that he'd asked you if you'd considered being a cop.'

'He was letting off steam. He wasn't serious.'

'Maybe.' Al tilted his head. 'Of course, you'd be working with McKittrick at times.'

Sam drew a deep breath, willing his expression to remain neutral, but Al chuckled.

'If you could see your face,' Al said quietly. 'For what it's worth, I wish you luck. She's got a good heart.'

'I know,' Sam murmured. 'But I'm not going to push her. She might demand a different consulting psychologist.'

Al shrugged. 'Then she does. She's not the only detective in Homicide, though. Unfortunately, there's lots of work to do, so the others will be knocking on your door. You can think about it if you need to.'

He didn't need to think about it. This was what he'd wanted to do for seventeen years. He'd be damn good at it. Plus, he was going to work with Kit.

She'd trusted him to keep her safe. To keep Rita safe. Maybe Kit would come to trust him with her heart as well.

Maybe.

He wouldn't push, and he was willing to wait. She was worth it.

Sam smiled. 'No need to think about it. I'm in.'

He couldn't wait to see what came next.

Game on, Kit.

Acknowledgments

Robin Rue, Claire Zion, Jen Doyle, and Liz Sellers for believing in this new series. Thank you all so very much.

The Starfish – Brian, Cheryl, Christine, Kathy, Sheila, and Susan – for the plotting help and for the questions you asked about my characters that made everything fall into place.

Andrew Grey for being my word count partner. Your daily encouragement made the words flow like water.

Martin Hafer for the background on the ethics of psychological professionals. And for feeding me when I was so busy writing that I forgot to eat.

Sarah Hafer for the editing.

Margaret Taylor for listening to my ramblings and for providing such valuable information.

As always, all mistakes are my own.